"DISPATCH, THIS IS UNIT 1244. DO YOU COPY?"

"1244, this is Dispatch. Go ahead."

"Diver One's safety rope was cut," Lou said. "Diver Two entering the water." Her hand shook as she put down the radio.

There was a startled pause before the dispatcher responded, "What is the status of Diver One? 1244, do you copy? Is there someone else on shore?" The questions increased in urgency as Lou fumbled to pull on her fins. She picked up the radio again.

"Status of Diver One is unknown. No one else is on shore. It's just me." Her voice wobbled on the last words, and she placed the radio back on the ice. She couldn't think about that now—not when Callum's life was on the line.

Closing her lips around the regulator mouthpiece, she slid feetfirst into the black water.

HOLD YOUR BREATH

KATIE RUGGLE

sourcebooks
casablanca

Published by Sourcebooks Casablanca, an imprint of Sourcebooks, Inc.
P.O. Box 4410, Naperville, Illinois 60567-4410
(630) 961-3900
Fax: (630) 961-2168
www.sourcebooks.com

Printed and bound in Canada.
MBP 10 9 8 7 6 5 4 3 2 1

To Mom and Dad.
As promised, here's the disclaimer:
None of the bad parenting in this book is
based on my childhood memories.
Love, Katie

Chapter 1

JUMPING INTO A HOLE CUT IN THE FROZEN RESERVOIR was a stupid idea. In fact, of all the questionable decisions she'd made since abandoning civilization for her tiny mountain cabin seven months ago, this was probably the worst.

At least, Lou mused wryly, it was a beautiful place in which to do a dumb thing. The sun lit the snow-capped mountains circling like sleepy sentinels around them, and the wind chased powdery snow across the frozen reservoir. Despite the cold, it still smelled strongly of fish.

"Ready for some ice-rescue training?" Derek bumped his neoprene-covered arm against hers. He seemed much too cheerful for a guy about to dive into glacial water.

"No."

"Aww, Lou." When he tried to pat her head with one of his bright blue gloves, she ducked out of reach. "Nervous?"

"Of course not. Why would I be nervous about jumping into a hole in the ice and swimming around in thirty-two-and-a-half-degree water? Why did I join the Field County Rescue Dive Team and not the Jamaican Whatever again?"

"Because *I* would not be on the Jamaican Dive Team," Derek answered. "And I make it worth the cold."

"Yeah, not really."

"Hey!" He smacked her arm, she laughed and whacked him back, and then it evolved into a full-fledged slap fight. The blue-nitrile shade of their gloves made them look like life-size cartoons, and Lou couldn't hold back another laugh.

"Sparks!"

Callum's bellow froze her in place. She shot Derek a wry glance before turning to face their team leader. She took careful, deliberate steps in the clumsy dry-suit boots, as humiliation was better served in small doses. Being caught goofing off was bad enough. She didn't need to fall on her ass, as well.

"Yes?" She eyed his scowling face. It was too bad about his surliness, since Callum was a joy to look upon otherwise, in a gladiator-meets-drill-sergeant kind of way. His blond hair was military short, and his eyes were a startling and beautiful blue against tanned skin. His jaw was square, and his body... Taking a deep breath, she carefully did not check out the neoprene-wrapped perfection below his neck.

Because...*damn.*

"What are you doing?"

Somehow, answering "Fooling around with Derek" did not seem like the best idea. "Uh...nothing."

He stared at her, heavy frown still in place. "It didn't— Never mind. You're like a terrier with ADD. Why can't you stand still for five minutes?"

"Because..." She shot a glance at Derek. The traitor had taken several steps back and was pretending to examine a seam on his dry-suit sleeve. "He... I just... Um, the gloves..."

Callum let the silence hang for several seconds.

When he eventually turned away from Lou, she let out the breath she'd been holding and shuffled over to rejoin Derek. Once there, she punched him lightly—well, sort of lightly—in the kidney.

"Ouch." He gave her an injured look. "What was that for?"

"Why am I always the one who gets in trouble?"

"Because you're the one who starts it."

"Do not," she protested, realizing she'd gotten a little loud only when Callum's eyes focused on her again. Dropping her gaze, she studied the half-frozen puddle in front of her boots. It seemed as if every single time she did something embarrassing, Callum was there, watching her with *the look*—a mix of exasperation and irritated bafflement. The sad part was that, even after three months of getting *the look*, Lou still wasn't able to smother the obnoxious butterflies that fluttered in her belly whenever she was the center of his attention.

"You done?" he asked. At her nod, he jerked his chin toward the icy reservoir.

Lou fell in line with the six other divers, taking slow, exaggerated steps to avoid tripping over her own neoprene-wrapped feet or slipping on the ice. As they reached the large opening that had been carved out earlier in the day for the training exercise, Lou peered at the water, frowning.

"What's wrong?" Derek asked, stepping up beside her and following her gaze as if looking for the answer to his own question.

She shrugged. "All that ice around the edge makes the water look really cold."

Bumping her with his elbow, he snorted. "It *is* cold,

genius. It's literally freezing, which explains all the hard stuff we're standing on."

Lou elbowed him back. "Dork," she grumbled.

He smirked at her.

"The ice is just under ten inches here," Callum announced in his schoolteacher tone—the one that always made Lou want to act up like a contrary third-grader. "Is that thick enough for a group of people to walk on?"

"Wouldn't it have been better to confirm that *before* we left shore?" Lou muttered, making Derek snicker. Callum sent a sharp look her way.

"It's thick enough," Chad answered, taking a step toward Callum. "It'd even be okay to drive on it."

"Drive what?"

"A car or light truck," Chad said quickly. "For anything more, twelve inches would be better."

"That's what she said," Derek whispered loud enough to make everyone except Callum laugh. Even Chad grinned before dropping his chin to hide it.

Callum let his gaze fall on each person in turn. The chuckles died, replaced by awkward coughs.

"So this ice is safe?" he finally asked when silence had fallen over the team members.

"Yes." Chad was the first to speak up again, and Lou winced. He'd obviously already forgotten the four hours they'd spent watching training videos that morning.

Wilt gave a slow, sad shake of his head. "No ice is safe," he said in the Arkansas drawl he held on to even after forty years in Colorado. Lou liked Wilt. He was a soft-spoken man who kept quiet unless he had something important to say. When he spoke, everyone shut up and listened. Wilt was in his sixties, with a thick mustache that drooped over his mouth, giving him a perpetually mournful expression.

"Good, Wilt," Callum said. "Glad someone was paying attention this morning. We have to be especially careful of weak spots after the warm spell last week. Even though it's been cold the past couple of days, the ice probably hasn't recovered yet."

Chad's shoulders sagged. Knowing all too well how it felt to be under the heavy weight of Callum's displeasure, Lou shot him a sympathetic glance. He avoided her gaze.

"Okay!" Callum clapped his blue-gloved hands together. "Everyone in the water. First time in is the hardest, so it's best to get it over with."

Lou eyed the water doubtfully, shuffling a little closer to the edge of the hole. She had a lot of scuba diving experience, but most of it had been in tropical locations. This was new to her.

"What if my suit has a leak?" Chad asked. Lou whipped her head around to stare at him. Hell. She'd never thought about a leaky suit. Her newly panicked gaze flew to Callum's face.

"Your suit is buoyant enough that it won't matter, even if it fills with water to your armpits." Callum waved a dismissive hand. "You'll still float."

Slightly relieved but trying not to think about how freaking cold thirty-two-degree water up to her armpits would be, she turned her attention back to the opening in the ice. Derek had already taken the plunge.

"C'mon in," he said, letting his legs float to the surface and leaning back as if he were in an easy chair. "The water's fine."

Deciding to just get it done, Lou took a breath and jumped in. When her head went under, she instantly realized her mistake. Once the shockingly cold water hit her face, her lungs clamped down, squeezing out all her oxygen. She didn't even try to figure out which way was up but just let her suit float her to the surface instead.

She felt a tap on the back of her hood and yanked her face out of the water. Callum was close enough for her to see the deep creases between his eyebrows.

"You good?" he asked.

"Y-yep."

After examining her face carefully, he shook his head. "Never do anything halfway, do you, Sparks?"

Since she didn't know if that was a compliment or an insult, she kept quiet. Her legs kept wanting to float to the surface behind her and tip her onto her front as the others climbed in more carefully. Scowling, she tried to force her lower half down but ended up flailing unsuccessfully.

"How are you staying upright?" she asked Callum, craning her neck to keep her face out of the water as her legs headed for the surface again.

"Tuck them to your chest and then push them straight down." He swam toward the icy ledge as she struggled to master her buoyant suit. She finally managed to shove her legs down so her body was more or less upright.

"Ha!" she crowed, slapping the surface in victory. "Got you down, bitches!"

"Did you just call your legs 'bitches'?" Derek asked from directly behind her, making her jump. Her upper body tilted forward, but she got herself back under control.

"Yep. Occasional evidence to the contrary, I am in charge of *all* my body parts."

"Glad to hear it."

"Everyone out!" Callum bellowed, levering his body onto the ice with ease. "Exit the water on your front like a seal and then roll away from the edge. Remember, the more you can distribute your weight, the less likely it is you'll go through the ice."

Lou flattened her hands on the ice and tried to hoist her body out of the water, but it looked a lot easier when Callum did it. Her legs, damn the rogue bastards, floated forward and up, catching under the ledge. She managed to slam the edge of the ice into her belly, driving out her breath.

"Nice, Lou," Derek mocked as he slid gracefully onto the solid surface. "You're like a *special* seal."

"Oh, shut up," she muttered, panting, as she hauled herself out of the water.

This, she could tell, was going to be one hell of a day.

———

"Sparks!" Callum bellowed. "You're up!"

She sighed, relinquishing her spot on the rope where she'd been helping to pull the "victims" and their rescuers out of the water and across the ice. It was like a lopsided game of tug-of-war—all brute strength and teamwork—and she'd actually been getting to like that part of training, despite the hard work. But now that she wasn't pulling, she noticed her eyelashes had frosted over, and her neck and the top of her chest were clammy from the water that had leaked into the suit after her full-body plunge.

Trudging over to Callum, she lifted her arms so he could wrap the end of the rope around her middle. Although she'd watched three of the guys perform an in-water rescue, she was still nervous. The ice-rescue veterans had made it look easy, but she had a feeling her first time wouldn't go so smoothly.

Callum handed her the victim's harness, which looked like a skinny pool noodle. It was attached to her rope with about six feet of line. That way, the victim would be first out of the water, and she'd be behind him, in a position to help lift him onto the ice.

"When you get to the victim, carabiner should be in your right hand," Callum instructed. "The other end goes in your left. Get control of your suit before trying to save anybody. Approach the victim from the side or back, talk to him, harness him up, signal the guys to start pulling, and lift your knee to help boost him onto the ice with your thigh. Once you get your hands on him, do not let go of your patient. Got it?"

"Yes." Her voice sounded a little uncertain, so she firmed her jaw and tried again. *"Yes."*

Callum's mouth quirked up on one side. If it had been anyone but Callum, Lou would've thought he was holding back a smile.

Okay. Okay, she could *do* this.

She approached the edge of the ice, crawling when she was ten feet out and then moving to her belly and sliding across the last yard. Swinging her legs around, she dropped feetfirst into the water, careful to keep her face above the surface this time. She looked back at where Callum stood on the ice. He bumped his closed fist on the top of his head, the signal for *Are you okay?*

She answered in the affirmative with a matching fist-to-head bump before heading toward her "victim."

Holding her face out of the water, she swam toward Phil, who clung to the ice on the other side of the opening with melodramatic panic. Lou had to bite back a groan when she saw how he was putting every ounce of community-theater experience into his role of drowning victim.

Coming up next to him, she tried to get her legs underneath her as she spoke. "Hang on, sir. I'm Louise Sparks with the Field County Dive Team. We're going to get you out of here."

Phil's pretend struggles increased, and his thrashing hand slapped the water, splashing it into her face. Air left her lungs again at the breath-stealing cold, and her legs floated up behind her. *Damn it.* When she could move her body again, she drew her knees up and pushed her feet straight down, glaring at her grinning victim.

"Oops," Phil said. "Sorry, Lou."

"Uh-huh," she muttered as she moved around behind him. "I'm hooking this harness around you, sir, so the team on shore can pull you out."

She struggled to reach around Phil's wide girth, wishing she'd gotten skinny Wilt as her victim instead. The dry-suit gloves made her fingers thick and unwieldy, and she fumbled with the carabiner. To make matters even more silent-swear-worthy, Phil had resumed his melodramatic struggling.

"Don't make me drown you," she snarled, jerking her head back so his flapping elbow didn't connect with her eye.

"Where's your compassion, Lou? I'm a panicked,

hypothermic tourist here." The bastard sounded as if he were about to laugh.

"I'll show you compassion," she muttered through gritted teeth. "And if you're hypothermic, shouldn't you be getting tired and sluggish?"

"That sounds threatening." Phil was definitely laughing, the ass. "As soon as you save me and I get out of the hospital, I'm going to file a complaint with your superior."

"That's where you're wrong—there is no one superior to me," she said, letting out a relieved grunt when she finally succeeded in hooking the carabiner through the metal loop of the harness.

Phil laughed and then wiggled several feet sideways, pulling his slick, neoprene-covered body free of her grip.

"Never let go of your patient!" Callum yelled. "Once you put your hands on him, you *do not* let go until he is being lifted into the ambulance, understand?"

With a heavy sigh, Lou tried to maneuver behind Phil again, but he was surprisingly agile for such a big guy. Plus, the training had been tiring, and she still had to help hoist Phil's bulk out of the water. Clenching her jaw, she lunged toward him, managing to latch her arms around his waist.

"Got you!" she crowed, but her satisfaction was quickly overruled by irritation as her legs floated up behind her *again*, curving her spine into an awkward partial backbend. With Phil's body in the way, she couldn't pull her knees up very easily. After several unsuccessful attempts at getting her legs underneath her, she kicked out in frustration. But instead of passing through unresisting water, her booted foot hit hard against something.

"What the hell?" she mumbled, looking over her shoulder. She couldn't see whatever it was through the murky water. It had felt fairly firm, although it had moved with her kick. She was tempted to thump it with her boot again, but reconsidered.

"What?" Phil had finally realized she was ignoring him. He quit his fake struggling, twisting his head around to follow her gaze.

"I kicked something." She kept staring at the water, as if she'd suddenly develop X-ray vision. Her arms were still locked around Phil's middle. No need to get yelled at for making the same mistake twice.

"The Mission Reservoir Monster?" he asked in his best spooky voice.

"What's taking you so long?" Callum called from the ice. "For Christ's sake, Sparks, your victim would be dead by now. Just complete the recovery, and let's get his body out of the water so we can notify his next of kin."

"You gave up on me so quick, Cal," Phil whined. "Aren't you even going to start CPR?"

"No way," Derek yelled back. "He knows where those lips have been."

"What's the problem?" Callum didn't sound amused. He *did* sound annoyed.

"There's something under the water. I kicked it."

"Shark?" Chad suggested.

"Seriously?" Derek scoffed. "In a freshwater reservoir?"

"Maybe," Chad muttered with a shrug.

"Well, it didn't bite me, so hopefully that rules out both the Reservoir Monster and all woman-eating fish."

Moving a few feet closer, Derek peered at the water. "If it's anything valuable, I call dibs."

"No way!" Lou protested. "I'm the one who kicked it. Finders keepers!"

Callum expelled an impatient sigh loud enough for Lou to hear, even across the twenty feet that separated them. He moved to the edge of the ice and slid gracefully into the water. As he swam toward them, Lou turned back to scan for the unidentified object.

At first she thought she was imagining it, but she could definitely see something down there, and it was getting larger and more distinct with each second. She wondered if her kick had knocked whatever it was loose, allowing it to float to the top. As she stared, holding her breath, the faint shape got closer and closer, until a large, gray mass bobbed to the surface. Lou gave a muffled shout, her arms tightening around Phil. A part of her knew what it was as soon as it surfaced, but a larger portion refused to accept it.

No. No way. *No way.*

"Is that a body?" Derek yelled from the ice.

"Yep, that's a dead guy," Phil said, his voice as casual as if it were a beer can floating next to them and not the waxy gray back of a corpse.

"Huh." Derek didn't sound too freaked out about it, either. "Lou, I'm good with finders keepers, then. You can have it."

She couldn't respond. For once, no words would leave her mouth. All she could do was cling to Phil's middle and try to breathe. It wasn't working.

As he pulled up next to them, Callum looked at the peacefully bobbing mass of flesh. "Fuck."

Lou's lungs had locked up again, and she felt as if her face had been dunked back into the frigid water. She couldn't tear her eyes away from the bloated body.

"Hey, Cal?" Phil still sounded much too calm. "Where's the head?"

Chapter 2

LOU DIDN'T KNOW WHY SHE'D THOUGHT FOR A SINGLE moment that calling her mother was a good idea. It had been an impulse, an in-shock drive for comfort that had made her momentarily forget the reality of what her mom was actually like.

"Mom?"

"Louise? Is that you?"

"Yeah. I...um, well, I..." She trailed off, not sure how to go about telling her estranged mother that she'd just come face-to...well, neck...with a waterlogged, headless corpse.

"Of course you can, dear."

Lou paused. *What?* "What?"

"Of course you can come home."

"What? No!" It was beginning to sink in just how bad an idea this had been. Lou didn't have the patience for the upcoming discussion, even on noncorpse-discovery days.

"Oh, don't worry about anything. Your stepfather and I won't even say a word about this silly...hiatus of yours. I'll book you a ticket out of DIA and email the boarding pass to you. You'll be home by Wednesday."

"No! Seriously, Mom, do *not* book a flight for me." Lou closed her eyes and let the back of her head hit the dive van. She'd holed up in the van, which was really a converted ambulance, to get some privacy for her anticipated nervous breakdown. It would be nice to be able to get around to that breakdown so she could just get it over with, but she'd been dumb and called her mother first and was now paying the price.

A heavy sigh gusted through her cell phone. "Louise Dutton Sparks, don't start second-guessing yourself now. Coming home is the right thing to do."

"My home is here now, Mom, in Colorado," she explained for the thousandth time. "I'm not going back to Connecticut."

"Don't be ridiculous, Louise," her mom snapped. "That…shed you live in is not your home. It doesn't even have running water."

"It does too have running—" Lou cut herself off with a brisk shake of her head, reminding herself not to get sucked into one of her mother's arguments. In all of her twenty-six years, Lou had never won a single one. "Whatever. Never mind. I have to go."

"So, I'll email you that e-ticket then."

Lou started thumping her head rhythmically against the side of the dive van. "No. No ticket. I'm not going to Connecticut."

Her mom tsked. "I don't know why you insist on being stubborn. I've been *trying* to reach you for good-ness knows how long now. And Brenton told your step-father the other day that you're not returning his phone calls either. We didn't raise you to be rude, Louise."

Oh God.

"Now's really not the time, Mom."

The rear door of the dive van flew open, making Lou jump. Callum's backlit figure filled the opening. It was almost ridiculous how broad his shoulders were.

"Gotta go, Mom. Love you. Bye." Lou ended the call while her mother was still sputtering.

"What was all the banging about?" he asked.

She shrugged and waved a hand toward the side of the van. Example one gazillion and three of Callum catching her at her most embarrassing moments. "My mother." To her surprise, he didn't press for details. After he stared at her for a moment, he seemed to accept her nonexplanation.

"Help me out of this, would you?" He turned and presented her with his back. After the coroner and sheriff had been called, Callum and Wilt had changed into less buoyant dry suits and scuba gear so they could dive and look for evidence. Lou had stayed on scene, intending to do her job and help get the body out of the water, but Callum had taken one look at her shivering miserably along the sidelines and sent her back to the dive van to change.

Chad had also been sent back to the van, although he was currently pacing in the parking lot. He hadn't fared as well as Lou and had puked up his guts at the first glimpse of the body.

Sliding her cell phone into her dive-team jacket pocket, she shifted toward Callum, pulling the Velcro loose and then unzipping the heavy, waxed zipper that ran the length of his back. Even with everything that was going on, Lou couldn't help but notice that the neoprene did nice things to his ass. It wasn't the first time she'd made the observation. She wished she could be as oblivious to his obnoxiously perfect form as he appeared to be to her much-more-average one, but sometimes he just couldn't be ignored. And at those times, it was almost impossible to control the stupid things that came out of her mouth.

"First body?" he asked, peeling the suit off his massive shoulders. His thermal underlayer had a wet ring that spread from his collar halfway down his chest, outlining the shape of his pecs.

She shivered. "Yeah."

"Doing okay?" He wasn't looking at her. Instead, he was stepping out of his suit, his focus on his feet.

She considered the question. "I think?"

The uncertainty in her voice brought her a quick glance. He considered her for a long moment, but then must have decided she wasn't going to collapse in shock. "Good. Rob wants a word."

The idea of reliving the past hour was not appealing. Lou made a face that was wasted on Callum, since he'd grabbed the back of his thermal top and was pulling it off over his head. Her heart sped up, though she blamed it on the upcoming chat with the sheriff. It had absolutely nothing to do with the beauty and definition of Callum's stupidly perfect chest. "Maybe I should, you know, recover here a little longer?"

"You're fine. Go."

She sighed and went. The half second of sympathy from her team leader was obviously over.

Climbing out of the dive van and slamming the rear door behind her only a little bit harder than needed for the latch to catch, she looked around and saw that poor Chad was throwing up again. Derek must have been enlisted as babysitter, since he stood fairly close, although far enough away to avoid any splatter. He caught her gaze and waved her over. Suddenly glad that she had to talk to the sheriff, she made an apologetic face and pointed toward the ice. In return, Derek offered a rude gesture that she pretended to ignore as she moved toward Rob.

Field County Sheriff Rob Coughlin was easy to spot. Not only was he the size of an ex-college-football star, but he also had what Lou could only describe as *presence*. She imagined it was useful in emergency situations. Even if he hadn't been wearing the tan uniform, she could've pegged him as both a cop and a leader.

The sheriff saw her coming and focused his attention on her. "Louise," he called out when she got close enough for him to greet her without actually yelling.

"Hey, Sheriff." They'd met a couple of times in passing—even worked a Search and Rescue op together once—but this was the first time they would actually have a conversation, or interrogation, or whatever. Up close, he didn't lose any of his appeal. His dark hair was mostly covered by his hat, leaving only his lightly silver-flecked sideburns exposed. Midday stubble created just a shadow of a scruff over his cheeks and jaw. Everything about him was hard but appealing—from the lines of his face to the muscles in his body. Maybe not grumpy-Callum-level appealing, but still. She couldn't complain.

"Rough training session, huh?" Although the corners of his eyes crinkled in sympathy, he never lost that watchful appraisal.

She gave an affirmative shrug.

"Let me just get your basic information, and then I'll get your statement." He touched something attached to his duty belt, and she cocked her head to see what appeared to be a digital recorder. At his prompting, she gave him her full name, date of birth, address, phone number, and pretty much every other piece of personal data she had.

Once finished, he asked, "Why don't you run me through what happened?"

"Okay." She tried to organize her thoughts, not wanting to be *that* interviewee, the one who sounded so dumb the cops all played the recording over and over at roll call. "We had ice-rescue classroom training all morning and then headed here after lunch for the practical."

"Why not Verde Reservoir?" Rob interrupted. "Wasn't that the original plan?"

"I guess." As the newbie on the dive team, Lou just went where she was told. "Oh, wait—I do know this answer. Callum mentioned that the thaw a few days ago had melted a bunch of the snow in the parking lot. All that water refroze, so the steep hill at the entry is like an ice slide right now. We'd never have been able to get the dive van up that. Plus, he said the ice on Verde is more unpredictable, so I think he was glad to have an excuse to switch to Mission."

He nodded and gestured for her to continue.

"We got suited up and headed over to the hole in the ice. After we practiced getting ourselves in and out of the water for a while, we moved on to getting other people out. It was my turn, and I'd gotten the harness around Phil. He was pretending to be a panicking victim, so he moved away from me toward the north side of the hole. I...ah"—this was the embarrassing part—"couldn't really keep my legs from floating up behind me, because of the dry suit, so I got a little frustrated and ended up kicking...um, the dead guy. I must've knocked him loose or something, because he floated up to the surface."

The sheriff watched her impassively, not saying anything. She didn't know what else to add, so she just shrugged and joined him in silence.

"You see a lot of dead bodies?" he finally asked.

She paused before answering, examining his expression and trying to figure out where he was going with that line of questioning. "My first, actually."

"Huh." Rob darted a look toward the still-heaving Chad before refocusing on her. He really did have the serious-cop gaze down pat. "You're pretty calm about it."

"That's thanks to the years of practice in suppressing my emotions." Too bad she didn't have more luck suppressing her smart-ass mouth. "Or maybe it was because I called my mom after…you know, the dead guy appeared. After our conversation, annoyance took precedence, so I forgot about being horrified and nauseated. I'm sure I'll have nightmares for weeks to come, though—about the dead body, I mean, not about the call to my mom."

The sheriff smiled, dissolving his poker face into a disarmingly attractive expression. Laugh lines had formed around his pretty brown eyes. "I have a mom like that, too."

Was *everyone* in Field County improbably attractive—and completely out of her league? "Why did he float up now?" she asked, changing the subject.

"Sure you want to know?"

"Not really." She chanced a look at his face. "But it probably can't be worse than what I can come up with using my imagination. Hit me."

After a long stare, he raised one shoulder in a shrug and jerked his chin at a small gray-haired woman talking to one of the deputies. "The coroner theorizes that the victim probably had been in the water for a few months, but it wasn't until the recent warm-up that he started decomposing. Decomposing bodies float. His ankle was tied to a twenty-pound weight that Callum and Wilt just pulled out of the water. When you kicked the victim"— Lou had to hold back a wince at that—"the cord hooked to the weight pulled free, allowing the body to rise."

She blinked at him, fascinated and disgusted.

When she didn't say anything, he continued. "If you hadn't disturbed the body, he still would've reached the surface this summer. When decomposition is far enough along, even the weight wouldn't have kept him submerged."

The coroner, who had joined them during the sheriff's explanation, added in a gravelly smoker's voice, "So you basically kept a summer tourist from being scarred for life by having a headless corpse pop up next to his pontoon boat. Good job."

Lou eyed the other woman's deadpan expression and wondered how to respond. "Oh. Um, good." Time to change the direction of the conversation. "Hi. I'm Lou Sparks. I'm a new member of the dive team."

"Belly Leopold." She took Lou's hand and gave it a single strong shake. "Field County Coroner. I'm not new."

"Belly?"

"Belinda. Don't call me that."

"As long as you don't call me Louise."

"Deal." Belly turned back to the sheriff. "Can I grab you for a sec, Rob?"

"Yeah, we're done," he said before lifting an eyebrow at Lou. "Unless you have anything else to add?"

"Nope. Kicked a dead guy so he popped up right next to me. That's pretty much it."

The coroner smirked. "Yeah, you'll fit in around here just fine, newbie."

"Thanks?"

As the two walked away, Lou realized she hadn't asked something important. "Hey, Sheriff," she called. "Who is it—do you know?"

"Not yet," he said without breaking stride. "And you should call me Rob, now that you're one of our divers."

"Huh." Lou glanced around, but no one seemed to be paying any attention to her. She followed behind Rob toward the emergency vehicles parked on the shore. None had risked driving on the newly rehardened reservoir, so they were hauling all the evidence across the slick stretch of ice to the shore. They'd loaded up the body onto a Stokes basket—a sort of floating stretcher—and covered it with a blanket. Two EMTs were in the process of pulling it across the ice like a grisly sled. The basket hit a rough patch in the ice and bounced hard enough for the blanket to slip, exposing the corpse's right side.

Lou cocked her head and took a couple of steps closer to the body. The shape of the arm was strange, ending too bluntly. She sucked in a breath.

"They cut off his hands, too," she muttered to herself, turning her head when Callum's deep voice responded.

"Yeah. Delays ID."

"Was it done before or after?" she asked, bracing herself for the answer.

"Death, you mean? You'd have to ask Belly."

Lou thought she might be happier not knowing. She looked over her shoulder at Callum, who was frowning at the corpse as one of the EMTs hurried to readjust the blanket.

"How can they not know who he is?" Lou asked. "Do that many people disappear around here? I kind of figured it's more of a one-missing-guy-a-decade kind of place."

He shrugged, finally turning away from the receding body. "Hard to keep track of people out here. Lots of them don't want the government—or anybody, really—in their business. More than one census taker has been greeted at the door by the business end of a shotgun."

The idea that someone could be murdered and missing for months without anyone noticing struck Lou as sad. "So, this guy never returned to his solitary cabin, and his neighbors just figured he'd developed a serious case of agoraphobia?"

"Could be." Callum's eyes narrowed, and Lou followed his gaze to a young-looking deputy carrying a hand weight. He fumbled with it, barely stopping it from falling onto the ice. "Or it could've had something to do with the cultists over by White Bear Peak, or that antigovernment group that's taken over the old Miller compound. There's an MC outside of Liverton, too."

"Emcee?" The thought of a murderous master of ceremonies just wasn't computing.

"Motorcycle Club."

Sometimes Lou was very glad Callum couldn't read her thoughts. "Ah."

"Should've kept on my dry suit."

"What?" She looked at the deputy and winced. Instead of just fumbling, he'd dropped the piece of evidence this time. Glancing around, most likely to see if anyone was watching, he picked up the weight. "Isn't that only a twenty-pounder? Why is he having such a hard time carrying it?"

"No idea, but that dumbass is going to figure out a way to get himself in the water."

They both watched as the deputy finally made his way to shore. Once he stepped onto solid ground, Lou exhaled. Only then did she realize she'd been holding her breath.

"Amazing," Callum muttered, finally turning away from the deputy.

"You know him?"

He snorted. "Unfortunately."

"I smell a story."

"You know Walsh? With Fire?"

She thought for a second. "Ian Walsh? Big guy? Looks like he should be every single month on the firemen's calendar, posing in just his bunker gear without a shirt and showing off those tattoo-covered pecs?"

Callum paused, a muscle ticking at his jaw. "How do you know about his tattoos?" She opened her mouth, but he spoke again before she could answer. "Never mind. I don't want to know. Ask him sometime about Lawrence hitting a bison with a month-old squad car. Going ninety miles an hour."

After considering that for a second, she said, "That doesn't make him an idiot. Maybe he was responding to a call and couldn't stop when he saw the bison. I hit a deer a week after I moved here." She made a face at the memory. That had been a traumatic day. Not quite as bad as headless-corpse-discovery day, but still, it hadn't been fun.

His mouth twisting in disgust, Callum shook his head. "He *was* responding to a call. A bison-in-the-road call."

"Oh." It was her turn to pause. "Yeah, that was dumb."

"Just one story of many."

"Ah."

They stood in surprisingly tense silence for a few moments, until a full-body shiver made her hug her middle.

Callum eyed her sharply and then jerked his head toward the dive van. "Go check that all our gear is stowed. Grab the puker and Derek to help. We'll head out soon."

"Is Rob done talking to everyone on the team?" Great—now that she let herself notice the cold, her teeth were chattering.

He shrugged. "If not, he knows where to find us. Go."

She trudged toward the opening in the ice, collecting harnesses and ropes. There were ten or so water-logged…things…that hadn't been there during training lined up about fifteen feet from the edge of the water. From the manila-colored tags hanging from each piece, she assumed they were what Wilt and Callum had pulled out of the water during their evidence-hunting dives.

After spending months, if not years, in the water, the objects were indistinguishable dark lumps. Trying to look innocent as she coiled a rope, Lou shuffled a few feet closer. The closest one looked like… She tilted her head and squinted. A tackle box, maybe?

"Hey."

She jerked her head up as she focused on the speaker,

a blond deputy standing on the other end of the evidence line. He didn't look familiar, but she didn't know many of the cops by name, except for Sheriff Coughlin, and now the unfortunate Lawrence. "Hi."

"You're the new girl on the dive team, right?"

She nodded. "Lou Sparks."

"Chris Jennings." He took a couple of steps closer, carefully placing his feet to avoid trampling the evidence, and held out his gloved hand. "Heard you were the lucky one who found him."

She made a face as she shook his hand. "Yeah. Lucky me."

With a sympathetic smile, he gestured at the line of items. "Well, I'd better get back to hauling the evidence over to the crime-scene vehicle. Doubt any of this crap is actually related to what happened to the floater, but better to bag and tag than miss anything."

"Need some help?" she asked, trying for nonchalance. If she carried them, she could see some of the potential evidence up close. Plus, the deputy seemed like a chatty one. More information straight from the sheriff's office wouldn't hurt. She felt a strange connection to the anonymous headless guy, an urgent need to give him back his name and identity. No one should be dumped like garbage and forgotten.

"Nah." He grinned at her again. He was an attractive guy, but he didn't wake up any butterflies in her belly. Maybe she only went for the surly type. "Thanks, but it's better if I do it. Chain of evidence and all that."

"Sure. It was nice to meet you."

"You too." With another smile, he carefully hoisted the tackle box and headed toward the shore.

She watched him walk carefully away. "Huh."

"What are you looking at?" At Derek's voice behind her, Lou turned and slipped. Flailing her arms, she tried to catch her balance, dropping the neatly coiled ropes to the ground. As soon as she had her feet under her again, she punched him in the midsection.

"Ass!"

"What?" He covered his stomach with one arm, although she knew she hadn't hit him that hard.

"Don't sneak up behind me like that," she growled, giving him an openhanded smack on his shoulder before reaching for the scattered ropes. "Especially not on headless-dead-guy-discovery day."

"You've made it into a *day*?" he asked. "Nice. Can we get it off of work?"

She recoiled the rope. "No day off, but there is one good thing about HDGD day. Callum was civil, actually civil, for about six minutes. Straight."

"Really? That's impressive. I think the previous record was twelve seconds. Nice subject change, by the way."

"What?"

"I saw you checking out Deputy Chris." He grinned. "Your eyes were firmly on that cop's ass. Don't deny it."

She gave him a lofty and glacial stare. "I was thinking."

"About what? Deputy Chris's bitable backside?"

"You know, I'm telling Artie you've been ogling deputies behind her back," Lou teased. Derek got the same sappy smile he always did whenever Artie was mentioned. The two were sickeningly and adorably devoted to each other. Lou tucked the coils of rope over her shoulder. "Actually, I was thinking about statistics."

"Boring. And doubtful."

"But true." She gave a final glance at the remaining objects and headed for the shore, although not before getting a good look at the evidence lined up next to her. "I was considering the likelihood of having such a high number of improbably attractive people in the Field County Emergency Services."

"I *knew* you were thinking about his ass!" Derek puffed out his chest. "And thank you. I agree."

"Yeah…" She drew out the word, looking him up and down. "I'm thinking you're an outlier."

"Hey!"

Ignoring his protests, she headed toward the ambulance to collect the newly emptied Stokes basket from the EMTs.

———⁓⁓⁓———

Headless-dead-guy-discovery day just kept getting better and better.

Lou stared at the flat tire on her Chevy pickup—her second flat in the past week—and felt her shoulders droop.

"Haven't you gotten ten-ply tires yet?"

She didn't look at Callum but continued glaring at the deflated tire, as if she could fix it with the power of her sullen gaze. "No. It's on the wrong list."

"Wrong list?"

She sighed. "I have my must-have list and my want-to-have list. Load E tires are on my want-to-have list."

"What's on your must-have list?"

"Food. Propane. Firewood." She resisted the urge to kick the flat tire. "Tire patch kit."

"Did you get your tire patched after last time?"

"Of course," she huffed. After a long moment of

silence, she gave in and kicked the deflated rubber after all. It didn't make her feel better. In fact, it hurt her toes. "I just haven't picked it up from Donnie's yet."

"So no spare."

She flexed her aching toes. "Yes, just...not here. I'll, uh, figure something out. No problem."

Callum stalked toward his own truck. Biting her lip, she watched him open the driver's side door, wishing she had the courage to ask for help. The other guys had scattered as soon as they'd arrived at Fire Station One, where the dive team was based. She and Callum had rinsed the dive suits and equipment, then hung them to dry before coming out to the parking lot and discovering her flat.

After climbing into his truck, he didn't shut the door. Instead, he shot her an expectant look. "You coming?"

"Oh, thank you, baby Jesus." She hurried over to climb in the passenger side. "Can you give me a ride home?"

"No. Donnie stays open 'til six, so we should make it in time to pick up your tire."

With a frown, she buckled her seat belt. It was a good dozen miles from the fire station to Donnie's Auto Shop. "You don't have to take me all the way there. Home's fine."

"I'm not leaving you in the middle of nowhere without a vehicle."

"Um...okay. Thanks." She squirmed a little, playing with the seat belt strap. Dusk had fallen quickly as usual, the sun dropping behind the mountain peaks to the west and turning the undersides of the clouds a dull red. The flat expanse of the high plains stretched out to their right, while a vertical cliff paralleled the left side of the road. Smaller rocks were scattered along the snow-packed shoulder, reminding Lou that rockslide season was approaching. The dramatic scenery couldn't keep her mind off of the grisly discovery at the reservoir, though. "Think the sheriff is still out on the ice?"

He shrugged. "Probably. Doubt he'll bring in the state investigators until tomorrow, though."

"State investigators?"

"Colorado BCA." At her blank look, he elaborated, "Bureau of Criminal Apprehension. They help out the smaller law enforcement agencies with forensics, investigations, that sort of thing."

"Oh." She thought about that for a moment. "Rob seems pretty competent."

"He is, but it's been a few years since there's been a murder in Field County—one like this, at least."

"You mean because of the headlessness?"

"That, and, if there is a murder, it's usually obvious who did it. Domestics, drunken arguments, things like that."

"Right."

After a few minutes of quiet, Callum looked at her, opened his mouth as if he were going to speak, and then closed it again with a shake of his head.

"What?" she asked, curious. It wasn't like him to be twitchy or uncertain.

He didn't answer for what felt like a long time. Then suddenly, he said, "You did well today, Sparks."

"Thanks." She blew out a breath, surprised when it came out shaky. She thought she'd worked through the shakes and had arrived at sheer exhaustion. "I didn't feel like I did well. I kicked the poor, dead bastard."

"It got him to the surface, didn't it? The killer was

probably hoping he wouldn't be found for another three months." He paused before continuing. "You handled yourself well. Didn't get hysterical or even puke like Chad."

"Poor Chad."

Callum gave a short shake of his head. "Needs to toughen up before summer season."

She winced but had to ask. "Lots of bodies?"

"Some." He glanced at her. "You'll do fine. Just get good tires on your truck so you can get to calls."

"I'll move it up on my list." Obviously, those ten-ply tires were the bone Callum was not going to stop chewing. She was a little proud of herself for her calm, nonsnarky response. It was best not to aggravate the man driving twenty-five miles to pick up her patched tire and, hopefully, help her change it.

"Do that."

As they approached a county road intersection, the lone streetlight briefly illuminated the interior of the truck cab. Lou's casual glance at Callum turned into a stare. He was actually smiling! It did strange things to her insides, turning the unpleasant churning from the day's events into something lighter and warmer.

Darkness overtook the truck again, and that fleeting smile was gone. Callum remained silent, so Lou rested her head back and closed her eyes. She'd been right when she'd thought it was going to be a hell of a day—and it wasn't over yet.

Donnie had heard about the body and really wanted to talk about it. Lou just wanted to pick up her tire and go home, so she let Callum handle the conversation. It was nice to use his surliness for good instead of evil. After ten minutes of receiving grunts and monosyllabic replies to his questions, Donnie gave up and led them to her tire. Her still-flat tire.

"Couldn't fix it, Lou. Sorry." He lifted his hands in a helpless gesture. "It had a slice, a big one, about four inches. Almost looked like someone cut it with a knife."

"After the grader evens out the gravel road by my house, sometimes the blade sharpens the edges of the embedded rocks." She poked at the cut that had killed her tire. "Could it have been from that?"

"Maybe." Donnie looked skeptical. "Doubt the grader's been by recently, though. I don't know about your road, but mine's still pretty snow-covered. There's a chance the plow blade could've sharpened a rock, I guess." By his tone, it seemed he thought that chance was a very small one.

"Huh." Examining the slash again, she felt her whole body droop. God, she was tired. "I have another flat. Any chance you have a tire on hand that would fit?"

"I ordered you one last week after looking at this. Tried calling you, but your phone wouldn't let me leave a message."

She resisted the urge to bang her head against the auto shop wall. "Sorry, Donnie. Voice mail stops working every so often on my phone. I need a new one. It's on my list."

"Which list?"

She ignored Callum's comment. "Thanks for ordering the tire for me. What do I owe you?"

A little proud at how she managed to repress her wince

at the amount, she pulled out her battered bank card. Her hand shook only a little as Donnie took it from her.

"That did look like it was done with a knife," Callum said quietly, leaning so his mouth was close to her ear. "You been annoying anyone lately?"

"Besides you?"

"Yes."

"Nope." Rubbing her forehead with the heel of her hand, she shrugged. "No one that I know of, at least. I might be ignorantly aggravating random people, though. I wouldn't put it past me."

He reached up to gently squeeze her shoulder before pulling away. "I'll take a closer look at the other flat when we get back to the station."

At the thought, she felt her stomach clench. "That's probably another tire Donnie won't be able to patch. Shoot. Guess ten-ply tires just jumped even higher on my list."

"You know," Donnie said, handing back her card, "you might want to wait on getting those Load E tires until you figure out if anyone's stabbing holes in them."

Her teeth ground together, but she managed a tight smile. "Thanks."

"Anytime." His face grew serious. "And let me know if you hear anything more about the guy you found in the reservoir. I might call a couple of guys I haven't seen in a while, just to make sure they're okay."

She murmured something noncommittal and backed toward the door. "Thanks, Donnie. Can we just back up Callum's truck to the garage bay?"

"That'll work. Have a good one!"

"Too late." Lou sighed.

The second tire had definitely been slashed. Even Lou, despite her lack of experience, could tell that the long, even cut had not been inflicted by a rock.

Frowning harder than usual, Callum examined the ruined tire. "Where were you when the other tire went flat?"

"I was at my day job. The Coffee Spot."

He shot her a look. "I know where you work, Sparks."

"Right. I knew that. I think this day has just turned my brain into goo." She tugged her cap down over her ears. Now that it was dark and the wind had picked up, the mostly empty parking lot was even colder than before. "I was parked in back, in that dirt lot off the alley."

"What time?"

"I closed that night, so probably seven thirty? Quarter to eight, maybe? It was well after dark, I remember. I could tell something was wrong with my truck, since it looked uneven, but I thought I'd just parked with one wheel in a low spot or something. That halogen light in the parking lot casts some funky shadows. It didn't register in my brain that it was a flat until I was right up next to it."

He didn't say anything until after he lifted the tire with enviable ease into the bed of her pickup. Dusting off his gloves, he turned to look at her again. She braced, since she knew his "lecture face" all too well. It was not her favorite expression.

"You were alone?"

"Leaving work?" She knew where this was headed. "Yeah. It's really slow after five in the winter, so Ivy schedules only one of us to close. Plus, since Sylvia quit a couple of weeks ago, we've been shorthanded. I'm scheduled to work by myself for every shift this week."

"Huh." He pulled his dive-team baseball cap halfway off his head before yanking it back into place. "Don't like that."

Releasing a silent sigh, she restrained herself from rolling her eyes. Barely. "Can I get a lecture rain check? It's really cold."

He changed to her second-least-favorite expression— irritation—but gave a short nod. "Get home. Lock your doors."

"Yes, Dad," she said, grinning at him to soften the sarcasm. "Thanks. I really appreciate you helping me out tonight."

He didn't acknowledge her thanks but just said, "File a report with the sheriff about those tires."

"Will do. First thing tomorrow." She saluted and climbed into the cab, leaving her door open as she fired up the engine. Her faithful truck turned over immediately, as usual. She patted the dash.

"Did you just *pet* your truck?"

She shrugged. "She's a good truck."

Shaking his head, Callum headed back to his own vehicle. Lou could hear him muttering under his breath until he shut his cab door—but before he'd turned away from her, she'd caught the smile on his gruffly handsome face.

———

In the shadows of a nearby shed, he watched the taillights of her pickup turn out of the fire station lot. That

big guy in the baseball cap thought he was being helpful, but his interference was just delaying the inevitable. Turning away from the now-empty parking lot,
he started the half-mile walk to where he'd parked his
car. As he unlocked his tense fists, stretching his fingers
wide, he felt the anger screaming for release.

He took a deep breath, then another. He just needed
to be patient. Soon, this would all be over.

Chapter 3

SINCE SHE DIDN'T START WORK AT THE COFFEE SHOP until noon, she fulfilled her promise to Callum and pulled up to the sheriff's office just after eight the next morning. She stopped by Donnie's on the way, to pick up the first damaged tire and yet another intact spare.

As she pushed open the front entrance marked "Field County Sheriff Department," she looked around with interest. Although she'd been living in the area for the past seven months, Lou hadn't had the opportunity to visit the stout, blocky building on the north end of town until now. It was, she figured, probably a good thing not to be too familiar with law enforcement offices.

The friendly blond deputy from the day before greeted her. "Lou, right?"

She nodded, racking her brain. She was horrible at remembering names, but his had fortunately managed to stick in her memory. "Chris?"

"That's me." His smile widened. "What can I do for you?"

Making a face, she gestured in the direction of the parking lot, where her truck was sitting—hopefully still on four inflated tires. "I wanted to make a report. I've had a couple of slashed tires over the past week."

His smile dropped. "Sorry to hear that. You're sure it was deliberate? The roads around here can be tough on tires."

"Yes, unfortunately. Donnie noticed the first one, and Callum and I both agreed the second one looked cut. They're out in my truck if you want to take a look."

"Sure thing. Hang on a second." He ducked back into the office closest to the reception area. When he reemerged, he'd pulled on a jacket and was carrying a small notebook and a camera. The portable radio on his duty belt beeped as he turned it on. "I'd been doing some research on the computer. You learn to make sure to log off around here. If you stay signed in, one of the other cops is going to get on your email, and that's never good. Everyone in the department gets invited to your place for steak and lobster, or somehow your resignation letter gets sent to Rob, or some other crazy thing."

She blinked, absorbing this. "I don't know if it's a good thing to admit, but I'd probably fit in pretty well around here."

With a laugh, he held open the door, allowing her to step out first into the parking lot.

"Were you working on the case of the dead body?" She winced a little. When she said it like that, it sounded like the title of a very uninventive British mystery.

"Yeah." He eyed her carefully as they half walked, half slid over the snow-coated asphalt. "You doing okay? That's a pretty traumatic thing to have happen."

Her nod turned into a shrug halfway through. "Mostly. I had some crazy dreams last night. I'll be fine, though. We all have to experience our first dead person sometime."

He looked across the parking lot, expression distant. "True."

When he didn't elaborate, she moved to open her tailgate, revealing the tires. Chris frowned as he tugged the closer one toward him, leaning in to examine the gash. He took a couple of pictures and then pulled a small ruler out of his pocket. Holding it below the cut, he took a few more photos and then repeated the process on the second tire.

Turning off the digital camera and tucking it into one of his many BDU pockets, he flipped open his notebook and grabbed a pen. "Let me just write down your plate number, and we can go inside where it's warm for the rest of this." With one hand, he closed her tailgate.

"Do you agree that someone did this on purpose?" She huddled in her coat as he scribbled down the numbers. Just in the short time they'd been outside, the cold had crept through her layers. Tiny shivers were vibrating through her, making her voice shake.

Giving her a sharp look, Chris urged her toward the building with a hand on her upper back. "Looks that way. Where were you parked when it happened?"

"Behind The Coffee Spot the first time." A sheen of ice on the ground caught her eye, so she carefully shuffled her boots across the slippery patch. "Yesterday, my truck was in the Fire Station One parking lot all day."

"This was two separate incidents?"

"Yep."

"Hmm."

They walked back into the warmth of the lobby, and Lou shivered, this time from the relief of escaping the cold. Chris led her to the back office, tapping a key fob against the sensor next to the door. When a small green light flickered, he twisted the handle and held it open, standing to the side so she could enter.

The room was cramped, barely big enough for the

desk and two battered chairs it contained. A computer that looked like it had been through a lot of hard use sat in the center of the desk. Chris gestured toward one of the chairs, and Lou took a seat.

"So." Chris sat back in his chair. "Who'd you piss off?"

She frowned. "That's the second time someone's asked me that in the past sixteen hours. Have you been talking with Callum?"

With a laugh, he said, "Nope. It's just the obvious question."

"I can't think of anyone. Seriously, I'm a very likeable person."

He laughed again. "I can see that." Tapping his pen against his notepad, he stared at the Field County map hanging on the wall. "You live in Burton Valley, right? So, some of your neighbors are the Taylors, Gene Wentworth, Terry Buck…who else is out there?"

"The Moonies own the place next door, but they live in Arizona and have only been out a couple of weekends this winter. Oh, and the father and son who have the same jacked-up teeth are in that trailer about a half mile south of me."

"Right!" He snapped his fingers. "How could I forget Tim and Tim Junior Helling?"

"How indeed?"

He started the pen tapping again. "Any trouble with any of them?"

"No. The older Helling freaks me out a little when he talks about how the perfect world population is eleven million people, but he's always pretty polite about it. I'm about sixty percent sure he'd allow me to stick around with the others."

"Yeah, I've heard that theory from him a few times. He's harmless, though. How about any of the other neighbors? Hard to imagine it's one of them. You have a pretty nice bunch out there."

She shot him a sideways look. "You almost sound a little disappointed that I don't have any real crazies within spitting distance."

"Well, their sanity is not helping us widen our suspect pool."

"True." She thought for a moment. "Vic and Missy Taylor are sweethearts. Vic used their skid steer to blow the snow out of my driveway in January. Unfortunately, the county road was still blown over with three-foot-high drifts, but I could drive up and down my driveway if I wanted."

He motioned for her to continue.

"Gene's been pretty friendly. After his last stroke, though, he's really gone downhill. He was telling me how he can barely see ten feet in front of him. I don't think he should be driving."

Frowning, Chris made a note. "Thanks. I'll check it out. How about Terry?"

She shrugged. "I don't think I've ever met him. Wait—does he drive a black pickup with a blue topper?"

"Yes."

"We've waved when our trucks have passed each other on the road, but that's about it."

"Hmm." He flipped through the pages in his notebook where he'd been scribbling as she talked. "How about before? Where are you from?"

"Connecticut." She was already shaking her head. "The only people I aggravated there were my parents, and they wouldn't even come out here to visit, much less skulk around dark parking lots stabbing my tires."

"No ex-lovers, boyfriends, stalkers, roommates, rivals?" he rattled off, making her stare and then laugh.

"An ex-boyfriend, but he wouldn't do anything like this."

"You sure about that? People can surprise you."

"Positive." Despite the ugliness of their breakup, the ridiculous thought of Brent tramping around in the snow slashing tires made her smile grimly. "He's not a fan of getting his hands dirty."

"What's his name?"

"Brenton Lloyd."

Chris scribbled in his notebook and then looked at her. "Any other possibilities?"

"Not that I can think of. Sorry. I lived a very boring, nonconfrontational life."

"Okay." He closed his notebook and stood. "I'll do some digging. In the meantime, keep your eyes open. Park in well-lit, heavily trafficked areas as much as you can. Don't be closing the coffee shop by yourself. Here." He handed her a card. "Call me if anything else happens or you remember something that might be relevant."

"Got it."

His serious expression faded and was replaced by a hint of a smirk. "Hang around Callum as much as you can. Don't think he'd mind."

"Uh, yeah, no. I annoy him. Greatly."

The smirk turned into a full-on grin. "Just saying. He couldn't keep his eyes off of you at the reservoir yesterday, and I wouldn't say he looked annoyed. Befuddled, maybe."

"Befuddled?"

"Befuddled."

"I think *you* might be the befuddled one, Deputy Chris, if you think Callum Cook has any interest in me."

He laughed. "Deny it all you want. But you're not the dashing law enforcement officer with the keen eye for observation."

With a snort, she turned for the door. "Keen eye, my ass."

As she walked through the lobby, a harassed-looking Rob barged through the front doors. He stopped his forward charge just short of crashing into her.

"Sorry about that, Lou," he said.

"No harm done." She eyed his frown. "Rough day? *Another* rough day, I mean."

"State investigators are here." His scowl started to return. He looked a little worn around the edges. On him, the exhausted look was surprisingly appealing. Although she wasn't interested in Rob that way, she was surprised he'd managed to remain single. The stoop of his shoulders made her want to watch over him as he took a much-needed nap, and she couldn't be the only woman who felt that way. "Which means dealing with the usual dick-measuring."

Confused, she asked, "But I thought you asked them to come?"

"I did. It's just the typical bullshit that happens when you put a bunch of people who are used to being in charge together on one crime scene. Too many alpha dogs always leads to a snarl or two." He shook his head and looked at her sharply. "Enough about that. Did you need to talk to me?"

"No, Chris already took my report."

"Report?"

She shrugged. "Someone slashed a couple of my tires."

Rob looked over her shoulder, and she turned to see Chris joining them. "I'll have the report to you by the end of my shift," the deputy said.

"Good." Rob turned back to Lou. "Sorry to hear about your tires. I'll make sure we look into it. You'll have to excuse me now. I just need to pick up a couple of things before heading back out to the scene."

"No problem." She took a step toward the door. "Good luck with the whole dick-measuring thing. Thanks, Chris."

Both men lifted their chins in the exact same good-bye gesture, forcing Lou to have to quash a smile before it could make it to her lips.

The two men moved toward the office and, as she reached the door, she overheard Rob ask, "Any luck here?"

"Not yet. No one in Field County matching his description—well, the neck-down description—was reported missing between last October and January. I even stretched it a couple of months and checked August and September. I'm working my way through the missing-person reports from the entire state, but that's going to take me a while."

"Okay. Keep on it. We've got no way to identify the victim right now, even though the state's dive team is pulling up a ton of shit out of the water that they're calling 'potential evidence.' I'll..." He went silent for a second before raising his voice. "Did you need something else, Lou?"

"No." She sent him a sunny smile over her shoulder. "I'm good for now. Thanks!"

Knowing she couldn't stall and listen any longer, she pushed open the door and stepped out into the frigid wind.

—⁂—

Lou's shift at The Coffee Spot had just started when Callum shoved open the glass door, sending the attached sleigh bells swinging. She grimaced. When she'd first started working at the coffee shop, she'd enjoyed the Christmassy sound. Now, however, familiarity had definitely bred contempt.

"What's that look?" Callum asked a little snappishly as he approached the counter.

"Those bells. I want to rip them off and hurl them into the street for a semi to squash."

"Oh." He blinked. "I figured it was me."

Lou looked back and forth between the bells and the man, pretending to consider. "Nope," she finally said. "The bells are more annoying."

Instead of his usual glare, he just ignored her. He must have been in a good mood.

"Coffee?" she asked.

"Yeah." He scowled at the menu, written on an oversized whiteboard and pinned high on the wall behind Lou. "Just black coffee. None of the fancy, sugary stuff."

"Got it." Grabbing the travel mug he held out to her, she headed for the pot of plain house brew. "*Manly* coffee."

Callum eyed her as if checking for sarcasm. She wasn't sure why he bothered. With her, sarcasm was guaranteed, a free bonus to go with his caffeine fix. "Did you talk to the sheriff about your tires?"

"Yep." She handed him his filled mug as he passed her a five dollar bill. After she gave him his change, he tucked everything she'd returned to him in the tip jar. Lou bit back a pleased smile. "Thanks. I went in first thing this morning, as a matter of fact. Well, second thing. I picked up a spare and the first stabbed tire beforehand. The sheriff wasn't there, though—not until I was leaving, at least. I talked to one of the deputies."

"Chris Jennings?"

"That's the one." She grabbed a wet cloth to wipe the counters. They were already clean, but Lou needed something to look at besides Callum…especially with Deputy Chris's comments running on repeat in her brain. "He was really thorough. I thought they'd blow me off, especially with a murderer running around, but he seemed to take it seriously."

"Huh." As he took a sip of coffee, he watched her over the top of his mug. "I bet he did."

That brought her head up. "Why?"

He was quiet for a moment and then said, "He's a… thorough guy."

That did nothing to appease her curiosity. She tossed the cloth into the sink. "What's that mean? Don't you like him?"

"He's fine." Callum sliced his hand through the air as if to physically end that detour. "Did he have any ideas about who might be doing it?"

"No." Leaning on the counter, she twisted the tip jar in circles until he stopped her with a big hand over hers. "I couldn't think of anyone who didn't like me."

"Hmm."

"That's what Chris said." His hand was still over

hers. Heat was creeping up her arm from where his palm covered her fingers, and she knew a blush was imminent. *Thanks, Chris.* Now she was the one who was befuddled.

"What'd he say?" he asked, seeming unaffected.

"Hmm."

"That's not helpful."

She shrugged. "Maybe he had some ideas he wasn't sharing. Figuring out who the dead guy is should be his priority, anyway."

"Had he?"

"Had he what?"

"Figured out who the dead guy was?"

"Nope." She flexed her fingers. Had he ever touched her for this long before? "Rob got back as I was leaving. I happened to overhear a little bit of his conversation with Chris about that."

Finally moving his hand, he propped an elbow on the counter, tipping his head toward hers in a silent request to continue.

"No one in Field County went missing around the time the coroner thinks the dead guy was dumped in the reservoir—no one who looks like our guy, at least. Chris's checking all the people who disappeared in Colorado during that time, but he hasn't found anyone yet."

Looking thoughtful, Callum took another sip of coffee.

"Do you think you should mention your theory about the cult? Or the militia group?"

He shook his head. "Rob's a smart guy, and he's been doing this a while. He'll look at all the possibilities."

"Hmm."

A corner of his mouth lifted. "Now *you're* doing it."

She laughed but sobered quickly. "It's just... Rob said that they don't have any leads in finding out who he is—well, *was*. It doesn't sound like state will be much help, either. I feel kind of responsible for him—the dead guy, I mean. Because I was the one who found him, I think. I really want to help figure out who the poor guy is. His family is probably frantic."

"Or they think he went for cigarettes and never came home."

Horrified, she stared at him. "That's even worse! His kids will think that he abandoned them. His wife probably thinks he was having an affair and... Okay, that's it. I'm going to do a little digging."

His eyebrows were raised in his *please-return-to-reality* expression. That was probably her third least favorite of his faces. "The entire Field County Sheriff's Department is working on it, *with* the Colorado BCA. You really think you have resources they don't?"

"I'm tenacious."

With a sigh, he said, "You've already pissed off someone enough that they're sticking knives in your tires. Do you really need to annoy more people by muddling around in a murder investigation?"

"Yes. I mean, I won't annoy people. I'll be discreet."

He snorted.

"I can be discreet."

Those damn eyebrows were up again.

"I can. Discreet and tenacious. Two of my best traits."

Rubbing his forehead as if he had a headache, he sighed again and tugged his hat back into place. "Fine. We'll do some research. *Discreetly*."

"We?"

"Yes. God knows what trouble you'd get into on your own. At least if I'm there, I can make sure you don't aggravate someone into sticking a knife into *you*. Now top off my coffee—please. I have to get to work. My real work, not this Nancy Drew shit you're dragging me into."

Stunned into silence and stupidly thrilled at the idea of spending more time with Callum, she did as he asked. After grabbing his newly filled travel mug, he stomped out the door, making those stupid bells ring again.

She stared after him for what felt like a long time. "Huh."

It was a relief to leave the coffee shop at the end of her shift to find all four of her truck's tires still fully inflated. Lou did feel a smidgen of guilt at disregarding the don't-go-anywhere-alone advice both Callum and Chris had given her, but she hadn't had a chance to talk to Ivy about scheduling a second person for evenings. Not that she'd really tried too hard to find that chance, since she was dreading Ivy's reaction. Her boss could be a bit of a bear, especially when it came to the coffee shop's bottom line. Having two people working the slow winter evenings was going to be asking a lot.

Lou had parked in the well-lit front lot, though, so she was following *some* of their advice, at least. Although her boss was probably not going to like her taking up a customer's parking spot, it was the lesser of two Ivy-related evils.

With a sigh, Lou turned the key, patting her truck's dash when the engine fired smoothly. She'd fight those battles when they came, she figured, reversing out of her parking space. When she pressed on the brake, the tires slid across the icy pavement for a few feet before slowing. Lou winced, glad that hers was the only vehicle in the lot.

The town of Simpson was as quiet as a ghost town as she drove the few blocks to the highway that would take her most of the way home. It was a tourist town, far enough away from the ski resorts that half of the shops closed for the winter. Summer was the busy time, when the road through town was bumper-to-bumper RVs and SUVs stacked with bikes and kayaks.

Now, only a few vehicles traveling in the opposite direction passed her on the nine-mile stretch to her turnoff. Plows had piled the snow twelve feet high on either side of the gravel road. Her headlights bounced off the white wall, making her feel as if she were in a tunnel—a tunnel that was slowly closing in on her. A claustrophobia-induced shiver touched her spine, so she reached for the radio preset buttons, looking for a distraction.

The DJ on a local station was in the middle of reading the news. Normally, that consisted of bake sale announcements and road closures, but the DJ's voice had an urgency usually not heard in the lost-pet report. Lou turned up the volume and caught the tail end of what had to be a story about the body found in the reservoir.

"…remains unidentified. If anyone has any information, please contact the Field County Sheriff's Department at—"

Lou punched the off button, interrupting the DJ mid-sentence. All day, between making lattes and serving muffins, her thoughts had kept returning to the dead

guy—*her* dead guy. Although she had been flabber-
gasted when Callum offered to help with her unofficial
investigation, she was also relieved. She couldn't just
continue to *think* about what happened. She had to *do*
something. Especially when it looked like the actual
authorities weren't going to get anywhere. Wasn't it
always the plucky loners who solved the case in all
the movies?

Or got themselves killed, she thought.

Pulling up to her gate, Lou sighed. The wind had
blown the dry, light snow, piling it into drifts across her
long driveway. She hopped out of her truck and hurried
to unlatch the gate. Shoving it against the fluffy piles,
she used it like a snowplow to scrape the snow clear.
Once the gate was open, she let out a relieved breath. If
she wasn't careful to keep it clear, the wind would pack
the drifts into frozen concrete, and no amount of shoving
would have made them budge.

Climbing back into her truck, she drove through the
gate and then stopped to close it. Visions of an automatic
gate that opened and closed with a touch of a button—a
button located in the cozy warmth of her truck, of
course—danced in her head, but an automatic gate was
so far down on her "want" list that she shouldn't even
be dreaming about it.

The rest of her driveway was still pretty decent,
although she had to back up to get a running start to
plow through a couple of places where snow had drifted
more heavily.

"Just three more months," she muttered to herself
as the wheels spun, flinging snow high into the air like
an uncapped blender. "The rest of March, then April,

then May, and then June will be here, and the snow will melt." Hopefully. Maybe. "Summer has to come sometime, right? This is not fricking Antarctica!"

The tires finally caught and pushed the truck through the deep spot. Relaxing a little, she flexed her fingers, forcing her hands to release their death grip on the steering wheel. The rest of the short distance to her tiny cabin was manageable, and she tucked her pickup as close to the south side of her house as she could get.

Climbing out of her truck, she locked the door before swinging it shut with a thump. The sound made Lou realize how quiet it was. Evergreens surrounded her property, blocking any view of a neighbor's house or the road. Her cabin defined the term "middle of nowhere."

The wind blew through the trees, shifting the branches and their accompanying shadows. *Anything could be out there*, she thought, images of bears and mountain lions and horror-movie madmen flashing through her mind. With a shiver, she hurried toward the cabin door. If she allowed herself to think about what might be lurking in the shadows, she'd never be able to sleep that night.

On her way inside, she paused just long enough to grab several pieces of firewood from the stack, juggling them as she struggled to unlock her door. Nerves made her clumsy, and she almost dropped the keys twice. The dead bolt finally released, and she half fell inside as the door opened. Dumping her armload of wood onto the tile floor with little regard to the mess of bark she'd have to sweep up later, she leaned back against the door until it closed with a thump.

She was home. Safe. Completely alone.

Vulnerable.

Lou spun around, twisted the dead bolt, and then stared at the locked door, nerves jangling. She'd grown up in the city, where alarm systems and locks were the norm. In Field County, most of the people she'd talked to about it confessed to rarely locking their doors. Lou wondered if the higher percentage of shotgun ownership partially explained that. Most people in the area knew not to walk into someone else's home without an invitation. A couple of months ago, she hadn't given the locks a second thought.

But the tire-slashing had ratcheted up her paranoia. It made her uneasy, the idea that there was someone out there so enraged that he or she was willing to damage her personal property. It made it worse that she had no idea who it might be. She'd managed to drive someone to the point of criminal retaliation, and she'd had no idea she was even doing it. Not to mention there was an honest-to-God murderer on the loose.

With a shake of her head, she broke her focus on the lock and started shedding her outerwear.

Fifteen minutes later, she was curled up on the couch next to the woodstove, wearing her favorite fuzzy socks and long underwear—a clothing item that, up until four months earlier, she'd never dreamed she would own, much less wear. Now, it was her loungewear of choice. Gazing down at the red-plaid flannel, she smiled, imagining what her mother's reaction would be to seeing her now.

She pulled her laptop closer and pressed the power key. Her electricity was limited to what was produced by a few solar panels and an ancient propane generator, but she'd learned to charge her phone and computer during the sunny part of the day. At night, she'd unplug everything except her refrigerator and use candles for light as much as possible. Candles didn't use any electricity. Plus, they smelled good.

But the one thing she knew she had to have when she'd moved into her new rustic home the previous August was Internet. There was roughing it, and then there was just plain nuts, and not having Internet was solidly in the second category. The monthly satellite Internet fee required her to eat more meals consisting of ramen noodles or peanut butter than was probably healthy, but, in her mind, having Internet was worth a few cheap meals.

Opening a web browser, she stared at the search bar, considering. Finally, she decided to go for the obvious and typed in "missing person Field County Colorado." A few of the results looked promising, including a site on missing people in Colorado. She clicked on that one. Once the website loaded, she was immediately overwhelmed by the sheer number of possibilities, and she felt sympathy for Chris's plight.

She surfed through different sites for about an hour, until she started yawning. Closing the browser window, she felt a little disappointed by her lack of results. The idea of investigating the case was exciting, but she wasn't sure how to start. To figure out who killed the man, she needed to know why. To figure out the motivation, she had to know who. Of the five "W"s, she had about half of one—the "what."

With a discouraged sigh, she opened her email. One from her mom popped up immediately, which didn't help her mood. She really hoped there wasn't an e-ticket attached. If there was, though, maybe she could exchange it for a flight to Hawaii or something. Sunshine and a warm beach would be a nice change from the frozen mountains.

Her finger hovered over the touchpad as she debated whether to open it or not. But she figured she'd probably dwell on it more if she didn't read it, so she reluctantly clicked on it. Immediately, she regretted the click.

"Louise," she read out loud, "I am very disappointed...blah, blah, blah...your stepfather agrees... blah, blah, and more blah...disrespectful to Brenton... come to your senses...blah and blah...your mother."

She hit the delete button with some satisfaction, although she did have one regret. "No trip to Hawaii, then. Bummer."

—∿—

He'd never been so cold. The wind was brutal, leaving him shaking, his hands and feet numb. The other side of the pine tree would have provided more of a windbreak, but he didn't want to move out of the concealing shadows. He'd learned to put caution before comfort.

Tucking his head, he buried his mouth in the upturned collar of his coat, allowing the damp heat of his breath to warm his skin. She was torturing him, making him hide in the dark and frigid night just to get a glimpse of her. Resisting the urge to stamp feeling back into his feet, he stayed perfectly still and watched.

Time passed—either hours or minutes. It was hard to keep track of things like that. He straightened as her bedroom window lit, pooling warm light on the snow. As his heart accelerated, he walked toward the cabin, step by cautious step. He hated to leave the cover of the trees, but the lure of seeing her was too great. The clearing stretched between him and Lou, the light surface of the snowdrifts silhouetting him, but the reward outweighed the risk. He focused on that square of light, drawing him closer and closer to the cabin.

Once he saw her framed in the window, he knew the hours of silent vigil had been worth it. She faced away from the window as she pulled her shirt over her head. The warm lamplight brought out the peach and gold in her skin.

She was so beautiful and, at the same time, so careless with his feelings.

Reaching behind her with both hands, she unhooked her bra, allowing it to slide down her arms. At the sight of her bare back, his breath caught so hard he almost choked. Although he kept silent, he couldn't stop himself from moving forward until he was just a few feet from the window.

He watched, mesmerized, as she stripped down to her panties. That body, that gorgeous, elegant body, was *his*. She might not realize that yet, but she would. He'd make sure of it.

Risking another step forward, he held back a disappointed sound as she pulled on her shapeless flannel pajamas. Once she was sharing his bed, she wouldn't wear such ugly things. He'd buy her delicate and expensive lingerie, the kind her luscious body deserved.

She finally turned to face the window. At first, he ducked automatically, before he realized that she couldn't see him. To her, the window was a wall of darkness, while he saw every detail of her life. A small, smug smile curled his mouth. This moment of power and superiority almost made waiting in the cold worth it.

His victorious thrill lasted until the light blinked out, leaving him exposed. He knew he had hours before she went to bed. Although he was tempted to circle her cabin and watch her through the living room windows, he forced himself to wait. It was too early for that. Once she was sleeping, he could look all he wanted.

So he returned to his hiding spot in the trees, growing colder and angrier with each passing moment. When the bedroom window lit again, just for a few moments, he allowed himself to move toward the cabin. His muscles had grown stiff, and his gait was awkward. Despite his discomfort, he had to catch himself before he ran toward the cabin. What had started out as practicality had grown into an obsession.

As he drew closer, there was no scream of discovery, no shotgun pointed at his face, so he dared to cross the final few steps until he was looking right into her window. He was close enough for his breath to leave condensation on the glass. Silently, he wiped the fogged spot clear with his sleeve.

She was in bed, curled in her usual position on her side. As he watched her sleep, time blinked forward again, until the numbness in his toes turned to a burn he couldn't ignore. Soon. Soon, he wouldn't have to haunt frozen forests and abandoned parking lots to see her. She'd be right next to him in his bed. Where she belonged.

This needed to work. It *had* to work. Nothing was right without her.

Chapter 4

"So…?"

It had taken her the entire dive-team training session to finally corner Callum. They'd been forced inside Station One by low temperatures and a biting wind, so they were polishing their first aid skills, checking equipment, and practicing with the rope-filled throw bags that were used to get a line from a rescuer on shore to someone in the water. When Callum moved away from the group to retrieve a stray throw bag, she saw her chance and followed.

"So?" he repeated, sounding distracted as he watched the others. "Chad throws like a fucking five-year-old girl." He glanced at Lou. "No offense."

"Why would I be offended? I'm not a five-year-old." She paused. "Though for the record, I *am* a girl, and I'm more accurate with the throw bag than half the guys on the team. Anyway, I wanted to talk about our…research project."

The slightest of grimaces crossed his face.

"Oh, no, no, no," she said. "None of that."

"None of what?"

"You're thinking of backing out." Lou planted herself in front of him, her fists on her hips. "There will be no backing out of this. I need your help. I realized last night that I have no clue what I'm doing."

His eyes shifted over her shoulder, as if he were

wishing he were away from her and back in the safety of numbers. Lou tipped her body slightly to the right so she could put herself in his line of sight.

"Please?" She bounced a little on the balls of her feet. "C'mon, Cal, you've been dive-team leader for how long now? Share your wisdom. Be my sensei. Lead me on the path of criminal enlightenment."

He exhaled heavily, and she gave another tiny hop of excitement, knowing she had him. "You're just going to harass me until I do anyway."

"That's right!" She beamed at him.

"Fine. Wait until everyone's left, and we'll talk." Glancing at his watch, he bellowed, "Time's up! See you all in two weeks. It's CPR recertification, so attendance is mandatory."

Several groans and mutters met his announcement as the dive-team members began to gather the equipment. Lou started stacking chairs.

"What are you so happy about?" Derek grumbled, grabbing her stack of chairs and carrying it to the storage room. "CPR training blows. Or do you enjoy sucking face with those creepy plastic dummies?"

Lou just grinned, starting a new stack of chairs. Not even CPR recertification could dampen her happiness. "Oh please, you drama queen. We all have our own breathing masks. It's not like in junior high babysitter certification where all that was between you and the last girl's spit was a funky-tasting alcohol wipe."

"Whoa." Derek blinked. "That image is...disturbing."

She smirked at him and hauled her chair tower into the storage room, dumping the stack by the one Derek had just deposited. A small, pained sound next to her brought her head around. Callum was eyeing the slightly lopsided, uneven stacks with a scowl.

"What's wrong?" she asked, looking from the chairs to his face and back.

"It's fine." One look at his twitching jaw muscle told her that it was *not* at all fine. When he reached out to straighten one of the chairs that hung a little drunkenly on top of its brothers, realization dawned.

"It's okay," she assured him, taking a step back. "It won't hurt my feelings if you rearrange them."

"It'll hurt mine," Derek objected as he entered the small room with the last few chairs. "I worked really hard to get these arranged exactly the way I wanted them. It's like art. Chair art." He tipped the newly straightened chair so it drooped askew again.

Callum glared at Derek, who was shifting another chair so the legs were misaligned.

"Stop," Lou scolded, although she couldn't completely erase the laughter from her voice. She gave Derek a push toward the door. "Don't torture his OCD soul."

The hard gaze shifted to Lou, and she held up her hands defensively. "Not that I'm saying you have OCD or anything. You just like things to be organized. Really, really organized." When Callum didn't look any happier, she gave up trying to appease him and just focused on getting Derek out of the storage room with another hard shove.

"Ow!" he whined as she herded him like a sheepdog, but he gave in to her less-than-gentle nudges and stepped through the doorway. As he entered the main training room, he gave a yelp at the sight of the huge digital clock on the wall. "It's late! I'm going to run. See you kids later."

"See you," Lou responded, waving as he grabbed his gear and headed to the parking lot. She turned back to the open storage-room door and stopped abruptly. In the short time it had taken for her and Derek to exchange good-byes, Callum had moved the chairs into perfectly even, exactly aligned stacks, arranged in two rows with almost frightening precision.

"Wow." Lou couldn't look away from the Stepford chairs. "That's…um, tidy."

With a satisfied grunt, Callum turned to face her. "Want to do some research?"

She beamed at him. "Yes, please. Here? Or do you want to go to my place?" With an inner wince, she thought of the lived-in look of her cabin. It was never actually dirty, but it was rather messy. Maybe taking Callum to her place wasn't a great idea. "Or here is fine, too."

He opened his mouth as if to speak, then closed it again silently. His gaze had moved to something behind her, so she turned around to look through the doorway into the training room to see what had distracted him.

"Hey, Cal." It was firemen-calendar-centerfold himself, Ian Walsh. "And it's Louise, right?"

"Lou," she corrected, although she couldn't help smiling. She also might have batted her eyelashes, just a little. Ian was just too perfect, as if he'd been modeled after someone's sexy fireman dream.

Callum moved around her, bumping her shoulder on the way. She shot him a surprised look. Callum was many aggravating things, but rude was normally not one of them. He didn't seem to notice her miffed gaze, too busy giving Ian the glare of icy death.

"Walsh," he said. "Need something?"

"Forgot my phone," Ian explained, apparently unoffended by Callum's chilly tone. Instead, one side of his mouth quirked up in a half smile. "I'm addicted to the thing."

"Oh, me too." Lou knew she was gushing, but she couldn't help herself. In her defense, she was pretty sure that anyone with a hint of estrogen would gush when looking at Ian Walsh, especially when he was wearing that smile. Ian was the definition of swoon-worthy, even if she couldn't help but think he wasn't *quite* as handsome as a scowling Callum. "If I'm away from it too long, I start getting the shakes."

That brought a full-out laugh from Ian. "Don't forget the imaginary bugs crawling on you."

She nodded mock-solemnly. "They're the worst."

Callum cleared his throat. "Your phone?"

"Right." Ian sent her another grin and winked before crossing the training area toward the locker room on the other side. Lou couldn't help but watch him walk away. *Whoa*.

"Quit drooling, Sparks!" Callum snapped, dragging her attention back to him.

"Oh please," she said dismissively, waving a hand. "Who could resist looking at that eye candy?"

He just glared. "Me."

She resisted the urge to mention that, as the resident iceman, Callum did not count. Instead, she just reminded him, "Research?"

"Sure you can tear yourself away from Walsh?"

"Quit being pissy, and let's identify a dead man."

"I'm not being pissy." He still sounded pissy.

"Fine. Research?"

"Fine."

—✺—

"'Research' isn't some new euphemism for getting laid, is it?" Lou asked, looking around at the sparse scattering of patrons at the Simpson Bar.

Callum made a sound that could have been a swallowed laugh. It was hard to hear it over the country music blaring from the overhead speakers. He didn't answer her question. Instead, he headed to the bar.

Lou followed him and slipped onto the bar stool he had politely pulled out for her. She turned to give a social smile to the thin woman occupying the next stool and then blinked in surprise. The woman was none other than Coroner Belly.

"Oh! Hi!" Even as the words left her mouth, Lou winced inwardly. There was way too much enthusiasm there. "Sorry," Lou added quickly. "I just didn't recognize you at first. I'm Lou, one of the dive-team members? We met yesterday at the…uh, reservoir."

Belly's chilly expression thawed considerably. "Right! The cute little blond diver who kicked the corpse. I remember you now."

"Oh, um. Right." Her voice lost a lot of its enthusiasm at the reminder. "Is that how people are going to identify me now? As the person who kicked a dead guy?"

"Oh, for God's sake." Belly took a long drink of her beer. "I said you were cute, too, didn't I?"

"Sorry?"

"Hey, Bel," Callum said. "They figure out who that guy is yet?"

After another drink from her bottle, Belly answered, "Nope, poor bastard."

"Huh." The bartender approached, and Cal held up three fingers and pointed at Belly's beer. "Poor bastard is right."

"And his poor family," Lou added. "Probably thinking he walked out on them when he was actually murdered. So sad."

The bartender set three beers in front of them. Lou reached for her purse, but Callum was quicker, pulling out some bills and handing them to the server with a nod of thanks.

"Thank you. I'll get the next round," Lou said. Callum made a sound that could've been agreement but most likely wasn't.

"Thanks, Cal," Belly said as she finished off the remains of her beer and reached for the next one, almost in the same motion.

"Something's bothering me," Lou said slowly, not sure if she was crossing a professional line but unable to ignore this sterling opportunity to ask some of the questions that had been plaguing her. "Whoever cut off the guy's hands, it…well, it wasn't when he was *alive*, was it?" She almost didn't want to hear Belly's answer, just in case it wasn't the reassurance she wanted, but it was worse not to know.

"Nope," Belly said. "Don't worry about that. Definitely postmortem."

"That's good. Not good about the cutting part, of course. That he wasn't alive when… I mean, I'd rather not be feeling it if someone was going to chop off my hands, if I had to choose, although I probably wouldn't get a choice in that situ…um. Right."

Her babbling cut off at the heavy weight of one of Callum's hands on her shoulder. Closing her mouth with a snap, she stared at her beer and started picking at the corner of the label.

"Much better to be dead if someone's going to chop off your hands with a Sawzall," Belly agreed.

Swallowing, Lou had to ask, "Is that how the murderer did it? With a Sawzall?"

"Yep. The head, too. Messy business. Didn't know what the fuck he was doing. Guess we're not looking for a surgeon or a butcher or even someone who hunts much."

Making a conscious effort not to meet Callum's gaze, Lou gently probed, "How old was this guy—the victim, I mean?"

"Sixty-five-ish." To Lou's surprise, Belly seemed perfectly willing to share. "Caucasian, diabetic, five-ten or thereabouts, one hundred and fifty pounds, gray hair—although the hair on his head might be different from the hair on his body—probably died of some kind of head trauma."

"How can you tell it was head trauma if he, ah, didn't have it on him? His head, I mean."

"Well, it had to be, didn't it?" Belly asked. "The rest of him was fairly healthy—except for the diabetes—so it was either a bullet to the head or something hit him really hard. I'd need to see the head to tell you for sure."

"Oh, that makes sense." Lou thought for a second. "How'd you know he had diabetes?"

Belly gave her a flat look. "Do you really want to hear about a dead man's pancreas?"

"Um…not really." She was pretty sure she wouldn't be able to understand what the coroner told her, anyway.

"Plus," Belly added, turning back to her beer, "he was missing two toes on his right foot."

"Had they been amputated before he died, or was it part of the whole Sawzall thing?"

"Amputated. Few months before, I'd guess. Pretty common for diabetics. Nerve damage and poor circulation can lead to nonhealing foot ulcers. If they're not treated quickly, the resulting tissue damage can require part of the foot or leg to be amputated." Belly sounded impressively coherent for a small woman with several beers under her belt. Glancing at Callum's untouched beer, Lou realized that Belly was the reason Callum had brought her to the bar. The coroner was their research source.

"Hmm." Great, now she was doing the humming thing again. Lou tried to think of any other questions she could ask the coroner. "He didn't have any birthmarks or tattoos or anything, did he? I don't remember any, but I was a little distracted by the dead body and the shock and everything at the time."

Belly gave a short laugh. "Yeah, you have a pretty good excuse for not noticing his back had been ripped to shit at one point, a long time ago. Looked like shrapnel scars, from Vietnam, I'd guess—just a guess, mind you, since he's about the right age, plus he had an Army tattoo on the left side of his chest." She patted halfway between her breast and collarbone. "Served our country and then someone chopped him up and tossed him in the reservoir. There's respect for you." Turning her head, she spat in the general direction of the floor. Lou hurriedly yanked her foot back before the loogie could land on her boot.

"Thanks, Bel." Callum gave Lou a light time-to-go pat on her shoulder before tossing another bill in the bartender's direction. "Have a good night."

"Yes, thanks for talking with us, Belly," Lou echoed as she slid off her stool. "Good-bye."

Belly waved, focusing on her beer as they moved away from the bar.

———⁓———

"I feel kind of dirty," Lou admitted as they walked through the bar's snow-packed parking lot.

Callum's eyebrows rose almost to his hairline. "Excuse me?"

She gave an uncomfortable shrug. "Like we took advantage of Belly's, you know, tipsiness or something."

"Oh." He was quiet for a moment. "She wouldn't have said anything to just anyone, if that makes you feel better. She also, most likely, would have shared all that with you sober."

"Really? What makes me special? I just met her, so it's not like she really knows me well."

Callum stopped at the driver's door of her truck as she pulled it open. "You're one of us now."

Cocking her head to the side, she just stared at him, confused.

"Fire, paramedics, cops. Search and rescue. You're not just the barista making Belly's coffee anymore — you're her colleague."

"Oh." A warm sensation slipped over her at the thought of being part of a group, of a family consisting of not only the dive team, but of all Field County's first responders. It was a nice feeling…comforting.

"Just make sure you keep the information confidential," he warned. "What we see on the scene or hear from others, like Bel, stays among us, got it?"

She climbed into the truck. "Got it."

When he unexpectedly leaned closer, her breath caught with a sudden mix of panic and startling hot anticipation. Mostly panic. Maybe. Seemingly unaware of her response, Callum reached an arm out and flicked the gaudy pendant hanging from her rearview mirror.

"This is illegal, you know. It obstructs your view and could create a blind spot."

She blinked, crushing any possible disappointment into rubble. "Oh."

With a frown, he glanced around the cab. "Don't you ever clean your truck?"

"Of course." The touch of disapproval in his tone made her clench her molars as she gave him a wide grin showing lots of teeth. "Once a year, whether it needs it or not."

The appalled look on his face made her laugh for real.

"Good night, Cal."

Stepping back, he checked to make sure she was clear of the door before closing it. He lifted a hand and watched as she backed out of her parking spot. When she turned onto Main Street and headed for the highway and home, she glanced in her rearview mirror.

Callum was still standing where she'd left him, illuminated by the sodium lights of the Simpson Bar parking lot, looking gorgeous and strong and achingly alone.

Chapter 5

THE NEXT DAY, AN UNSEASONABLY WARM SPELL brought hordes of people out of hibernation and directly to The Coffee Spot. It was late afternoon before the shop emptied, and Lou finally had the chance to pull out her laptop and log onto the Internet.

But before she had time to do anything else, the sleigh bells from hell jangled, announcing the entrance of yet another customer. Biting back the curses that wanted to escape, she closed her laptop and plastered on a smile.

"What can I get…oh, Cal!" Her fake smile morphed into a real one. "Thank God. I've been dying to talk with you. My brain wouldn't turn off last night. I just kept thinking about everything Belly told us, so now I have a gazillion questions."

Although he wasn't smiling, his expression was slightly more pleasant than his usual dark scowl. He held out his travel mug, and Lou filled it while still talking.

"We now know a lot more. I mean, HDG had—"

"H-what?" he interrupted.

Flushing a little, she explained, "HDG, as in Headless Dead Guy. Sorry, I know that's insensitive, but I had to call him something, so I've been referring to him as HDG in my head, and it just slipped out."

Callum looked more amused than offended. "The job— the dive team, not the coffee job—tends to make all of us more callous. Just watch how you talk around civilians."

"That's what the initials are for. So I don't actually say the words 'headless' or 'dead.'" She grinned. "Anyway, now we know he'd been in the Army, had diabetes, and was missing two toes. So I'm wondering if we should check out the nearest veterans' hospital? Or maybe a VFW or something?"

He sipped his coffee, considering.

"I like your idea about the VA hospital, but how are you planning on getting any information? With HIPA, they won't give out patient information to random people."

Making a face, she admitted, "You're right. I hadn't thought it out that far." She rested her chin on her cupped hand, her elbow propped on the counter, and thought. "So we probably won't get any information from the staff, but what about the other patients?"

He nodded slowly. "The VA hospital in Denver is probably too large for that to work, but the closest VA outpatient clinic is in Connor Springs, just about twenty miles from here. Want to take a field trip?"

"Yes!" Bouncing up onto her toes, she restrained the urge to flip the sign in the window to "Closed," lock the coffee shop door, and head to Connor Springs that very moment. Reality intruded, and she sighed, lowering back down to her heels. "I'm off tomorrow— would you be able to get away from work?" As the team leader, Callum was the only paid staff member on the dive team. From what Lou saw, he earned every penny of his paycheck, often working twelve-hour days dealing with local board members and still taking calls at night.

"Yes. Board meeting's tomorrow evening, so my morning will be free. I'll pick you up at eight."

Wiggling around in a tight circle, she did a little dance of excitement. "Field trip!"

When she finished her final rotation, Lou realized that Callum was watching her, frozen with his travel mug halfway to his mouth. With a shake of his head, he pushed off of his stool and headed out the door.

"Don't you want me to top off your coffee for you?" she called after him, but the only answer she received was the wordless clang of the bells against the door.

She stared at the green leaf lettuce as if it had done something to offend her.

"Six dollars," she muttered under her breath, eyeing the wilting tips of the leaves balefully. "Not worth it."

With a sigh, she poked around in the stack of lettuce bunches before giving up on greens. As she walked to the measly display of apples, she knew she had no one to blame for her lack of fresh produce except herself. If she had sucked it up and gone to Denver that morning, she wouldn't be poking through expensive and unappealing vegetables and fruit at the local grocery store.

She hated driving to Denver with a passion, though. Too many people, too much traffic, too…everything. Plus, if the weather took a turn for the worse, she could get stuck there overnight, which meant her woodstove would go out, and her pipes could freeze. Lou found she could get away with ordering almost everything she needed online, but fresh food remained a challenge. When she'd lived in Connecticut, she'd never considered fresh vegetables a luxury. The difference between her former life and current existence boggled her mind sometimes. She couldn't believe it'd only been seven months since she'd escaped to the mountains.

Roaming the aisles with little enthusiasm, she was examining an on-sale jar of bread-and-butter pickles when her nose twitched. There was a nasty smell floating her way—body odor and pot, mostly, mixed with patchouli. She turned her head and immediately identified the source. Smelly Jim. Of course. The bearded man was an occasional coffee shop visitor, requiring a cappuccino and, once he left, half a spray bottle of cinnamon air freshener and the windows open for as long as possible before the customers started complaining about the cold.

"Hey, Jim." Lou took a casual step back, as if to get a wide-angle look at the pickle selection.

His head whipped around, and he glared at her suspiciously for a long moment before his expression finally cleared. "Lou. Hey."

"How're things?" she asked.

He paused again, although not quite as long this time. "Bad."

"Oh. Sorry about that."

"Yeah." Without saying anything else, he stalked to the end of the aisle and disappeared in the frozen-foods section. Unfortunately, his smell lingered.

Dropping the jar of pickles into her handbasket, she darted for the cashier and, hopefully, fresher air. But as she whipped around the hot-chocolate display at the end of the aisle, she almost ran headlong into someone.

"Rob!" She backpedaled a couple of steps and lowered her voice. "Sorry about that. Smelly Jim was just in that aisle, so a quick exit was necessary—for my lung health, I mean."

A quick smile touched his mouth. "Understandable. You should smell the inside of his trailer home."

"No. Thanks, but I'll pass." She glanced at the teenager leaning against the handle of Rob's shopping cart. The kid was a shorter, skinnier carbon copy of the sheriff. "Hi."

The boy flipped his bangs out of his eyes and gave her a grunt.

"Tyler." The sheriff's voice was quiet, but his son must have heard the warning, because he straightened from his slouch and even met her eyes.

"Hey." It still sounded sulky, but at least it was an actual word.

"I'm Lou." She grinned at him, amused by his angst. The poor sheriff had his hands full with this one. "Nice to meet you."

"You just move here?"

With a shrug, she said, "Sort of. Depends how you define 'just.' It's been about seven months, but some of the old-timers think people who moved here twenty years ago are newcomers."

Rob gave a snort that Lou took as agreement.

"I'm on the rescue dive team," she told Tyler. "That's how I met your dad."

"Oh!" Recognition made his face light. "You found that dead guy in the reservoir. The headless one."

Rob gave his son a sharp look. "I didn't tell you that."

"School, Dad," Tyler muttered. Lou had to hide a grin at how the kid patronized his intimidating father. "It's, like, gossip central there. We probably hear stuff before you do."

Lou's ears perked up at that. "Anyone at school have a guess who it is?"

"Well, Braden Saltzman's uncle is one of those militia guys, and Braden thinks it's them. Because of the no-head thing. Like, he talked when he shouldn't have, and so they cut his head off as a warning. Braden said that head is probably mounted on the wall in their compound—"

"I think that's enough." The sheriff didn't raise his voice, but it still cut through Tyler's macabre theory with the sharpness of a blade.

The kid dropped his head, glower firmly back in place.

"We'd better go. Good to see you, Lou." He headed toward the dairy section, one hand pushing the cart and the other on his son's shoulder.

"Bye," Lou called after them, a little disappointed not to hear any more of the high school set's theories. She could have used Tyler and his friends for a brainstorming session.

Swinging her almost-empty basket, she headed for the cashier, grabbing a couple of candy bars on the way. She had to make her trip to the store worth it, after all.

"Hey, Doris," she greeted the cashier.

"Hi, Lou." As she started scanning the items, Doris asked, "You hear about the dead guy in the reservoir?"

"Yeah."

"Sad." Doris tried three times to scan the pickle jar, and ended up just punching the code in by hand. "Everyone's trying to figure out who the poor guy could be."

"Any ideas?" Lou figured that the more people she asked, the greater the chance of finding someone who actually had valuable information.

"Could be anyone." She punched the button to total the amount and watched as Lou ran her debit card through the scanner. "That wind around here just drives people nuts. When Helen Napping lost it and killed her husband that really nasty winter about twenty years or so ago, I think the wind made her do it. Why, all that blowing and blowing could make someone just"—she clicked her fingers together—"snap."

Lou stared, resisting the urge to step back from the sweetly smiling woman. "Uh…okay." She took her receipt and single bag of groceries. "Thanks, Doris."

"No problem, sweetie. Have a nice day!"

Lou forced a smile and hurried away.

"I've been thinking about one of our theories today," Lou announced as soon as Callum answered the phone with a terse greeting. "A kid reminded me of it, but I think it still might have some validity."

"Sparks?"

"Who else calls you with random theories?"

"Why are *you* calling me with random theories?"

"Because you're my research partner."

"I'm going to pick you up in less than twelve hours," he said. "This couldn't wait until then?"

Lou tucked her blanket around her toes. "I suppose. It's just that all the information we've discovered is circling around in my head. I figured it would help to write down everything. Then I started thinking that we really need a murder board."

"A murder board?"

"Like in the crime shows. A big whiteboard that shows how all the clues are connected. You don't happen to have a big whiteboard, do you?"

There was a pause. "Yes."

"Seriously?"

"Why would I joke about having a whiteboard?"

"I just… Why?"

"Does it matter?"

"I guess not. We have our murder board then—or we will, once we get wild with the dry-erase markers."

Another pause. "So, are you coming over then?"

"Now?"

"You're the one who wanted to do this tonight."

"Right." She frowned at her blanket-wrapped legs. "I'm in my pajamas."

"So change. Or don't change, and just throw a coat over the top. My house is heated, you know."

"Okay." Eyeing the light layer of snow clinging to the outside ledge of her window, Lou suggested, "Or you could come to my house."

"Whiteboard, remember? I'm not dragging that big-ass thing to your house."

It was her turn to sigh before she began untangling herself from the blanket. "Right. Okay, give me a half hour."

She ended the call, took a step toward the door, and then froze.

"Frick. I'm going to Callum's house." Her stomach started rolling with nerves and something she tried very hard to pretend wasn't excitement. "Stop it," she told herself. "It's not a date."

Despite repeating those words to herself, she couldn't stop herself from hurrying to the bathroom to check the state of her hair.

———

Thanks to her uncontrollable need to primp, it was closer to forty-five minutes when she pulled up to Callum's house on the edge of Simpson and parked in the driveway. His home was a tidy two-story with cedar siding that blended well with the scattering of pine trees backing his property. Since she didn't see his truck, she assumed he'd parked in the garage. Either that, or he had bailed and was at the Simpson Bar, hiding out until she gave up and went home.

Although the snow was light—just flurries, really—the wind had a snap to it that made her hurry up the steps to his wraparound porch. Callum opened the door before she had a chance to knock.

"Oh, good," she sighed as she slipped by him into the warmth, unzipping her coat. "It's freezing out there."

His gaze ran from her booted feet up to her stocking hat. He didn't mention the yellow flannel pj's with their pattern of white ducks, but his expression said plenty.

"I took your advice and kept on my pajamas," she stated the obvious, before toeing off her boots and placing them on a mat next to the door. Lou didn't tell him that she'd been tempted to change into nonpajamas, but she didn't want him to think she'd made an effort, since an effort would mean that she thought of this visit as a date, which she most assuredly did not. Pulling off her gloves and jamming them into her coat pockets, she then wiggled out of her thick coat. Her hat joined the gloves in one of her coat pockets. When she didn't see a hook or coatrack, she offered the coat to him with a quizzical tilt to her head.

"Let me take that," he said with heavy sarcasm, but he accepted the coat and turned to hang it in a nearby closet. While he was arranging it to fall just so on the hanger, Lou took the opportunity to look around his house.

They were in the living room that, thanks to the open floor plan, was also the kitchen and dining room. Everything was perfectly neat, and she was once again relieved that they hadn't met at her place after all, cold drive or no. Her messy house would have given Callum a stroke. Plus, the promised whiteboard was arranged in the middle of the living area, at just the right distance from the couch.

"It's perfect," she breathed, admiring the professional-looking board, complete with wheels and a box of markers in a full spectrum of colors. "I couldn't have special-ordered a better murder board."

"I aim to please." His sarcasm was still firmly in place as he ushered her closer to the couch, with a hand on her back. It felt warm and uncomfortably good.

"Your house is nice," she said, sitting down on the sofa and tilting her head back to admire the lofted ceiling. "I've never been in here before."

"I don't invite many people here," he admitted. "Want something to drink?"

"No, thank you." She felt a sudden awkwardness, as if the research session really was morphing into something closer to a…well, a date. Fumbling for the small notebook she'd tucked into her pajama pants' pocket, she asked, "Um…did you want to see my notes?"

Sitting next to her on the couch—although not close enough to make her brain shut down—he held out his hand in a silent request. She passed him the notebook.

While he flipped through the pages, she nibbled on the inside of her cheek, suddenly embarrassed by her amateur sleuthing. More than anything, she wanted him to be impressed by her, for him to think she was intelligent.

Shutting down those thoughts firmly, she reminded herself that turning herself inside out to gain people's respect was a slippery downward slope. Twenty-six years with her parents had taught her that.

"What's this?" he asked, jerking her out of her darkening thoughts.

Scooting closer so she could see her writing, she read out loud, "'Tyler Coughlin arrow Braden Saltzman, militia, lesson.' That's not perfectly clear?" She laughed when he gave her a look. "I ran into Rob and his son at the grocery store this afternoon. Braden's a kid at Tyler's school who had a theory that our guy's headlessness was a lesson for the other militia members. Apparently, Braden's uncle is one of the top militia dogs, so Tyler considers him a local authority on the subject. He also mentioned the possibility of the victim's head being mounted on the wall in the compound as a reminder not to speak out of turn. Although I'm paraphrasing here."

"Hmm." Callum turned back to her notes.

"I wish Tyler would've shared more high school rumors, but Rob shut him down pretty quickly. I know it's a crazy theory, but there might be a hint of truth in gossip."

Closing the notebook, Callum tapped it against his thigh, looking at the blank whiteboard thoughtfully. "I think we should focus first on what we know about the victim. If we start considering possible scenarios too early, we might try to make them fit, rather than looking at where the facts lead us."

"Good idea." Excited, Lou bounced to her feet and grabbed the whiteboard markers. "Can we start listing known facts?"

Callum grinned, softening the harsh lines of his face and making him so beautiful that it temporarily erased every thought in Lou's brain. The iceman actually had dimples! "You're just dying to dirty up that clean surface, aren't you?"

It took Lou a moment to recover from the force of his full-wattage smile. Clearing her throat, she forced herself to grin back at him. "You know it. Now let's get started before I just start drawing random rainbows and stick people." Pulling out a green marker, she tapped it against her mouth, thinking, before yanking off the cap and drawing a straight line across the top of the board.

Even before she added any notes, he guessed her intention. "Timeline. Good idea."

She couldn't stop the pleased smile that crept over her face. Turning more fully toward the board to hide her happy expression, she made a vertical mark close to the right side of the timeline and scribbled "HDG Found in Reservoir" with the date the body was recovered.

"When did the coroner think he was dumped?" Callum asked, flipping through her notes again.

"October through January, I think." She drew a bracket below the timeline in red, writing "October 1" on the left side of the bracket and "January 31" on the other. Along the bottom of the bracket, she wrote "HDG Dumped in Mission Reservoir" and added out loud, "Although Chris mentioned checking disappearances as early as August." She smudged out "October" with her finger and wrote "August" instead.

Clearing his throat, Callum said, "There's an eraser next to the markers." When she just looked at him, he changed the subject. "It was a fairly warm fall. I can't imagine the body would've stayed submerged so long if it were in the reservoir in August."

She shrugged. "True, but better to make the box too big than too small, right?" When he agreed, she kept the first of August as the initial date on her bracket. "Is that all we have so far for the timeline?"

"What about the amputation of his toes?"

"Yes!" Using a purple marker, she created another bracket. Labeling it "HDG: Two Toes Amputated," she put the initial date as April and the final date as December. "Think that's a wide enough spread? Belly mentioned it was probably done a few months before he died."

Callum said, "I think that's good. We already know that he was most likely killed closer to October than August, so there's plenty of cushion in there if Belly was off in her estimation."

"Okay, so let's list what we know about our HDG." She grabbed the blue marker and wrote as she talked. "Male, Caucasian, gray hair, approximately sixty-five years old, five-ten, one hundred and fifty pounds, U.S. Army tattoo on his chest, old shrapnel scars on his back, two toes amputated from his right foot, diabetic. Anything else?"

"Bel thought he'd been in Vietnam, but that was an educated guess, based on his age and the age of the scarring."

"I think we should include it." Lou put it on the board, although she added a question mark behind it.

"There's the obvious, too." When Lou just looked at him, he elaborated, "The missing hands and head."

"Right!" She scribbled that down as well. Gazing at the spotless two-thirds of the whiteboard, she asked longingly, "Can we write out just a few theories on that side?"

"Nope. Only the facts, ma'am."

"Fine," she sighed. "Throw some more facts at me, then."

By the time they'd wrapped things up for the night, there was still a tempting amount of empty space on the whiteboard. With great self-restraint, Lou capped her marker and handed it to Callum, who put it with the others in perfect spectrum order.

"Hopefully, we'll have more to add after our field trip tomorrow," she said, before glancing at her watch. It was already after eleven. "Speaking of that, I'd better get home, or you'll have to drag me out of bed tomorrow morning."

"You could stay here," Callum offered.

She whipped her head around before she could temper her response. "Um...*stay*?" she repeated.

His cheeks darkened as she stared at him. "I'd sleep on the couch. I mean, you could have my bed. If you didn't want to drive home tonight." He suddenly looked irritated. "Never mind. I'll pick you up at your place tomorrow at eight."

"I...well, thanks. My woodstove needs to be stoked, but I appreciate the offer." Wincing inwardly at her stiffly formal tone, she tried to relax and speak normally. "Besides, you know I'd be waking you at two a.m. to discuss some new, wild theory my sleeping brain conjured up."

Although he nodded, he still looked uncomfortable. She moved toward the door, pulling her coat out of the closet and jamming her feet into her boots. Once she had her coat zipped and was wearing her hat and gloves, she didn't have any excuse not to look at him, so she met his eyes.

"Thanks. For letting me come over and use your whiteboard and everything." Why he always reduced her to sounding like a stammering seventh-grader on her first date, she didn't know. She *did* know that right now everything was awkward and uncomfortable, and she wanted to leave. "Okay. Um...bye."

Callum held the door for her. "Bye. Drive safely."

"Will do." She saluted him and hurried down the steps, tripping on the last one. Although she stayed upright, she had to pinwheel her arms to catch her balance. Apparently, she was incapable of being anything but a walking disaster in Callum's presence.

"Careful," he warned, his voice sharp.

She waved, her attention on the ground in front of her feet as she walked the rest of the way to her truck without any more mishaps. She started the engine and rolled down the window. "See you tomorrow," she said, waving as she backed out of his driveway.

He raised a hand, his figure silhouetted in the doorway. He looked so solitary standing there that she felt a twinge of guilt for not accepting his invitation to stay.

Her truck tires slipped sideways as she went around a turn. They caught the surface of the road when she straightened the wheel, but the slide had brought her back to the present. After that, she concentrated on driving, pushing Callum into a dark corner of her mind.

Later. She'd think about all that later.

How long had he been sitting there? How many minutes or even hours had passed since she'd disappeared into that house? He wasn't sure, but it had been long enough to knot his hands into fists and sour his stomach.

When he'd watched her leave her cabin and hurry to her truck earlier, disappointment had swamped him, knowing that his favorite part of the day—watching her sleep—would be delayed. Curiosity had crept in as he ran to his own car before her taillights could disappear completely. She never went anywhere in the evenings. Where was she going?

He'd managed to catch up to her. That was one good thing about this forsaken place—tailing her was easy with so few vehicles on the roads. As she'd pulled up to a house, he'd cut his headlights and rolled to a stop in the shadows a half block away. Even from a distance, though, he'd recognized the same guy who'd helped her with her tire.

"Boy Scout," he'd muttered, as the door swung shut behind the pair. "What's she doing there?"

Whatever it was, it was taking a long time—at least, it felt like eons had passed since she'd stepped through the doorway into the warmly lit house. He knew she wouldn't be doing anything...wrong. She wasn't like that. She was faithful.

But...what were they doing in there?

Although it wasn't as cold as the forest, he realized he was shaking. Keeping the lights off, he cranked the engine of his car to warm the interior. The front door of the house swung open, making him jump and bang his knee on the underside of the instrument panel. He scrambled to turn off the motor, worried that they'd hear it.

He almost couldn't watch them. What if they kissed good-bye? Rage bubbled from where he'd held it to a simmer. If he touched her—if *she* touched *him*—then he wouldn't be able to restrain himself. When she trotted toward her truck without either of them making contact, all the air in his lungs exited in a whoosh. There'd been no touching. Good. That was good.

As she started up the truck, he watched the man framed in the doorway. He could be a problem. Not a huge one, but it wasn't good for her to be distracted right now. It might delay the plan, and he didn't know how much longer he could be without her.

He followed her home, careful not to be obvious. It would be a bad time for her to get suspicious. Maybe that was the solution, though. Maybe she was too comfortable in her miserable little life. Maybe he needed to give her a little nudge, just hard enough to send her running into his arms.

Smiling, he waited for her to duck back into her cabin. It bothered him to miss watching her sleep, but this was better. If he was lucky, too, he could get a glimpse of her without that obtrusive pane of glass between them. Maybe, if he dared, he could even touch her, just the lightest brush of fingers against her skin.

It seemed to take forever for the cabin to go dark, but that could just be his impatience warping time. He forced himself to wait an endless amount of time past when the last light was extinguished before slipping out of his car.

He moved closer, keeping his footsteps as quiet as possible in the muffling snow. As he lifted his boot onto the bottom porch step, it creaked under his weight. He froze, listening for any movement, but the cabin stayed quiet and dark. Daring to try the next step, and then the next, he reached her front door.

His hand reached out and grasped the doorknob.

———————

Lou woke suddenly from a heavy sleep, pulse racing.

Inhaling a deep breath, she forced herself to calm down and take inventory. A nightmare hadn't woken her. Had it been a strange sound? She listened intently, but her heart was still pounding in her ears, deafening her to anything else. She glanced at the clock, which read two twenty a.m.

A creeping anxiety sent a chill up her spine. No matter how hard she tried, she couldn't escape the feeling that someone was out there—watching her.

"Don't be stupid," she whispered, but her voice didn't sound like her own. It was just the investigation getting her amped up—her head was filled with tire vandals and murderers. It was nothing.

It didn't feel like nothing.

She *had* to check it out. No way was she getting back to sleep now.

Pushing back the covers, Lou slid out of bed, wincing at the creak of the wooden floor beneath her weight. She crossed the room and reached for the light switch, but hesitated and pulled her hand back without turning on the light. It would make her too vulnerable, not to be able to see outside. Besides, the moon was full enough that her bedroom was fairly bright.

Her house was isolated, and there wasn't a clear view of her place from any of her neighbors or the road, so she didn't have any window coverings. She'd figured the bears and coyotes could peek at her all they wanted. Now, though, the dark squares of glass made her feel exposed and queasy.

Carefully placing her feet to avoid the floorboards that creaked the loudest, she crept into the living room. All looked normal, everything still as it was when she went to bed, except the fire in the woodstove had burned down to glowing red coals, putting off just enough light to turn her furniture into ominous shapes.

Still, she couldn't quite shake the feeling that something was *off*.

The kitchen was visible from the living area, but she crept around the breakfast bar to check the spaces she couldn't see. The pantry door was cracked, making Lou frown. *Didn't I shut that?* she wondered as she reached for the doorknob. Her fingers slipped on the cool metal, and she realized that her palms were sweating.

She hesitated, her hand on the knob. She was being ridiculous, right? No one had broken into her house only to hide in the pantry. Besides, if there *was* someone in there, she didn't think she wanted to know. Maybe she should just return to bed and be blissfully ignorant.

Not that she'd be able to sleep, wondering if she'd been wrong.

Annoyed at her wishy-washiness, Lou tightened her fingers and gave a hard twist. The door swung open— and a dark shape lunged at her.

With a shriek, she jumped back, twisting out of reach. Something fell to the floor with a loud smack. As Lou stared at what was just an innocent broom lying on the floor, she resisted the urge to kick it. It wasn't the broom's fault she'd turned into a horror-movie cliché. Trying to ignore her too-quick breaths, she bent to pick up the fallen broom. After putting it back in the pantry, she closed the door.

Her stomach tightened as she glanced at the black windows of the living room again. The exposed glass brought a prickling feeling of unease that made her long for blinds. She was tempted to grab the blanket from the couch and use it as a temporary curtain, but she shook off the idea. It was just nighttime nerves making her crazy. There was no one out there.

As she moved toward the bathroom, the only unsearched room left, her heartbeat pounded in her ears. The wind had died down earlier, and Lou almost missed it. Without the usual whistling and groaning, everything was quiet—too quiet. The silence felt almost watchful. Chewing on the inside of her cheek, she pushed the bathroom door open and forced herself to step inside.

The light from the fire didn't reach very far into the small room, so the corners were draped with heavy shadows. The shower was the scariest, its heavy curtain hiding who-knew-what. Although she was tempted to back out of the room and go back to bed, pretending like she'd checked behind the curtain and her little home was secure, Lou knew she needed to see for herself if she ever wanted to sleep again.

Her hand shook as she reached toward the closed shower curtain. Her obvious fear annoyed her, and she yanked the covering aside with more vehemence than she'd planned. The rings rattled against the curtain rod, making her jump, even as she realized that no one was crouching in the shower. Her exhale shivered even as she smiled. At least her life hadn't turned into a scene from *Psycho*.

After adding some firewood to the stove, she double-checked that the front door was locked and then headed back to her bedroom, peeking into the closet before crawling back into bed. Even though she'd just checked every space in her home big enough to hide even the smallest of people, Lou still felt like she was being watched.

"Silly," she scolded her paranoid brain as she snuggled into a ball, tugging the covers to her chin. As she drifted to sleep, the thought of seeing Callum in just a few hours crossed her mind and made her smile.

Her fear was forgotten—for now.

Chapter 6

OF COURSE SHE SLEPT LATE. WHEN HER BLURRY EYES finally focused on the face of her cell phone, it was seven minutes before Callum was supposed to arrive. Jumping out of bed, she immediately tripped on the voluminous covers she'd dragged with her, and Lou sprawled across the floor, banging her left knee painfully.

Grumbling and rubbing her knee, she untwisted the blankets from around her legs and piled them back on the bed. Grabbing a pair of jeans from the floor, she frowned at the mud-crusted hems and tossed them back in the corner. She and Callum were headed to a clinic, so she should probably wear something a little less dirty. It seemed only sanitary.

The next pair of jeans she snatched appeared to be fairly clean, or at least didn't have any obvious dirt. She did a smell test and immediately rejected three shirts before pulling on a long-sleeved crewneck and topping it with an Avalanche hoodie. Her socks were sort of a good match, although they were slightly different shades of blue.

As she darted for the bathroom, she heard the diesel grumble of Callum's truck. Lou swore. Of course the guy couldn't be late just once in his life. Her teeth received about five strokes of a brush, and her hair got a couple less than that. She used the toilet, even trying to pee quickly.

It was probably less than a minute after he pulled up

to her cabin when she ran for the front door, but she could still hear him grumbling on the porch.

"I know! I'm late—sorry!" she babbled as she yanked open the door to find a scowling Callum. He didn't seem to be focused on her, though.

"What the hell's on your door?"

Lou blinked at him, confused. That wasn't the complaint she'd expected. "What?"

"That." He stabbed a gloved finger toward her opened door, and she followed the gesture to where he was pointing.

"Gross." Frozen trickles of amber goo ran down the exterior of her door. "What is that?"

He gave her *the look*. Biting back a sharp comment, she reminded herself not to poke the bear, or it was going to be a long day. Callum *was* giving up his morning to help her with Operation Identify HDG, after all. "That's what I asked you," he said with exaggerated patience.

Instead of shutting the door in his face and immediately returning to bed, she focused on the light brown streaks, poking one with her finger. It was frozen, but still oddly sticky. She smelled her finger.

"Don't lick it!" Callum grabbed her wrist and pulled her hand away from her face.

This time, she couldn't hold back an eye roll. "It's fine." Tugging her arm free, she stuck her finger in her mouth just to bug him. "It's honey," she mumbled around her fingertip.

Witnessing his horrified and completely grossed-out expression was very satisfying. "You just... I can't believe you put it in your *mouth*..."

"What? It's just honey." Pulling her finger out of her

mouth, she examined it closely. "Besides, doesn't cold
kill germs and bacteria and such?"

"I can't…" He couldn't seem to think of anything
more to say.

"Get in here." She grabbed his forearm and pulled
him through the doorway. "You're letting out all
the heat."

He allowed her to tug him inside, and she swung the
door closed once he was clear of it. The heat seemed to
help him recover from his germ-phobia-induced fugue
state. "Why is there honey on your door?"

She shrugged. "No clue." When he eyed her narrowly, she planted her fists on her hips. "Why would I
put honey on my door? That's crazy!"

"Then who? It couldn't have just appeared there."

"I don't know! Someone who wants to set a trap for
Winnie the Pooh? Who puts honey on a door?"

His expression turned thoughtful. "You think someone wanted to attract a bear?"

"No, sorry, that was just a joke. Not one of my best,
but then I just woke up about eight minutes ago, so I'm
not really on my game yet."

"You woke up eight minutes ago?" And critical
Callum was back.

She sighed. "I had a rough night. I woke up really
early because I thought I heard…" Her eyes went wide.
"I'm an idiot!" She yanked the door open and hurried
outside, ignoring her coatless state. From her perch on
the top of her tiny porch, she examined the three steps
leading down to the snowy ground.

The wind had blown off most of the light snow from
the previous evening, so all that remained on the steps

was a dusting of white powder caught in the corners and cracks. She popped back into her cabin to yank on her boots, and then she jumped off the porch into the foot of old snow heaped around the foundation of her home.

"What did you hear last night?" Callum asked, his proximity startling her. She hadn't realized he was walking next to her as she circled the perimeter of the cabin.

"Nothing. I mean"—she made an impatient gesture—"something woke me, but I don't remember what it was. I did a tour of the cabin, decided I was paranoid, and went back to bed." She shivered. "I hope whoever it was wasn't watching me."

"I wouldn't count on that," Callum said grimly, pointing toward some impressions in the snow. Her stomach twisted as she took another step closer and saw distinct boot prints in the drift right outside her bedroom window.

———

Chris was at her house within a half hour after she called him. His serious expression sat oddly on his normally cheery face.

"Your stalker is changing things up on us," he said as he climbed out of his squad car. "I'm not liking this new development."

"Me neither," Callum said, his words clipped.

"Me third." Lou gestured at the door. "What do you think the deal is with the honey?"

Chris shrugged. "Not sure. Maybe he thinks you're sweet?"

"Why stick knives in my tires if he likes me so much he's giving me compliments with condiments?"

"Lou thinks he might've been trying to attract a bear," Callum said, and Chris looked at her with interest.

"Not really. I actually said Winnie the… Never mind." She waved her hands, flustered. "I mean, that would be stupid, right? It's like a plan thought up by a five-year-old."

"It fits better with the slashed tires MO." Chris leaned in close to the door to examine the frozen rivulets. "It does look like honey."

"It is honey," Lou affirmed. "I tasted it."

The deputy's head whipped around. "Are you a toddler? Don't be putting random shit in your mouth. Especially shit left by your stalker."

With a sheepish shrug, Lou carefully didn't look at Callum. "Fine. No more taste-testing the evidence. It just seemed like the easiest way to identify it."

"Nope. Bad idea. You can use all your senses in an investigation except taste." After Chris took some pictures of the door, he stepped back and turned to Lou. "Show me these boot prints."

She led the way, followed closely by Callum, with the deputy taking up the rear. As she pointed toward the tracks beneath her bedroom window, Lou was unable to hold back a shiver that had nothing to do with the cold. When Callum gave her shoulder a quick squeeze, she jumped and looked at him in surprise. Reassuring gestures felt strange coming from Callum. She was more used to getting withering looks and barked commands from him. His focus was on Chris, however, so he missed her startled glance.

"Will these prints help?" Callum asked.

Chris took some photos, then laid his small ruler in

one of the prints and took some more before answering. "If we have a suspect, then yes. Definitely. Every shoe or boot wears differently, so they're almost as unique as fingerprints. If we have probable cause to think some-one's responsible, we can get a warrant to check out the guy's footwear. Most people know better than to leave their fingerprints around a crime scene, but not as many think about shoe prints. We had a burglary about four months ago where all three suspects were tied to the scene by their tread."

He opened a shoebox-sized case and pulled out what looked like an old-fashioned shaving brush and a small jar of black powder. After dipping the brush into the powder, he held it over the print and tapped the brush handle.

"What are you doing?" Leaning closer, Lou watched, fascinated, as the black powder drifted over the print in the snow.

Chris repeated the process of photographing without and then with his ruler. "The fingerprint powder gives the boot impression more definition in the pictures. We could also do a mold of the print, but I usually don't have much luck with that. The casting material heats up as it sets, which melts the snow. The conditions have to be perfect to get a good cast. I like pictures better." Tucking away his equipment, he stood. "Did you follow the prints?"

Giving him a "duh" look, Lou said, "Yes."

Chris laughed for the first time since arriving at her house. "Right. Of course you did."

"He came from the trees over there, to her window, around to the front of the cabin and back to the trees,"

Callum said, gesturing toward a stand of evergreens that separated her property from her neighbors'. "I think he parked at the Moonies' place, watched from the cover of the woods until he knew Lou was sleeping, and then did the honey thing."

Making a face, Lou added, "And the creepy peeping thing."

Without looking at her, he gave an affirmative grunt. Although Callum's face was carefully blank, she could tell he was pissed. Deeply pissed.

"The Moonies have visited their cabin only twice since I've lived here," she said, deciding to focus on her stalker and worry about Callum's mood some other time. "It's been empty for the past two months. Do you think this person might be staying there?"

Callum shook his head. "The boot prints end at their driveway, and there are fresh tire tracks. The snow covering their front and back porches is undisturbed."

"Tire tracks?" Chris asked with interest. "This is my lucky day, forensically speaking—boot prints *and* tire tracks. I'll go check it out."

As the two watched the deputy plow through the snow—a safe distance from the boot prints so as not to disturb the evidence—Lou shot a sideways glance at Callum.

"What?" he snapped. Since he was still watching Chris, she wasn't sure how he saw her look.

"Why are you so angry?" she asked. "Is it that I'm wasting your morning with my stalker drama?"

That made him focus on her. "What? No, of course not."

"Then…?" She let her voice trail away, hoping he would fill in the blank.

"You really don't know?" he asked. When she shook her head, he looked away again, readjusting his baseball cap. "I'm angry because some asshole is harassing you. He was fucking *watching* you while you were sleeping."

"Oh." It was her turn to look away from him. She shifted her weight, uncomfortable and pretty sure she would've preferred dealing with his anger rather than his concern. At least she would've known how to respond to his irritation—she'd had plenty of experience with *that*. "Yeah…hmm." Giving up on her search for something fitting to say, she settled for the always-appropriate hum.

"You can't stay out here alone." Callum obviously didn't have a problem finding words. "You'll stay at my house until they catch this son of a bitch."

Startled, she turned to face him again. "Um…no. My woodstove needs to be fed. And I'm not going to let him drive me out of here." Plus, the idea of staying with Callum was much too appealing for her peace of mind.

"Fine." The small muscles at the corner of his jaw were twitching. "I'll stay here then. I have propane heat as a backup for my woodstove, so my house will be fine." When she just stared at him, his face reddened, and he looked away. "I'll stay on your couch."

"I don't think that's a good idea," she said slowly, imagining him living in the midst of her mess. "It's almost a twenty-minute drive to Station One from my place, compared to three minutes from yours. Won't that cause an issue for dive-team calls?"

"I'll work it out."

She opened her mouth, frantically trying to think of another logical reason he couldn't stay with her that had nothing to do with the tumbling mix of nerves and excitement the idea produced, when the sight of the returning deputy had her closing her mouth. "We'll talk about this later."

"Nothing to discuss," he said, and she glared at him—which he ignored.

"I'm going to head down the road to the end of the Moonies' driveway, see if I can tell which direction this guy turned once he got on the county road," Chris said once he got close enough for them to hear him. "Call me if anything else happens, even little things."

"Will do. Thanks, Deputy Chris."

"No problem, Lou." He gave her a wink along with his usual grin. "You might think about installing one of those wild-game cameras outside of your cabin. They're motion-activated, so you could get lucky and get a shot of your guy if he returns."

Her stomach tightened at the thought of how much one of those cameras would cost. "I'll look into getting one. Thanks."

Turning to Callum, the deputy said, "I assume you're going to be staying with her?"

"Hang on a second," Lou protested again, but she was soundly ignored by both men.

"Yep," Callum said, and the two men exchanged a look.

"Good." Chris glanced at Lou and laughed. "Settle down, Tinker Bell. It never hurts to have someone around to watch your back."

She opened her mouth to protest, but the deputy turned away and headed for his squad car before she could decide which offended her more. All she could do was make a wordless sound of irritation.

"Tinker Bell," Cal said thoughtfully as Chris carefully turned the SUV around and headed down her driveway. "It fits. You're little and blond and feisty."

Lou glowered at him. "Tinker Bell's a huge bitch."

Although he shrugged, a grin twitched at the corners of his mouth. Glancing at his watch, he changed the subject. "We're not going to be able to get to the clinic and back in time for me to get to my one o'clock meeting. When's your next day off?"

Grimacing, she said, "Not until next Wednesday. If we leave early tomorrow, though, we could get back before my shift starts at noon. Unless you can't get another morning free?"

"Tomorrow should work." He headed for his truck. "I'll see if Wilt's available to respond to any calls while we're gone."

"Great. So I'll see you tomorrow at, what, seven thirty or so?"

He gave her a hard look over the hood of his truck. "Good try. I'll be here tonight after the board meeting." Scowling, he added, "I'd rather you not be alone at all, especially after it gets dark. Why don't you attend the board meeting with me?"

Appalled, Lou stared at him, hoping her expression fully conveyed her horror at the idea. "Why don't you just shoot me in the face, because I think I'd prefer that to sitting through a two-hour meeting where people squabble about county ordinances and the acceptable decibel level of old Mr. Zarnecki's generator."

His eyebrows rose. "You've been to one of these meetings then? I haven't seen you there."

Shaking her head, she explained, "My mom is very

much into civic responsibility, and she dragged me, kicking and screaming, with her. Also, when I was in high school, our neighbor was in a grudge match with my stepdad. Their weapons were city ordinances and arcane state laws about fence lines and swimming pools and tree branch heights. It got pretty ugly. My mom insisted I attend the city council meetings with them in a show of familial support."

He blinked. "Sounds brutal."

"It was. So, no, I'm afraid I must decline your kind invitation to the board meeting tonight. But I do promise to stay inside with my doors locked and my shotgun within easy reach."

"Good." He opened his truck door.

"Um, you do realize that last part was sarcastic?" she asked. "I mean, not the locking the door part, since I will do that, but the shotgun thing. I don't actually own a shotgun."

He looked at her as if she'd just said she didn't believe in eating food. "Okay," he finally said. "I'll bring one of mine."

She paused to digest that. "Ah…okay. So it's a shotgun kind of sleepover then. Good to know."

With an amused snort, he climbed into the driver's seat and slammed the pickup's door. His truck came to life with a roar. After lifting his fingers off the steering wheel in a manly wave, he followed the deputy's example and executed a neat three-point turn before heading down the driveway toward the county road.

Although she was shivering, she watched him leave, turning to enter her cabin only when his pickup disappeared from sight and she could no longer hear its engine. But as she walked inside, her trembling got worse instead of better. Her warm little home felt foreign and too exposed, as if her stalker had, through his uninvited nighttime visit, turned her walls transparent.

She hovered in the entryway for a few more seconds before grabbing her laptop and her truck keys. Hopping into her own pickup, she headed to town.

Lou loved libraries, all libraries. They'd been her refuge and her comfort when she'd been growing up. Even the tiny, underfunded Simpson Library made her stomach warm with a feeling of happy familiarity.

After waving to Bart, the sole librarian, and getting the usual suspicious glare in return, she set up camp in the back corner. Although several rows of shelving provided some privacy, she knew from previous visits that Bart was sure to make multiple passes through the stacks closest to her, making a big show of reshelving books. Lou was pretty sure his real motivation was to check that she wasn't doing anything shady, like tearing out pages of reference books or using her penknife to carve "Lou + Callum" in the wooden table.

This mental image brought a flood of worries about Callum, his new status as her roommate, and all the potential awkwardness that situation could have. It was hard enough being near him at training, and that was when he had on multiple layers of clothing. Living with him was going to create a bunch of uncomfortable situations. Undressing and showering and brushing her teeth with him in the next room seemed so…*intimate*. Just the thought of the upcoming night made her skin heat. With enormous effort, she shoved all Callum-related thoughts out of her mind and focused on HDG research.

Although Callum—damn, she just thought about him again!—had warned her about trying to force facts to fit favorite theories instead of letting the facts form the theories, she figured it wouldn't hurt to do a little Internet research. Since the conversation with the sheriff and his son was fresh in her mind, she started surfing the web for information about local militia groups.

There was nothing specific about the antigovernment group Callum had mentioned, the one that had taken over the old Miller compound, but there was oodles of information about militias. It was fascinating, especially when she thought about how the local group was located less than ten miles from her cabin.

She was engrossed in reading about an illegal weapons raid on a compound in Michigan when a voice made her jump.

"Lou, right?"

Her first instinct was to slam her laptop closed, but she settled down quickly, realizing that she wasn't doing anything wrong. Instead of acting like she'd been looking at porn, she glanced up casually and saw the sheriff's son smirking at her from across the table.

"Yeah," she said, belatedly answering his question. "Hi, Tyler."

"What are you doing here?" Pulling out the chair across from her and flipping it around, he straddled the seat and laid his arms over the back.

"I needed a change of scenery," she said, lowering the top of her laptop, since it looked like Tyler was settling in for a chat. She didn't mind too much, though.

Despite the sulky attitude, he seemed like a nice kid, and her eyes were starting to get a little fuzzy from staring at the computer screen without a break. "How about you? Shouldn't you be in school?"

"It's been out for, like, an hour." He jerked his chin toward the clock on the wall. It was almost four thirty.

"Wow. I didn't realize I'd been working on the computer for so long." She scrunched up her face. "No wonder I can't focus my eyes anymore."

"I do that sometimes." At her questioning look, he clarified, "Get caught up in the computer. Just messing around online, and then I realize that I've just wasted hours doing nothing."

Reaching her arms overhead, she stretched out her tight muscles. "Yeah, it happens." Cocking her head to the side, she regarding him curiously. "So what are you doing in the library instead of…well, whatever kids do after school nowadays?"

He snorted. "Yeah, 'cause you've been done with school for, what? Like, two years?"

"High school? Try eight years."

"Yeah? You look younger."

Lou turned what wanted to be a laugh into a cough. Was this little punk *flirting* with her? "You never answered my question." When he looked confused, she added, "Library?"

Dropping his gaze to the table, he shrugged. "Dad's at work, so the house is really quiet. I come here to do homework sometimes. Bart's not the best company, but…" He shrugged again as his words trailed off.

She felt a surge of empathy, his explanation sharply reminding her what it felt like to be that lonely, awkward kid. Maybe he hadn't been flirting. Maybe he was just desperate for company. He looked uncomfortable and a little embarrassed, so she changed the subject.

"Did your friends have any other theories about the guy found in the reservoir?" Once the words were out of her mouth, she regretted them. What kind of person tried to pump a teenager for information on a dead guy, especially when that information came from other clueless high schoolers?

But Tyler immediately sat straighter, his eyes brightening. He didn't seem to mind the topic. "Tons. It's all anyone talks about at school. Simpson isn't the most exciting place, you know. The only stuff that happens is, like, some girl broke up with some guy or, you know, the Masons' shed burned down or whatever." He smiled.

Actually, with headless, floating dead guys popping up in reservoirs and tire-slashing, honey-dribbling stalkers on the loose, Lou could've done with a little less excitement lately. Instead of saying this, she just made a noncommittal sound that could have been interpreted as agreement.

"Some people have some crazy ideas," Tyler continued, "like that there's a serial killer living in Simpson, or that some occultists cut his head off as, like, a present to the devil, but the most popular theory is he got on the bad side of the Freedom Survivors."

"Freedom Survivors?"

"That militia group outside of town."

Lou made a face. "What kind of name is the Freedom Survivors? It makes it sound like they survived freedom."

He shrugged. "What would you call them?"

"If I got to pick the name?" She thought for a moment.

"How about Liberty or Death? Or maybe Soldiers of Freedom?"

"Like the video game?"

"No, like—" She was interrupted by someone clearing his throat. The throat-clearer sounded annoyed, so she was not too surprised to see that it was Callum.

"Hi," she said with a sunny smile, knowing that would aggravate him even more. She had to take her fun where she could find it.

"Sparks," he said, politely enough, although there was a growl somewhere underneath her name. "Is there a reason you're not answering your phone?"

She glanced down at the coat hanging over the back of her chair. The phone was buried in one of the pockets, silenced as was only polite in a library. "The ringer's off."

Closing his eyes, he looked a little pained. "Would you mind turning your ringer *on* for the remainder of the day?"

"Sure." She glanced at the clock. "I should head home anyway."

"Have you eaten yet?"

"No." As if on cue, her stomach growled. "I'm starving, actually."

"Want to go to Levi's for some barbecue?"

Her eyes widened. "With you?"

"If you want to sit at separate tables, we can." He really was the king of sarcasm. Before she met him, she'd thought she'd ranked pretty high in sarcasm royalty. Callum made her feel like an amateur.

She smiled. "I might take you up on that. Only if you're especially irritating, though."

He either grimaced or suppressed a smile—she wasn't sure which—and then turned to the teenager listening in on their conversation. "Tyler."

"How's it going?" Tyler asked flatly, his expression surly again.

Callum obviously took the question as a greeting rather than an actual inquiry, because he turned to Lou and asked, "Ready?"

Nodding, she stood and pulled her coat off the back of her chair. As she shoved her arms into the sleeves, she looked at Tyler. "Thanks for sharing your theories with me. Good luck with that homework."

"Sure, whatever."

She grabbed her laptop, slid it into her bag, and gave Tyler a final wave. He just lifted his chin in response without looking at her, his eyebrows pulled down in a glower. He focused on the top of the table, rubbing his thumb over a nick in the wood with almost violent force.

As Callum escorted her past a scowling Bart and through the exterior door with his hand on her lower back, she eyed him curiously. "How'd you know to look for me here?"

He tipped his head toward her truck, parked on the street in front of the library.

"Oh." She grinned. "Those are quite the investigatory skills. I chose well when picking my HDG research partner."

He just shrugged in obvious agreement, which made her laugh. The barbecue place was only six blocks away, so they left their trucks parked at the library and walked.

"Did you find out anything interesting from Rob's

kid?" he asked. His hand still hadn't left her lower back, which was a little distracting. Nice, but distracting.

"Just that he's lonely, doesn't like going home to an empty house, *does* like to hit on older women, could be a little jealous of you because you get to eat barbecue with the wonder that is *moi*, and works on his homework in the library after school. Also, there are some crazy stories about our HDG circulating around the high school that involve serial killers and devil worshippers. Oh, and the local militia group has a really stupid name."

He blinked, apparently processing. "He hit on you?"

"That's what you pulled out of that mess?" She frowned. "The poor kid's lonely, like I said. Where's his mom, do you know?"

"Sydney had some mental health issues—probably still does. She'd take off for a week or a month and then come back to Rob and their kid for a while. She left for good about nine years ago."

"Poor kid," she said again. "Poor Rob."

He gave her a sharp look. "Don't get all sappy for the sheriff."

"I'm not getting sappy for the sheriff," she huffed. "I just feel bad for the guy—single dad, messed-up ex-wife…"

"Why do women always want to fix broken men?" he grumbled.

Stopping in front of Levi's, she turned to face Callum. "I don't want to fix him or do anything to him. He is nice—and really hot, of course—but he kind of intimidates me, to be honest. He's so…in control of things. Official."

"So I'm not official? You're obviously not intimidated

by me." He nudged her toward the door, and she started walking again.

"You're official." As she stepped through the door that Callum held open, she tried to figure out the difference between the two men and put it into words. "You're just...*my* official. It's different." She closed her eyes briefly when she heard the words come out completely wrong. "Never mind."

But Callum apparently didn't want to drop it. "I'm *your* official, huh?"

"And I am intimidated by you sometimes." She waved at Levi's wife, Bonnie, and took a booth in the corner. Callum did some quick maneuvering so he could have his back to the wall. Since she really didn't care if she had a clear view of the restaurant and everyone in it, she settled on the other side of the booth without complaint. "Just not so much anymore, especially since we've started the HDG research. Now it feels like we're partners, rather than the drill sergeant/peon relationship we had before."

Bonnie arrived with menus, a couple of glasses of water, and two straws, dispensing everything with the competence of years of experience.

"Sometimes I think it would be nice to get that intimidation factor back," he said after Bonnie left. Despite his words, it looked like he was holding back a smile.

"Never going to happen." She blew her straw wrapper at him, giggling when she hit him on the chin.

"Callum. Lou." The male voice brought up both of their heads. Lou flushed at being caught acting like an eight-year-old. An *immature* eight-year-old.

"Rob," Callum said while Lou gave the sheriff a

dorky little wave. A few seconds of awkwardness followed when no one said anything further. Although she knew there was no way Rob had overheard their earlier conversation about him and his ex-wife, Lou still felt a little guilty.

"Want to join us?" she asked, more to break the uncomfortable silence than anything. Callum's face flattened into an expressionless mask.

"Thanks, but we're not staying to eat. Tyler's in the car—he mentioned you were headed here. I just wanted to let you know, Lou, that Chris told me about the incident last night."

She nodded, holding back a wince. The afternoon of militia research and dinner with Callum were doing a pretty good job of distracting her from her stalker, and she hated being reminded.

"We'll do our best to find whoever's doing this," Rob said.

"Thank you," she said sincerely. "Chris was really thorough in his investigation today. I know you guys are working hard on this, and I appreciate it—especially since you have bigger issues to deal with right now."

Rob gave her a wry smile. "Despite that, we still want you to feel safe."

"Thanks." She figured it would be silly to pass up an opportunity to further her research. "How's the other case going? Any luck finding out who the"—she paused before saying *headless* or *dead guy*—"victim in the reservoir was?"

"No." Rob's answer was definite and did not invite further questioning. He immediately followed up with his good-byes before heading toward the door.

Lou took a sip of her water as she watched him leave the restaurant. "The sheriff is not as generous in sharing information as our pal Belly."

"No, he is not." Callum leaned back against the booth. "Rob doesn't see many shades of gray when it comes to the law. It's part of why he's so good at what he does."

It was almost funny to hear Callum, of all people, talk about someone being too rigid. "Can I ask you a question?"

Despite his cautious expression, he nodded.

"Exactly how bat-shit nuts is our local militia group?"

Callum blinked before relief washed over his face. "I'd say somewhere in the mid-range. Why?"

"Actually, now I'm more interested in what you *thought* I was going to ask that made you so nervous."

With a shrug, he took a drink of water. Lou figured it was to stall long enough for him to think of an evasion rather than out of actual thirst. "I don't know. Something personal, I guess."

She tapped her fingertips together, evil-genius style. "Which means you have all sorts of juicy personal secrets hiding in those closets of yours."

From his flat look, she gathered that she wasn't going to be unearthing any of those secrets anytime soon.

"Fine. Let's talk about the antigovernment type of crazy rather than our own personal neuroses. When you say 'mid-range' nuts, would that include the possibility of homicide?"

One of his shoulders lifted slightly.

"I'm going to interpret your semishrug as a yes. Do you know any of the members?"

"I'm acquainted with a few."

Lou waited a few seconds, continuing only when she was certain that he was not going to elaborate on his answer. "Do any of your acquaintances seem particularly...murderous?"

After closing his eyes and looking pained, Callum sighed. "No."

"Sure?"

"Yes."

"Okay." She frowned at him, spinning her glass of water in circles. "Do you think HDG's head is mounted on the wall of the sadly named Freedom Survivors' compound game room? Could he have been a member? Or maybe he was actually a journalist trying to infiltrate the local militia group for a career-making exposé?"

"I thought we weren't going to try proving wild theories."

"But..." Her whine was interrupted by Bonnie's return. After they both ordered the ribs without ever having looked at their menus, Bonnie topped off their water and left them to their conversation.

"No, I don't."

Since she'd been expecting to have to argue just to get him to talk theories, she was startled at his direct answer...as well as a little confused about exactly which question he was answering. "You don't what?"

"I don't think there's a head mounted in the Freedom Survivors' game room."

"Oh." Oddly, she was a little disappointed. After reading militia stories all afternoon, her imagination was ready to take off at a full-on gallop. "Why not?"

"To my knowledge, they haven't reached *that* level of crazy. I've asked around some, and the consensus is that they're just a bunch of preppers who have a big gun collection and like to run drills. They're not going to be chopping off some guy's head and tossing him in the reservoir because he spoke out of turn. If they *are* responsible for killing this guy, they've reached a serious new level of fucked-up and have hidden it well."

That didn't disprove anything—but it didn't prove it either. Since he seemed more open than usual about discussing theories, she asked, "How about the motorcycle club?"

Callum looked thoughtful. "Don't really know enough about them to comment on that. You know who's a member, though?"

"Who?"

"Your crush."

She barely prevented herself from blurting, *You?* When she just looked at him, mentally fumbling away from that potential disaster, he grimaced.

"Calendar boy? With the sexy tattoos?" He said *sexy tattoos* in a falsetto that made her snort, although she still didn't know the identity of this so-called "crush." When she continued to stare blankly at Callum, he sighed. "Walsh? The guy whose ass you couldn't take your eyes off of the other night?"

"Ian? The fireman?" She had to think about that for a moment. Her brain immediately went to the obvious image. "Whoa, Ian on a motorcycle. Just when I thought he couldn't get any hotter."

Callum made a disgruntled sound, and she bumped him with her foot under the table. "I'm just messing with you, Cal."

"Did you *kick* me?"

"It was barely a nudge," she scoffed. "A little love nudge."

His face went still, and his eyes flared with sudden heat. As she realized what she'd just said, she clapped a hand over her mouth, instantly making her slip of the tongue so much more obvious. They stared at each other for a long, charged moment.

She finally couldn't take it anymore and mumbled through her fingers, "So, about the dead guy…"

The intensity of Callum's stare eased as his mouth relaxed into a half smile. "What about him?"

The arrival of their food stalled any further discussion. To Lou, it was a welcome relief from the earlier tension. If Callum was going to be sleeping over at her house tonight, it probably wasn't good to bring up the whole "love" topic…or sex, or lust, or anything having to do with his body touching hers. Her ears grew hot at the thought, and sudden warmth pooled low in her stomach, although she tried to convince herself the spicy sauce on her ribs was to blame.

After she worked her way through half her plate, she sighed and looked at Callum. "Think Ian will talk to me?" At his sharp look, she added, "Not in a fifth-grade crush kind of way. Do you think he'll talk to me about whether the MC might be involved in HDG's death?"

"No."

"Oh." She poked her baked beans with her fork, frowning.

"If they had something to do with it, he's not going to rat out his club, Lou."

That made sense, although it did make things harder. "Not even for his emergency-services sister? I thought we were a club, too."

Although she meant it mostly as a joke, Callum answered seriously. "He grew up in the MC. I think it's hard for him, balancing both the club and Fire. There are guys on both sides who don't trust him because he straddles that line."

"That must be hard." She took a bite of the beans. After she swallowed, she asked, "Did you grow up around here?"

"Yeah." His expressionless mask fell back into place. It wasn't until she was faced with robot-Callum again that she realized how much he'd opened up over the past few days.

"Did you know him? Ian, I mean."

"Not really." He crumpled his napkin and tossed it next to his cleared plate. "You done? I should get to the meeting."

She stared at him in horrified disbelief. "You cannot eat at Levi's and not have the berry-apple crumble. You just can't. It's…sacrilegious!"

His scowl eased slightly.

"Besides"—she glanced at her watch—"you have oodles of time to get to the meeting."

"Fine!" He threw up his hands. "I'll have crumble."

"You will have crumble," she told him with a mock-frown, pointing her fork at him, "and you'll like it."

The last remnants of his icy countenance melted away as he laughed. When Bonnie arrived at the table, Lou asked for a box for her leftovers and ordered two crumbles with ice cream. Her glare dared Callum to argue, but he just watched her with an amused twist to his mouth.

With a contented sigh, Lou leaned back against the booth, patting her stomach. "After I eat here, I always feel like I'll never be hungry again. That never turns out to be the case, though."

Callum grunted. "Guess you won't have room for that crumble, then."

"Touch my crumble and die."

He smiled again, but it slid too fast into a frown. "I wish you'd go to the meeting with me tonight."

"Remember how I said I'd rather get shot in the face? That still applies."

His frown deepened as he tried to scowl her into submission. It didn't work. Her aversion to civic-type meetings of all sorts had been beaten into her years ago. She easily ignored his displeasure…especially when Bonnie slid their heavenly crumbles in front of them. She also left a box for Lou's leftovers, and the check.

"Mmm," she hummed around a bite. "Besides, there's another reason I can't go. I have stuff to do."

"What stuff?" For a guy who was ready to leave before getting his crumble, he was packing away the dessert at an impressively rapid rate.

"Peeper prevention," she explained after swallowing another mouthful. "I picked up some window shades at the hardware store before going to the library today."

For some reason, maybe because it was a reminder of how he was stuck sleeping on her uncomfortable couch for an undetermined amount of time, this didn't seem to make him any happier. "Wait until I get there, and I'll help you hang the shades."

Her spoon clanked against the glass bowl as she set it down firmly. "Are you saying that I'm incapable of hanging shades on my own?"

"No." He obviously saw the warning signs of an imminent explosion and was hurrying to backtrack. "I was just offering to help."

"Uh-huh," she said, eyeing him suspiciously as she picked up her spoon again.

He was quiet for a moment before asking, "Do you need to borrow my drill?"

"I have my own drill, thanks."

"How about some drywall screws?"

"Got 'em."

"I have a level in the truck you can use."

"Why would I need that to hang shades?" At his aghast look, she laughed. "Kidding, of course. I have a level. I am fully stocked with tools, despite being in possession of a vagina."

His mouth opened and then closed again as his cheek-bones darkened with a flush. Lou was a little proud that she'd managed to embarrass him. Getting him to smile was the best, but she'd settle for ruffling his feathers.

"Ready?" she asked, digging in her purse for her wallet.

"Put that away," he growled, tossing bills on the table.

"But—" As she started to protest, he shut her down with a look. "Thank you," she said meekly, instead. "I get next time."

"No, you don't," he said, sliding out of the booth. "You have tires to buy."

"Ugh." Standing, she felt her stomach sink at the reminder. "At least the honey thing is a cheaper fix. I hope. Actually, I have no idea how to get frozen honey off of a wooden door. Do you think just soap and hot water would work?"

He shrugged. "Probably. We'll figure it out."

His words sent a rush of warmth through her. As he escorted her toward the door, she told herself that the cozy feeling was because he was there to help. She loved her little cabin and was fiercely protective of her new ability to survive on her own, but there was something so reassuring about having another person—a capable person—with whom she could share the load. Over the winter, she'd had some panic-filled moments when her truck wouldn't start or her generator stopped working. She'd survived, but it would've been nice to have had another pair of hands, especially a pair controlled by Callum's practical, intelligent brain.

Lou immediately warned herself not to get used to that warm and safe feeling. The only brain and hands she could rely on were her own. There was no way she could let herself backslide and become that meek, help-less, and useless person she used to be.

"Where'd you go?" he asked, giving her shoulder a nudge.

"Hmm?" She blinked, realizing that they were almost to the library, where the trucks were parked. "Oh! Sorry. Just thinking about…stuff." Stuff too personal to share, *especially* with Callum.

His mouth quirked. "Well, pay attention on the drive home."

"Yes, sir." She resisted giving him a salute, but she did stand at attention. She felt it was a fair compromise between well-earned respect and her need to mock him.

"Text me when you get there."

"Will do." She climbed into the driver's seat and cranked the engine.

"Hang on."

Lou waited as he did a full circle of the truck, inspecting all four tires. Although he didn't seem to see anything amiss, he was still frowning when he returned to her open door.

"Why don't—" he started, but she cut him off before he could ask her to go to the meeting for the umpteenth time.

"No."

After a glare, which she ignored, he stepped back so she could close her door. She cranked down the window so she could hear him, even though she knew perfectly well what he was going to say.

"Be careful."

It was like she was psychic. "I will. Promise. I'll see you after the meeting."

He just nodded, and she faced front, her hand reaching for the gearshift. Before she could shove the truck into drive, however, he said her name.

When she turned toward him, an inquiring smile forming, he suddenly reached forward, slid a hand around the back of her neck, tugged her close, and kissed her—a hard, breathless, short press of his lips against hers. Her smile dropped away in shock, and she stared at him, eyes wide, as he quickly backed away.

"See you later," he said, turning and walking toward where his own truck was parked. She continued to stare well after he climbed in and started the engine.

"Callum," she said softly, touching her lips.

She could feel the burn of his stubble, and her stomach tightened with sudden, unmistakable heat. "Callum, what the hell?!"

Chapter 7

SHE BLAMED THE POOR JOB SHE DID HANGING THE shades on Callum's kiss. It had taken up a great deal of her brainpower over the course of the evening, and that was why her window coverings were just a hair lopsided. Lou backed toward her bedroom door to get a better look at the finished product. If she squinted and tilted her head to the right, they didn't look *that* bad. Besides, any installation or repair in which she didn't need to resort to duct tape and her staple gun was considered a success.

After putting away her tools, she looked around the cabin. Before hanging the shades, she'd done a whirlwind job of cleaning, and her house looked considerably neater than it had when she'd left that morning. Hopefully, it was clean enough not to provoke Callum into some sort of OCD-triggered seizure.

She lit the candles scattered around the cabin. The multiple flickering flames filled the rooms with a warm yellow light. It was very…romantic. She hurried to blow them all out again, not wanting Callum to think she was trying to set a mood.

Shaking her head, she stepped away from the last extinguished candle and scowled. It was silly to waste electricity just because she didn't want to give Callum the wrong impression. Or *was* it the wrong impression? Her hand drifted to her lips for the thousandth time since Callum had kissed her, and she yanked it away in irritation.

Needing something to do, she grabbed a bucket from under the sink, stuck it under the tap, and turned on the hot water. While it was running, she squirted some dish soap into the stream and watched it bubble. She tossed in a scrub brush and a cloth and took everything to the front porch.

After she'd been scrubbing at the frozen honey for less than a minute, she heard the rumble of an engine. Looking over her shoulder, she saw headlights approaching. Although the logical part of her brain knew it was Callum, her stomach still jumped with nerves until she recognized his truck as it backed into the spot next to hers.

He was frowning as he climbed the porch steps. "What are you doing?"

"Scrubbing. The soap and water seems to be working. I was kind of worried I'd have to resort to Goo Gone."

This explanation didn't seem to appease him. "Where's your coat? And boots?"

She glanced down, surprised to see she was just in her flannel long underwear and socks. She'd been in such a flustered rush to distract herself from his kiss that she'd stormed out without her outerwear. As if on cue, she started to shiver. "Um, I didn't realize I wasn't wearing them."

Reaching past her, he swung the door open and waited for her to go inside. After picking up the bucket, he followed her, closing and locking the door behind them. "That can wait until tomorrow. Go by the stove and get warm."

She curled up on her usual spot on the couch, grabbing a blanket hanging on the sofa arm and wrapping it around her. "How was the meeting?"

"Same as always," he grumbled as he toed off his boots before reaching down to line them up parallel to each other on the mat. "Bitching and boredom. That pretty much covers it."

"I'm so glad I didn't go," she said, laughing when he gave her a look.

He hung his coat on the hook next to hers, and his ever-present baseball cap on the next one down. Then he picked up the bucket and dumped the soapy water into the kitchen sink. He rinsed off the scrub brush and cloth before arranging everything in the optimal position to dry.

Lou realized she'd been staring at him. Not only was his backside exceedingly attractive, but his methodical way of performing tasks was a little mesmerizing. He seemed to fill all the available space in her cabin, as well as take up all the oxygen. That would explain why Lou suddenly was having a hard time breathing.

When he turned, the items apparently having been arranged to his satisfaction, Lou managed to tear her gaze away. Callum crossed over to the couch, pulled his radio off his belt, and set it on the end table. Then he plopped down on the sofa, on the opposite end from Lou, but still close enough to make every one of her nerve endings start to buzz. If she reached out, she could touch him. As soon as the thought occurred to her, she flushed and tucked her hands between her knees. *Stop thinking like that*, she told herself sternly. It would be easier if Callum wasn't so incredibly touchable.

With a groan, he tipped his head against the top of the couch. "I feel like I could sleep for a week."

As if those were the magic words, the dive-team tones sounded from his radio. Lou's radio squawked in stereo from the bedroom.

This time, Callum's groan was in protest, not relief, as the dispatcher relayed the call. "Complainant reports that his dog went through the ice on the east side of Verde Reservoir…"

Lou darted into the bedroom to grab her radio and yank on some pants before returning to find Callum on his own portable. "1210 and 1244 are both en route to Station One, ETA fifteen minutes."

Lou's eyebrows shot up. Callum was planning on driving *fast*.

"Copy," the dispatcher said, her voice echoing through both radios, reminding Lou to turn off hers. They both quickly donned their coats and boots, grabbing their hats off the hooks.

"Your truck?" Lou asked, opening the door.

Callum nodded, listening to Wilt and then Derek call in that they were also en route to the station. He tossed his keys to Lou before switching the radio to the channel dedicated to the dive team. Shocked that he wanted her to drive his truck, she gaped at the keys in her hand for a moment before circling around the hood to the driver's seat. Callum headed for the passenger side while talking into his radio.

"Wilt, you're closer. Can you grab the dive van and meet us at Verde?"

"Copy," Wilt's easy drawl confirmed, right before Derek chimed in that he'd be at Station One in two minutes.

"Good, Derek, ride with Wilt," Callum directed. Releasing the talk button, he turned to Lou. "Verde's not far. You know the back way?"

"Kind of," she said, getting a feel for his truck as they bumped over her snow-rutted driveway. As expected, the fluffy drifts from a few days earlier had hardened into rocklike mounds. "I know I turn right up here."

"That's correct." He turned off his portable radio and switched to the one in his truck. He let dispatch know they were heading straight for the reservoir. Immediately after the dispatcher acknowledged Callum's transmission, Med One, the ambulance, came on to announce they were also on their way.

"Not that I don't love dogs," Lou said tentatively as she turned onto the county road and accelerated, "and I feel kind of like an evil person for even saying this, but wouldn't some people say we shouldn't be risking the dive-team members' lives to save an animal?"

"If we don't rescue that dog, someone else—someone who doesn't have the right equipment or training—is going to go after it. Then we have a person *and* a dog to rescue. Same with wildlife going through the ice."

"Makes sense. Plus, I don't think I could leave a dog to drown, so I'm all for it. Turn left here?"

"Yes."

The truck fishtailed going around the corner, and Lou tightened her grip on the steering wheel. As she accelerated, the truck steadied.

"Good job, Lou," Callum said, and she relaxed a little, sending him a quick smile before refocusing on the road. "The next turn comes up fast, right past that tree."

"Got it." The squatty evergreen did a pretty good job of hiding the narrow lane, but Lou managed to make the turn without overshooting it. Although the road was plowed, months of snowfall had reduced the width of the passable area until just one vehicle could fit. Lou said a silent prayer that no one would be coming from the other direction.

The radio crackled, and then Wilt's voice announced that Dive Rescue One—meaning the dive van—was headed to the scene. As the dispatcher responded with a "copy," Callum checked the truck clock.

"We should be arriving around the same time as Rescue One, as long as you keep up your speed."

Taking that as a suggestion to take it up a notch, Lou eased her foot down on the accelerator, praying once again that they wouldn't encounter any other vehicles on the narrow road.

"Switchback coming," he said mildly.

"I'm impressed," she said, feeling the antilock brakes shudder beneath her foot as they skidded on the packed snow.

"With...?"

"How well you're dealing with not being in control." She made the three-hundred-degree turn with only a minor slide to the left. "I'd be clinging to the door handle at the very least. I figured you would've had to drive by the time we left my driveway, even if you had to sit on my lap to do it."

"Another switchback. And I don't always have to control everything."

"I see it." The sharp turns slowed her down more than she would've liked, but she figured it would take them even longer to get to the reservoir if they ended up in the ditch, so it was worth the extra ten seconds it took to slow for the switchbacks. "And don't give me that. I've seen your house. And your gear locker. And your truck. And the horrified look you gave *my* house, and my gear locker, and my truck."

"Just because I'm neat doesn't mean I'm a control freak. There's a steep hill coming, and you'll turn left at the bottom."

"Thanks." The hill presented no problems, and the regular turn felt easy after the two switchbacks. "And yes, you are a control freak. It's not a bad thing, especially as our dive-team leader. You keep everyone safe that way."

"Keep following this road. It'll take us around to the east side of the reservoir. Does the control thing put you off?"

"Put me off? Of you, you mean?" She looked at him in surprise.

"Watch the road."

"Sorry." Her head whipped back around to face the snow-rutted path they were following. She saw emergency lights in the distance, approaching from the opposite direction. "There's Wilt and Derek."

"I see them. So, does it?"

"Not at all. It does make me want to scatter a handful of paperclips in front of you, though." A thought occurred to her. "Isn't this road to the reservoir covered in ice? Wasn't that the reason you moved ice-rescue training to Mission Reservoir?"

"Yeah. Just get down as best you can. Try to stop before going onto the reservoir. We'll worry about

getting back up the hill once the dog is out of the water."
He paused. "And what the hell's up with the paperclip
thing? I'm organized, not Rain Man."

She shrugged. "I don't know. I just want to add a
little chaos to your life. I should turn in here, right?"

"Right. Slow and easy."

Lou held her breath as the truck slid down the icy
slope, turning until the pickup was at a diagonal angle.
It felt like they were on a wheeled sled more than in a
steerable vehicle. The brakes weren't helping, and she
had an anxious moment when she thought they would
just keep going until the truck was out onto the ice.
Please don't let me drown Callum's truck, she thought.

But then the slope flattened, and snowdrifts helped
to slow their forward momentum. They eased to a halt
several feet from the shore. Her breath left her in a
relieved rush.

"Nice lighting placement," Callum said as he opened
his door. Lou looked out on the ice and realized what
he meant. The truck was angled so the headlights illuminated the broken ice and dark water surrounding the
head of a struggling light-colored dog.

"Shit. Owner's in the water, too." Callum's calm tone
contrasted with his speed as he jumped out of the truck
and ran for the back to get his gear. It took a second for
his words to register before Lou realized there was a
second hole in the ice, this one containing a person.

"Hang on, buddy!" Callum called to the person struggling to pull himself out of the water. Pieces of ice broke
and sank beneath his flailing arms. "We'll get you out
of there."

"Oh man," Lou breathed, her stomach plunging to

her toes at the sight of the two struggling victims. It was one thing to train, to pretend that Phil really was drowning, but this was reality—a true life-or-death situation. She grabbed for her portable radio and twisted the power knob, waiting impatiently for the beep letting her know it was working. She relayed the information about the second victim while hurrying to join Callum at the tailgate.

He'd already gotten his dry suit on halfway, so she held it up so he could thrust his arms in the sleeves. Her hands shaking, she pulled the hood over his head, zipped the back, and secured the Velcro flaps, following his movement as he reached into the bed of the pickup to pull out the rope and harness.

As she hooked the rope around him, red-and-white flashing lights lit the area, and the dive van crested the hill. Lou saw the brakes lock up as the van made the same sliding descent as Callum's truck.

"Watch out," he warned, but she was already moving. They scrambled back ten feet and watched as the dive van slid to a stop next to the truck. Lou refocused on fastening the rope around Callum's midsection. Harness in hand, he jogged along the shore, looking for the most direct line to the man in the water. Lou followed, her gaze locked on the victim's slowing struggle.

As Callum headed out onto the ice, leaving her on shore with the other end of the rope, Lou realized that she didn't have her tug-of-war team behind her this time. She sent a frantic glance toward the dive van to see Derek and a dry-suited Wilt grabbing equipment from the back of the van, and she mentally begged them to hurry. Endless shoveling and stacking firewood had given her more upper-body strength than she'd ever had before, but the idea of hauling two good-sized men out of the water and across the ice by herself made her shake.

Callum was crawling toward the mostly submerged man. Although she couldn't make out the words, Lou could hear him talking to the victim, his voice low and reassuring. Sliding on his belly across the final stretch, Callum slid feetfirst into the water just as the ice cracked beneath his weight. He had the harness fastened around the man's chest in seconds, and the part of Lou's brain that wasn't completely terrified had to admire his dexterity. She knew from their aborted training session that it was harder than it looked.

"Oh no," she breathed. Callum was giving her the "pull" sign. She hauled on the rope, and it was much easier than she'd expected. Glancing behind her, she saw Wilt and a grinning Derek. Relief spilled over into a beaming smile. "My tug-of-war team is back!"

Wilt, obviously not getting her reference, blinked quizzically. Turning back toward the reservoir, Lou focused on getting the two men to safety. Callum had boosted the victim onto the ice and was holding him in a bear hug from behind. The ice was cracking and sagging beneath their combined weight, threatening to drop both of them back into the frigid water. With Derek's regular command of "*Pull!*" they hauled on the rope, dragging the two men across the ice until it held solid beneath them.

The ambulance had arrived, but the EMTs had wisely left the vehicle on top of the slick slope and made their way to the shore on foot. As they helped Callum wrap warmed blankets around the victim and buckle him into a Stokes basket, Derek hooked a rope around Wilt. Confused for a moment, Lou realized with a flash of guilt that she'd completely forgotten about the dog.

Looking at the original hole in the ice, she didn't see anything except water, and her stomach clenched. She joined Derek on the rope as Wilt headed out on the ice. Lou strained her eyes, trying to get a glimpse of the dog in the harsh light and shadows created by the truck's headlights. Her breath caught when she thought she saw a muzzle poking out of the water.

It was torture, watching Wilt make his cautious way across the untrustworthy ice. Although she wanted to scream at him to hurry, she knew it would only delay the rescue if Wilt were to unintentionally go into the water too far from the dog. The ice must have been threatening to crack beneath his feet, because he started crawling and then slid to his belly after moving just a few feet farther.

When he finally reached the opening where the dog had fallen through, Lou realized she was muttering, "Oh please, oh please," under her breath. Wilt swung his feet around and dropped into the hole. He reached beneath the water, feeling around for what seemed like ages, and finally hauled the dog to the surface, propping its front half against the ice so he could secure the harness around its middle.

She was so caught up in the drama of the rescue, Derek had to shout, "Pull!" before Wilt's gesture registered.

"Sorry!" she yelped, before yanking hard on the line. Even with them down one person on the rope, it was easier this time. Wilt's dry suit slid easily over the ice, and, although the dog was fairly large, it still weighed considerably less than its owner. As they drew closer, Lou could see the dog's wet fur was already beginning to whiten as the water froze, and her throat clenched at the stillness of the furry body.

"I should've driven faster," she whispered, thinking of all the places she'd hesitated instead of speeding up. If they'd gotten there just a little earlier, maybe the owner wouldn't have tried his own rescue, and Callum could've gotten the dog out right away. Gritting her teeth, she gave a final haul on the rope that brought Wilt and the dog to the shore.

Callum hurried toward them with a second Stokes basket and several warmed blankets. The dog's owner was gone, and Lou realized that the EMTs and Callum must have hauled him up the icy slope to the ambulance while she'd been focused on the second rescue. Dropping the rope, she rushed over to where Callum was taking the dog from Wilt. She hovered over them, feeling desperately unhelpful as she watched Callum and Derek wrap blankets around the too-still animal.

"Is he okay?" she asked, crouching down fairly close but out of the way of the rescuers. Although she didn't want to distract them, she couldn't take another second of not knowing if the dog would live.

"Heartbeat is faint, but present," Callum responded, helping to lift the swaddled dog onto the stretcher. "Respiration slow and shallow. I can't take his blood pressure. Our equipment doesn't fit."

"Are they going to take him in the ambulance?" she asked.

He nodded. "It's going to take too long to get either

of our vehicles up the hill. Dispatch has the Connor Springs emergency vet on call heading to the hospital. She'll meet the ambulance there."

"Good." Her smile was shaky. "Think they're going to be okay?"

His gaze was steady, so confident and trustworthy that she knew she would believe anything he said at that moment with all her heart.

"Yeah. I do."

––––––

Callum and Wilt were stripping out of their dry suits, the ambulance having headed toward the hospital in Connor Springs, when the County road-maintenance truck they'd asked dispatch to request arrived to coat the icy reservoir road with sand and salt. After that, Callum's pickup made it to the top of the hill in one try, although the dive van took two.

Trying to control her shivering, Lou waved at Wilt and Derek as they pulled away in the dive van. She headed toward the driver's door of the pickup, only to stop short before she ran into Callum, who was headed toward the same destination. Relieved, she changed course to the passenger side. Now that the adrenaline was leaving her system, she was shaky and exhausted—so exhausted that she would probably fall asleep thirty seconds after sitting down. It was likely best if she didn't drive.

"Aren't you tired?" she asked through a yawn.

He glanced over at her. "Not too tired to drive. You can sleep if you like. I'll be fine getting us home."

It was a sign of her fatigue that Callum calling her

cabin "home" didn't send her into a state of panic. In fact, it warmed her insides.

"Thanks." Now that sleeping was an option, she didn't feel as tired. Blaming that on her contrary nature, she rested back against the seat, watching Callum's profile. "That was crazy—in an amazing way. I mean, they both would have *died* if we hadn't been there. It's hard to wrap my brain around that."

"Yeah. It is amazing." Callum turned his head to smile at her. "Best feeling in the world." He looked happy—tired, but happy. It was just how she felt. Her eyes drifted shut as she relaxed against the seat, trusting Callum to get her home safely.

She must have dozed, because it felt like the trip back to her house took no time at all before Callum was backing in next to her truck.

"Sorry," she apologized, sitting up with a jerk.

"Why?" He frowned at her as he turned off the engine. "I told you it was fine if you slept."

"I don't know." Tilting her head to the side, Lou stretched her neck and yawned. "Just an automatic thing, I guess. Plus, I feel bad about making you drive us home while I snored, when you have to be just as tired as I am."

"It was fine." He got out of the cab and circled the truck to open her door.

She blinked, staring at him. After the long evening and her too-short nap, everything felt fuzzy and unreal. Callum opening her door as if they were on a date was just...strange. Shaking off the weirdness of the moment, she climbed out of her seat and thanked him.

Callum closed her door and headed for the back of

the pickup. He opened the topper and lowered the tailgate so he could pull out his gear. The water coating
everything was already beginning to freeze.

"Mind if I hang this up inside?"

"Of course not," she said, reaching toward the dry
suit. "I can help haul everything."

"Got it," he said with a shake of his head while she
closed the tailgate. "Thanks."

They headed toward her front porch but had made
it only a few steps before Callum stopped. "With some
asshole wandering around here at night, we'd better lock
the trucks."

"Mine's locked," she said, shrugging when he shot
her a surprised look. "You can take the girl out of the
city, and all that. Where are your keys?"

He stopped trying to shuffle the gear in his arms and
tilted his head toward his right side. "Coat pocket."

For some stupid, ridiculous reason, sticking her hand
into his pocket made her blush. Lou feigned casualness
as she grabbed his keys, pressed the lock button on his
fob, and returned them to his pocket.

"Thanks." Although his voice was even, he was
watching her in a way that made her think he'd either
seen her blush or was just now noticing the awkwardness of the moment.

Either way, it was embarrassing, so she turned and
hurried up the porch steps, digging for her house key.
"No problem."

"Hang on," he said as soon as she'd unlocked the
door. Stepping back so Callum could enter first, she
watched him leave his gear by the door before making a
quick sweep of the house. When he returned to the main

room, he gave a jerk of his head that she took as an all clear, so she stepped inside.

They worked quietly to strip off their outerwear before hanging Callum's wet gear. They'd need to rinse everything at Station One the next day, since Lou's small kitchen sink was not up for the task. Most of the gear dangled from the coat hooks by the door, but they stretched his dry suit over a couple of straight-backed chairs that they pulled away from her kitchen table.

"You can use my shower," she said, eyeing his damp thermal shirt. "I'm just going to crash, so the hot water is all yours."

"Thanks." His eyes flicked to the couch. "Do you have a pillow I could use?"

Her gaze followed his to her short, not-very-comfortable couch. The idea of finding sheets and pillows and pillowcases and blankets was suddenly overwhelming. She turned to look at Callum.

"Would it be weird if you slept with me?"

It was several long moments before he spoke. "It... well, I..."

Even in her exhausted state, she was a little proud she'd reduced the mighty Callum to stammering. "Not like in a sex way," she tried to explain, stumbling more than usual over her words. Her sense of pride faded when she fumbled even more than he did. "Just in a loss-of-consciousness way. That couch isn't really that comfortable to sit on, much less sleep on. I have only one bed, but it's big, and I'm really tired, so I wouldn't, like, attack you in your sleep or anything." She paused. He was still staring at her. "If you wouldn't be comfortable with it, that's fine. I'll just grab you some sheets and a pillow and stuff."

She looked around, trying to clear her muddled brain and figure out where she kept the extra bedding. Remembering that she had some blankets in the hall closet, she figured it'd be a good place to check. As she started to turn, she was stopped by Callum's hand on her arm.

"It's fine."

It was her turn to stare at him. "Um…which one is fine—the sleeping on the couch, or with me?"

"With you."

"Good." Her breath rushed out in relief. "I have no idea if I actually own another set of sheets."

He gave her an appalled look. "Don't you ever change your bedding?"

"Of course," she huffed. "I wash them and then put them right back on the bed."

"Oh."

With an amused snort, she said, "You were about to change your mind about sleeping on the couch, weren't you?"

He just grinned, picking up a backpack he'd left by the door when he'd first arrived that evening before the call. It seemed like days had passed since then. As he headed toward her bathroom, she stood still and watched him, dazzled by that huge, flat-out-beautiful smile. There were those *dimples*.

Shit. She was in so much trouble.

The wind wouldn't stop. He pressed his hands flat against his ears, barely holding back a scream of frustration. It blew and blew, never ceasing, and it made him crazy.

But he couldn't just stay like that forever. Eventually he dropped his arms to his sides and moved through the trees, staying in the blackest shadows. The worst part of the wind was that it disguised other sounds—sounds like the crunch of snow under boots or the brush of moving fabric. Someone was following him. He knew it, but the wind hid whoever it was from him. The back of his neck burned every time he was watching her.

He reached the tree line and paused, scanning the cabin. The days were starting to run together, blurring time around the edges. He was late, and he'd probably missed her changing. It was okay, though. He'd still get to watch her sleep, to see her relaxed body and peaceful expression. He realized he was almost at the cabin, but he didn't remember moving from the trees. It was getting worse.

He quietly approached the darkened window, his heartbeat speeding up as it always did. Maybe tonight he'd try the door, and it would be unlocked. He pictured her with her hand on the dead bolt, deciding to leave it open, just for him. Instead of sneaking inside, he'd walk through the cabin, knowing that she'd be waiting in her bedroom, in her bed…

He stopped abruptly. Instead of the usual darkened room, all he could see were closed shades. She'd blocked him. *Him!* How could she do that to him?

His chest started to burn as he moved around to the front of the cabin. It was time to make her understand that she was his. He'd tried to be gentle, to give her time to realize that she belonged with him, but now she'd shut him out. His anger growing, he rounded the corner of the cabin and jerked to a halt.

The man's truck was there. She'd put up shades and had another man staying the night. His confidence that she was faithful shredded, and he could hear his ragged breathing. He knew he needed to be quiet or he'd be caught, but he couldn't control it. His imagination was going wild as he thought about what was going on behind those covered windows. The rage was close, the kind that made him deaf and blind to everything until afterward, when he had to face what he'd done.

This time, he welcomed it. They needed to pay.

Chapter 8

Lou woke with a start.

Although she had heard the saying, "asleep before her head hit the pillow," she'd never experienced it until the night before. As she'd changed back into pajamas while Callum showered, she'd thought she'd be antsy, anticipating him so close to her, but a syrupy blackness had swallowed her mind as soon as she had gotten into bed and curled onto her side.

Now she lay still, hunting in the darkness for clues about what woke her. Callum lay next to her, his breaths deep and even. She didn't think that was what had disturbed her.

No light was creeping in around the newly hung and only slightly crooked shades, and she twisted, reaching for the cell phone on her nightstand so she could check the time. It was two thirty. Her brain flew to the memory of the morning before, when she'd woken in the same way. Her stalker could've been watching her at that moment.

Her gaze shot to the covered window. She eased out of bed, not wanting to wake Callum until she had solid proof they should be concerned. Besides, the cabin was small. If her stalker was close, Lou's scream could bring Callum running within a couple of seconds. She tiptoed across her bedroom floor toward the door.

"What's wrong?" Callum's voice, husky from sleep, made her jump.

"Sorry," she whispered. "I didn't mean to wake you."

"You didn't answer my question. And I'm up. You don't need to whisper."

"Right." She should have known she couldn't dodge his question. He was a master at spotting evasion—she'd seen him in action during training. "I was just checking on…things."

Shoving down the covers, he swung his legs off the bed and stood. "What things? Did you hear something?"

"No. Maybe." When he just cocked an eyebrow at her, she sighed. "I woke up. I'm not sure why. I just wanted to check things to see if there was anything to actually get alarmed about or if it was just my overactive brain."

Frowning, he moved around her so he could leave the bedroom first. "Don't be checking things by yourself. That's why I'm here."

"Fine." Stepping behind him, she gave him a nudge. "Then go. Investigate."

Callum shot a quelling look over his shoulder before starting his search of her house. She stayed behind him as he checked the dimly lit living room and kitchen. When he reached to open the pantry door, she flinched. This time, though, the broom stayed put. They moved to the bathroom. It was nice, having a shield between her and her own overactive imagination. Still, she jumped at the rattle of shower curtain rings as Callum yanked it open, revealing a shadowed, empty tub.

He headed toward the front door and began pulling on his boots. Unlike her fearful stumble around the house, his search had been quick, but thorough, and she was impressed by his technique.

"Were you in the military?" she asked.

"Yes."

"What branch?"

"Marines."

"Did you like it?"

He paused in the middle of reaching for his coat. At first she didn't think he was going to answer, but he finally said, "I did. I liked the order and the discipline. After growing up in chaos, the structure was…reassuring."

Shocked that the normally reserved Callum had actually shared something personal, she was quiet as he eased open the front door and slipped through it. The short rush of cold air that blew in before he closed the door behind him brought her back to reality. She hurried from window to window, watching Callum's progress around the perimeter of the cabin.

With him gone, the dark shadows inside the house regained their menace. He disappeared around the corner of the cabin, and she ran for the next window, not able to breathe until she could see him again. Once he was back in sight, Lou made a face at herself. How had she returned to being a scaredy-cat in just the short time he'd been outside?

He paused for a minute outside her bedroom window, staring hard at the ground, but then he continued his circuit. Lou looked away from him for a moment, her eyes scanning the landscape. The trees were huge and menacing—not only in their ability to hide all sorts of frightening things in their shadows, but also their own shapes turned nightmarish in the dark. The tree limbs bobbed and dragged, potentially hiding someone who might be using the tree line as cover *right now*, staring back at her.

The door flew open, making Lou jump and swallow a scream. Bringing in another gust of frigid air, Callum reentered the cabin, stomping the snow from his boots onto the mat just inside the door. "It's clear. I want to take another look at those tracks outside your bedroom window once there's daylight, though. I think there might be fresh boot prints, but it's too hard to tell in just the moonlight."

A shiver coursed through her at the thought that her stalker might have returned while she was in a deep sleep. Knowing that the shades would have blocked his view helped, and having Callum there helped even more, but it was still unnerving to be watched.

"Go back to bed where it's warm," Callum said, having apparently seen her shake and misinterpreting the cause. "I'll be there in a minute."

She turned toward the bedroom. The woodstove caught her eye, and she started to make a detour in its direction. Since she was up, she might as well feed the beast. Besides, she didn't want to go back to the shadowed emptiness of the bedroom without him.

Callum's voice stopped her. "I've got it. Go to bed."

Although he was bossy, he was also helpful, so she ceded firewood duty to him. She did give him a "careful, Buddy" look, however, so he'd know her easy-going nature had its limits. Lou wasn't sure how seriously he took her nonverbal warning, since he laughed, although he quickly turned the sound into a strangled cough.

Even worse than entering the darkened bedroom by herself would be admitting that she was scared, so she made her way—albeit slowly—into the room. Not allowing her gaze to travel to the windows and whoever

might be lurking outside, she slid into bed and pulled
the covers up to her chin. Lou felt like a six-year-old,
afraid of monsters under her bed. She hated that someone could do this to her.

This time, she definitely did not fall asleep as soon
as her head hit the pillow. Instead, she stared at the pine
ceiling until Callum returned and slid into bed next to
her. Opening her mouth to ask one of the dozen questions hovering in her throat, Lou suddenly realized that
she didn't want to think about it anymore.

"Tell me something else you liked about being a
marine," she asked instead.

There was that pause again, the one that made Lou
hold her breath in anticipation, not knowing if Callum
would share something about himself or if he'd shut her
down, as usual.

"I suddenly had brothers, guys who had my back, no
matter what. I liked that."

She tried to let her breath out silently, so Callum
wouldn't know she'd been holding it. "What didn't
you like?"

She heard the bedclothes rustle, as if he were shifting
positions, but she was too afraid of breaking the spell
to turn her head and look at him. "Leaving. It was hard,
after I was out. I felt…I don't know, pointless." He
made a small sound of frustration. "That's not the right
word. It's hard to explain. I was lost for a while until I
joined the dive team. Then I had another new family in
search and rescue."

It seemed so big, so important, what he'd shared with
her that she didn't want to diminish it with platitudes.
So, keeping her mouth shut for once, she just reached

out and found his hand. Lacing their fingers together, she squeezed hard, smiling when he squeezed back.

—*∾*—

Dawn light was creeping around the shades when Lou awoke. Her first impression was of toasty contentment, and she smiled as she snuggled into that lovely warmth. When she realized the source of that heat was Callum pressed against her back, his arm wrapped around her middle, her eyes went wide.

With a sleepy grunt, he pulled her closer. Lou swallowed as her heart went crazy. This was *Callum* wrapped around her like a possessive grizzly bear. Should she get out of bed? Go back to sleep? Roll over and kiss him senseless like she'd been wanting to do for months?

The last option was the most tempting. She bit the inside of her cheek, trying to build up the courage to do it. After all, he was the one treating her like a body pillow, so technically he'd made the first move. So what if he'd been unconscious at the time? Plus, there had been that kiss—the kiss that they were apparently going to pretend never happened.

Taking a deep breath, she started to turn when she felt him stiffen. Then he was gone, leaving her back and her heart cold. Before she could recover from his sudden abandonment, there was a rattle of shades, and light poured into the room. With a groan of disappointment, she shoved her head under her pillow, wanting to hide from his rejection as much as from the sun.

"Time to get up," he announced.

"Five more minutes."

When he didn't respond, she figured he'd agreed to her request—at least until he jerked the covers off of her.

"Why do you hate me?" she wailed from beneath her pillow. Although she tucked her knees into her chest, the cold air wouldn't allow her to fall back asleep.

"We need to leave now if we want to get to the clinic and back before your shift starts." He did not sound at all contrite about torturing her. With a groan, she reluctantly sat up.

She yawned as he stared at her head with a bemused expression. "What?"

"Your hair. It's…" As he trailed off, his hands made an exploding type of gesture.

"Whatever," she grumbled, shoving a few strands out of her eyes. "At least I don't have your morning face."

"What?" It sounded like he was trying not to laugh.

"Never mind." She slid off the bed and shuffled toward the bathroom. "Give me fifteen minutes, and then we can go."

At his disbelieving snort, she stopped and scowled at him. "What?"

"You're really going to be ready in fifteen minutes?"

"Fourteen and a half, now." She slammed the bathroom door behind her before shouting, "And make yourself useful in the meantime and cook breakfast!"

<center>~~~</center>

She'd been kidding—well, kind of kidding—when she'd hollered at him to cook, but there was a definite smell of bacon in the cabin when she emerged from the bathroom twelve minutes later, smug about her speediness. After she threw on some warm and not-too-smelly clothes, she followed her nose to the kitchen, where Callum was indeed slaving over a hot stove. Leaning against the wall, she enjoyed the view of him standing at the stove, his sleeves pushed up to reveal his muscled forearms, lining up the strips of bacon into perfect formation.

"You know," she teased, "you could have your own calendar. You'd only be wearing an apron in this shot. Although that's kind of asking for spitting bacon-grease burns, isn't it?"

He flushed, and she realized she was getting pretty proficient at making him turn red. "Did you want breakfast or not?" he grumbled, forking the bacon onto a paper-towel-lined plate.

"Yes." She reached over to steal a piece, but he smacked her hand before she could reach her prize. "Ow. Did you happen to notice my twelve-minute prep time?"

"Wait for the eggs. And yes, very impressive."

"You're making eggs, too? I might just keep you."

Although he was trying to hide it, a smile was fighting to break free. "You're on toast duty."

Lou glanced at the digital display showing the charge left in her batteries. "If you want me to use the toaster, I'm going to have to turn on the generator. The sun's not high enough yet to produce much power. That's what happens when you get up at the crack of dawn."

He just gave her a look. "We don't have to have toast."

"No, it's okay." Heading for the front door, she said over her shoulder, "If you made bacon and eggs, the least I can do is make toast."

Throwing on her boots but skipping the coat, she ran outside to the small shed that housed her generator. She

opened the valve that allowed propane to the generator and reached for the start switch. A strange hissing
sound and the strong smell of propane made her hesitate.
Instead of turning on the generator, she pulled her hand
back and closed the valve.

Trotting back to the cabin, she made a face. There
always had to be something going wrong. Why couldn't
she just eat bacon with Callum in peace?

Inside, she nudged her temporary chef aside to grab a
spray bottle from under the sink.

"What's up?" he asked, turning off the burner, immediately slipping into calm and competent mode. It was
like he could smell the start of a potential crisis.

"Propane leak," she said, squirting some dish soap
into the bottle and filling it the rest of the way with
water. She grabbed her coat on the way out this time.
Callum followed her silently. As they crossed the
yard, the only sound was the crunch of snow beneath
their boots. Although she had on her brave face, Lou
couldn't help glancing around at the surrounding trees.
Everything was still and quiet, without even a breeze or
the chatter of a squirrel. It felt like the forest was holding
its breath, watching.

"Leave the door open, would you?" she asked as they
both entered the shed. "There's no other light in here."

After she opened the valve again, she sprayed the
soapy water in a stream where the propane line connected to the generator. When no bubbles formed,
she frowned.

"Am I crazy, or do I hear and smell a leak?"

"You're not crazy." Taking the bottle from her,
Callum began spraying the length of the propane line.

At about the midpoint, large bubbles formed, and Lou closed the valve.

"This was cut." Callum's voice was grim as he examined the slice in the line.

Leaning her chin on his shoulder so she could see the hole as well, she growled, "That's it. My tires and front door are one thing, but you don't mess with someone's toast!"

"This isn't funny, Lou."

"I know." She sighed, standing. "It's scary and dangerous and becoming really expensive. Joking in the face of adversity is just what I do."

There was a loud bang, and everything went dark. With a yelp, Lou grabbed Callum's arm, needing something to hang on to in the sudden blackness. There was no one in here with them—she *knew* that. And yet, she couldn't help but feel a hot breath against the back of her neck…couldn't help but imagine hands reaching for her in the dark.

"It's okay," she reassured herself more than Callum. "The door just blew shut."

"There's no wind."

"It had to be the wind." Lou released her death grip on his arm and shuffled in the direction of the door, holding her hands in front of her. "The alternative is too freaking scary."

"I'll get it." Catching her, Callum gently tugged her behind him. She grabbed a fistful of the back of his coat and followed him the few steps to the door. He opened it slowly, peering around outside before stepping forward to allow Lou out of the shed.

Although it was a relief to escape the darkness, standing outside felt almost as nerve-racking. Her gaze darted around the snow-covered ground, looking for tracks of some kind or any kind of evidence to prove or disprove that someone had been here…though she wasn't sure yet which she preferred.

"Do you think he was here last night?" She examined the packed snow around the shed entrance, looking for a boot track matching the ones under her window.

"Could be." Callum closed the door behind him. "Or he could've done this two nights ago, and we just didn't notice. When was the last time you ran your generator?"

"Three days ago?" She squinted in thought. "Maybe four? I know I didn't turn it on yesterday, so the propane line could've been cut at the same time as the honey thing."

Cocking his head, he looked at her. "But you don't think it was."

With a shrug, she moved around to the other side of the shed, still looking for tracks. "I'm probably being paranoid—"

He interrupted with a snort. "Are you paranoid if someone's really after you?"

Her smile was more pained than amused. "Something woke me last night—or this morning, I guess. It's just a feeling, but I think he was out there."

Callum waved her toward the front door. "Let's eat and then go to the clinic. You can call the sheriff on the way to Connor Springs."

Climbing the porch steps, she asked, "Shouldn't we wait for Rob to get here?"

"He knows the way, and you don't lock your generator shed." With a disapproving look, he added, "You probably should."

"It has a lock," she protested. "I'm just not exactly sure where the key is."

He grunted, and she resisted the urge to make a face. Callum was the only person she knew who could fit a reprimand into a single wordless noise.

"Eggs," he said, "and bacon. Can't waste bacon."

"Definitely not!" she agreed with appropriately theatrical dismay, and then laughed when he gave her a look. But her laughter died as Callum headed into the house, leaving her alone on the porch. Lou paused, skin prickling, and twisted her head to scan the trees. She couldn't help but wonder if someone was there even now, watching. Waiting.

Wanting to hurt her.

It was still fairly early when they reached the VA clinic. A few people were scattered around the reception area, but there was still a sleepy feel to the place. She and Callum exchanged a glance, and he headed toward one of the waiting people, a man about HDG's age, who was frowning at the news playing on a TV mounted to the wall.

Lou made her way to the check-in desk. "Excuse me."

The tired-eyed receptionist with a nametag reading "Tina" gave her a smile. "Good morning. Checking in for an appointment?"

With a shake of her head, Lou said, "I'm actually here about my uncle. He had two toes amputated recently— well, several months ago—and I wanted to check if he was showing up for his aftercare appointments."

"Did he sign the waiver giving you access to his records?"

"Of course," she lied.

"What's his name?" Tina asked, tugging the computer keyboard closer.

"Grant Dutton," she said, giving her grandfather's name.

After typing in the name, Tina asked, "Is that D-U-T-T-O-N? I'm not finding anyone by that name."

That was because her grandfather had never been in the military, and he definitely hadn't visited the Connor Springs VA clinic. "He, um, has some mental-health issues, so he sometimes uses a different name."

The receptionist looked up from the computer screen and frowned. "He wouldn't be able to use a different name here. We offer services for veterans. We don't just take anyone off of the street."

Lou tried to look confused. "I don't know why he's not in your system, then. Do you remember seeing him here? He's about five-ten, a hundred and fifty pounds, sixty-five, gray hair, has diabetes, and he had those two toes on his right foot amputated last year."

Tina's lips flattened. "That describes a lot of patients, and I can't really talk to you about anyone without verifying that they gave you access to their records. I'm sorry."

Although she was disappointed, Lou hadn't expected to get much information from the staff. "I understand. Do you happen to know of any local support groups for amputees or diabetics? My uncle actually lives in the Simpson area, so anything around there would work the best."

"Sure." Tina seemed relieved to be able to help with something. Her fingers tapped on the keyboard, and then she pulled several sheets of paper out of the printer. "Here you go. I included ones in the Denver area, too."

Lou smiled as she took the printed pages. "Thank you."

As she turned away from the check-in desk, she scanned the waiting area. Callum was leaning against the wall next to the entry doors. When she caught his eye, he shook his head. He must have struck out with the other patients. She pushed away the disappointment as she crossed to where he was standing. That had been an extremely long shot.

As soon as they were back in the truck, she shared the gist of her conversation with Tina. Holding up the support-group lists, she gave them a shake. "I figured we could check with the coordinator of each of these, see if they recognize my 'uncle' and know what name he was using."

"We'll probably run into the same privacy issues as you did at the clinic," he cautioned.

"I know. I just like to be doing *something* to figure out who this guy is. Who knows"—she shrugged— "maybe we'll get lucky." When he sent her a smile, she eyed him suspiciously. "What?"

It was his turn to shrug. "You're doing a good thing. According to the word around Station One, the cops really have hit a dead end. Sounds like the BCA and the local guys are doing more fighting than investigating."

"We need to keep looking. I feel kind of responsible for him."

"Because you were the one to find his body?" Callum asked, turning onto the highway.

"And because I kicked him," she admitted. "There's some residual guilt."

He just shook his head at her, looking amused.

"Honestly?" She stared out the windshield. "Out here, it's too easy to disappear, to become nothing."

"That could never happen to you. You know that, right?"

"Not now, maybe. When I first moved out here, though, who would've looked for me?"

"No maybe about it," he said harshly. "If you go missing for five minutes, every cop, firefighter, diver, and search and rescue member is going to be looking for you, and we won't stop until you're safe again. Got it?"

Smiling, she turned her head to look at his profile. "Got it."

―⁓―

Rob was leaving her driveway when she and Callum returned. Reversing the sheriff's department SUV, he backed along the driveway until he stopped just in front of her cabin. Callum pulled up next to him, rolling down his window so their driver's doors were side by side.

"I didn't get much," Rob admitted as soon as Callum's truck rolled to a stop. "The snow is so packed that there wasn't much for boot prints, and I couldn't find any fingerprints on the propane line or the doorknob to the shed. I took some pictures, and I'll make a report, but that's about all I can do for now."

Callum tightened his fingers around the steering wheel. "Any idea who might be doing this?"

"No!" Lou burst out in frustration aimed more at the situation than at Callum or the sheriff. "I keep trying to think of who I've annoyed—other than you—and I can't think of anyone. I look at each person who comes into the coffee shop, wondering if it could be them, but I just can't picture anyone I know being a freaky stalker! Seriously, no guy has even asked me out since

I arrived, so I don't even have a short list of the rejected and resentful."

There were a few seconds of silence before Callum said mildly, "I was talking to Rob, actually."

"Oh. Sorry." She paused before waving a hand toward the two men. "Carry on then."

Rob smiled at her but sobered quickly. "Afraid I'm right there with you, Lou. We have our couple of troublemakers, the people we usually look at when there's been a theft or some minor damage to property. I haven't been able to connect any of these guys to you, though."

With a grimace, she said, "It makes it worse, actually, that I have no clue who it is. It makes me think it could be anyone, which is why I'm mentally accusing *everyone*."

To her surprise, Callum ran a hand across her shoulder and gently squeezed the back of her neck. In the months he had known her, he'd so rarely touched her—or anyone, that she'd noticed—that any physical contact made her jump. The sparks that lit her skin when he touched her didn't help, either.

"Don't get discouraged, Lou," the sheriff said. "As a rule, most criminals are pretty dumb, and I'm guessing your guy isn't a rocket scientist. He's been destructive, but not violent." He kindly left off the implied "yet." "He'll screw up, and we'll get him. No one messes with one of ours."

"Thanks, Rob."

He shifted his truck into drive. "Let me know when he does something else. And stick close to that guy of yours." With a final lift of his chin in farewell, he eased his squad SUV away from them and headed down the driveway.

Lou was blushing. From the heat she could feel radiating from her cheeks, it was quite a bright blush, too. Although Callum didn't say anything, she could sense his gaze on her very red profile.

"Shut it," she growled.

"I didn't say a word."

And that just made it worse. "Yeah, well, you were thinking some words."

"Yeah. I was." The look he gave her made her cheeks fire even brighter, and she scrambled out of his truck. The sound of his laughter followed her all the way into her cabin.

Chapter 9

WORK DRAGGED. LOU TRIED VERY HARD NOT TO LOOK at each customer as a potential threat, but it was difficult. Plastering on a fake smile, she attempted to keep her suspicious glares to a minimum.

During the mid-afternoon slump, she was cleaning the bathroom when the sleigh bells on the door jangled.

"Be with you in a moment," she called as she stripped off her rubber gloves and washed her hands. Lifting the hinged portion of the counter, she slipped through to find a deputy waiting. He looked familiar, with a compact frame, reddish-blond hair, and a cropped mustache. She couldn't remember where she'd met him until she read his nametag.

"Deputy Lawrence," she greeted him.

Although his nod was a little stiff, he looked pleased to be recognized. Lou wondered if he'd forgotten that he wore his name pinned to his coat. "And you're…?"

"Lou," she finished when he paused. "Lou Sparks. Dive team. We met in passing the other day at the… um, reservoir." She'd discussed the event so much with Callum that she didn't know how to politely refer to finding HDG when talking to others.

"Right. You were the one who discovered the body." His face screwed up in a grimace. "That's created a lot of work for us."

She blinked, unsure how to respond to the hint of

accusation in his tone. "Um…sorry to hear that. Would you like something to drink?"

"Yeah, a large mocha with whipped, please." His gaze dropped to her chest. "So…you're on the dive team."

"Yes."

"As what? The mascot?"

She choked and almost spilled the steaming milk. "Uh, no. As an actual, real-life diver."

"Seriously?" His tone told her how very much he disapproved of that.

"Seriously." *Deputy Jackass*, she added in her head.

Although she was pretty sure Deputy Lawrence was not going to be one of her favorite people, she kept a pleasant expression on her face as she prepared his drink. "How's that investigation going?" she couldn't resist asking as she topped his mocha with whipped cream.

"I can't talk about the case to civilians," he said stiffly.

"Of course," she said, ringing up his order with a mental shrug. So much for sharing information among the search-and-rescue family.

"Although," he said slowly as he pulled out his wallet, "there have been some interesting developments."

"Like what?" She accepted his cash and handed back his change. None of the money made it into her tip jar.

After pocketing his wallet, Lawrence leaned closer, resting his elbows on the counter. "There's a possible connection with a motorcycle gang."

"Really? The club in Liverton?" Despite the deputy's rather slimy manner, she couldn't resist the lure of new information.

"*Club*," he repeated with a slight sneer. "They can

call themselves whatever they want, but it won't change what they are—a law-breaking gang of thugs."

"Um…okay. So, what's the connection?"

He leaned even closer, and Lou had to resist taking a step away from him. She wasn't sure why he had to be so close. It wasn't like there were any other customers in the shop who could possibly overhear. "There was an item caught on the weight holding down the body. It has the gang's symbol on it."

"Really?" She was quiet for a few seconds as she processed this. "That seems sloppy of them."

"We think it might be a signature. You know, the killer wants everyone to know not to mess with the club."

"Gang, you mean?"

"Yes, of course." He eyed her suspiciously but didn't seem to notice the sarcasm, because he continued, "This information needs to be kept confidential, since those Hells Angels wannabes have their guys planted everywhere, even in the county emergency services."

That confused her for a few seconds until realization hit her. "You mean Ian Walsh?"

His mouth twisted like he'd tasted something sour. "Fire should've never let one of them join. His loyalty is always going to be to his gang of criminals."

"Why can't he be loyal to both?" Lou asked with true curiosity. "From what I've heard, Ian's a good firefighter."

Lawrence drew back, his lips pulled into so tight a line that they pretty much disappeared. "You can't play both sides of the law."

"But—"

"Excuse me." He pushed away from the counter

abruptly. "I have to go. We're really busy with this murder case."

"Okay," she said to his back as he hurried to the exit. "Thanks for coming."

He paused by the door. "What time do you get off?"

"Uh," she said, trying to think of a way to deflect. "By the time I get done cleaning and closing, it's pretty late."

"I don't mind late. How about I give you a"—his grin was so slimy that it made her want to smack him—"police escort home?"

Swallowing the urge to gag, Lou forced a polite smile. "Thanks, but Callum already offered. Some other time, maybe?"

His lips tightened again underneath his mustache. "Sure." The palm of his hand smacked against the door as he plowed through it.

"Bye!" she called after him, but the only response was the flat jangle of the sleigh bells as the door closed behind the deputy.

She took a step toward the bathroom to continue cleaning and then stopped, pulling her cell phone out of her pocket. Before she could talk herself out of it, she pulled up her contacts list and tapped on Callum's name.

"Sparks," he answered after a single ring. "Everything okay?"

She could hear voices in the background. "Sorry, are you busy?"

"No, hang on." There was some muffled talking and then silence. Several seconds later, he spoke again. "I'm glad you called when you did. That meeting with the regulator reps was over a half hour ago, but they wouldn't *leave*."

"No problem." She grinned. "I'm shocked you didn't just kick them out."

"I try to be diplomatic."

"You do? Since when?"

"Why did you call?" She could tell he was trying to sound irritated, but amusement leaked through into his voice.

"Deputy Lawrence paid me a visit," she said. "He made a big deal about not being able to give me any information about the HDG case, and then proceeded to tell me there was something with the Liverton MC's logo on it attached to the weight holding down the body."

"Hmm."

"That's what I thought. Lawrence had a theory that the murderer intentionally left this item so no one would risk messing with the MC, but it doesn't seem to fit. Lawrence really wants the killer to be in the MC, though, since he has his hate on for Ian Walsh."

"You caught that?"

"Hard not to." Although he couldn't see her, she rolled her eyes. "He came right out and said Ian shouldn't be a firefighter since he's also in a, and I quote, 'gang of criminals.' How do Rob and Chris stand working with this guy?"

"I don't know," Callum said. "But ever since the bison-versus-squad-car incident, Lawrence has had it out for Walsh. I think it's a combination of embarrassment and the fact that Ian makes me look tactful in comparison."

She snorted. "I almost feel bad for Lawrence, except that spending time with him just wiped away any possibility of sympathy for the man."

After a grunt of agreement, Callum abruptly changed the subject. "Did you get your report done on the incident last night?"

"Almost." Finishing the report was next on her list after the bathroom was cleaned. "Give me a half hour unless I get an unexpected rush of customers, and I'll email it to you."

"You there alone?" he asked sharply.

Lou made a face. She'd been hoping to delay this conversation. "Right at this moment?"

He didn't respond to her evasion but just waited until she spoke again.

"I'll talk to Ivy." She sighed. "She was just in such a cranky mood when she was in here earlier, so I didn't want to ask her to put another person on this shift to close with me."

"When will you talk to Ivy?"

"Soon." At his silence, she sighed again. "Tomorrow."

"Fine. See you tonight."

"About that…" she started, but then realized he'd already ended the call. With a shrug, she pocketed her phone and headed for the bathroom to finish her cleaning. She'd worry about their ever-increasing intimacy—and how much she was starting to like it—later.

After pulling on her rubber gloves, she started scrubbing the sink, humming a little in an effort to distract herself from thinking about Callum. She turned on the hot-water tap and heard the clang of sleigh bells.

"Frick," she muttered, stripping off her gloves again. The bathroom was never going to get cleaned. She washed her hands and left the restroom.

"Sorry for the wait." She forced a cheery note into her voice as she headed for the front desk. "What can I get…" Confused, she looked around the shop. No one was there. Frowning, she looked out the window, but the parking lot and street were empty. In fact, there were no people in sight, at all. She'd sworn she'd heard the bells, but she must've imagined it.

"All of this stalker stuff is driving me crazy." After a final puzzled glance around the empty shop, she returned to the bathroom.

———

Callum showed up a half hour before closing.

"You know," she said, reaching for his travel mug, "your phone etiquette could use some work."

Arching an eyebrow, he relinquished his cup. "Decaf, please, or I won't sleep."

"Normally," she continued, filling his mug, "one says 'good-bye' before ending a call."

"Not if one is irritated that his…ah, the other one will be alone at work again, after repeatedly being asked to have someone there with her." He accepted his coffee. "Thank you."

"You're welcome." She changed topics. "Any thoughts about the whole thing I mentioned earlier? Before you hung up on me?"

"I didn't 'hang up' on you. 'See you later' is an acceptable way of ending a call." He took a sip of coffee and shot a glance at a couple sitting at a corner table, who were trying to act as if they weren't avidly listening to his and Lou's conversation. "And yes. We'll discuss that when we get home."

"Which home?" She started taking the pastries out of the case in her usual preclosing ritual.

"Either works for me." Eyeing her over the top of his mug, he continued, "Just thought you preferred to stay at yours."

"I do. At least, I did." Grabbing a plate, she plunked a cranberry white chocolate scone onto it and set it in front of Callum. "Eat this. It's going to be another forty-five minutes before we get out of here. Wait." She snatched the plate back as he reached for it and popped the scone in the microwave. At the gentle *ding*, she pulled the scone out and put the plate in front of Callum again. "Now eat it. It's better warm. Thinking about having some crazy dude wandering around my house while we sleep is creeping me out. I'm not sure whether it's better to be there or not while he's doing his stalker thing. And that just makes me mad, since my cabin's been my sanctuary since I ran away from Connecticut."

He took a bite, chewed, swallowed, and took a sip of coffee before speaking. "Ran away?"

Going back to relocating the pastries, mainly so she'd have something to focus on besides Callum, she shrugged. "My parents were a little controlling, and I was a lot passive. They picked where I went to school, what courses I took, who I dated, which law school I attended…"

He choked a little on a bite of scone, so she leaned over the counter and smacked him on his back. Clearing his throat, he repeated, "Law school?"

"Yes." Lou made a face. "It was so boring. I don't know how I made it through, much less passed the bar exam."

"Bar exam?"

She cocked her head to the side and studied him. "You okay? You're repeating everything I say. It's not like you."

"I'm just surprised. I didn't expect... You are not very lawyer-like."

"I'm not. I hated it—law school, the firms where I interviewed, everything about it. But I'd just floated along, doing what my parents said, until I was twenty-six." Making a face, she studied a crumb that had fallen onto the counter. "Pathetic, huh?"

"No." At his answer, she looked up and caught his gaze. He didn't look judgmental—more...thoughtful. "A lot of people do what others expect of them, even if they hate it. At least you realized you wanted out and made it happen. Why move here, though?"

She laughed, feeling lighter at his easy acceptance. "I knew they would never follow me here, or even visit for too long. It was Simpson or Alaska, and I didn't think I could stand the twenty-three hour nights, so here I am."

"You're rather remarkable."

A blush worked its way up her neck. "Thanks, but I'm really not."

"You are. Staying alone in your cabin, working here, joining the dive team... You're surviving and helping others in a place most people can't imagine living."

Clearing her throat, Lou glanced at the couple who had given up all pretense of not listening. "Hey, guys, we're closing in a couple of minutes. Can I get you anything else for the road?"

"No, thanks," the woman said, tossing her long

dreadlocks over her shoulder. "And way to find your own soul's path."

"Yeah," the guy agreed, standing up and gathering their empty cups. He had matching dreadlocks, although his were slightly shorter. "That's awesome."

"Thanks." Slightly bemused, she watched them leave, the sleigh bells bouncing merrily against the door as it closed behind them.

"So my house, then?" Callum's words brought her attention back to him.

"Yeah. Maybe we could alternate—one night at your house and then one at mine?" He nodded, and she gathered the pan of dirty dishes and carried it into the back. "It's a plan, then. I'm going to stop by my place tonight and then first thing tomorrow to feed the woodstove." As she returned to the front, she grinned at Callum. "There is one good thing about this."

"What's that?"

"I get another crack at that whiteboard of yours."

―⁂―

Dressed in flannel pajamas—this pair light blue with lavender fish printed on them—and thick, fuzzy socks that did not match each other in any way, Lou stood in front of the whiteboard, brown marker in hand. After leaving the coffee shop, she and Callum had stopped by Lou's cabin to feed the woodstove and pick up her overnight bag before heading to his house. He'd made dinner—a very tasty stew. Who knew that Callum was a genius with the Crock-Pot?

"How do we want to do this?" she asked. "Should I give the MC their own section?" She touched the tip of the marker to the board but then hesitated, looking at Callum over her shoulder. "What's their name—the MC, I mean?"

"Liverton Riders," he said.

As she scribbled it on the board, she made a face. "The groups around here really need a course in creative naming," she muttered. She underlined the club's name and then added the new information. Underneath that, she scribbled Ian Walsh's name and stepped back to read over what she'd written.

"Lawrence mentioned that the evidence was found on the weight," she said thoughtfully. "Did you or Wilt notice it when you pulled it out of the water?"

Stepping up next to her, Callum frowned. "No, which is strange. Not that we're infallible, especially in that murky reservoir where visibility is shit, but we're pretty thorough. Wilt's a perfectionist, so he's going to hate that we didn't catch it."

"*Wilt*'s a perfectionist?" she murmured, grinning when he shot her a look before returning his attention to the board.

"I'd like to know exactly what that piece of evidence is," he said.

Lou nodded. "Do you think we could talk to Ian now? He might have an idea what it is. Plus, I'd kind of like to give him a heads-up about this—do you think that's wrong? Would I be aiding and abetting?"

When Callum just grunted, staring at the whiteboard, she turned to face him.

"Was that a 'yes' grunt or a 'no' grunt?"

"That was a 'let's keep our mouths closed for the time being' grunt."

Her grunt was unhappy.

"If the MC did kill HDG," Callum said with more patience than condescension, "do you want to be the one who screws up the investigation?"

"No," she agreed reluctantly. "I just don't want to screw over Ian. He doesn't seem like a killer."

"No, but one of his MC brothers might be."

She shot him a glare.

"What?"

"I hate it when you out-logic me."

He grinned. "You're tired. Why don't you go to bed? The whiteboard will still be here in the morning."

Her stomach dropped with nerves. "Um…so where am I sleeping? I mean, the couch is just fine. It's a lot more comfortable than my couch, so I could easily sleep here if that's where you want to put me. Or anywhere is okay, actually—"

"Lou." He cut off her babbling. "Upstairs."

Relieved that he'd just made the decision without any awkward conversation—not including her nervous monologue—she headed for the spiral stairs. The loft covered half of the lower level, looking over his living room. Except for a walk-in closet on one side and a bathroom on the other, the bedroom took up the entire space.

"My bed is even bigger than yours," Callum murmured close to her ear, making her jump. She hadn't realized he'd followed her up the stairs.

"Um… I can see that." Flustered, she hurried into the bathroom, more because she wanted to hide than because she actually needed to use the facilities. After completing her nightly bathroom routine, though, she felt calmer, ready to face Callum and his very large bed.

He wasn't upstairs, which made it easier. She crawled under the covers, turning from one side to the other, unable to settle. It had been easier the night before, when pure exhaustion had won over awkwardness. Forcing herself to lie still on her left side, she closed her eyes.

Her brain was whirring so loudly that she missed Callum's reentry. When the bed sank on one side, her eyes snapped open, and she flew to a seated position, staring at Callum, who was sitting on the edge of the bed in just a pair of shorts. Her gaze landed on his pecs, and she was incapable of yanking her eyes away. *God, he's gorgeous*, she thought, stomach tightening. Even seeing him as often as she had recently, sometimes his physical perfection just knocked the breath out of her.

"Sorry," she said, settling back with a false air of calmness when she finally forced herself to look at his face. "I didn't hear you come in, so you just startled me a little."

He smirked, so she was pretty sure he saw through her facade of nonchalance. Raising his arms over his head, Callum stretched. Lou's eyes bulged when she saw the play of muscles in his back. The man seriously deserved his own calendar. As he twisted around to slide under the covers, she snapped her eyes closed and then turned on her side again, facing away from him. Spending time—especially seminaked time—with Callum was a bad, bad idea. Before, she could only imagine what his muscles looked like shifting under his skin. She hadn't even known until recently that he *had* dimples. Now, these details had implanted themselves into her daydreams, turning a simple crush into something so much more.

"'Night, Lou."

"'Night."

It took a long time for her to fall asleep, her body thrumming from Callum's proximity and her mind churning with thoughts of waterlogged bodies and faceless stalkers. But his steady breathing filled the room, allowing her muscles to finally relax.

Callum was there, so she was safe.

———

All the time. He paced a path between the trees, snow crunching beneath his boots. She was with the asshole all the fucking time! His fingers tightened around the diver's knife, pressing an imprint of the handle into his palm. He needed to get her alone, and then he could show her exactly how he felt about faithless whores.

The wind picked up a notch, and he tipped his head back, wanting to shout at it to shut up. The need for silence was grinding on his nerves. He shouldn't be the one skulking in the trees, freezing. He should be in her cabin, in her bed, and the guy she was screwing shouldn't exist at all.

He smiled bitterly. He could take care of that.

In a lull between gusts, a silence fell. His head turned as he eyed the surrounding trees. It was too quiet now. There was a rustle of dead vegetation, and he eased closer to a pine tree, his gaze searching for the source of the sound. Nothing moved, nothing even breathed, but he knew someone was there. Someone was always there.

With a final frustrated glance at her cabin, he melted into the shadows.

Chapter 10

SHE WAS STANDING ON TIPTOE, REACHING FOR THE package locker key in her post office box, when she smelled him.

"Hey, Jim," she said without turning to look. Her fingertips brushed the plastic end of the key and managed to slide it farther out of her reach. Lou bit back a bad word. Sometimes it sucked being short. "How're things?"

"Bad."

"Oh?" Bouncing off her toes in a little hop, she finally snagged the key, although she scraped her knuckles on the box door on her way down. "Ouch."

"They're always watching me."

"Who?" She turned to face Smelly Jim, shaking her hand to ease the sting.

"Government agents." He took a step closer, and Lou breathed through her mouth. "They're watching you, too."

"I know someone is," she muttered, thinking dark thoughts.

Jim seemed pleased she was taking him seriously. "I've seen him."

"Really?" It was probably just part of Jim's delusion, but maybe he had actually seen someone following her. "Anyone you know?"

Jim shook his head, and Lou felt a pang of disappointment. It would've been so easy if Jim could've just told her the name of her stalker. If Jim didn't know the guy, then he wasn't a local. Smelly Jim knew *everyone* in town. In fact, Lou would not be surprised if Jim had dossiers on everyone he'd ever met stored in his trailer.

"What did he look like?"

With a sound of disgust, Jim spat out, "Typical fed."

"Uh… I don't know what that means. Was he tall or short?"

"Average."

"Okay." Although she reminded herself not to get too excited about eyewitness testimony from Smelly Jim, she couldn't completely quash the bubble of hope that rose in her chest. "Dark hair or light?"

He shrugged. "Couldn't tell. He was wearing a hat."

"Oh." She tried to think of other descriptors. "Was he a white guy?"

He nodded, and Lou felt that surge of hope again.

"Glasses?"

"Dark ones, yeah."

"Beard?"

"Nah."

"Mustache? Any kind of facial hair?"

Smelly Jim thought about that for a second. "Nope."

"What did his face look like? Handsome, ugly, scar, big nose, anything?"

Making a face, Jim said, "Kind of a pretty boy. Soft-looking."

"What was he wearing?"

A change came over Smelly Jim's expression, and he stared at her suspiciously. "Why are you asking me all these questions?"

Thrown off guard, she hesitated, then said tentatively, "So I can figure out who's watching me."

The hardness in his face didn't ease. "Are you working for *them*?"

"No!" She scrambled to get back to their normal odd, but fairly easygoing, footing. "They're following me, too, remember?"

Obviously, he didn't, since he stomped out of the post office, sending mistrustful glares over his shoulder. Lou sighed and then pulled out her phone, intending to call Callum and fill him in on her conversation with Smelly Jim. However, when she saw the time on her phone's screen, she yelped. She had only five minutes to grab her package and get to work, or she'd be late. Repocketing her cell phone, she bolted for the package locker.

Of course the lock was sticky, but she finally managed to wrestle it open and grab the box containing a couple of months' worth of toilet paper she'd ordered. She sprinted for her truck while muttering a prayer under her breath that all four tires would be intact. When she saw that everything was fully inflated, she let out a huff of relief and climbed into the driver's seat.

She flew into The Coffee Spot with thirty seconds to spare, but Ivy still gave her a sour look.

"Sorry!" Lou apologized, despite the fact that she wasn't really late. If she was going to bring up the whole not-being-alone thing with her boss, she wanted to start the conversation off on a good note. However, judging by Ivy's expression, it wasn't going to go well. "I ran into Smelly Jim at the post office, and we started talking…"

"Talking? With Smelly Jim? That's why you're late?"

Lou debated giving Ivy the entire rundown of Jim's possible sighting of her stalker, but she looked at her boss's closed expression and went with just a silent nod instead.

Ivy let out a gusty sigh as she reached beneath the counter, pulling her purse out of the cubby. "I have to pick Briana up at the sitter's, since there's no preschool today. There's a lunch order for the guys at the hardware store. I left the ticket in the back, and you'll need to put that together before Deedee picks everything up in a half hour. See you tomorrow."

The last sentence was thrown over her shoulder as Ivy rushed out the door, leaving Lou with an open mouth and still no company at closing time. She closed her mouth and sighed.

"Callum is going to be pissed," she said in a singsong under her breath.

As she headed to the back, she called Callum and put the phone on speaker so she could make sandwiches for the guys at the hardware store and talk at the same time. Normally she didn't miss her Bluetooth, but this was a rare exception. It was one of many things she'd abandoned in a back-to-basics purge when she'd moved to Colorado.

"Sparks," he answered, his voice pulling her out of her nostalgic moment.

"Callum," she responded as she spread chipotle mayo. "Do you want the good news—well, odd and sort of interesting news—or the bad news first?"

"Bad."

She made a face. She'd rather have told him the odd and interesting news, while hoping that he'd forget all about the bad news by the end of the conversation. "You sure?"

"Lou…"

"Fine." She sighed. "Ivy had to bolt out of here as soon as I arrived for my shift, so I still haven't talked to her about adding another person to be here at closing."

"Okay." Surprisingly, he didn't sound too upset. "I'll come by after work."

"You don't have to do that," she said. "You have to be getting sick of this place." *And of me*, she added silently.

"I'm not sick of that place."

She hoped that also meant he wasn't sick of her either. Shaking her head to rid herself of her uncharacteristic insecurity, Lou said briskly, "Good. See you later, then. Want to hear about the odd and interesting part now, or do you need to go?"

"Let's hear it."

As she layered lettuce and sliced tomatoes on the sandwiches, Lou gave him the truncated version of her talk with Smelly Jim. "So," she concluded, "I don't know if this is all a figment of his imagination, or if he really was describing my stalker."

"Hmm." There was a pause, which Lou used to start filling the take-out boxes with the completed sandwiches, chips, and cookies. "If he did see your stalker, then that rules out anyone local."

"I was thinking that, too," she said excitedly. "His description was pretty sketchy, but I thought I'd call Rob—" The jangle of bells cut her off mid-sentence. "I think Deedee just came in for her sandwiches. Can I call you later?"

"If you have time. Otherwise, I'll see you after five."

"Five?" She blinked in surprise. "But that means you'll have to be here over two hours…hello?" She looked at the phone and saw the call had been ended. "Grrr. That man and his lack of good-byes." Raising her voice, she called, "I'll be right out!"

After stacking the filled take-away boxes into plastic bags, she carried them to the counter. Instead of Deedee, she saw the sheriff waiting for her.

"Rob!" she said in surprise, putting the bags on the counter. "I'm glad you stopped by. You'll save me a phone call. Coffee?"

"Sure. A large, please." When she turned to grab a cup, he asked, "What phone call is that?"

"To your office," she explained as she poured the coffee. "Room for cream?" When Rob shook his head, she topped it off and placed it on the counter so she could put a lid on the cup. "I had a chat with Smelly Jim earlier."

Rob didn't say anything, but he cocked his head. She took that as a signal for her to continue.

"As I'm sure you know, it's hard to know what's fact and what's…um…imagination with Jim." Lou propped her elbows on the counter. "He was talking about people watching him, and then he mentioned seeing a guy following me, too. I figured it wouldn't hurt to get some details, although Jim was pretty vague. He said it was a white guy, average height, no facial hair, kind of a pretty boy—soft-looking, he said—and that he wasn't from around here. When I started asking what the guy had been wearing, Jim kind of shut down and then left."

Halfway through her recitation, the sheriff had pulled out a small notebook and a pen and started scribbling. When she mentioned the part about the man not being local, Rob's head came up, and he looked at her. "Not from around here? That's interesting."

"I thought so, too." Not able to stand still, she started wiping down the counter. "And Smelly Jim seems to know everyone in the area."

"Thanks, Lou." He tucked away his notebook and pen in his shirt pocket. "I'll add this to the report and pass it along to Chris. He's starting to view your case as a personal challenge."

"Well, I'll be glad when it's over." Even though that was mostly true, she felt a pang at the thought of losing Callum as her personal bodyguard and bed-warmer. She cleared her throat, dragging her thoughts away from the memory of a rumpled and sleepy Callum waking her that morning. "Anyway, I kind of hijacked our conversation. Did you just come in for coffee, or did you need to talk to me about something?"

"Right." His hard-eyed cop look was back. "I—"

The bells jangled as Deedee pushed open the door and stepped inside the shop. The sheriff went silent.

"Hi, Deedee," Lou greeted her, hurrying to grab the bags of sandwiches she'd prepared. "How are you?"

"Eh, so-so." Deedee looked as if she'd been left in a dehydrator a few years too long. Her tanned skin was heavily wrinkled and loose over her wiry frame. Lou had no idea how old the woman was—she could've been anywhere from sixty to ninety. "I think our warm spell is over for a while. Snow tonight. Hey, Sheriff."

"Deedee," Rob said politely.

"Ugh." Making a face, Lou rang up the total and accepted Deedee's money. "I wouldn't mind skipping over the next three months of winter and heading right into spring. I've had enough of snow for a while."

"Yeah," Deedee agreed, taking her change and

hoisting the bags of sandwiches off the counter. "Wish the snow would skip over us and land on the ski resorts where they're happy to have it."

"Amen, sister." Lou waved as the woman stepped out the door. She turned back to Rob.

"I discovered," he said when she gave him an expectant look, "that one of my deputies shared some confidential information with you."

It took a second for the connection to click into place. "What information was that?" she asked slowly. He hadn't mentioned Lawrence by name, and, as unappealing as the deputy was, she'd rather not throw him under the bus if she could avoid it.

He gave her a pointed look, as if he could read her thoughts. "The evidence found in the reservoir that links the murder to a certain local organization?"

She nodded silently.

"Are you planning on sharing this information with anyone?"

"No," she said, since she'd already shared it with Callum, and they'd agreed to wait before potentially sharing it with Ian—so technically, she wasn't planning on sharing the information with anyone...at least yet.

"It would be best if you kept this knowledge to yourself," he said, leaning a little closer. "I would hate if you were on the radar of that particular club. With them, it's best if they don't know you exist."

"Right," she said as she repressed a shiver. She definitely did not want the MC after her.

Rob watched her as he took another sip of his coffee. "Have you been doing some investigating on your own?"

Lou shrugged, not sure how much she should share.

Was poking her nose where it didn't belong a crime? Jessica Fletcher hadn't seemed to run into any legal trouble when she'd done it in every single episode of *Murder, She Wrote*. But then, maybe it was a bad idea to be taking cues from an ancient television show. "Nothing serious. I just feel somewhat…invested, I guess, after finding him. It seems so sad that no one knows who he is."

"Be careful. Like I said, it's better to remain anonymous sometimes. There are some groups that make their own laws." He tapped a finger against the counter, eyeing her thoughtfully. "I wonder if this has something to do with your case. Maybe someone is trying to warn you away from asking questions."

She jolted at the idea that her stalker might also be a murderer, but then common sense intervened. "I don't think they're related. My tire was slashed for the first time before the body was discovered."

"Still," Rob said, looking unconvinced, "leave the investigating to those of us with the tools to do it. You're a nice woman. I'd hate for you to get caught up with some not-so-nice people because you're trying to do the right thing. Okay?"

Although she nodded, she wasn't convinced. Visiting the VA clinic and scribbling on a whiteboard seemed pretty harmless. But she figured it was the sheriff's job to protect people like her.

"Thanks, Rob," she said.

"No problem." He pushed the door open and glanced back at her one last time. "Think about what I said?"

"Of course." She'd think about it. She probably wouldn't follow his advice, but she'd definitely think about it.

———

It had started snowing by the time Callum arrived at The Coffee Spot, heavy flakes clinging to his hat even after he knocked it against his leg before stepping inside the shop. The recent warm-up had been too pleasant and too early to last, since snow usually continued to fall well into May.

"How's the driving?" she asked, pouring decaf into his mug.

He sat sideways on the end counter stool and propped his back against the wall. "Somewhere between not-that-bad and shitty."

Making a face, Lou peered through the front windows into the almost-night. "It's just going to get worse as it freezes. You should head home now instead of waiting for me. No reason for both of us to play slip-n-slide on the highway later."

Instead of responding, he just gave her *the look*. "Where's my scone?"

"Fine." She held up her hands in an *I-give-up* gesture. "When we're both hanging out in the ditch later, I get to say 'I told you so.'"

"Scone?"

"Coming. Jeez." Pulling the covered scone out of its hiding spot behind the counter, she popped it into the microwave. "You remind me of British royalty when you demand your scone with that haughty expression."

"Why were you keeping it back there?"

"You would not believe what I had to do to save this scone for you," she said, placing it in front of him. "There was an accident that closed the interstate east of Rosehill this afternoon, so everyone got detoured through here. They'd been sitting in traffic for *hours* before they got to Simpson, so I had carload after carload of cranky, hungry skiers in here for about two hours straight. They ate everything." She gestured at the empty pastry case like a game-show hostess. "Exhibit A. About twenty minutes after the mad rush started, I realized there was one—one!—cranberry white chocolate scone left. Luckily, the person ordering at the time was one of those unsweetened-green-tea types who would never, ever eat all the carbs and processed sugar contained in that scone." She nodded toward the tiny piece remaining in Callum's hand. "However, there was a hungry-looking snowboarder behind her, and his eye was already fixed on your scone. Being the quick thinker that I am, I pointed out the window and yelled, 'Moose!' When everyone in the shop stampeded to press their noses against the windows, I tucked your scone under the counter where snowboarder boy couldn't get his grubby little mitts on it."

Having finished the last bite of his hard-earned scone, Callum was leaning against the wall, smiling. "What'd they do when they didn't see a moose?"

"You know how people are. Someone got a glimpse of Roger Thornton's dog running around the back of his house and yelled, 'I see it! I see the moose!' and then everyone else claimed they saw it, too. It was half a Bigfoot hunt and half 'The Emperor's New Clothes.'"

"Isn't Roger's dog a beagle? How could that be mistaken for a moose?"

She shrugged. "Who knows? What matters is that you got your scone, and a bunch of city people get to tell their friends they saw a moose while they were in the mountains. It's a win-win."

He sipped his coffee while watching her, the corner of his mouth pulled up in a crooked smile.

"What?" she asked.

"Things are not boring when you're around," he said, placing his mug on the counter and carefully lining it up with his now-empty plate.

"Thanks?" She grabbed his plate, ruining whatever perfect symmetry he'd just achieved, and added it to the dishpan of dirty dishes. "I'd actually kill for some boring moments right about now. Between HDG, my stalker, potentially murderous motorcycle clubs, militias with poorly thought-out names, and visits from the sheriff, I think I'm due for a few minutes of monotony."

"Visits from the sheriff?" As always, Callum picked the pertinent fact out of her rant. "Did he have anything interesting to say?"

"Yes and no," she said slowly, picking apart the earlier conversation in her mind. "I didn't get any new information about HDG. He found out that Lawrence had blabbed about finding that evidence, so I think he wanted reassurance that the loose lips ended with me. I said it was in the vault, although I didn't mention you'd visited the vault before I locked it tight." There was some unintended innuendo to her words, but she refused to fixate on it.

"Was that all?" The smirk was gone. Callum's expression was all stoic focus now.

"He gently warned me away from investigating HDG on my own."

"How so?"

"He said he didn't want me getting mixed up with the MC, or anyone who would chop off a dead guy's head. I told him my investigation was pretty innocuous so far—although I didn't mention the 'so far' part."

"Hmm."

Since Lou was unable to translate the hum, she asked, "Thoughts?"

He opened his mouth but closed it again when the sleigh bells jangled. Lou glared at the intruder.

"Whoa!" Derek backed into the door he'd just entered. "Whatever I did, I'm sorry. Don't kill me, please!"

"What?"

He walked up to the counter. "You were giving me the face of impending death."

"Sorry," she apologized. "It's not you. It's those stupid sleigh bells."

Glancing at the door, he turned back to her with raised eyebrows. "Yeah, I see how they'd make anyone rage-y. Are you calm now, Lulu, or are you going to spit in my coffee out of displaced anger?"

"Lulu? That's not going to be a thing now, is it?"

"Why? Does it bug you?"

"No." The denial came out too fast, and she winced.

"Liar. Lulu the Liar."

She sighed, resigned to having a new, hated nickname. "I might consider the spitting thing if you annoy me."

"I'm never annoying." He sat on the stool two down from Callum. "Hey, brave leader. It's kind of late for you to be out, isn't it?"

Callum narrowed his eyes. "It's not even six."

"Exactly. Aren't you missing a scheduled reorganization of your sock drawer?"

"Please," Lou snorted. "As if his socks would ever be disorganized."

Derek laughed. "True. Sad, but true."

"While you two analyze the state of my sock drawer," Callum said, standing, "I'm going to use the bathroom."

"Good timing," Lou said approvingly. "It's freshly cleaned after the hordes came through here. It was not pretty after the last of them finally left. Not pretty at all."

"Okay," Callum said slowly. "Thank you for rectifying the situation."

"You're welcome."

With a shake of his head, he walked to the restored bathroom. Once the door closed behind him, Derek turned to Lou.

"What did you do to him?" he asked in a hushed voice. "Did you get him addicted to happy pills? Did you give him a personality transplant? Hypnotism? You have to tell me, because I have a bet going with Artie."

Lou stared at him. "I didn't do anything to him. What the hell are you talking about, crazy man?"

"Please. Don't tell me you haven't noticed."

"Uh…noticed what?"

"He's smiling. All the time now."

"He is not. He hardly ever smiles."

"No, he hardly ever *used* to smile," Derek corrected, pointing a finger at her. "But now you two are joined at the hip, and he's turned into Mr. Giggles."

"Please," she said skeptically. "As if Callum would *giggle*."

"Maybe not," he conceded, "but he is smiling an abnormal amount, and on him, it's just creepy. You know those greeting cards with a human smile stuck onto some poor puppy or kitten?"

With a grimace, she nodded. "Unfortunately."

"That's what it's like, all those happy smiles on Callum's face." Sitting back, he frowned. "It's not right."

"Whatever. Are you saying he can't be happy?"

"No, I'm saying he's *not* a happy person. Never has been, at least since I've known him, and that's been *years*. But now you have him all hopped-up on mood enhancers—"

"I do not!" she interrupted him loudly.

"You don't what?" asked Callum, emerging from the bathroom.

"Nothing," she said, glaring at Derek. "He's just nuts."

A half smile tugging at one corner of his mouth, Callum looked at Derek. "Agreed."

"Since Lou won't tell me," Derek started, turning to the other man, "I'll ask you. What's going on with the two of you?"

Callum gave him an even look. "Is that any of your business?"

"Yes!" Derek yelped, throwing up his hands. "I'm dying to know, and that makes it my business."

"Plus you have a bet going with Artie," Lou interjected.

"Zip it," Derek growled before turning back to Callum. "So…are you guys going at it like wild animals?"

Unable to stop the flush creeping up her face, Lou turned to grab a cup to hide her red cheeks. "Did you want a coffee or not, Derek?"

"Are you going to give me all the details of your torrid affair?" he asked.

"No!" she and Callum said in loud unison.

"Fine." Derek slid off his stool. "Then no coffee. But I will find out the truth. You cannot hide good gossip from me." With that final pronouncement, he left the shop, leaving the bells to ring in the newly fallen silence.

Lou glared at them. "I really hate those bells."

She replaced the cup with unnecessary care, restacking it perfectly in order to avoid looking at Callum.

"Sorry," he said, bringing her gaze to meet his in surprise.

"Why?" she asked. "You didn't have any part in the creation of Derek."

That brought a slight smile from him, but it disappeared quickly. "I'm the reason everyone thinks something's going on between us."

"Have you been bragging about getting me into your bed?" she teased, although she focused on rubbing at a nonexistent spot on the counter with her thumb. Her blush was dying to reappear, and she wasn't sure she could hold it back if eye contact was involved.

"No, of course not," he said quickly. "I've just been... ah, more cheerful than usual lately."

"Oh." Lou didn't know how to respond to that. "That's...nice?"

"It is, except you know the guys on the dive team and at the station. They're worse than old women when it comes to gossip. They've noticed we've been spending time together and are trying to match that with my... improved mood."

"Okay," she said slowly, giving herself time to find the right words. "Do they? Match, I mean."

There was a pause, during which she almost took the skin off of her thumb by rubbing the counter so hard. "I believe so," he finally said, and her gaze snapped to his. "I find I'm happier when I'm with you."

She swallowed. "Thanks. I'm happy to be with you, too."

Their eyes met across the counter. Her breath caught in her chest, and she couldn't stop her hand from reaching toward his. When she was just an inch away from touching him, though, she lost her nerve.

Before she could retreat, Callum caught her fingers.

Her gaze bounced from her trapped hand to his face as he started to lean toward her. She froze, her lungs burning with the need for air and her muscles tight with anticipation, watching him move infinitesimally closer, closer…until the sound of the sleigh bells made her jerk away.

Biting back a swearword, Lou gave the trio who'd just entered a smile that was more gritted teeth than welcome. "Hi." Why did her voice sound like she smoked a pack of cigarettes a day? Clearing her throat, she tried again. "What can I get you?"

Chapter 11

By THE TIME HER LAST CUSTOMERS LEFT, IT WAS TIME to close the shop. Callum had retreated into his corner, his expression as closed and unreadable as the very first time she'd met him, and she couldn't help glancing at the tight slash of his mouth with a pang of regret. The last hour would've been very different if the three local teenagers hadn't decided to walk the four blocks from their house to the coffee shop for dinner. Instead of making stilted conversation with Callum in front of their adolescent audience, she probably could have been kissing him. The thought made her smile.

"Ready?"

Lou jumped. "What? Oh! Right. Um…just a second." She grabbed the tray from the cash register, almost dropping it in her flustered state, and then practically ran to the back where the safe was located. She took a few moments just to breathe, to calm her silly heart.

"Stop," she commanded her brain.

"Did you say something?" Callum called from the front.

"No," she yelled back. "I mean, yes, but it had nothing to do with you."

There was a pause. "Okay."

Squeezing her palms against her temples, she took another deep breath. It didn't help. Her heart was still hopping around in her chest. Letting her hands drop to her sides, she gave up. It was time to accept the fact that

she was going to behave like an idiot in front of Callum.
It was unfortunate but, at the same time, inevitable.

Blowing out a shaky sigh, she went to grab the
mop bucket.

—∿∿—

Driving on the snow-packed highway finally got her
brain off of Callum and his unbearably sexy mouth. At
a crawl, she led their mini-convoy of two through the
swirling snow. Even going impossibly slowly, she still
felt the tires slide sideways as she maneuvered around
a curve. There weren't many other vehicles on the
highway, for which Lou was grateful, since oncoming
headlights reflected against the snow and blinded her for
a few panicky seconds.

When she finally reached the turn-off onto the county
road, she relaxed her tight shoulders and stretched her
fingers, sore from clutching the wheel. Although the
snow was deeper, the gravel beneath allowed her tires to
grip the surface. Lou reached her driveway without any
issues and guided her pickup into the ruts she'd already
created in the frozen drifts. The new snow hadn't filled
her old tire tracks in completely—at least not yet.

After stopping in to feed her woodstove that morning,
she'd left the gate open, since drifting snow had been
predicted, and Lou had figured it would be better if the
gate was stuck in the open position. Finally reaching
her cabin, she backed into her usual parking spot with
a relieved exhale. She felt as if she'd been holding her
breath for the entire drive home.

Callum backed in next to her truck, maneuvering his
pickup through the snow with a confidence she envied.

Hopping out of the truck, she landed shin-high in a fresh mound of snow.

"If Mr. Stalker makes a visit tonight," she said as Callum rounded the hood of his truck, "we'll definitely see his boot prints tomorrow." She glared at the flake-filled sky. "If this snow ever stops, that is."

"If he does try to visit tonight," he responded grimly, "he'll end up in a ditch instead."

"Hopefully."

Moving to pick up an armload of wood, she was stopped by Callum's hand on her shoulder. "I'll get it," he said, giving her a gentle push toward the door.

Her independent side wanted to protest, but it was overruled by her tired-and-lazy side, so she just thanked him and unlocked the front door.

As she held the door, he carried in a huge armload of the split logs with ease. She narrowed her eyes at him.

"What?"

She closed the door behind them. "That's the second time in five minutes I've coveted your abilities and/or strength."

The corner of his mouth lifted. "Are you jealous of my wood-hauling skills?"

"Yes," she admitted, kicking off her boots before heading for her bedroom. "And your driving-in-snow acumen."

"Wait." His teasing expression disappeared as he toed off his own boots and dumped the wood into the box next to the stove. "Let me check the house first."

She gave him a go-ahead wave of her arm and returned to the woodstove. When he returned shortly, he maneuvered his body between her and the stove.

"Let me," he ordered, his attention on the smoldering

remains of the fire. She took a couple of steps back out of his way, and continued watching him for a few moments. He added wood methodically, with a precision that bespoke a well-thought-out plan. She grinned, shaking her head.

"What?" he asked, carefully placing another log.

"Just admiring your fire-laying technique. I usually use the chuck-it-in-and-hope-it-burns method."

"That's just wrong," he said, although she caught a hint of amusement in his voice. "Go ahead and get changed. I know you're dying to put on pajamas."

He wasn't wrong. Her flannel pajamas were calling her name quite loudly, in fact. She headed to her bedroom, leaving him to focus much too intently on the layout of the firewood.

Closing her bedroom door behind her, she started to move to the dresser when she stopped. Something wasn't right. Sweeping her gaze over the space, Lou eyed the bed, the nightstand, the closet door, the dresser, the desk. Everything seemed to be in order and in the same semi-neat state that she'd left it, but something was…wrong.

She scanned the room again before shaking her head. First she was hearing imaginary sleigh bells, and now there was this weirdness. Lou decided she needed to hop off the bus to crazy town, change into her pajamas, and then join the hot man waiting in her living room.

Striding to her dresser, shedding clothes as she went, she pulled out some lavender flannel pajama pants with hippos wearing tutus. Instead of grabbing the matching, rather boxy top, however, she gave in to vanity and yanked a silky tank top from the drawer.

Once she was dressed, she stood in front of her mirror, tugging down her tank. Her arms and the top part of her chest felt very…bare. Despite her bottom half being encased in flannel, Lou felt naked. Losing her nerve, she grabbed a hoodie, pulled it on, and zipped it to her throat.

She headed for the door but was unable to resist checking out the room a final time. There was nothing out of place, nothing to explain why her stomach was churning.

"That's because there's nothing wrong, crazy girl," she said out loud and left the bedroom.

As she entered the kitchen, she inhaled and then closed her eyes with a blissful smile. "What is that heavenly smell? Are you planning on feeding me again?"

"Dinner. And yes."

"Is it chicken soup? It smells like chicken soup." When she spotted the large pot on the stove, she hurried over to lift the lid. "When did you have time to make this? It took me less than five minutes to get changed. Are you some kind of cooking magician?"

"I put it together at lunch and then left it in the fridge at the station." He leaned back against the counter, watching her with a half smile.

Picking up a big spoon propped neatly next to the stove, she gave the soup a stir. Frowning suspiciously, she asked, "Did you make this from scratch? You're making me feel a little inferior, Martha Stewart."

"Not really," he answered. "I roasted the chicken and cut up the vegetables, but I used prepared broth."

"Prepared broth?" she repeated in a mock-appalled tone, replacing the lid. "Horrors!"

He rolled his eyes at her, and she grinned.

"You got that from me—the eye-rolling thing," she said proudly. "I'm so glad I'm corrupting you."

"Do you want some soup or not?"

"I don't know." She sighed. "I heard it was made with"—she lowered her voice to a scandalized whisper—"*prepared broth*."

Moving so quickly that she didn't have time to dodge, he caged her against the edge of the counter, with an arm bracketing each side. Startled, she could only stare at him as he leaned close.

"You have a smart mouth," he said quietly, his gaze firmly focused on her parted lips.

"Uh-huh," she agreed, not caring if she sounded brainless. It was hard to care about anything when he was looking at her like that. She marveled at how his usually cool and closed expression was now so intense, hungry. "Sorry."

He leaned in another inch, moving his gaze slightly higher so he met her eyes. "Don't be. It's grown on me."

"Yeah?" Lou realized her breath was coming in quick puffs, and her heart was drumming as if she'd just run a couple of miles.

The corner of his mouth kicked up in that devastating half smile of his. "Yeah."

And then his lips were on hers.

When her brain had gotten away from her in the past and she'd imagined what kind of kisser Callum would be, she'd figured he would kiss like he lived—neat and organized, with structure and a need for complete control. It had been hard to tell what he was like when he had kissed her outside the library, since it had been

over before she'd realized what had happened. The
reality of his kisses, his *real* kisses, was nothing like
she'd imagined.

In real life, the kiss was wild, spinning immediately
out of control. As soon as their lips met, they both
ignited, grabbing at each other as if they would launch
into space otherwise. Lou's hands found his shoulders,
her fingers trying to get a purchase in the unyielding
muscle beneath his shirt, while Callum cupped the back
of her head with one hand. As his other found her hip,
yanking her tight against him, he stepped forward, trapping her in place.

The edge of the counter dug into her lower back,
but she didn't care. All that mattered was getting closer
to Callum, pressing against him as if she could bury
herself inside of him. His teeth closed on her lower
lip, sending shocks of pleasure through her, and she
gasped. He immediately took advantage of her parted
lips, stroking into her mouth with a swipe of his tongue,
taking possession as if she and all of her body parts
belonged to him.

She made a sound, low and needy, and yanked at
his shirt, wanting skin-to-skin contact. In the tiny, still-
thinking portion of her brain, she worried that they were
going too fast. The kiss had barely started, and she was
already trying to strip the man. That faint warning voice
faded as she pulled his shirttails free and burrowed her
hands beneath the fabric.

As her fingers met the skin over his stomach, he
groaned into her mouth. Sinking his fingers into her hair,
he kissed her harder, devouring her mouth. She welcomed the increased pressure, her senses torn between

the feel of his mouth and the rigid strength of his abs under her fingertips.

There was no softness to him, no yielding, but that didn't scare her. It just made her want more of him, more kissing, more touching. Her need turned fierce, and she nipped at his bottom lip as her hands slid around his hard sides to his back. His growl made her flush with heat. His muscles shifted and strained under her palms as he pinned her tighter against the edge of the counter, the pressure of his kiss dipping her into a slight backbend.

Her ears were ringing, and she vaguely wondered if that was the sign of a truly amazing kiss, until Callum reluctantly pulled away from her.

"What?" she asked, trying to follow his retreating mouth for a second, until she realized the sound she heard was his cell phone. With a groan, she dropped her forehead against his chest, where it connected with a thud that made Callum chuckle.

"Cook," he answered his cell, the roughness of arousal still lingering in his voice. He paused. "You didn't."

His body stiffened with what Lou was pretty sure was irritation. Feeling slightly awkward, she let her hands slip from his shirt and took a step to the side. His free hand squeezed her hip before releasing her.

"I'd expect this from Chad or Phil, but not you."

Even though the reprimand wasn't directed at her, Lou hid a wince. Callum had perfected the *I'm-disappointed-in-you* tone, which was intended to create maximum guilt in the recipient.

"I'm out at Lou's. Isn't anyone closer available?" Although his tone was brusque, the look he shot Lou was still burning with frustrated need. "Fine. I'll be there in half an hour." He glanced out the window over the kitchen sink and grimaced. "With the road conditions, it'll be closer to forty-five."

"What's up?" she asked as he stomped over to the door, where his boots were neatly placed. Melting snow still clung to them, and Lou eyed the slush a little sadly. She'd been envisioning an evening of homemade chicken soup and a cozy fire and making out with Callum. The joys of the first two paled with the loss of the third.

"Wilt put the dive van in a snowdrift." He jerked on his coat with short, angry motions. Apparently, she wasn't the only one disappointed by the interruption.

She frowned, confused. "Why was he driving the dive van? Did we miss a call?"

Jamming his cap on his head, Callum practically snarled, "No. He parked it in the lot so he could power-wash the station floors. When he went to drive it back inside, he miscalculated and backed it into the ditch."

"Wow. Poor Wilt."

"Poor Wilt?" Callum repeated. "I don't have any sympathy for him. He's interrupting my…evening." His eyes, still hungry, raked over her. Lou had the urge to pull her hoodie around her more tightly, but at the same time she wanted to strip naked. Before she could do either of those things, he gave a final wordless grumble and stomped out the door.

"Bye!" she called before it closed.

Callum stuck his head back inside. "Lock this."

She nodded.

"Do not go outside." His light blue gaze felt like it

burned her. "Do not open this door for anyone except for me. I don't care if it's Santa Claus. Is that understood?"

Resisting the urge to salute, Lou simply said, "Understood."

He continued staring at her for a long second before giving her a short nod. "I'll be back as soon as possible. If you hear anything outside, call the sheriff, but do not unlock this door."

"Cal." Moving to the door, she gave the hard line of his mouth a quick kiss and then gently pushed him back a step. "I've got it. No opening the door to anyone, not even mythical old guys. Now go help Wilt out of the ditch. Drive carefully. I'll be fine." Giving him a smile to soften her dismissal, she closed the door and turned the dead bolt. It locked with a solid clunk, and she leaned against the door. If he'd stayed for even one more minute, staring at her with that fiercely protective look she found equal parts aggravating and irresistible, she would've dragged him back inside the cabin and had her way with him, snowbound dive van be damned.

It was only when she heard the rumble of Callum's truck starting that she pushed away from the door. With a sigh, she headed for the kitchen. The soup was bubbling gently and smelled amazing, but she turned off the burner. Between Callum driving in the storm and their unexpectedly mind-blowing make-out session, Lou's stomach was knotted. She'd wait until he returned to eat.

She fidgeted, playing with the soupspoon. The familiar nervous restlessness that seemed to be her constant companion lately when she was alone rose up in her, making her chest burn. She resented how her stalker had turned her cabin from a refuge to a source of fear. Her gaze settled on the bottle of whisky she'd bought the previous fall. It was mostly full, only missing the single shot she'd taken on Christmas evening after a disastrous phone conversation with her parents.

"What the hell," she muttered, reaching to grab the bottle. It wasn't like she was going on any dive-team calls that night after Callum's strict instructions not to leave the cabin. Unscrewing the cap, she took a drink right out of the bottle, wincing as it burned all the way down.

Coughing, she squinted at the bottle. "I feel like such a mountain woman." Her voice was husky from the residual burn of the alcohol. "Drinking whisky straight from the bottle while getting snowed in at my log cabin."

After a second swig, she coughed again and screwed on the top, placing it back in its usual spot on the counter. Turning toward the living room, she suddenly felt the room rock from side to side, and she grabbed the edge of the breakfast bar to steady herself.

"Whoa. Am I that much of a lightweight?" She took a tentative step toward the couch. The floor seemed to hold steady, so she tried another one. By the time she'd reached the sofa, the cabin was shifting under her feet again, and it was a relief to sit. When she tipped her head back against the cushion, the room spun. Lou squeezed her eyes closed, but her brain kept whirling until everything went black.

The wind sounded strange. It was roaring and crackling at the same time. Lou frowned, but her eyes didn't want to open, so she listened to the weird-sounding wind for another second. She was so tired, and her head pounded in time with her heartbeat. Her limbs felt heavy, as if weighted down. She was so nice and warm. All she wanted to do was sleep, so she let her brain drift…until a stinging on her hand made her start awake.

Her eyelids lifted, revealing a blur of orange. Blinking rapidly, she forced her vision to clear, and then immediately wished she hadn't. Flames were everywhere. Glowing yellow and red and all shades in between, they leapt and played like living things.

Her cabin was on fire, and she was trapped inside.

Lou shoved herself off the couch in a panic, but her legs went soft, and she tumbled to the floor. Pushing to her hands and knees, she fought for control of her limbs. It was as if her body didn't belong to her, like she was a clumsy puppet. Her arm collapsed beneath her, sending her down to land painfully on her elbow.

As she looked up, she got her first clear view of the burning cabin. Fire rippled up the walls and across the ceiling, enclosing her in a flaming trap. Burning chunks of wood fell to smolder on the floor, and a small piece of flaming material landed on her hip. It took a second before she felt the burn, and she swatted it off of her, smacking the fabric of her pajama pants until she was sure no embers remained. Everything was wrong. Her thoughts were scattered and hazy, and she couldn't make sense of what was happening. Fear joined the smoke in clogging her breathing.

Out. The word rang sharply in her brain, piercing the confused fog of her thoughts and her rising panic. She tried again to stand, but she hit the floor hard, sending pain radiating from her hip. With a groan, she started to crawl across the floor in the direction of the door.

Smoke pinched her lungs, making every breath hurt. She coughed once but then held back the need to do it again, afraid she'd never be able to stop hacking once she started.

Out. Squinting, she hunted for the door with watering eyes. The room was both too bright and too dark at the same time, making it hard to see anything. Lou forced herself to think. This was her home. She knew where the door was. Crawling next to the couch, she yelped as a chunk of burning wood fell, bouncing off her calf.

Her body was heavy and her thoughts sluggish. A large part of her brain wanted her to hide and cry and try to go back to sleep. Maybe this was just a nightmare—a horrible, realistic, *painful* nightmare. Despite the blurriness of her mind, however, she knew it was real.

Shoving back the panic that wanted to overwhelm her, she clung to her one goal—finding the door. Through the door would be cold and snow and relief from the heat that burned her, inside and out. Her shoulder bumped something—a wall. That was good. The door was in a wall. All she had to do was decide to go left or right.

Her eyes were useless, tearing so heavily that everything was a blur, flames and darkness melding together. She groped the wall, trying to feel something—anything—familiar that could give her a clue about where she was. Her fingers bumped something soft and heavy, sending it swinging.

She dug through the thick sludge of her thoughts, trying to identify what she'd found. When she clutched it harder, it fell onto the floor in front of her, the silky surface brushing her cheek on the way down.

"Ski pants!" she tried to say, but she choked on the

words and the smoke and her clumsy tongue. With the realization that she was under the coatrack, she knew exactly where the door was. The smoke was thicker there, clogging her lungs and stinging her eyes so badly that a constant flow of tears blurred her vision. The few feet seemed endless as she crawled toward the exit, escape so close she could almost taste her relief.

Pushing up onto her knees, she grabbed the doorknob and toppled back, pulling it open as she went. Cold air rushed inside, soothing her overheated body and making the flames behind her roar with renewed fury. Her arms shook as she pushed herself back to her hands and knees, and a semihysterical part of her mind wondered if she'd be reduced to rolling. That was what she was supposed to do in a fire, right? Stop, drop, and roll?

She tried to clamp down and close off the odd thoughts, but it was getting harder and harder to hold on to her plan. *Out.* She was so close. All she needed to do was make it through the doorway, and then she'd be free of the inferno, of the raging heat and too-bright darkness and smoke that made it impossible to breathe or see. One hand in front of the next, a forward slide of one knee and then the other—all she could focus on was moving forward an inch at a time.

Her head bumped something, making her look up. It looked like…legs?

"Oh, thank God!" she rasped, hardly able to force any sound from her stripped and raw throat. "Help! Help me, please!"

There was no answer from the person in front of her, no movement at all. Rocking back onto her knees, she looked up and up at the figure. From her vantage point, the person towered over her like a giant. She swayed, blinking her tearing eyes, and the form seemed to shrink to normal—almost small—size before growing to a terrifying height again. When her blurry gaze reached his face, she sucked in a painful breath that tore at her throat. In the flicker of shadow and light, he looked like a monster.

Then her eyes cleared slightly, and Lou realized it wasn't a nightmare in front of her, but a person wearing a self-contained breathing apparatus. *Fireman!* was her relieved thought, although that didn't seem to fit. Except for the SCBA mask, he wasn't wearing any bunker gear. Instead, he was all in black, from his boots to his hat.

"Please," she tried to say, although it came out as a rasp. *Why is he just standing there?* she wondered, her voice shrill in her mind. *Why isn't he helping me?* She reached toward the figure, wanting to catch hold of his arm, but he shifted out of reach. Confused and swaying, Lou stared at him.

Then the man lifted a booted foot, placed it in the center of her chest, and *shoved*.

Even as she tumbled back into the burning cabin, Lou couldn't comprehend what the person had just done. The door slammed closed as she lay sprawled in the entryway, shock holding her motionless. Then it all suddenly clicked into place. Her stalker. Her stalker had likely drugged her, had set her cabin on fire…and now he was going to watch as she burned alive.

The realization sent a surge of rage through her, clearing her head and smothering her panic. Okay. If she couldn't go out the front door, then she'd just need to find another way out of the cabin. There was no way she'd let that asshole win. She was going to get out— even if it killed her.

As the flare of anger burned out, though, terror crept in its place. Just outside the door was someone who wanted her dead. She struggled to crawl, to pull herself back into the burning house, away from the killer. Fear stole the last of her coordination, though, and she lurched forward, cracking the point of her chin against the floor.

Darkness threatened to dim the flames, and she tasted something metallic mixed in with the thick flavor of ash in her mouth. The horror of the murderer so close to her forced her back to her hands and knees, and she started a slow, crawling shuffle toward where she thought her bedroom was.

The floor was getting hotter. She could feel blisters forming on her palms. Her knees stung—either from being scraped on the hard floor or from burns. Either way, Lou had to ignore the pain. Her hand bumped something, and she snatched it back before it could burn her. It hadn't felt hot, though, so she tried again, reaching out tentatively to discover the back corner of the couch.

Her body drooped in relief, but she pressed forward, keeping her shoulder close enough to brush along the back of the sofa as she moved. The smoke stung her eyes, covering them with a haze of tears. She could barely see, and then even that was gone as the flames roared upward, whiting out her vision. Her lungs caught with each breath, but she blamed it on the smoke. She wasn't sobbing. She wasn't.

A rain of sparks danced across her back. Her yelp of pain came out as more of a hoarse huff of air, and she shoved over onto her back to smother them before they could burn her. It ran through her head on repeat—the image of her pajamas going up in flames, her skin charring, the pain… Her puffs of breath turned into legitimate sobs she couldn't seem to stop. Tears rinsed her eyes, and her vision returned for a moment. She immediately wished it hadn't.

An enormous beam—black and glowing red, like it had just been tossed from hell—lay across the couch, dropping sparks and burning bits onto the floor…and Lou. The now-flaming cushions were the only thing keeping the beam from crushing her. With rasping, desperate sobs, she rolled, escaping from the threat.

Her evasive maneuver left her in the center of the room, disoriented and unsure of which way she should go. A growing sense of dizziness reminded her that every breath was poison and her time was running out. The entire room was ablaze, bright and deadly.

She desperately tried to plan, not to curl up and wait to burn, to die. Bathroom? The only window was too high and too small for her to fit. Living room? She might be able to squeeze through the opening in the ancient crank-style windows, but they opened to the front of the house, right where *he* was waiting. The thought of the horrific figure who'd left her to burn destroyed the tentative hold she had on her sobs. They ripped through her, painful and hoarse. If she managed to escape the horror inside her ruined cabin, he'd be waiting—waiting to finish what the fire had started. Either way, she was dead.

Please, her mind begged. *I don't want to die!*

Darkness was creeping around the edges of her blurred vision. Her skin felt dry and so, so hot. Lou struggled to push herself to her hands and knees, but her arms slipped out to the sides, dropping her on her front. Her mind screamed at her to move, to get out of this nightmare of smoke and heat and blinding flames, and she tried to pull forward in a belly crawl. Her arms weren't working right, though, and she didn't know where she was going.

She turned her head, blinking away tears from smoke and regret. That thing with Callum was so new, and she'd never know how their story would end.

Or maybe she would. Maybe it would end with her dying in her cabin.

Knock it off, the voice in her head, the only part of her that wasn't pathetic and whining, ordered. *Move.*

Forcing her heavy, uncoordinated arms in front of her, she dragged her body forward an inch and then two. She didn't know where she was going or what her plan was, but she did know that she wasn't going to give up and die, sniveling and helpless. Another pull, and she advanced painfully slowly across the floor.

A large shape interrupted the pattern of the flames, and she blinked her watery eyes to clear them. When she saw the human figure running toward her, she started shoving herself backward. *He's inside! He's inside and going to kill me!* her brain shrieked. But then his face—blackened and familiar and so beautiful—was close to hers.

"Callum?" she mouthed, unable to force any words from her roasted throat. He was talking to her, but she couldn't hear over the roar of the fire. That was okay, though, because it was enough that he was there, hoisting her off the floor and against his chest. She allowed her body to go limp. It wasn't up to her to save herself anymore. Callum had come for her.

As they approached the door, Lou opened her mouth, trying to force words through her burning throat. She had to warn him about the attacker—what if he was still out there? Before she could speak, the masked figure appeared, and her words of warning emerged as a hoarse, almost silent scream that was swallowed by the thunder of the flames.

She braced for an attack, but Callum ran toward the man, rather than away. Squinting through watery eyes, she realized that this man was in full bunker gear and was urging them out of the open door, rather than kicking them back into the burning cabin. Callum flew through the doorway, and the cold air washed over her for the second time that night. She sucked in breath after breath, exhaling in a hacking cough that shook her entire body.

The firefighter ripped off his SCBA mask, revealing Ian's furious face. "Put her down, Cook, so I can check her."

Callum's arms tightened for a second before he started to lower her. Before her socked feet could touch the snow, however, he lifted her again and walked over to sit her on the back bumper of one of the fire rescue trucks.

Another firefighter, Steve, hurried over to them with a med bag and a stack of blankets. Ian opened the kit, but when Steve moved to wrap the blanket around Lou, Callum grabbed it.

Instead of looking offended, Steve dropped his now-empty hand on Cal's shoulder and gave it a squeeze. "Get her covered then. Anyone else in there?"

It took a moment to register that the question was directed at her. Lou shook her head as Callum tucked the blanket around her without his usual precision. When she looked at his hands, she was startled to see that they were shaking. Ian fit an oxygen mask over her face and then fished her hand out of the blanket so he could clip something over the end of her finger. A muscle worked along his jaw the whole time. Lou watched it, a little confused.

"Why are you so mad?" she asked in a croak of a voice.

His narrowed eyes met hers as he dug through the med kit with more force than necessary. "Because Cook acted like a reckless asshole."

Her glance flicked to Callum, whose own jaw was clenched tight. Steve was urging him to sit down next to her.

"Cal?" she repeated doubtfully.

"*Reckless*. Like fucking jumping in a fucking frozen reservoir without any fucking gear." Ian emphasized each swearword with a hard yank on the unrolling blood pressure cuff. He reached for her arm, which she offered a little tentatively. As pissed as Ian was, though, he was still gentle as he wrapped the cuff around her bicep.

Callum adjusted his cap, leaving additional black streaks on the bill. "I know. But *Lou* was in there."

"And I was going to get her out. I was putting on my *gear*. So I could go in the burning cabin and not *die*." Ian pulled a pen out of his pocket and wrote something on his hand before taking her pulse. Snowflakes landed on her cheeks, making Lou realize how cold she was, despite the blanket. She leaned against Callum, who immediately wrapped an arm around her shoulders and pulled her close. His hands were still shaking, she noticed.

"That was pretty dumb, Cal," she rasped. Air scraped at her raw throat, making her wince.

"Don't talk," he ordered, and kissed the top of her head. "And it wasn't a thought-out decision. You were in the cabin. The cabin was on fire. I had to get you out."

Ian just grunted, but he put a truckload of irritation in the sound. "You'll be fine, but you need to get checked out at the hospital. Medics are on their way, but they got caught on the wrong side of an accident on the highway, so they're still twenty minutes out."

"I'll take her. We'll be halfway to Connor Springs by the time the ambulance gets here." Callum stood. Raising a skeptical eyebrow, Ian looked at Steve.

"BP is a little high, but he seems fine to drive." Steve smirked. "Doubt you could stop him if he wasn't, anyway."

Ian met Callum's gaze, both men coolly appraising the other. "Oh, I think I could manage."

"Guys?" Lou cleared her throat, which brought on another spate of coughing. Callum rubbed her back until she could speak again. "Instead of having a pissing contest, don't you think you should go dump some water on my house? You know, the one that's burning?" Although she tried to make her tone joking, her stomach felt like it was collapsing in on itself. The rescue truck blocked her view of the fire, but she could see the orange glow lighting the area and hear the muted roar of the flames even over the rumble of the pump truck.

Ian patted her blanket-covered knee. "We're on it."

Knocking Ian's hand off of her leg, Callum lifted her into his arms for the second time that night. As he carried her around the rescue truck to his pickup, she buried her face in his neck. It was weak of her, she knew, but she didn't want to see the flames eating what remained of her cabin. Instead of facing reality, she squeezed her eyes shut and breathed in the smell of smoke and Callum.

She was safe.

For now.

Chapter 12

THE LIGHTS FROM THE ONCOMING PICKUP SEEMED abnormally bright through the driving snow, making him squint and tilt his face. His fingers yanked at the steering wheel, and then he pounded on it. The car began to slide on the icy road, and he grabbed the wheel again, regaining traction. What had just happened?

He'd lost control before, but never like this. Never where he couldn't remember anything. Had he actually tried to kill her? The rage that had been burning inside him for months had been chilled by the realization that he'd actually attempted to burn her—his soul mate—to death.

Air hissed between his teeth. Why had he done that? Why? He needed her.

Things were spinning out of control—*he* was spinning out of control. It was time to take her, whether she was ready to go or not.

Although she'd braced herself for the worst during the hair-raising drive back from the hospital, the reality was even uglier than she could've imagined. Floodlights mounted on a rescue truck illuminated the scene, and Lou almost wished for darkness so she didn't have to see the pathetic remains of her little cabin. She wrapped her arms around her middle, hugging herself through

Callum's heavy coat as she surveyed the destruction of everything she owned. Even her truck was only a black-ened skeleton.

The site was a mess of churned-up mud, half hidden by a fresh layer of still-falling snow. The tender truck was linked by hoses to the pump truck, supplying water to the firemen who were still mopping up, soaking the charred remains of her home to make sure no smolder-ing embers remained. Icicles had formed where water leaked out of the hose connections, and vapor from the firefighters' breath merged with the lingering smoke.

The smell was horrible, and Lou wondered if part of that was from her truck. It was a good thing she hadn't wasted money on those ten-ply tires. She choked back a laugh that threatened to turn into a sob. Standing silently next to her, wearing an extra coat he kept in his truck, Callum rested the heavy and comforting weight of his arm across her shoulders. She sighed, leaning into him as tiredness sank deep into her bones and her feet went numb in the boots one of the nurses had grabbed from the hospital's lost and found for her.

"Lou." The gravelly voice of the fire chief brought her head around.

She attempted a smile of greeting but failed miser-ably. "Hey, Chief." Talking didn't hurt as much as it had earlier, although she sounded like a three-pack-a-day smoker.

Pushing up the face shield to the top of his helmet, the chief sighed. In the harsh artificial lights, the lines on his face were more pronounced, and his nose and cheeks were blotchy red with cold. Normally, Winston Early was a cheerful guy, quick to smile, but tonight he looked almost as weary as she was. "I'm so sorry, Lou. By the time we got here and Cal got you out, it was pretty much already gone. Even with this snow, the wood-frame construction, especially as old as your place was, went up in minutes."

Trying to control her wobbling chin, she nodded. "I figured not much would be left."

"Lou." Rob joined their small group. "You okay?"

With a small shrug, she bit her cheek to keep from crying as she shifted her weight. "We both checked out okay. Except for some smoke inhalation, I'm fine. It's just things that burned. *All* my things, but still."

Callum rubbed her upper arm in silent support.

"Did you find the guy I told you about? The one who kicked me back into the house?" she asked, looking back and forth between the fire chief and the sheriff. She'd called the sheriff on the way to the hospital to tell him about the would-be killer.

"Not yet," Rob said, exchanging a glance with Early.

"Did anyone see him leaving?" she pushed, not liking the look passing between the two men. "Were there any footprints or witnesses or…I don't know, any evidence to tell us who he is? Ruining my tires is one thing, but he tried to kill me tonight!"

Cal's fingers tightened around her upper arm, his body vibrating with tension next to hers.

"Lou," Rob said in a calm voice. "We'll find him. Did you remember anything else besides the SCBA mask and his black clothing? Height? Build?"

"He looked really tall, but my vantage point was off, since I was on my knees," she said, feeling guilty for not noticing any details. Pressing the heels of her hands into her still-stinging eyes, she tried to bring up the mental picture. "An average build, maybe on the thin side? Sorry I'm not being more help. My eyes were watering from the smoke and the heat, plus that whisky messed me up."

"Whisky? You'd been drinking?" Rob exchanged another look with Early, and Lou mentally cursed herself for bringing up the alcohol.

"One drink. There was something wrong with that whisky, though. I told them about it at the hospital, so they drew some of my blood to test."

Rob's gaze sharpened. "You think it was drugged?"

"Yes."

After scribbling something in his small notebook, Rob flipped it shut and dropped it in his pocket. "We'll be able to tell you more after we take a look tomorrow during daylight." The sheriff's tone had a ring of finality to it. "I'm the fire marshal for Field County, so I'll be heading up the investigation. I promise you that we will find whoever did this. Now go get some rest."

Although Lou set her chin stubbornly, she knew she wouldn't get any answers until the following day. She held back her multitude of questions and just said, "Thank you, Rob."

"Of course, Lou. I'm just sorry you have to go through this." He shot a quick glance at Callum and then looked at Lou again. "Do you have a place to stay tonight?"

Lou opened her mouth to answer, but Callum beat her to it with a short but definite "Yes."

"Good. Go home and get some sleep, if you can. Nothing more you can do here except get cold. Colder," the sheriff amended, his sharp eyes on her huddled posture.

With a final glance around at the destruction of her hard-won but cozy life, she gave a defeated nod and let Callum steer her down her driveway. They'd parked the truck almost at the road, since emergency vehicles lined her driveway. As they passed one of Fire's rescue trucks, Lou saw a familiar face and stopped.

"Ian," she called, and the firefighter turned from where he was reloading equipment.

"Hey, Lou, Callum," he said, walking over to them. "You two okay?"

"Yes." She had a feeling she was going to be getting that question a lot over the next few days and weeks. "Thank you for your help."

With a shrug, he said, "Least I could do for two of ours. I'm still pissed at Cook for running into a burning building in his fucking baseball cap and BDUs, but he got you out of there, and you're both okay. I'm just sorry we couldn't save your place."

"Nothing you could've done," Callum said, and Lou nodded.

Ian rubbed the back of his neck. "Still sucks."

With a choked laugh, Lou said, "That it does. Thanks again, though."

He gave another nod and headed back to the truck.

Leaning against Callum as she watched him walk away, Lou said, "I really think we should tell him the sheriff's office thinks his club was involved in HDG's murder."

He gave the back of her neck a gentle squeeze before urging her to start walking again. "Tonight's not the best time to make decisions."

"Yeah, you're probably right." She sighed as she

trundled through the snow toward Callum's pickup. The drifts looked almost blue in the moonlight. Tipping her head back, she stared at the clearing sky, letting Callum guide her steps.

"One good thing," she said.

"What's that?"

"It stopped snowing."

"Yeah." He tucked her closer against his side. "That is good."

Chapter 13

BY THE TIME CALLUM HELPED HER OUT OF HER coat—his coat, really—and she kicked off her lost-and-found boots, Lou was swaying with weariness. While Cal hung the coat with a precision that even a sleepless night couldn't mar, she leaned against the mudroom wall.

"Callum," she said softly.

"Hmm?"

"My house burned down." She started to cry.

"Oh, Lou." Callum dropped the coat on the floor and pulled her unresisting body into his arms.

"Someone tried to kill me." The idea seemed so foreign, so abhorrent. "I almost *died*."

His grip tightened until it was almost painful, but she welcomed the security of his hold.

"And my truck," she wailed, the loss of it hollowing out her chest. "I loved that truck so much."

"I know." He rubbed her back as she sobbed against his collarbone.

"All my stuff." After pausing to take a shuddering breath, she continued, "I know they're just replaceable objects, but they were important to me. They were the only things I brought with me from my old life. Now I have nothing."

After a long pause, he said, "You still have these pajama pants. They're very nice. I especially like the...dogs?"

With a laugh that was more sob than anything, she corrected shakily, "Hippos. They're hippos."

"They're very nice hippos."

"Thank you." She hiccuped.

"And you don't have nothing," he soothed her, running a hand up and down her spine. "Whatever I have, you can use. Like my pickup. You can share my truck."

"Thanks. I like your truck."

"And you can stay in my house as long as you like."

"I like your house, too."

"You can eat whatever's in the Crock-Pot."

This time, her laugh was more solid. "Score. I love the contents of your Crock-Pot."

He paused so long she started to doze standing up, startling awake when he finally spoke.

"And you have me."

Her heart began beating very fast. She was tempted to make a joke but screwed up her courage instead, and met his gaze. "Good. I think I like you the best. Even more than the contents of your Crock-Pot—and that's saying something."

His contented rumble made her glad she'd been brave. "We're going to find him, Lou," he said, his expression fierce as he stared into her eyes. "We're going to find that fucker. He won't hurt you again."

"Okay," she whispered, overwhelmed by his intensity and the matching emotions that stirred in her. "But can we sleep first?"

"Okay." Callum scooped her up and carried her through the kitchen and up the stairs.

"You don't have to carry me," she protested,

looping her weighted arms around his neck. "You must be exhausted."

"I'm fine." He brought her into the bathroom, carefully lowering her legs until she was standing upright. After he watched her for a minute, most likely to make sure she wasn't going to keel over, he turned to start the shower.

Lou unzipped her hoodie and let it drop to the floor. When Cal caught a glimpse of her in her tank and pajama pants, he blinked several times before heading for the door.

"I'll...uh, get something for you to wear." Still facing away from her, he paused in the doorway. "Will you be okay by yourself?"

"Sure," she said, although she wasn't sure if her legs would support her for another minute. Since she wasn't about to strip naked in front of Callum, though, she'd just have to be tough. Her voice must have held more confidence than she felt, since Cal left, closing the door behind him.

The hot water felt amazing, except when it stung the minor burns and scrapes that were scattered over her body. The water ran gray at first as it washed the soot from her skin. She helped herself to Cal's shampoo and soap, finding comfort in the thought of smelling like him. Her energy didn't last long, though, so she rinsed quickly and turned off the water.

She was toweling off when Cal knocked on the door, opening it immediately after and giving her just enough time to clutch the towel to her chest. A quick downward glance showed that she had all the vital parts covered—barely.

His stare earlier was nothing compared to how his eyes raked over her now. Since he appeared to be frozen into place, Lou reached out and snagged the T-shirt and shorts dangling from his paralyzed hand. When she pulled gently, they popped free of his fingers. The movement seemed to wake him from his daze.

"Sorry. I'll just…" He turned and almost walked into the edge of the door, jerking back just in time to prevent a collision before dashing out of the bathroom.

If she hadn't been so exhausted, Lou would've laughed. Instead, she just concentrated on dressing without falling. She was tempted to forgo brushing her teeth, but soot seemed to have settled into every corner of her being, including her mouth, so she grabbed the toothbrush she'd used the last time she'd stayed there. By the time she opened the bathroom door, the floor was tilting, reminding her of the drugged whisky.

That, in turn, reminded her of the fire and her terror and the murderous figure in the doorway. Callum must have been waiting for her, since he scooped her up before her legs could fold beneath her and carried her to his bed. Even with all the horrors of the night churning in her brain, her body was done. Lou fell asleep seconds after he tenderly placed her on the mattress.

Daylight made it so much worse.

The sun made the new snow sparkle wherever it lay, covering mountain peaks in the distance, lining tree branches and fence wires, turning the landscape into a postcard. It made the wreckage of her former home look even more bleak and pathetic. Lou had thought she'd be able to scavenge a few things, but *everything* was gone, destroyed once by fire and a second time by water—both from the hoses and the snow. She wasn't even able to look at the charred shell of her truck.

"There's nothing left here," she said as Callum laid a hand on her lower back. Heat seeped through her coat to her spine, offering comfort. It was painful to look at the remains of her cabin and know that it had almost held *her* remains. If it hadn't been for Callum... She shivered. "Let's see what the sheriff and Winston have to say, and then we can go."

The chief and Rob were standing a discreet distance away, far enough to give her some privacy, but close enough to intervene if she started messing with their crime scene. Straightening her spine, she hoped it was enough to move her from "pathetic victim" to "stoically enduring survivor." From the expressions on the two men's faces as she approached, she doubted her efforts were successful.

"Lou," Early greeted her, examining her closely as if checking for fire damage or an impending breakdown. "How are you?"

"Hanging in there," she said with a tight smile. It was only the partial truth, but if she shared any more, she'd start blubbering again, and no one wanted to see that.

"Good," the chief said approvingly before giving the man next to her a nod. "Callum."

Rob cleared his throat after Callum returned Early's greeting. "Looks like arson."

She'd been expecting tear-inducing commiseration, so Rob's all-business attitude was a relief. Callum's hand, still on her lower back, tightened into a fist around a handful of her coat.

"The first ignition point was your bed." Early kept shooting wary glances at her, as if checking her reaction to his words. "It appears to have been soaked in accelerant, most likely gasoline, and then ignited. Gas was also poured over the floor in the bedroom and living room, as well as along the base of the walls. The second ignition point was in your kitchen. That's a pretty common occurrence with amateur arsonists—two ignition points. They figure the more the better."

"So this person broke in first? He was in my house with me?" The idea made her stomach want to turn inside out. Even though she wasn't looking at him, Lou could feel the tension radiating from Cal.

The sheriff nodded. "Did you lock the door last night?"

"Yes, I always do." She had a moment of doubt and paused, trying to remember the actual act of locking the door after Cal left the previous evening. She turned to Callum. "I did, right?"

"Yes." His voice contained the confidence hers lacked. "I heard you lock the door."

"I suspect the arsonist entered through the bedroom window," Rob said. "It appears the glass was struck by something rather than exploding from the heat of the fire. I'm sending pieces of the broken glass to the state lab for testing, as well as items they can test to determine what accelerant was used."

"If it wasn't gasoline, I'll eat my shirt," Early said.

The sheriff shot him a look. "We have to do definitive scientific testing—you know that, Winston. Otherwise, it'll all go to hell once we get to court."

"Yeah, yeah," the chief grumped. "Just saying. Been doing this for thirty years. I know what I know without some lab geek telling me how to wipe my ass."

If Rob had been just a hair less controlled, Lou was pretty sure he would've rolled his eyes.

A sheriff's department squad vehicle eased through the snow and frozen mud that had once been Lou's yard. Chris hopped out of the SUV and hurried over to them.

"I was just talking with Lou's neighbor, Terry Buck," he said as soon as he got close enough to be heard. His words were rushed, as if he was excited about something. "A few minutes before he saw the fire and called it in, Terry passed an unfamiliar car headed north on thirty-six. A"—he pulled a small notebook from his coat pocket and flipped it open—"dark-colored BMW sedan with Connecticut plates."

Lou swayed, feeling hot and then cold. She knew that car. "Are you fucking kidding me?"

The four men all stared at her, startled.

"What a vindictive *asshole*." Her voice, still hoarse, gave out on the last word. "I can't believe he would do this." Even as she spoke, though, she knew that wasn't true. Faced with the evidence, she *could* believe it. He'd always had a temper, especially when he didn't get what he wanted. And ever since she was sixteen, he'd wanted *her*—or at least the benefits a relationship with her would bring him.

"Uh, Lou?" Chris was the first one of the guys to speak.

"What?" she snapped, and then immediately felt bad. "Sorry, Chris. I'm just so…argh!" Anger and betrayal cut off her ability to form words.

"I take it you recognize the car?" the sheriff asked.

"Yes. I do." Yanking off her hat, she smacked it against her thigh a few times. "The *dickface* you are looking for is Brenton Lloyd of Glenview, Connecticut: opportunist, social climber, and dater of teens, as well as an employee and friend, unfortunately, of my stepfather, Mr. Richard Chilten."

"Ex-boyfriend?" Callum asked with an odd inflection to his voice that she couldn't decipher.

"As embarrassed as I am to admit it, kind of. My parents wore me down when I was sixteen and he was…I can't remember, twenty-seven or thereabouts. Completely too old for me, but I was in my compliant phase. We were together off and on ever since—I'd have a brave moment and break up with him, but Brent wouldn't leave me alone until I agreed to get back together. Ugh. When I look back on it, I can see how weak and stupid I was, but he could be persistent, even a little scary. But I never thought he could do something like this. He wanted to get engaged as soon as I finished law school, but the thought of being married to Brent…" She shuddered. "I kept putting him off until I heard him talking to my stepfather about taking over the business once we were married. I'd been dragging myself to law-firm interviews and hating every second of it. When I heard Richard basically selling me to that asshole, I just…snapped. That's when I told Brent we were through for good. I packed up and moved to the mountains."

"Why is he targeting you now?" Rob asked.

"Instead of when I first moved here? No idea." Trying to calm her whirling brain and think, she was silent for a few moments. "My mom mentioned that he was trying to get a hold of me." It wasn't a reason, but it was a possible place to start. She pulled out her cell phone.

"Who are you calling?" Chris asked. Both he and the sheriff stepped forward, as if preparing to rip the cell phone out of her hand if necessary.

"Not Brent," she hurried to assure them before her phone was confiscated. "I don't even have his number, since I deleted it from my contacts and erased all his messages without listening to them. I'm calling my mom." She found her mother's number and tapped it.

"Messages?" Callum and Rob said in stereo.

She nodded absently, listening to the ringing on the other end. "He... Hang on a sec. Hi, Mom."

"Louise."

Rob was saying something about not telling her mother about her suspicions, but Lou waved him off, turning away from the listening crowd of men. She could concentrate on only one conversation at a time, especially when that one discussion was with her mother.

"Do you have Brent's phone number?"

"Oh, good," her mom said instead of answering Lou's question. "Are you finally going to respond to him, then? It's about time. The poor man's been frantic."

Lou frowned. Once she'd heard the description of his car, she'd been positive her stalker was Brent. Now, her first doubt crept in. "Has he been around recently?"

"I wouldn't exactly say recently."

"When was the last time you saw him? Feel free to use precise dates."

"What is this about, Louise?"

With a sigh, Lou restrained the urge to throw her phone into a snowbank. Why couldn't her mom just answer the question? "I'm going to call Brent, but not if he's traveling or something." She winced. That had been weak.

Her mom wasn't buying her lame excuse, either. There was a pause before her mother spoke again. "What ridiculous thing are you planning, and why are you dragging poor Brenton into it?"

"I thought you were excited I was going to contact Brent."

"Not if you're up to one of your little schemes," her mom said. "Brenton is seriously interested in you, Louise. You already broke his heart once. I don't want you playing with his emotions."

"*Me* playing with—" It took an extreme effort, but she managed to bite off the rest of that sentence before it escaped in the indignant tone it deserved. "Fine. I'll be kind to Brent. Can I have his number now?"

"I'm having reservations about this," her mom snipped. "I don't believe you are taking my concerns seriously."

"I'm very serious about this, Mom." Taking a deep breath, she silently counted to three before exhaling. "Please."

The pause that followed seemed endless. "Very well," she agreed, although she still sounded reluctant. "I'll text you his number."

"Thank you." That was the most sincere thing she'd said to her mom in a long time.

"So, does this interest in Brenton mean you're considering returning to civilization, or are you still enmeshed in your childish rebellion?"

"Sor—Mom...can't...los—" With a satisfied poke of her finger, she ended the call.

The text came through seconds later, and Lou handed the phone to Rob. "Can you track his phone using the number?"

He scribbled the number into his ever-present notebook. Instead of answering her question, he started asking his own. "What's his full name?"

"Brenton Lloyd." When Rob raised his eyebrows, as if expecting something more, she clarified, "Brenton Michael Lloyd."

"Address?"

Lou rattled it off to him.

"You said he works for your stepfather. What's the company name?"

The interrogation continued for a while, long enough for Lou to go hoarse and start to feel the wind cut through her coat. When she shivered, Callum stepped forward, easing his bulk between her and Rob.

"Enough for now, Rob," he said, his voice calm but implacable. "She's cold."

The sheriff eyed him narrowly for a long moment, and Lou had the mad urge to hum the preshoot-out theme from an old Western. Rob broke the tension by flipping his notebook closed and tucking it into his pocket.

"You working today, Lou?" he asked.

"Shoot!" She yanked Cal's sleeve back so she could see his watch. To her relief, she had almost an hour before her shift started. "Phew. And yes. Noon to seven thirty, or thereabouts."

"Don't you want to take some time off?" Early asked, frowning. "After, you know…" He jerked his chin toward the remains of her house, but she avoided looking at the charred mess again.

"No," she said without hesitating. "I need to be busy, or I'll think about it too much. Working is good."

"I'll stop in this afternoon, and we'll finish this then." Rob tapped his pocket where his notebook was hiding.

She just nodded, resigned to more questions. It seemed to have become her life recently. The hard knot in her stomach seemed to have settled in permanently.

"Ready?" Callum asked, tipping his head toward his pickup—their getaway vehicle. He'd been a steady, quiet presence the entire time they'd been there, and she appreciated it more than she could ever say.

"Yes," she responded with such relief that he smiled.

As they moved out of earshot of the other three men, Callum tilted his head closer to hers. "Sure you want to work?"

"Positive."

He gave her an appraising look out of the corner of his eye.

"What?" she asked.

"You're just…very resilient."

"Not really." Lou made a face. "I'm a few short steps away from a major breakdown. I just don't want to hang around home…your house, I mean." Her new reality smacked her in the face, and she swallowed before continuing. "All I would do is dwell on everything. And probably rearrange all your stuff out of boredom, which would lead to *your* nervous breakdown. Going to work is best, I think."

After another careful look, he just nodded silently and opened the passenger door of his truck for her. After he circled the front of the pickup and climbed into the driver's side, she studied his profile.

"You know," she said thoughtfully, "there's been a lot of bad stuff happening—HDGs and stalkers and burning cabins and close calls with death and such."

"Yes?" Callum sent her a curious glance as he turned the key, bringing the pickup's engine to life.

"You're the good part of all this. Getting to know you was worth everything that happened." With a frown, she added, "Although HDG might not agree with that."

The skin over Callum's cheekbones had darkened to the color of brick, and Lou was pretty sure it wasn't all because of the cold. "Thank you."

"You're welcome." Leaning her head against the seat and basking in the heat beginning to flow through the truck's vents, she promptly fell asleep.

There were now two positives to almost dying: more time with Callum, and Ivy was being nice. Kindness sat oddly on her boss, like a coat that didn't quite fit, but Lou appreciated the effort. She also took advantage of Ivy's temporary fit of sympathy by asking if another staff member could close with her at night. Although the sweetness quickly soured, Ivy grudgingly agreed she would schedule two people to close, as soon as Sylvia's newly hired replacement was trained.

Buoyed by this concession, Lou stayed fairly positive for the busy first hour of her shift. Lou had the impression that the majority of those who stopped in were driven by curiosity. The news of her cabin burning had apparently spread across Field County quicker than the flames had eaten her home. Although her smile stretched thin when she was faced with some of the

more prurient gossips, most of the people offered real
sympathy and support.

The crowd was dwindling when Derek charged
through the door and behind the counter. As she stared
at him, mouth open, he grabbed her in a bear hug, lifting
her off her feet.

"Why didn't you call Artie and me last night?" he
demanded, giving her a shake. Although Lou tried to
answer, his arms squeezed all of the oxygen out of her
lungs. "I just heard about your cabin. Shit, Lou, are
you okay?"

Wiggling her hands between their bodies, she shoved
against his chest. He finally got the message and set her
on her feet. Taking a step back, he kept his hands on
her shoulders, giving her a shake to emphasize each
exclamation.

"I heard you weren't hurt. That was true, right?" He
eyed her closely. "You don't have any burns that I can
see. What caused the fire? Was it one of those candles of
yours? Damn it, Lou, I knew you'd forget you had them
lit one of these times. I didn't see your truck outside. Did
it burn, too? Ah man, you loved that truck."

Lou took advantage of his tiny pause and grabbed his
wrists. "Derek. Breathe."

"But did you—"

Not waiting for a break this time, she just interrupted
him. "Sit. I'll get you a coffee." Eyeing his face, she
amended, "A *decaf* coffee. Then I'll tell you everything,
okay? Right at this second, just know I'm okay. Cal's
okay. My stuff is gone, but it's just stuff. Everything is
going to be fine."

Although he still looked a little wild-eyed, he did

as she asked, circling around to the customer side of the counter with only a few fairly gentle nudges. As he plopped down on a stool, she poured his decaf coffee. Lou handed it to him, eyeing him carefully before deciding he was stable for the time being. Turning to the two people waiting in line who'd watched the previous scene with undisguised interest, she gave them a how-can-I-help-you smile.

"Hi, Lou." Naomi, who worked at the outdoor-gear store down the street and came in almost daily for her early afternoon pick-me-up, leaned over the counter and lowered her voice to a whisper. "Are you dating Derek now? Isn't he with Artie?"

"Of course not," Naomi's friend and coworker, Daryl, scoffed. He was jammed right up against Naomi so he could hear what she was saying, his floppy bangs not concealing the eager look in his eyes. "She's practically living with Callum. Everybody knows that."

"Because *everybody* never gets it wrong." Naomi rolled her eyes. "Her house burned down, genius. She has to stay somewhere."

Daryl blew a raspberry. "They were living together *before* her place got torched. Dude, you are so out of the loop."

"Don't call me 'Dude.'" Turning to Lou, who was watching their interplay with wide eyes, Naomi said, "So, Derek or Callum? Derek seems like more fun, if you want my opinion. If he's still with Artie, though, you'd better put down the man and back away slowly. She could totally take you."

Derek cleared his throat. "I'm sitting right here. I can hear you, you know."

"I *said* you were more fun." Naomi sighed. "Why are you offended?"

"Did you two want some coffee?" Lou asked, a little desperate to redirect the conversation.

"Just the usual—medium soy latte, extra hot." Naomi rattled off the order, even though Lou had made it dozens of times.

"Double-shot cappuccino." Tossing his hair out of his eyes, Daryl asked, "Do you think whoever lit your place on fire is the one who tossed that headless dude in the reservoir?"

"Someone *lit your place on fire*?" Derek's voice was back in the frantic range.

Focusing extra hard on steaming the soy milk, Lou shook her head. "I don't think the two things are related."

"Oh." Daryl sounded disappointed. "You found him, right? The headless dude, I mean? How freaky was that?"

Her smile was strained as she answered. "Pretty freaky. Do you want anything to eat?"

"Of course. Who do you think you're talking to? I'll take one of those seven-layer bars."

As she pulled out the pastry and set it on a plate, she asked Naomi, "How about you?"

"No, thanks. I just want to know which guy you're knocking boots with."

Lou could feel her cheeks reddening, so she spun toward the register to hide it. "Neither, actually."

Making a scoffing sound, Naomi held out a ten as she narrowed her eyes at Lou. "Please. You spend all that time hanging out with these hot, buff guys, and you're 'just friends'? I don't think so, unless you're rocking a cast-iron chastity belt."

Derek broke into a coughing fit, and they all looked over at him. "I'm fine," he said hoarsely. "Coffee just… went down the wrong way."

Turning back to making Naomi's change, Lou prayed for the conversation to end, but it obviously wasn't her day.

"Aren't you worried about, you know, things getting awkward? If you guys don't work out, I mean? It's kind of a small town, so it's hard to avoid people you don't want to see." Daryl spoke around a huge mouthful of seven-layer bar.

Naomi turned her narrowed gaze to her coworker. "You weren't that concerned about it when you were banging me in the storage room."

"O-kay!" Lou said more loudly than she'd intended. "Don't you two have to get back? Who's running the store?"

With a shrug, Daryl took another bite. "Put a sign on the door. You know, a 'be back in five' kind of deal."

"It's definitely been five," Lou said, grabbing the sparse remains of his bar and wrapping it in a piece of waxed paper. She handed it back to him, making a shooing motion toward the door. "There's probably a line of people waiting to buy something."

"Doubt it," Naomi said, although to Lou's relief she started moving slowly in the direction of the exit. "It's been dead."

"Like the headless dude!" Sputtering a crumb-spewing laugh, Daryl jammed the last piece of the seven-layer bar into his mouth. Balling up the waxed paper, he tossed it toward the garbage can across the shop. It fell to the ground a fair distance from the trash bin, and Daryl's shoulders collapsed.

"I've got it," Lou assured him, hurrying around the counter and toward the fallen wad of paper. "You've got a store to open. Off you go now!"

For once, the jangle of the sleigh bells was music to Lou's ears as the pair gave final waves and headed outside. She tossed the paper into the garbage.

"I really could've lived without the mental image of the two of them going at it in the storage room," she muttered, returning to the counter to grab a wet cloth. "Can you imagine what his kitchen looks like? Gross." The wet crumbs were everywhere. She squished up her face as she cleaned the pastry case.

"Forget them," Derek said. "Tell me what happened."

She did. From the punctured tires to the fire at her cabin, she gave him all the details of her stalker, the lovely Brenton Lloyd.

"You're sure this is the guy?" Derek asked when she finished.

"The car matches his, down to the Connecticut plates," she said, rinsing out the cloth. "The more I think about it, the more I can see him doing things like this. He always did have a short fuse. Well, at least hiring someone to do the small things. The arson seems flat-out nuts."

"I don't get it." He frowned, picking at the rim of his now-empty cup. "If you broke up with him last summer, why'd he go all stalker on your ass now?"

With a shrug, she reached for his cup, knowing that if she left it in his hands, it would shortly be in pieces all over the counter. "He's always been, I don't know, a little bit…off, I guess. My parents really pushed me to date him, but once I found out they were bribing him to

marry me, I knew I had to break things off with him—
for good that time." Her legs felt tired, so she rounded
the counter and sat on the stool at the end—Callum's
usual seat. When she realized she was smiling at the
thought, Lou hastily wiped her expression clear.

Luckily, Derek was too busy thinking about her
stalker's motives to notice. "Why now, do you think?"

"Not sure." She shrugged again. "Maybe it fully sunk
in that I wasn't coming back, or my parents could have
said something about me refusing to leave the mountains,
or who knows? Sometimes I wonder why I'm trying to
apply logic to the actions of a crazy person. This makes
me extra glad I turned down that plane ticket, though.
Despite everything that's been happening here, there's
no part of me that wants to return to Connecticut. I spent
too many years caught in that trap."

"Plane ticket?"

With a heavy sigh, she tipped her head back against
the wall. "Don't ask. After kicking HDG, I was a little
traumatized and obviously not thinking clearly. I figured
I needed my mom."

"HD—what?"

"Oops!" Her hand flew to cover her mouth. "Can you
pretend you didn't hear that?"

"No." He started to smile. "I'm curious now."

Groaning, she let her head bump the wall behind her.
"You're going to think I'm…I don't know, insensitive.
Crass, even."

He laughed. "Sweetheart, I don't know if you've
noticed, but almost every single person working as a
first responder is insensitive." Raising a mocking eyebrow, he parroted her, "Crass, even."

When she thought about it, it did seem to have a ring of truth.

"We have to be," he continued. "You can't see bad shit over and over without throwing up some defenses. It's either that or burn out. Some of the jokes the deputies tell..." He shook his head, although a smile tucked in the corners of his mouth.

"Headless Dead Guy," she said in a small voice, peeking at him to see his reaction.

Derek blinked. "The guy from the reservoir? Is that his nickname?"

"Maybe. But that's just between me and you. And Callum, of course."

"Ah." He leaned back, twisting his stool until he faced her. "Of course. So, the two of you *are* knocking boots, then?"

"No!" Grabbing a plastic coffee stirrer, she tossed it at him. Although it fluttered down harmlessly between them, Derek ducked as if she'd hurled a pot of hot coffee at him. "Not yet."

His eyes widened as he sat up straight, and she instantly regretted letting the words slip. "So, there's a plan to knock boots in the future then? The *immediate* future?"

As hot as her cheeks were, she knew her face had to be bright red. She lifted her hands to cover them, closing her eyes with an embarrassed groan. The sound of the sleigh bells made her eyes pop open again.

When Callum walked into the shop, she held back another groan at Derek's delighted grin. Callum raised an eyebrow, looking back and forth between the two of them.

"Hi?" she said, not sure why she raised her voice in question.

"Hi." Looking hard at Derek—who looked ready to burst into gales of laughter—Callum hesitated, then abruptly crossed the shop until he stood in front of her. Before she had any inkling of his intent, he leaned in and kissed her. It was short but hard, leaving her staring at him with startled eyes and tingling lips.

He turned toward Derek, although he stayed so close to her that he would just need to move a half inch for them to be touching. Lou blinked. How had they gone from three abbreviated kisses to full-on PDA?

"Derek." Callum lifted his chin in greeting.

"Hey, Cal." Derek's beaming smile did not dim at all at the other man's cool welcome. He opened his mouth to say something else, but whatever outrageous thing that was going to emerge was cut off by the sheriff's entrance.

"Rob!" Lou knew she sounded much too excited to see him, but she was dreading Derek's next quip. Whatever he was going to say, it was guaranteed to be embarrassing.

"Lou." Rob took her overeager greeting in stride. "Is now a good time to finish our discussion?"

"Sure." The shop was empty except for the four of them. "See you later, Derek?"

"You know it." His grin was still in place as he stood. "We have a discussion of our own to finish."

"No, we don't," she said quickly—too quickly, judging by the way Callum's head snapped around. Grimacing, she mouthed, "I'll explain later," at Cal, who, after a stiff pause, nodded. Derek was practically chortling as he pushed open the door, exiting the shop with a final wave. Sighing, Lou poured Cal's coffee into a to-go cup.

The sheriff eyed Callum, who returned his stare for a long second before turning to Lou and trading the coffee for a five-dollar bill.

"I'd better get back," he said reluctantly. When he leaned in this time, Lou was prepared, turning her face so his lips met her cheek instead of her mouth. She met his glower with a stern look of her own. PDAs required a prior discussion and agreement by both involved parties. He couldn't just go throwing his testosterone around because there were other males lurking nearby.

His irritated look slipped into his usual expressionless mien as he turned toward the sheriff.

"See you, Rob," he said before moving toward the door. "I'll talk to you later, Lou." That short statement was filled with all sorts of implications. She just smiled at him, although she probably looked like a pissed-off tiger with the way her teeth were set. His mouth softened into a barely there smirk right before he stalked out of the shop.

"It's getting serious, then? The two of you?" Rob asked, bringing her attention off the door and back to the sheriff's curious face.

"Is it Ask-Lou-About-Her-Relationships day or something?" she snapped, but immediately softened. "Sorry. Long day. Long week, actually."

"My fault," he said. "None of my business. I'd just been considering… Never mind." His voice turned brisk, and her curiosity ramped up to cat-killing levels. "I just had a couple more questions for you."

Rob covered some of the same ground they'd been over before, about Lou's relationship with Brent. She snorted a laugh.

"Guess it *is* Ask-Lou-About-Her-Relationships day," she explained, when Rob raised an inquiring eyebrow. "Never mind. I'm embarrassed to admit it, but my parents were so happy when I started dating Brent that I just went along with it. When I was in college, I'd try to end things with him, but he'd get really angry."

Rob frowned. "Was he abusive?"

"Not physically." She dropped her eyes to the counter. "He'd yell and threaten and throw things, but he never hit me. It was scary, though, and my parents would always push me to take him back, so it was just easier to be officially together and avoid him as much as possible." Lou cringed at how spineless she'd been. "I'd even find excuses to skip the twice-a-year family trip to Barbados because my parents invited him along." When Rob looked surprised—well, as surprised as the sheriff ever allowed himself to look—she nodded. "I know. Mom and Dad love this guy—probably more than me at this point. But I got to where I didn't want to be around him, to the point of giving up opportunities to scuba dive."

The corner of his mouth twitched. "You'll get plenty of chances now that you're on the dive team."

"Yeah, *cold*-water diving." Lou made a face. "Somehow, it's just not as fun as diving in a bikini with the tropical fish."

That brought an actual smile. "Guess not."

Afraid that her complaint made her sound like a

spoiled princess, she hurried to add, "The dive team is awesome, though. Helping to save people's lives is in a whole other realm than paddling around, looking at sea life. It's worth the cold."

"I get that," he said seriously. "That's why I do this job."

"Oh? It's not for the thrill of moving cattle off the highway?"

He grimaced. "Or getting to deal with the state investigators."

"Is the measuring contest still ongoing?"

His eyebrows flew up. "Did I mention that to you?"

With a grin, she shrugged. "I think you'd just come from the scene, so the annoyance was fresh in your mind."

"Probably." Glancing down at his notebook, he switched back into cop mode. "Tell me about any encounters you had with Mr. Lloyd since you stopped dating him."

Although there was little to tell, she did her best to comply with his request. They were interrupted a few times by customers, but the presence of the sheriff had all of them taking their coffee and hustling for the door.

"You can really clear a room," Lou said, putting the milk back in the small fridge after the third person practically ran out of the shop.

He looked a little uncomfortable. "Part of it's the uniform, and part is just me. I guess I tend to be... off-putting."

Cocking her head to the side, she considered him carefully. "You do have an air of authority. I think it's more that you're intimidating rather than off-putting, though."

"There's a difference?"

"Sure." She laughed. "I'd much rather be intimidating than off-putting."

The door opened again, this time admitting Tyler Coughlin.

"Hey," he said to both of them before turning to Lou. "Heard your house burned down. That blows."

"How did you…?" Rob shook his head. "School. Gossip. Got it."

"It's Friday, Dad," Tyler said with exaggerated patience. The Simpson schools were set up on four-day weeks. "But I don't have to be in school to hear about it. The whole town is talking." He sent Lou a sly look. "About the fire…and *other things*."

"Tyler," the sheriff barked.

The teenager's head dropped as he muttered, "Sorry."

Despite her blush, Lou waved it off. "It's fine. It's not news to me. Everyone and their brother has been in this afternoon, asking about the fire and…other things. Want something to drink?"

"Mocha?" he suggested, sending his dad a sideways look.

"Hot chocolate," Rob corrected, making Tyler roll his eyes but give in with a shrug.

"So who did it?" Tyler asked as she mixed chocolate with the steamed milk for his drink.

The sheriff cleared his throat.

Ignoring the wordless reprimand, his son continued, "I heard you, like, got trapped inside and almost died. Bet it was freaky in there. Did you get any burns?"

"Tyler!"

Shaking off the horrifying images the boy's

questions brought back to her mind, she handed Tyler his hot chocolate.

Repressively, Rob said, "I'll see you at home."

Tyler snorted. "Right. Because you'll be home before I'm asleep."

"Tyler," Rob said, sounding tired and guilty and frustrated and…all kinds of emotions Lou couldn't identify.

"See you, Lou," Tyler said, ignoring his father as he pushed open the door.

"Good night, Tyler," she called as the door swung closed behind him.

"Excuse me a moment," Rob said, following his son outside.

Lou could see them in front of the shop, although she half-heartedly tried not to watch their interaction. When Rob turned back toward the door, Lou hurried to busy herself, restacking plates that really didn't need restacking.

"Sorry for the interruption," Rob said as he returned. The professional mask was back in place, worried single father hidden again. His deeply tired look remained, though, and Lou had the same urge to help him as she'd had before. Something about the lost father-and-son pair brought out her nurturing side.

"No problem. Any more questions for me?"

Consulting his little notebook, Rob finally shook his head. "Not right now. I'll call if I think of anything else. You'll be staying with Callum at his house for a while?"

She nodded, feeling a little awkward admitting that.

"Good." He tucked away the notebook. "He'll notice if anything is wrong."

Making a face, she couldn't resist asking, "And I won't?"

"Sure," Rob said, although his expression didn't exactly agree. "It's always good to have a second pair of eyes, though."

"True." Plus, Lou had to admit that the idea of hanging out with Callum at his house was considerably more appealing than the thought of staying somewhere alone. Just the thought made her shiver. This, in turn, made her angry, since she'd been by herself and happy for over seven months, and Brent ruined that for her. At the thought of Brent, her hands tightened into fists. "Any luck finding him?"

"Not yet," Rob admitted. "But we have some solid leads we're following."

"Good." She hesitated to ask her next question, since it somehow felt as if she was admitting she was afraid. "Will you tell me? When he's in custody, I mean. So I know he's not running around somewhere." The idea made her glance out of the window into the approaching dusk.

"Of course," he said. "And, with a little luck, that will be sooner rather than later."

"Good." Lou glanced through the window again, hating that this ordeal was turning her into someone who flinched at shadows. Straightening her spine, she resolutely turned her back on the window and any watching stalkers. "Would you like something to drink for the road?"

Chapter 14

CALLUM WAS ACTING...DIFFERENT. FOR ALMOST TWO hours, while he'd sat on his usual stool, she'd been trying to put her finger on what was making him seem odd. Finally, after she'd closed the shop and climbed into his truck, she couldn't take it anymore.

"What?" It probably wasn't the most diplomatic leadoff to a discussion, but she was tired and tense and ready to get home—his home—and change into flannel pajama pants—her only pair now—and his weirdness wasn't going to allow her to get comfortable, warm pj's or no.

"You and Derek are friends," he stated. Since he hadn't really asked a question, she waited for him to continue. When he was silent for too long, she decided to give him a verbal prompt.

"Yes."

"And...?"

She turned in her seat so she could stare at him. "And what?"

His lips tightened in annoyance. "Are you...anything more?"

"More?" It was a little like having a conversation in pig Latin. She could pick up the gist, but it was maddening and made her want to smack him. "More than friends, you mean?" At his short nod, she blew out a breath. "No. Even if hell froze over and he broke up with

Artie, I'd never be tempted. He's like the brother I never wanted. How could I date that?"

Although he didn't smile, at least his mouth relaxed slightly. "Rob."

"Oh, for the love of Pete, just spit it out! What about Rob?"

That slight easing of his tension was gone. "Are you interested?"

"In Rob? Romantically? No. Sure, he's hot in a sexy-but-damaged kind of way, but there's no zing between us. And can you imagine me as a stepmother to a teenager? The poor kid would be traumatized." With a mock shudder, she purposely did not mention that the sheriff had implied his interest. Sharing that would not be helpful during the current discussion—or any discussion with Callum, actually. Instead, she asked, "What's with the line-up of possible love interests?"

Adjusting his baseball cap, he stared through the windshield with more attention than the mostly cleared road required. "I'm trying to understand," he finally said.

"Understand…?"

He flashed her an irritated look, which made her realize how few of those he'd been sending her way recently. Honestly, she hadn't missed them. "You."

"What about me?"

"Earlier, at the coffee shop…" He lifted his cap again and resettled it on his head. The amount of fidgeting was a sure sign he was off balance. "You didn't want me touching you."

"Is that it?" Flopping back against the seat in relief, she turned her head and grinned at him. "Jeez Louise, I thought you were breaking up with me or something."

"Break up with you?" He frowned. "I'm not the one turning away when *you* try to kiss *me*."

"Yeah, well, I'm not the one using PDA to mark his territory."

"What?"

"The only reason you kissed me was to prove a point to Derek and Rob."

"That wasn't why," he grumbled.

Ignoring that, she continued, "We haven't even really talked about it. What we are, I mean. We're basically living together, but we haven't even dated."

"We've gone on dates," he protested, totally missing the point. "We went to Levi's."

"Fine. We've gone on one date."

"Plus, we went to the bar together."

"Uh, that was to talk to the coroner about a dead person."

"Still counts."

"Does not."

"Does."

"Whatever. Two dates then. So, we're dating?"

"Yes."

"Are we exclusive?"

"Yes."

"Okay then." She smiled at him. "Are we good?"

Finally, he smiled back. "Yeah. We're good."

~~~

Lou decided that Callum's cooking more than made up for his lack of communication skills. After dinner, though, she couldn't settle. She did the dishes and cleaned the kitchen just for something to do. When Callum discreetly checked the cleanliness of the countertops before wiping them down again, she rolled her eyes and wandered around the living area.

He watched her over the breakfast bar as she roamed the space. Lou sat on his very comfortable couch and almost immediately popped back to her feet. Watching television was not going to happen. She was much too twitchy to sit still. If she stayed in one place too long, then she would start thinking about how someone—Brent—hated her enough to try to kill her. That would just lead to being petrified and sad, so she decided the solution was to keep moving.

Her gaze stopped at the woodstove, and she headed in that direction. The fire didn't really need attention, but she figured that poking at it would allow her to pretend to be useful.

"Stop," Callum ordered. "The fire is perfect. Do not mess with it."

Months of obeying that commanding tone during trainings and on calls made Lou stop in her tracks. "Sorry. I'm being irritating."

"I'm just not used to people being in my space." He looked relieved that his fire was no longer in danger of being assaulted.

She pivoted away from the stove, and the whiteboard caught her attention. "Can we talk about HDG? I just need to do…something."

"I can think of something to do."

It took her a moment of staring at him to realize he was flirting. "Oh! Um, better not right now. That's not very calming."

He stalked—actually stalked!—around the breakfast bar toward her. "We don't have to be calm."

"I...uh." Her mouth was suddenly dry, making it hard to swallow. She backed up as he advanced, and the image of an antelope being hunted by a mountain lion popped into her head. When her legs bumped into the back of the couch, she jumped, startled. He was just inches away from her, and he put both hands on the top of the couch, trapping her and reminding her of their kiss in her kitchen the night before. The memory brought back the reason that kiss was interrupted, and her hand flew to his chest, stopping him as he leaned closer.

When he went still, looking at her with an unreadable expression, she studied him, taking in the hard planes of his face and the concern in his eyes. Despite his predatory advance, it'd taken only the smallest amount of pressure against his chest for him to stop. It made her feel powerful and safe and so incredibly turned-on that she closed her hands, grabbing two fistfuls of his shirt so she could yank him toward her.

A rare look of surprise crossed his face before her lips crashed into his. It didn't take him long before Callum's stunned moment passed and he took over the kiss. There was no teasing this time, and little finesse. Their embrace was sheer raw need that had been building since their first real kiss in her kitchen.

She fumbled for the buttons on his flannel shirt, wanting to skip the fastenings and just rip and tear until he was naked. Her teeth closed on his lip, and he jolted. For a second, she felt guilty, worried that she'd been too rough, when his fingers threaded through her hair, and he yanked her closer.

Groaning against his mouth, she sank into him. She

needed him, needed this, needed the sensations crashing through her body to prove that she was still alive. Even as she fell deeper into the kiss, however, Cal eased back, his hands slipping to her shoulders and gently holding her away from him.

"What's wrong?" Her voice was still husky from smoke and want. "Is your phone ringing again?"

"No." He moved his hands to cup her cheeks. "But I don't want to take advantage. You've had a rough few days. Are you sure you want this?"

"Yes." Biting the inside of her cheek, she dropped her gaze to his chin. "Maybe?"

Leaning closer, he pressed a kiss to her temple and then stepped back, his hands dropping to his sides. "We'll wait until you're sure."

Now that her desire for him was settling back to its usual simmer, Lou knew he was right. It was too soon. She shifted awkwardly, looking anywhere but at Cal, much too aware that she'd just jumped the poor guy. "So…what would you like to do instead?"

His exhaled sigh was resigned. "Want to talk about the dead guy?"

"Can we?" she asked hopefully, her gaze returning to him.

He gestured toward the whiteboard, creating an opening for her to escape his too-tempting nearness. She took the out gratefully, hurrying over to the board and focusing much too intently on choosing a marker color. Magenta pen in hand, she looked over at Callum, who was still standing where she'd left him by the back of the couch.

"So," she said, underlining Ian Walsh's name.

"Should we tell him about the evidence that might impli-
cate his motorcycle club?"

Callum looked at her for a long second before circling to the front of the couch and sitting. "What do
you think?"

Tapping the end of the marker against her pursed
lips, she considered the question. "I want to tell him,"
she finally said, "especially after last night. My reasons
are more emotional than logical, though. I mean, he
braved a burning building for us. It just strikes me as
wrong that we're keeping this vital information from
him, you know?"

Leaning back against the sofa cushion, Callum looked
thoughtful. "What are the cons of telling him?"

She turned toward the whiteboard, picking an empty
corner and writing "pros" on the left and "cons" on the
right. Under pros, she put *Need to look out for fellow
rescuer*. After a short hesitation, she added, *Ian risked
life for us—should treat him with equal respect*.

"Okay," she said. "Cons." She scribbled, *Sheriff
warned Lou to keep her big mouth shut*. and *Do we want
to give MC this info (especially if they did it)?*

Taking a step back, she eyed what she wrote before
turning to Callum. "I care more about the second con
than the first. In case you haven't noticed, I'm not very
good at following orders."

His lips twitched. "I've noticed."

She grinned at him. "So, we're basically looking at
whether we want to risk indirectly sharing this information with the club, then."

With a nod, he leaned forward and propped his elbows
on his knees. "What could they do, if they did know?"

"You're being very Socratic-Methody tonight with all these questions," she observed, tilting her head to the side as she eyed him.

The lip twitch turned into a small grin. "Just trying to help organize your brain."

After considering this for a moment, she gave him a nod. "Actually, it is helping. Thank you." She paused. "What was the question again?"

"I can tell it's helping," Callum said dryly. "The question was, what could the MC do with this information if they did have it?"

"Ooh, good question. They could make the evidence disappear."

He changed an amused sound into a cough when she narrowed her eyes at him.

"We're brainstorming," she said sternly. "There's no laughing allowed in brainstorming sessions."

"Sorry." He gave her an impressively somber nod. "The evidence is safe in the state lab. I don't think this small, local MC has the reach to make it"—he cleared his throat—"disappear."

"Okay." She tapped the marker against her lips again, stopping when Callum gave her an odd look. "What?" Glancing down, she realized she had the marker upside down, and there was probably magenta ink all over her face now. "Shoot. Oh well, at least it's not a permanent marker. So, if the club has prior knowledge of the evidence, they'll be prepared when Rob interrogates them about it. That could mess up the case."

"It could." He didn't sound too convinced. "It's a stretch, though. They'll already know something's up, just because the sheriff's bringing them in for questioning."

"But they won't know what, specifically, he has on them, unless we spill the beans to Ian."

"Will that actually affect the outcome of the interview?"

Opening her mouth to answer, she closed it again to reconsider. "I don't know," she finally admitted. "They could have excuses prepared, I suppose. It's all so hypothetical, when the reasons I *should* tell Ian are so visceral."

"So what do you want to do?"

"Tell him." It just popped out of her mouth without her having to think about it.

After considering her for a long moment, Callum nodded. "Do it."

With a little bounce of excitement, she asked, "Now?"

He glanced at his watch. "It's pretty late, and you probably want to do it in person?" She nodded. "Tomorrow morning, then."

"Okay." Looking at the whiteboard, she said, "I think I'm going to start calling the diabetes and amputee support groups tomorrow, too. Unless you think I should visit in person?"

"No." Standing, he stretched his arms toward the ceiling. Distracted by the play of muscles visible even under his shirt, Lou temporarily forgot the question she'd just asked until he continued. "More snow's coming, and it's too dangerous to be driving that far. Most of the towns where the groups meet are over an hour from here."

Frowning, she replaced the cap on the marker. "Plus, I'm currently truckless."

He walked to where she was standing and rested a hand where her neck and shoulder met, massaging the muscles there. "Did you hear anything from your insurance company?"

"Not since I called them this morning." Leaning into his touch, she closed her eyes as his fingers dug into a particularly tight spot.

"Things will get settled quickly," he assured her, but she was too blissed-out to really listen. "I'll help you shop for a new truck."

When that penetrated, her eyes popped open. "That's okay," she said, slipping out from underneath his hand. "You're busy. I can do it on my own."

Crossing his arms over his chest, Callum gave her a heavy frown. "What's the problem?"

"No problem." She rubbed at a pink smudge the marker had left on her hand so she could avoid looking at him. "It's just that I can shop for my own truck."

He was quiet long enough that she gave in and met his gaze. It gave nothing away. Stubbornly, she stayed silent in what felt like an extremely awkward round of the quiet game.

"Are you regretting it?"

"What?"

"What we talked about earlier." He ran his hand over his shorn head, as if he were reaching to adjust his baseball cap and was surprised to find it missing. "Us."

"No!" For this conversation, she couldn't stay still. Crossing to the breakfast bar, she started arranging the apples and bananas sitting on a plate. "I just…" Balancing a banana on top of two apples, she sighed. "Moving here was really hard."

He grunted.

"It was the first time I decided what *I* wanted to do. Once I got here, I had to learn everything from scratch." She turned another banana into a teeter-totter by balancing it over a single apple and then rocking it back and forth. "I hadn't even mowed my own lawn back in Connecticut, and here I had to learn how to take care of my solar batteries and how to fix my generator when it wouldn't start and…just everything. I didn't even know how to start a fire when I first moved into my cabin. I thought it was a matter of throwing a lit match at a stack of logs."

When she risked glancing at him, Callum was still expressionless, but he was looking at her with an intense focus that made her shiver. She took that as a good sign and continued.

"It was really hard and scary, but I did it. Now, you make everything easy." Frowning, she spun the teeter-totter banana in a circle before it wobbled and fell off the apple. "And that's even scarier, because I just want to dump everything in your lap and lie on a fainting couch while you fan me with palm fronds and feed me grapes."

His slight choking sound brought her head around, but his expression hadn't changed. Turning back to the plate, she made a happy face out of two apples for eyes and a banana for a mouth.

"I don't want to go back to that helpless, weak person I was before." She flipped the banana over so it created a frown. "And I'm really tempted when I'm with you."

Although she didn't hear him cross the room to stop behind her, he was close enough to reach out and reflip the banana to a smile. "I worry about you all the time," he said gruffly, and she whirled around to face him.

"I don't want you to worry. I want to do such a good job taking care of myself that you don't have to worry."

"You're not the problem." He shifted closer, never

taking his gaze from hers. "It's snowstorms and killers and fires and that fucking stalker. When you're not with me, I'm constantly thinking about you."

As she stared at him, nerves and something else— something *amazing*—bubbling inside of her, she said quietly, "I think about you all the time, too."

"I do want to protect you. I do want to do things for you, to make your life easier." He brushed his thumb over her bottom lip. "Whatever I do, you could never be helpless. And you definitely could never be weak."

"But—"

He silenced her with a short, hard kiss. "Does discussing the HDG case with me take away from what you're doing?"

"No."

"Did having me help you last night and stay with you this morning in the aftermath of the fire make you weaker?"

She considered the question. "Not really. But I think I wanted you there too much."

With a shake of his head, he told her, "It's okay to have help. When we go on dive-team calls, we are never alone. We're stronger together, safer together. Getting a second opinion on what truck you should buy won't change what you've accomplished by moving out here and surviving."

When she was quiet for several moments, he added, "Okay?"

"I think so." He'd given her a lot to consider, and her brain chose that moment to go from full speed to a crawl. "Can I chew on what you said and let you know in the morning?"

Hooking an arm around her neck, he pulled her into a hug. "Of course." He kissed the top of her head. While she was debating whether to give in to the hug or pull away, her body decided on its own, sinking against his heat and strength. Giving her a final squeeze, he gently pulled away. When his hands left her shoulders, she swayed with exhaustion.

"Bed," he ordered, narrowing his eyes at her.

"Only if you come too."

Callum considered her. "Deal."

She didn't obey him because she was weak or helpless, her fuzzy brain decided, but because she was dead tired and longing for his cloud-soft bed. Turning to the stairs, she headed to the bedroom without even tossing back a flippant comment, and she couldn't help a pleased smile when he followed right on her heels.

Chapter 15

THE NEXT MORNING, LOU CALLED IAN AS SOON AS SHE figured it was late enough to be considered a reasonable hour. For some reason, pissing off a member of the local, potentially murderous MC seemed like a bad idea. Despite her patience, he didn't answer. When the call went to voice mail, she left a message asking him to call her back.

Although it was Saturday, Callum had headed to his office at Station One early that morning. He'd mentioned needing to catch up on paperwork. Even though he didn't say that he was behind because he spent so much time dealing with her problems over the last few days, Lou felt a guilty pang, knowing she was the reason he was working on a weekend.

He'd delayed leaving, standing next to the mudroom door as he'd eyed her with an unreadable expression. He'd been jangling his keys in a nervous, very-un-Callum-like motion.

"What?" she'd asked.

His eyebrows had pinched together. "Maybe I shouldn't go."

"Why not?"

"I'd rather not leave you here alone while that Brent asshole is roaming around."

Walking over to where he stood, she'd given him a light push. "Go. I'll be fine. I have my phone, and I'll

call you if anything happens. I'll even set your alarm."
He'd had a security system installed in his house the
day before. How he'd managed to do that on such short
notice after a snowstorm was a mystery. That promise
had done the trick, though, and he'd reluctantly headed
to Station One.

To occupy her jittery brain while she waited for Ian to
return her call, Lou started on the list of contacts for the
support groups. She began with the diabetes list, but she
was connected to voice mail for the first several phone
numbers. On the fifth call, someone answered, but he
flatly refused to share information about group members. The next live voice she'd reached was the husband
of the group coordinator. He knew the time and place of
the next meeting, but couldn't tell Lou anything other
than that. After that, call after call went to voice mail.

Ending the latest fruitless call, she sighed. This inves-
tigative work was frustrating. She figured it made sense
that not many people answered, though, since it was
Saturday morning. Punching in the next number, this
one for a group that met in the nearby town of Otto, she
hit "send" and waited for the recorded message.

"Hello?"

The live female voice startled Lou, and she sat up
straight. "Oh, hi! Sorry, I wasn't sure if I'd get anyone
on a Saturday. I had a question about the Otto Diabetes
Support Group?"

"Sure!" The voice warmed. "I'm Mary Dorring, the
coordinator. Were you interested in joining us? We
get together at seven on Tuesday evenings, in the Otto
Library's meeting room."

"Hi, Mary. I'm Lou. I'm actually calling about my

uncle." She figured she'd stick with the uncle story she'd concocted at the VA clinic. It was a little lame, but she couldn't think of any other way to find out someone's identity when she didn't know his name.

"Oh, is he the one wanting to join?"

"He's already a participant—or was. He disappeared on us a few months ago, so we—my family and I—are trying to locate him. I was hoping he's still been attending the meetings."

"Okay," Mary said slowly. "What's his name?"

"Grant Dutton, but he has a few issues with paranoia, so he might be using another name."

There was a pause. "I'm not sure how I can help you, then. I haven't met anyone named Grant Dutton."

"Well, he's white, sixty-five years old, about five-ten, a hundred and fifty pounds, gray hair, and he had two toes on his right foot amputated last year."

"Oh!" The brightness in Mary's voice put Lou on high alert. "Do you have another uncle named…oh, now what was it? Something unusual. Not Dexter, but something similar…Baxter! That was it!"

Lou blinked at the unexpected detour and scribbled *Baxter—brother?* next to Mary's phone number. "Um… yes! Uncle Baxter. Why do you ask?"

"He called just a few days ago, looking for his brother. The description matched what you gave me. He asked for a different name, though…maybe one of your missing uncle's pseudonyms?"

"Very likely," Lou improvised, her brain scrambling for an explanation. "They're really close. If anyone would know what name Uncle Grant was using, it'd be Uncle Baxter. Do you remember what the name was?"

"Oh dear. Let me think. It was Willard something. You don't hear that name very often these days, so I remembered that part. Willard…oh, what was it?"

In the pause that followed, Lou wrote "Willard" on the list under her previous note. Biting her tongue in an effort not to scream at Mary to remember, which would not be helpful, she underlined Willard's name several times, tearing the paper with the last violent stroke of her pen.

"I'm sorry," Mary said. "I don't remember the last name. You can check with your Uncle Baxter, though, can't you?"

"Um, sure." Racking her brain for a reason why she *couldn't* ask her uncle, she came up empty and gave a silent sigh. "Thank you for your help."

"Of course. Good luck locating your uncle."

"Thank you," Lou repeated. "Bye."

As soon as she ended the call, her finger was poised over Callum's name on the screen of her cell. She hesitated, though, not wanting to interrupt him yet again while he was working. The new information was chewing a hole in her brain, however, and she was dying to share it with him. Just as she decided to compromise and send him a text, the phone rang in her hand, making her jump.

It was Ian calling, and she hurried to accept the call. "Ian!"

"Yes." He sounded wary, and rightfully so. She didn't call him regularly—or ever—so her message, combined with her overenthusiastic greeting, must have struck him as very odd.

"I was hoping to talk with you," she said, pacing from

Callum's living room to his kitchen and back again, too wound up to stand still. "Can we meet?"

"Okay." His answer was slow in coming and even more cautious than his initial response.

"Good." After a short pause, she asked, "Today?"

"I'm in Liverton for the weekend," he said.

"I could meet you there," she said. Liverton was only a half hour or so from Callum's house. There was a silence that stretched long enough to make Lou wonder if the call had dropped. "Hello?"

"Don't think that would be a good idea," Ian finally said.

"It doesn't have to be at your…um, club." Lou wasn't sure what the correct terminology was for the lair of an MC. "We could meet at a coffee shop or something."

"Coffee shop?" He sounded like he was choking a little. "In Liverton?"

Lou ran through her limited memories of Liverton. It wasn't really on the way to anywhere, so she'd been through it only once the previous fall, and that was because she'd been lost. It was small, she recalled. Very, very small. And a large percentage of the residents owned several pickup trucks, most of which had been parked in the scrubby yards of the couple dozen houses and trailer homes. For some reason, the Livertonites liked to keep their driveways clear.

"Is there *anywhere* to meet in Liverton? A diner or a gas station or something? This shouldn't take too long."

Instead of answering, he asked his own question. "What's this about?"

"I'd rather tell you in person."

After another long pause, she heard him exhale. "Fine. I'll meet you at the Liverton Bar at eleven."

"The bar will be open that early?" she asked doubtfully.

"It's Liverton," he said, as if that explained it.

"Okay. Thanks."

With a grunt, he ended the call. Lou looked at her phone thoughtfully. When she'd seen him at Station One or even at the scene of her cabin fire, he'd been a lot more…easygoing. Relaxed. Definitely more friendly. With a shrug, she dismissed his abruptness and tapped on Callum's number. Although she hated to interrupt his work yet again, he had possession of a truck she needed to borrow.

——⁓——

It seemed that Callum and his pickup were a package deal.

"I could've gone by myself so you had more time to finish your work," she said as they sped along the highway toward Liverton. "At this rate, you'll never catch up on everything."

He just shrugged off her concern. "You weren't going to Liverton alone."

"Why not?" Lou cocked her head curiously. "It's just to see Ian."

Giving her a steady look before returning his gaze to the road, he said, "Ian's not just Ian, firefighter. He's a member of a motorcycle club—one that looks to be the sheriff's main suspect in a murder."

"Oh!" The mention of the murder brought her mind back to her earlier discovery. "Guess what? I might have found out HDG's name! Well, his first name, at least. Maybe."

"What?"

"I called some of the support group numbers, and one in Otto was answered by the coordinator, Mary. Mary didn't recognize our HDG, but she said someone named Baxter had called a few days ago looking for his brother, who matched HDG's description, down to the missing toes. Baxter said his brother's name was Willard something."

"Willard…something? His brother didn't know his last name?"

Lou shook her head. "He did tell her Willard's last name, but Mary couldn't remember what it was. She just remembered the Willard part because it was unusual."

"So you think Willard is our HDG?"

"It seems possible, doesn't it?" She twisted in her seat to face him. "If it was just a gray-haired guy, I'd think it was probably a coincidence, but two missing men, both with diabetes and eight toes? I think that lowers the odds of it being two different guys considerably."

"I agree." He shot her a sideways grin. "Nice work, Nancy Drew."

"So what's our next step?" she asked, smothering a proud smile at his praise. It warmed her more than was probably good for her future mental health.

He thought for a few seconds before he spoke. "I think we should pass this along to the sheriff's department. They have the resources for this information to really be helpful."

"I agree. I'll give Rob a call." They passed the small "Welcome to Liverton, Altitude 9,745 feet" sign. "Right after we've talked to Ian."

Callum turned left onto Second Street and immediately turned left again to park in the small gravel lot next to the bar. It was big enough for only five or so vehicles, and Callum took the last available spot. Glancing at the clock on the dash reading 10:53, Lou shook her head. Not only was the bar open before eleven, but it was packed, at least by Liverton standards.

She hopped out of the truck and joined Callum by the door. "You know," she said, glancing over her shoulder at the line of pickups, "this is why my truck has—had—such good self-esteem."

He didn't say anything but just looked at her with an expression of wry amusement mixed with a touch of bafflement.

"Anywhere else, my truck would've been considered a POS. But in Field County, she was a shining star of beauty…at least compared to most of the vehicles around here." Lou jerked her head to one pickup in particular, the color of primer except for the orange topper and army-green hood. A huge dent hollowed out the right side of the bed.

With a quiet huff of amusement, Callum ushered her inside.

The place was pretty much what Lou expected—a row of bar stools and a few Formica tables. The stools were all occupied, and everyone turned to look at them as they entered, making Lou feel like an actress in an old Western. If music had been playing, she was pretty sure it would've screeched to a halt.

Since none of the gawkers were Ian, Lou followed Callum to a table tucked in a corner. He pulled out a metal-framed chair with a vinyl seat bearing the requisite rip in it. Once she sat, he took the chair next to hers. She noted that he'd arranged them both with their backs to the wall, facing the door. Callum plucked the plastic-covered menu from its spot propped between the salt and pepper shakers.

The bartender, with her bleached hair and overtanned, lined skin, fit right in with the decor. She appeared to be doubling as the waitress, since she left her spot behind the bar and headed to their table. "What can I get you?" she asked in a raspy smoker's voice.

"Chicken wings?" Callum sent Lou a questioning look, tilting the menu in her direction.

"Yes, please." Leaning closer so she could see the options, she added, "And onion rings. Oh, and cheese sticks. Mmm…an order of mini-pizzas, too. The sausage ones."

The waitress nodded. "Anything to drink?"

"Just water," Lou said, and Callum held up two fingers.

As the server took their order to the kitchen, Callum gave her a look.

"What?" she asked defensively. "I'm hungry."

"That's about a year's worth of grease," he said. "You'll probably regret this in a few hours."

"Probably," she agreed with a shrug. "But it'll taste pretty good going down."

After the waitress dropped off their waters and then returned to her post at the bar, Lou watched Callum thoughtfully as he unwrapped his straw.

It was his turn to ask, "What?"

"I just realized that I've never seen you drink," she explained, stripping her own straw. "Alcohol, I mean. You ordered a beer once, when we talked to Belly, but you didn't drink any of it."

"That's because I don't." He flattened his straw wrapper and folded it in half with careful precision. "Not unless I'm on vacation and far away from Field County."

"Why's that?"

"Can't go on a call if I've been drinking," he explained, snagging her straw wrapper and pressing it smooth. "The dive team isn't that big. I think of how I'd feel if someone died because I decided to have a few beers. To me, it's an easy sacrifice."

"I never thought about that," she said.

"Why haven't I ever seen you have a drink, then?"

With a laugh, she admitted, "Because living out here in the winter is scary. I need to have all my faculties intact to give me the best chance of survival."

He opened his mouth to respond, but Ian Walsh walked through the door, catching both of their attention. The transition from his fire department bunker gear to lots of leather did not detract from his calendar worthiness. Sure, it'd be a whole different calendar, but she'd still hang it on her wall—or would have, if her walls hadn't all burned.

Lou waved, and Ian headed in their direction. As he pulled out a chair, she noticed his expression was unusually grim.

"Thanks for meeting me—us," she said.

In response, he gave a short lift of his chin. When the waitress headed in their direction, Ian shook his head. She retreated back to the bar.

"What's up?" he asked.

"Uh…" His locked-down expression was throwing her off her game. Ian had never been chatty or extra-smiley, but he'd been much more approachable than this hard-edged man sitting across from them. It was making her reconsider sharing the information with this dangerous-looking stranger. Shaking off her doubts, she decided she just needed to say it and get it done. "I heard something about the dead guy found in the reservoir that I thought you should know."

She could tell that she'd surprised him. Even though his expression blanked a split second after he let it show, Lou caught the slight widening of his eyes. He gestured for her to continue.

"There was an item—I don't know what—found on the weight that was holding the body down in the reservoir. It had the Liverton MC logo on it. There's a theory that it was intended to be the murderer's signature."

This time, his startled look was even more obvious. It also took him longer to regain his impassive expression.

"That's all." Lou gave a small shrug. "Sorry it's not much."

"You sure about this?" he asked.

"It was a pretty…reliable source," she said, picking her words carefully. "Plus, it was confirmed by an even more reliable source."

He nodded and stood. "Thank you."

"You're welcome."

Lou watched him stride toward the door. When he'd disappeared outside, she turned to Callum. "That was weird. *He* was weird."

"He's on MC turf now."

"Turf?" she teased. "Are you an extra in *West Side Story*?"

He rolled his eyes, but he was smiling. "Turf, territory—whatever you want to call it. He splits his time between two very different worlds. Are you glad you told him?"

After considering this for a moment, Lou nodded. "Yes. My gut feels like it was the right thing to do. Plus, I get mini-pizzas."

Callum's laugh was loud and free, and it made her proud she'd been the cause of that rare sound.

Not wanting a lecture on sticking her nose in where it didn't belong, Lou called Chris instead of the sheriff on the way back to Callum's and told him what she had learned about HDG's identity. After she finished her long and, admittedly, convoluted story, there was an extended silence.

"Why were you looking into this?" he finally asked.

She shrugged, even though he couldn't see her. "I kicked the poor guy's dead body. That created some feelings of guilt and ownership." She didn't add: *Besides, it sounded like you guys weren't getting anywhere*.

"Okay." Although his tone was fairly expressionless, Lou heard an undertone of "you are so weird."

"Think it'll help to have—well, possibly have—his first name? And his brother's name?"

"I'll definitely look into it."

Lou frowned. That had been a nonanswer worthy of Rob.

"Could you text me the name and number for the Otto support group coordinator who told you about this?" he asked.

"Sure." She shrugged off his un-Chris-like caginess. "I'll send that to you as soon as we finish talking."

"Thanks, and Lou?"

"Yeah?" She knew what was coming from his tone. So much for avoiding a stay-out-of-this lecture by calling Chris rather than the sheriff.

"This case is messy, and it looks like some pretty scary people are involved. Do yourself a favor and stay clear."

"Hmm," she hummed noncommittally, and changed the subject before he could press her for a more definite agreement to cease and desist her amateur investigation. "Any luck tracking down Brent?"

"Not yet." Chris sounded irritated. "He's proving surprisingly elusive for a soft city boy."

"I'm not surprised." When Callum looked over at her, brows raised, she shook her head, silently passing on Chris's answer. "He's always been proficient at self-preservation."

"Well, he hasn't been doing too well, lately—other than at dodging arrest," Chris shared. "He's run into some money trouble—the kind that has burly guys chasing him with baseball bats."

"Really?" Callum looked at her questioningly again, but, this time, she just mouthed "later" at him and returned her focus to her conversation with Chris. "How'd that happen? Not that I know the specifics, but I assume my stepdad pays him a pretty hefty salary."

"Brent was trying to run in some affluent circles, and he wasn't able to do that on his income, as generous as your stepdad is. Brent disappeared two weeks ago. He mentioned something about a 'family situation,' but your stepfather hasn't been able to contact him since. He's been worried."

Lou snorted. "Richard should be worried about what'll happen when I get my hands on that tire-slashing, cabin-burning creeper."

With a laugh, Chris joked, "After we bring him in, do you want five minutes in the interview room with him when the camera's off?"

"Is that an option?" she asked with real interest.

"Ah, no," he said, although he sounded amused. "There've been a couple of people who've tempted me, but I haven't gone over to the dark side yet—that one, at least."

"*That* dark side?" she teased. "Deputy Chris, how intriguing."

As Chris coughed and mumbled something, sounding flustered, Callum shot her a dark look. "Stop flirting with him."

Rolling her eyes, she refocused on the conversation. "Sorry, Chris. Let me know if Brent pops up somewhere, okay? It'll be nice not to imagine him lurking in the bushes wherever I go."

"Will do." Chris sounded as if he'd regained his equanimity. "And don't go looking for trouble."

She laughed. "I'll try, but it won't matter. Trouble finds me."

His sigh was heavy, and she could tell it was only half put-on. "Bye, Lou."

"Later, Deputy."

After ending the call, she sighed. "Everyone's being weird and cagey today." After finding Mary's number on her recent-calls list, she texted it to the deputy while filling Callum in on Chris's side of the conversation.

"What I don't get," she said when she was finished, "is

why Brent's fixated on me. If he has bad guys trying to squeeze the money he owes out of him, why doesn't he just disappear? It's not like I can give him anything more than a free coffee, especially now that he's burned all of my earthly possessions. And why does he want to *kill* me? I would think my being dead would defeat his purpose."

Frowning thoughtfully, he mused, "Maybe he just snapped, blaming you for the way his life has turned to shit?"

"But why?" Lou shifted to look at him. "All I did was date him, dump him, and then avoid him ever since. I haven't had a single conversation with him since I've lived here."

Callum pulled into the alley behind the coffee shop and eased to a stop. "You said he was supposed to take over your stepfather's business once you were…married." He muttered the last word between gritted teeth. "Maybe he blames you for not going along with that plan."

"I suppose," she said doubtfully. "My stepdad likes Brent a lot better than me, especially now. I can't see him handing off control of the company to anyone else, whether I'm Brent's wife or not. Whatever the reason, I just hope the cops find him soon. I'll be glad when I can quit looking over my shoulder for stalkers."

"I second that." He leaned back against the seat and rubbed his eyes.

"Once they nab him, I can concentrate on checking over my shoulder for murderers instead."

His head snapped to the side so he could shoot her *the look*.

Grinning, she opened her door and hopped out of the truck.

Chapter 16

IVY WAS COMPLETELY OVER HER FIT OF SYMPATHY. Lou already knew this from the grudging way her boss had agreed to cover the first half hour of Lou's shift when she'd called that morning. Lou had managed to eat a shocking amount of greasy bar food and then make it back to Simpson in just over an hour, so Ivy only had to tack ten minutes onto her shift. The way the other woman was acting, though, it could've been ten *hours*.

Lou was happy to see her affronted boss leave. When Smelly Jim entered immediately after Ivy had stalked out the front door, Lou began breathing through her mouth, but sent him a big smile. After all, he'd noticed Brent following her. Looking back, the description fit her stalker exactly.

"Sm—uh, Jim," she greeted him, wondering why he was standing in the doorway, half-in and half-out of the shop. "What can I get you?"

"Nothing." He seemed twitchier than normal, his eyes darting left and right. He must've decided to stay, because he took a step into the shop. When the door swung shut behind him, sleigh bells jangling, he jumped and whirled around, as if he'd heard gunshots.

"You okay, Jim?" she asked carefully.

"No." He shook his head, hard enough that the oily strands of hair protruding from his deerstalker hat slapped against his hollow, stubbly cheeks. "I know too much. They're after me." He took a couple of backward steps away from the door, until his back bumped against the ornate shelf holding sweeteners and sprinkles.

"Hey," she said gently, keeping her voice low and even. "You're safe in here. Why don't you sit at that corner table? You can put your back to the wall and watch through the front windows. I'll get you something hot to drink and one of the pastries." Although it was hard to tell under his thick layers of clothes, he looked thinner to her, his features sharpened to the point of gauntness.

"No." He shot a look at the table she'd indicated and then back at the door. "I'd be trapped."

"There's no way anyone could sneak up on you," she assured him. "You'd see them long before they made it to the door. If anyone's headed this way, you can escape out the back before they see you."

"They'll be watching the back." He shook his head again. "I just wanted to warn you."

"No need." Moving slowly and deliberately so she didn't startle him, she reached into the pastry case and pulled out a cinnamon roll, wrapping it in waxed paper. It was the largest thing in the case, and she figured the nuts would provide some protein. She had a feeling that Jim wouldn't stick around long enough for her to make him a sandwich. "The sheriff knows who my stalker is. You described him perfectly. It's a guy I knew back in Connecticut who apparently went off the rails. Here."

She held out the wrapped roll, and he hesitated, eyeing the pastry suspiciously.

"We bake them here," she told him, roll still extended toward him, taking a guess at the reason behind his hesitation. "I know everything that goes into them. It's safe." She hadn't actually supervised the baking of this particular roll, but she figured her small lie was for the greater good if it got him to eat something. When he finally reached for the roll, she bit back a grin of triumph.

"That's not what I needed to tell you," he said, closing his fingers around the roll. Then his gaze shot to the windows, and he swung around, knocking the pastry to the floor. "The back!" He stared at her, his eyes wild. "You promised I could go out the back!"

"This way." Lifting the section of counter, she stood aside to let him pass. "Straight through the kitchen."

He took off, and she heard a clang that she guessed was a baking sheet he'd knocked off the rack. With a sigh, she circled the counter to pick up the roll off the floor. Luckily, it had stayed wrapped, so she scooped it up and dropped it into a paper bag. With a marker, she wrote "Jim" on the bag, and then followed his path through the kitchen, although at a more sedate pace, retrieving the fallen baking sheet on her way.

When she heard the bells on the door jangle, she called, "Be right there." Jim had left the back door open, so she stepped into the alley. No one was in sight, so she tucked the bag on a ledge outside the door, making sure his name showed, and then weighted the folded top of the bag down with a rock the size of her palm. After a final glance around the alley and parking lot didn't reveal Smelly Jim, she pulled the door closed and headed to her waiting customer.

When she got a glimpse of who'd entered, she stifled a sigh, wishing she'd torn out of the shop on Jim's heels.

"Deputy Lawrence," she said, trying to sound as welcoming as she could with gritted teeth. "What can I get you?"

His face was scrunched in a grimace. "What is that smell?"

"Oh, right." Jim's mental state had distracted her from his odor. "Sorry. Smelly Jim just visited." She unlatched the window behind her and shoved it open as far as it would go. "He seems worse than usual—physically and mentally. Is there any way to get him some help?"

"You can call Field County Social Services," Lawrence said, settling on the stool closest to the wall. It bugged her that his annoying ass was contaminating Callum's usual seat. "He won't thank you for it, though. Probably just hide from them."

"Yeah." Gazing past the deputy, lost in thought, she nodded. "He definitely doesn't like any government types. Once he saw you coming, he flew out of here."

He frowned. "I didn't see him leave."

"I let him go out the back." Fingering a to-go cup hopefully, she asked, "Did you want a mocha?"

"You remembered." He looked so smugly pleased by this that she wished she'd pretended she hadn't. "Yes, please. And you shouldn't play along with his delusions."

With a shrug, she busied herself with making his drink to hide her annoyance. "No harm in letting him go out the back if that makes him feel safer."

"You're just encouraging his paranoia. If you agree with him that little green men are going to steal his brainwaves, it makes him believe it even more. You wannabe do-gooders..." He actually tsked.

Squeezing her eyes closed while she counted to five,

Lou wondered how Lawrence managed to survive working with so many people who carried guns. His fellow deputies must be better, more patient people than she was. "So," she said a little too loudly, "how's the murder case going?"

When he fell uncharacteristically silent, she glanced over her shoulder at him. His pale skin hid none of the blush that reddened his face and neck. "I…uh, can't share any information about that," he finally said stiffly.

Rob must've torn him a new one. Lou got an odd satisfaction from the thought. "Okay," she agreed easily, pressing a lid onto his cup and passing it to him. "Have you been on any other interesting calls lately?"

It was the wrong question to ask. By the time he'd finished his twenty-minute monologue, Lou had concluded that her definition of "interesting" was drastically different from Lawrence's. She was also shaking from cold. In desperation, she closed and latched the window, hoping that the residual scent of Smelly Jim would help drive the deputy out of the shop.

Unfortunately, it took another fifteen minutes before his radio crackled to life and the dispatcher called out his unit number. When Lawrence made a face and reached for his shoulder mic to respond, Lou was so relieved that she almost did a little dance.

"Sorry," he told her. "Got to go. Domestic dispute."

Lou just nodded, not mentioning the fact that she had a pair of functioning ears and had been able to hear the call just fine.

"I've been to that address before." Standing up, he pitched his cup toward the trash and missed. He glanced at her out of the corner of his eye, and the tips of his ears reddened. She politely pretended not to notice. "Erma Vann is probably chucking things at her wuss of a boyfriend again."

"You'd better get out there, then," she said, trying to use the force of her mind to shove him out the door, "before he gets injured."

He snorted, walking toward the exit. "Nothing he doesn't deserve. He needs to stand up and act like a man."

"Uh-huh," Lou muttered, distracted by the fact that he was apparently going to leave his discarded cup on the floor with the dregs of his mocha leaking onto the tiles. As much as she wanted him to leave, it would've been nice if he'd taken two seconds to pick up his trash.

"I'll see you later, Lou." He paused by the door. "Hey, would you want to…? Damn it!" The dispatcher's voice interrupted his question. Since Lou had a horrified idea of what he was about to ask, she made a mental note to find out which dispatcher it was and take her flowers in thanks for her excellent timing. As he snapped a response into his shoulder mic, he shoved the door open with his shoulder and gave Lou a final wave.

"Thank you, baby Jesus!" She sighed, letting her forehead rest against the counter. If he'd stayed any longer, she was pretty sure she would've found either a gun or a heavy, blunt object. If her jury was made up of people who knew Deputy Lawrence, she was pretty sure she would be acquitted of his murder.

After releasing a long-contained growl of frustration, she dampened a paper towel and circled the counter to pick up his abandoned cup. She cleaned up the spilled mocha and tossed everything, marveling at how she managed to hit the trash can every single time, unlike a great number of people frequenting the coffee shop.

Immediately after moving back behind the counter, she grabbed for her cell phone. "You're becoming a dependent ninny," she warned herself, even as she tapped his name on her screen.

"You okay?" Callum answered, and just the sound of his voice made her muscles relax. She hadn't realized how tightly she'd been holding herself since she'd started her shift.

Ignoring the voice in her head screaming, "Helpless weakling!" she said, "Yeah. Now."

"What happened?" She could hear a few other voices in the background on Callum's end of the call.

"Where are you?" she asked instead of answering.

He seemed to take this subject change in stride. "Hardware store."

"Yeah? Say hi to Deedee for me if you see her." Just the normalcy of the conversation was calming her.

"No."

Well, there went the normalcy. "No? Why not?"

"Because if I even mention you, she's going to take that as permission to ask a thousand questions about...us."

"Us?" She grinned. It was rare—and fun—hearing Callum sound so flustered.

"*I* don't even know the answers to these questions—not that I'd answer them, anyway."

"You could try 'no comment,'" she suggested.

His answer was a grunt. "Why'd you call? I know it wasn't to hear about Deedee's interrogation."

"Oh." Lou sighed. The misery of a few minutes before had already faded. "I've just had a really sucky shift so far."

"What happened?"

"Ivy was pissed, then Smelly Jim came in—acting super twitchy—and then, to cap it all off, our favorite deputy decided to hang out for forty-five minutes, telling me about Gordon Johnson sneaking his garbage into his neighbor's cans. I've never wanted to commit homicide so very badly."

His chuckle was low, but it still warmed her belly. "Poor Lou. You had to deal with the trifecta."

"I did," she whined, although there was a laugh buried underneath. "Can you stop by the shop after you get done with dodging Deedee's questions?"

"Yeah."

"Thank you! You need to sit on your stool to kill the Lawrence cooties."

"What?"

"Never mind. Have fun shopping. I'll see you soon."

"Shopping? You make it sound like I'm picking out a purse or something."

Rolling her eyes, Lou said, "Fine. Have fun on your ultramacho and manly errand, selecting and purchasing whatever gender-appropriate item you need."

"I will."

"And I'll lock the door and hide in the back until you get here."

"On the positive side," he said, "there isn't anyone *worse* than Lawrence who could come into the shop."

"Except for Brent," she joked.

Obviously, he did not find it funny, since he went

silent for a long moment, and then snapped, "I'll be right there."

"I was"—she realized he'd already ended the call—"kidding."

———

Once Callum arrived, the rest of her shift was fun. The crowd picked up as the afternoon transitioned to evening, so the time flew. When Lou realized it was almost closing time, she was surprised by how quickly her shift had gone.

"Thanks," she told Callum as he drove them the short distance to his house. "For staying for so long. It made it much more bearable-er."

His lips twitched. "Bearable-er? Don't think that's a word. How many years did you go to school?"

With a groan, she admitted, "Too many. And none of my classes taught me the important things, like how to fix a clogged toilet. The clever people on the Internet taught me that."

"Speaking of plumbing, you get to be my assistant tonight."

"Your assistant?" She turned toward him as they pulled into his garage. "Do I get to have mall hair and wear a bedazzled leotard?"

"I didn't understand most of what you just said."

"Like a magician's assistant? With big hair and all the sparkly stuff? Oh, never mind. It's not funny if I have to explain."

"Okay." He paused as they both got out of the truck, speaking again when she'd rounded the pickup and entered the mudroom as he held the door for her. "I need to fix the kitchen sink. Since I was going to do that this afternoon, you can help me tonight."

"Sure." She watched as he bent over, his back to her, to loosen his bootlaces. "You know, you'd make even plumber's crack look good."

His hand slapped over the back of the waistband of his jeans. Finding himself fully covered, he sent her an upside-down glare.

"I'm using my imagination," she told him, heading into the kitchen. Before she'd realized he'd caught up with her, there was a solid smack on her own butt.

"Brat," he murmured in her ear as he passed.

"Foul!" she yelled, rubbing her rear. "That's no way to treat your assistant."

He just gave her a wicked grin. It sat oddly on his normally austere countenance, but it looked good on him. Although she tried to hold her glare, it melted under the heat of his smile.

"Let's do this," she said, turning toward the kitchen sink and slapping her hands together so she didn't do anything stupid, like hurl herself at him and attach her lips to his.

"Don't you want to eat first?"

"Nope." There were too many butterflies in there right now. Food wouldn't fit. "Let's get this done. Unless it's a multihour project?"

"It's just a leaky flange, so it shouldn't be." He headed to a closet. "Unless the plumbing assistant really jacks it up."

"Hey!" she yelled after him. When he emerged from the closet, toolbox in hand, he grinned at her.

"So, what are we doing?" she asked, her eyes darting

to the kitchen sink so they wouldn't land on his too-tempting mouth.

He opened the cabinet beneath the sink, turning onto his side and sliding his head under the trap. "Get under here," he said when she hovered above him.

"Okay," she said doubtfully, "although I don't see how I can hand you tools in a bedazzled leotard in this position." She scooted until she was on her side mirroring him, her head and shoulders inside the cabinet. "You have an unsettlingly clean under-sink cabinet. Don't most people store, I don't know, rat poison and bleach under here?"

"Grab the flashlight. Is that what you kept under your sink?"

Her stomach lurched at the past-tense reference to her cabin, and she used the excuse of getting the flashlight to hide her expression from him. She'd forget about the fire for a few minutes, and then something would remind her, forcing her to experience the horror with painful freshness each time. When she was with Cal, it was easy to pretend she was safe and not scared all the time, and that there wasn't a psycho ex-boyfriend out there who wanted her dead. Although she knew it was a false bubble of security, she still wanted to dwell in it for a little longer.

"No." She turned on the light and aimed it at the drain piping. "I didn't really use bleach or rat poison. I had dish soap, a bag filled with plastic grocery bags, a stack of paper grocery bags, extra scrubbies, a bucket, extra hand soaps, and a few containers of Bar Keeper's Friend. Oh, and a big bottle of white vinegar I used for cleaning."

He'd been positioning the pipe wrench, but paused so he could stare at her. "How could you live like that?"

"It was organized. Well, sort of neatly kept. Maybe a little messy." She watched as he loosened the pipe with the ease of much practice, wanting to turn the conversation away from memories of her cabin. She couldn't think about her once-homey kitchen without picturing it engulfed in flames, and her nerves tightened. "So, how'd you learn all this stuff?"

"What's that?" he asked, his focus still on his work.

"This." She waved her hand at the interior of the cabinet. "Fixing things. You are intimidatingly capable."

"Necessity," he said shortly, unscrewing the nuts on the underside of the sink.

His curtness just made her more curious. "When you got this house, you mean?"

"No." Although she waited for him to elaborate, he remained silent. To encourage him to talk, she made the flashlight jiggle around the cabinet in a truly irritating way, if she did say so herself. With an annoyed grunt, he reached out and clasped his hand over hers, steadying the beam. "Fine. Growing up, if I didn't fix something, it stayed broken. Necessity."

When he ducked out of the cabinet and stood, she wondered if she'd pissed him off with her pushing. She stood as well and saw that he was removing the strainer from the sink. Once he'd lifted the flange, he stripped off a circle of rubber attached to it and attacked it with a wire brush.

"Didn't your mom fix stuff?" she asked, watching with interest as he scrubbed the sink where the flange had been with equal vigor.

"No."

"Why not?"

"Hand me the plumber's putty. And because she wasn't the type to learn to fix something. She was more the type to cry that it was broken and then bring home another loser who wouldn't fix anything."

"Here." After handing him the putty, she watched him apply it with careful precision and considered his use of past tense. "She's not around anymore?"

"No. Gasket, please."

"Uh…" Lou looked between the neat arrangement of tools and Callum's face. "What exactly does a gasket look like?"

He gestured with his chin at a packaged part sitting next to his toolbox.

"Ah." She pulled open the packaging and handed him the gasket. "Why didn't you just say the round rubber thingy?"

Although he attempted to give her *the look*, he was obviously fighting a smile as he accepted the gasket.

"I don't…umm." Even though she was dying to know the answer, she was also dreading the possibility that he would say yes. "Never mind."

"What?" Callum returned to his position under the sink.

Joining him, Lou resumed her flashlight-holding duties, watching as he began tightening the nuts he'd loosened earlier. "Do I remind you of her?" When he didn't answer immediately, nerves made her babble. "Because of the whole princess-of-chaos thing. I mean, I remembered you mentioning your childhood was chaotic, and my life tends to be chaotic, especially these past few weeks since I kicked a dead guy—oh wait, I guess it was earlier than that, because Brent was already shoving pointy objects into my tires—"

"Lou."

"Never mind. I've changed my mind. I don't want to know."

"Lou."

She finally dredged up the courage to meet his eyes. Unfortunately, she moved the flashlight to follow her gaze and he flinched back, raising a hand to block the glare. As he retreated, he banged his head against the edge of the cabinet opening. "Fuck."

"Ouch." Cringing in sympathy, she reached toward him and then pulled her hand back again before she did something to cause more damage. "See? Chaos."

His eyes were squeezed shut for another moment as he rubbed the injured spot. Shaking his head, he resumed his position in the cabinet. "Pipe wrench."

Lou handed it to him, handle first, with extreme caution.

"And no. You don't remind me of her. At all."

"Really?"

"Yes, really. You are smart, and you might not know how to do something, but you figure it out. You're tough and brave, and I respect you." Since he was focused on tightening the pipe as he said this, she was pretty sure he didn't notice her eyes get wet.

"Thank you." He might not have seen her threatening tears, but there was no hiding the waver in her voice. Darn it.

"I'm not saying anything that isn't true. Hand me that rag."

As she held it out to him, she gave a watery laugh. "I don't think you can technically call that a rag."

He wiped away any traces of excess putty. "Why not?"

"It's nicer than most people's guest towels."

With an amused snort, he examined the repair a final time. "Done."

"Nice work, doctor," Lou commended in her best sexy-nurse tone, turning off the flashlight. Although a smile lifted one corner of his mouth, it slipped away when he turned to face her.

"I like having you around."

The butterflies were back. "Good. I like having you around, too."

"It's too quiet when you're not here."

"Yeah?"

"Yeah. Boring, too."

"Oh." It wasn't the cleverest of responses, but she couldn't help it. His admission had stolen all her words.

They stared at each other for a long moment until she couldn't take the rising tension anymore. She had to say something.

"Now what?"

He seemed to be fixated on her mouth. "Now…"

"Yeah?" Her voice had gone husky.

Their faces were so close.

"I'm trying to be patient," he muttered.

She watched his mouth move, too entranced by the shape of his lips to really focus on the meaning of his words. "Uh-huh."

"You've had a very traumatic week." His face moved another inch closer to hers.

"Mmm." She could almost feel his exhale on her skin.

"I shouldn't…take advantage."

Lou felt the warm puff of air against her mouth as he spoke. "Yes," she breathed. "You should."

"Oh, fuck it." His lips crashed hard into hers.

Chapter 17

THE ENCLOSED SPACE QUICKLY BECAME LIMITING. With a frustrated sound, Callum shoved himself out of the cabinet. Grabbing Lou by the hips, he pulled, sliding her across the tile floor until her head cleared the opening. Once she was out, he flipped her onto her back and was on her again, his mouth as hungry for hers as if they'd been separated for years.

She matched his ferocity with her own, forgetting to breathe as they rolled over the hard kitchen floor, switching off who was on top. Without breaking lip-to-lip contact, they yanked at each other's clothes, only partially succeeding in getting naked. In a moment of lucidity, Lou realized she still had an arm in one sleeve of her shirt, and her bra was unhooked, but the straps were still looped over her shoulders.

Callum palmed the back of her head and urged her down for another kiss, and that second of clarity disappeared. What clothes she was or was not wearing didn't matter. All that existed was his mouth on hers and his hard chest against her partially naked skin.

She felt his stomach muscles flex as he sat, bringing her with him so she was straddling his lap. Clutching his upper arms at the sudden movement, she was immediately distracted by the truly impressive circumference of his biceps.

Pulling his head back to break the kiss, he rasped, "Just a second."

Lou stared at him dumbly as he reached above them and yanked at a drawer, pulling it completely off its runners. Although it didn't come close to hitting her, she still ducked as the contents spilled onto the tiles. Oddly, Callum did not seem upset by the mess. Instead, he was making it worse, digging through the scattered items and knocking aside those he didn't want. Finally, he seized a small box with a sound of triumph.

Realizing what he'd grabbed, she cocked her head curiously. "Why do you keep condoms in your kitchen?"

"Preparedness kit," he said before kissing her again, his teeth tugging on her bottom lip. A groan escaped her, sounding so hungry she would've been embarrassed if she wasn't so aroused. Leaving her mouth, he trailed a line of kisses down the side of her neck.

"Why in the kitchen?" she managed to ask, although her voice was as husky as a phone sex operator's.

"I have…a kit…upstairs, too," he explained between kisses. "Everything…I might…need…in an emergency." His lips touched the spot just behind her earlobe, making her shudder. "Flashlight…matches…Leatherman…first aid kit…"

Although her body was screaming for her to shut up and just let him continue the wonderful things he was doing with his mouth, she couldn't let it go. "Sex is an emergency?"

He chuckled, and the vibration against her skin drew goose bumps. "It feels pretty urgent to me now." His teeth scraped lightly against the tendon running up the side of her neck.

"Agreed." Pushing him onto his back, she followed him down, finding his mouth with her own. As her lips met his, she could feel him laugh before the kiss combusted.

Every nerve ending flamed, making her frantic. His mouth worked its way down her throat, nipping and licking as she arched her head back, giving him better access. Everything in her was focused on where they touched, where his lips and hands moved across her skin, leaving flares of pleasure in their wake.

Rolling them over again, Cal moved down even farther, the scruff of his cheek scraping against the sensitive skin over her collarbone. The roughness contrasted with the hot slickness of his lips and tongue, and she arched her back as she groaned, frantic with need.

When first his hands and then his mouth found her breasts, she almost went out of her mind. Her fingers clutched at the back of his head, but his hair was too short to grip. As he sucked a nipple into the heat of his mouth, she grabbed at the back of his shirt and yanked.

"Cal," she gasped. "Please. I need you."

He met her gaze, his normally icy blue eyes burning. "Sparks."

That's all he said. It was just her name, but it told her everything. Their playing ended, and they focused on just shoving the necessary clothes out of the way. He fumbled with unwrapping the condom in a very un-Callum-like way, swearing under his breath, but managed to don the prophylactic before Lou grew desperate enough to grab it from him and do it herself.

Then he was inside her.

They both stilled, staring at each other. It was…Lou didn't have a word for how perfect he felt in her. She'd always mocked the cheesy romantic phrases like "you complete me" or "two halves of the same soul." But Callum felt like he fit. He fit with her and she fit with him, as neatly as that last piece of a puzzle snapping into place.

He started to move, driving all philosophical notions and soppy clichés out of her head. Everything turned to motion and pleasure and driving heat, until she couldn't stay still anymore and rolled them both. After a moment of resistance, Callum shifted to his back, and she followed. Straddling his hips, she took control, loving that she could, that they could trade back and forth without Cal insisting on being the boss all the time. As she watched his face—his beautiful, tightly drawn face—she began to raise and lower her body. His expression, usually so closed, broadcasted everything he felt as she moved above him. When she tightened around him, his head tipped back and he groaned. A pleased smile curved her lips as she flexed her fingers, digging her short nails lightly into his chest. Driving Cal crazy was as fun during sex as it was all other times. As excitement started tightening her muscles, Lou moved faster, finding a rhythm and an angle that was exactly what she needed to drive her over the edge. Her body stiffened as she came, and she called out his name, her fingers digging a little deeper into his unyielding flesh.

As soon as she climaxed, he flipped her onto her back again. Even in her fog of pleasure, she felt a shudder of excitement at the ease with which he moved her. When he was on top, he started thrusting in hard, quick strokes that prolonged her orgasm and brought him along with her. He shouted as he reached his peak, which surprised the tiny corner of her brain that was still functioning. Callum was so controlled in all areas of his life that she assumed he would be as calm and stoic in bed, as well.

He was not calm *or* stoic at this moment. No, he was more of a sweaty, panting, limp, and heavy mess, and Lou loved him for it. All except the heavy part—as more and more of his weight rested on her, her shoulder blades were starting to grind painfully into the tiles. His kitchen floor was *hard*.

"Hey, Cal?" she wheezed.

His response was a grunt.

"Need...to...breathe..."

"Sorry." He flipped onto his back to lie next to her.

Sucking in a relieved breath, she rotated so her head rested on his belly, her body perpendicular to his. Cal's hand stroked the damp strands of hair off her face. She focused on the ceiling, feeling the rise and fall of his stomach as he caught his breath. As quiet settled over them, Lou wondered what he was thinking and then immediately wanted to slap that thought right out of her brain. She'd wallowed in enough sex clichés for the evening. His breathing gradually slowed while she concentrated on the view in front of her.

"Your ceiling beams are really pretty."

"Thank you."

A silence followed, but it wasn't awkward. Lou was still unable to resist the urge to break it. Propping herself up on her elbows, she asked, "Want to go to bed and do this again?"

He was on his feet in a second, yanking his jeans

and boxer briefs up over his hips so he could walk. "Definitely."

With a laugh, she accepted his hand so he could help her stand. Instead of stopping once she was upright, he kept her momentum going until she was lying belly down over his shoulder in a fireman's carry.

"Not loving this," she grunted as he headed for the stairs. "You do know that most people who need to be carried like this are unconscious, right?"

Callum just laughed.

Despite the discomfort, she smiled at the sound. Plus, her current position gave her a really good view of his ass. All in all, it wasn't a bad place to be.

Sunday morning was, in a word, awesome.

After an active night, they lounged in bed until a slothfully late hour, when hunger drove them to the kitchen. Since pancakes were the one thing that tasted good when she made them, she manned the griddle, wearing one of his flannel shirts. Because it was fuzzy, smelled deliciously like Callum, and kept her warm all the way from her shoulders to her knees, she decided to steal it.

As Callum was a bit possessive about the bacon cooking, she ceded that portion of the preparations to him. That did not, however, mean she didn't peer over his shoulder and make pithy comments.

"What is that?"

He gave her a how-do-you-not-know-this look. "A bacon screen."

"Oh." There was a pause. "So…what is that?"

His sigh was deep and long. "It keeps the grease from splattering."

"Oh. Awesome." Lou flipped a pancake. She'd tried for a C, but it had spread into more of an oval blob. The L was better—at least it *was* until she tried to double flip it, and it landed on the edge of the griddle, permanently disfiguring the pancake.

"It is. This way, I don't have to clean the stove after I make bacon."

She nudged him aside so she could open the oven door and pull out the pan of cooked pancakes. "But you'll clean the stove anyway."

He didn't deny it.

She added the blobby C and mutilated L to the stack of pancakes and slid them back into the oven to stay warm. "So now you'll have to clean the stove *and* the grease screen?"

"What's your point?" He sounded a bit snappish.

"Nothing." The corners of her mouth tucked in as she fought her grin. Leaning closer, she hooked a finger in the waistband of his jeans and tugged. His eyebrow went up in question, but he allowed himself to be drawn closer to her. Standing on her tippy toes, she gave him a quick, light kiss and then released him.

"What was that for?" His voice was much warmer now. Apparently, kissing canceled out the criticism of his grease screen.

"Just 'cause I felt like it."

"Yeah?" It was his turn to tug her toward him. "Well, I feel like it, too."

His kiss was not quick, nor was it light. It was deep and hard and thorough, and left her leaning against the counter, panting for breath when he finally released her. Grinning, he returned to his bacon.

"Whoa," she muttered under her breath, fanning herself with the spatula she still held in her numb fingers.

His grin widened.

Callum's bacon was, not surprisingly, perfect. Her pancakes, despite their unfortunate shapes, tasted good, although Lou was pretty sure she'd like anything she ate in her current happy daze. Once breakfast was done and Cal took over cleanup, however, she started to feel the usual restlessness as she fought off thinking about things like fires and deaths and ex-boyfriend stalkers.

"What are you doing?"

Tugging on her stocking hat, she said with what she thought was a commendable lack of condescension, considering the answer was obvious, "Dressing."

"You're going outside?"

"I am."

"You don't have to be at work for almost two hours."

"So?"

"So why are you going outside?"

"I'm feeling twitchy. I need to burn off some energy—and some pancakes."

His grunt still sounded confused.

"Want to come?"

"Don't we spend enough time outside on calls and training and doing daily life tasks?" he asked.

"But this will be fun."

He didn't look convinced.

"Please?" She tried her most winning smile.

"I still think you're insane." Despite his words, he moved toward his coat.

"That's nothing new," she scoffed.

Although he snorted, she saw a smile fighting its way to the surface. "C'mon. Let's go so you can run off that energy."

Bouncing out the door in front of him, she jumped off his deck into the two-foot drifts covering his back yard. Callum followed more slowly, shaking his head.

"I think you absorb all the caffeine from the coffee shop or something," he commented, eyeing her as she scooped snow into a mound. "It's not normal for anyone over the age of five to be this peppy."

She grinned, rolling her large lump of snow into an even bigger ball. "What can I say? I'm a mutant. This snow is awesome, though. It's never this wet up here." Normally, snow in Simpson was either powdery fine or frozen into rocklike drifts.

Once she had a decent-sized ball, she started on another.

"Snowman?" Callum guessed, eyeing the large lump of snow critically.

"Of course."

"Your lower section is uneven."

"So fix it."

So he did.

They were laughing. *Laughing*. While Brent was in the woods, frustrated beyond sanity and freezing, they were having fucking *bonding* time. Her gaze turned in his direction, and he shifted behind the trunk of the tree next to him, although he kept her in his sights. She barely paused before turning back to the man.

It was like Brent was invisible, so easily dismissed.

The way she looked at that guy, on the other hand, as if he was the center of her whole world, made Brent feel unhinged.

He started to pace. That guy needed to go. Once *he* was gone, she'd refocus on Brent. He'd become her sun, the person she couldn't live without. He stopped pacing so he could listen. That feeling was still there, the one that told Brent he wasn't alone. That person was always there, watching him and trailing him, judging his every movement.

The wind gusted through the trees, making the branches squeak and sway.

"Stop!" Brent hissed in an almost silent exhale. He wasn't sure if he was talking to the wind or his stalker… or maybe his own brain.

—〰—

Lou stepped back, eyeing the snow person. "Wow. I've never seen a snowman that…uh, symmetrical."

Callum just gave a satisfied nod. "Where are you going?" he asked.

"Our extremely symmetrical snowman is missing limbs," she said over her shoulder as she tromped through the snow, heading toward the woods. "I'm going on an arm hunt." He started after her, and she shook her head. "I'll be right over there. Why don't you fix his face while I grab a couple of sticks?"

"Fix his face?" Cal scowled, peering at the snowman. "What's wrong with his face?"

Struggling to hide a grin, Lou said, "I'm not exactly sure. It just seems…goofy, somehow. Maybe his eyes are uneven?" She bounded toward the woods before she started laughing. When she reached the first line of trees, she looked back to see Callum with his frowning face close to the snowman's perfectly aligned features. Lou had to cover her mouth with her gloved hand to hold back the laugh that wanted to escape.

She turned her attention to the ground, but snow had covered most of the fallen branches. When she peered deeper into the woods, she could just make out a fallen pine tree, propped against a boulder. Lou made her way to the needleless skeleton and snapped off two small branches that would work as snowman arms. After a short hesitation, she broke off another four so Callum could choose the best two from a selection.

As she pivoted away from the dead tree, a small sound caught her attention. She stopped, listening. The noise didn't repeat. In fact, Lou's stillness made her realize how quiet everything was. There were no animal noises or branches creaking in the wind or rustling pine needles. It was just…silent.

A shiver shot up her spine, and she forced her feet to move quickly toward Cal's yard. *Nothing's out there*, she told herself firmly. It was just the whole Brent thing making her paranoid. Despite her stern mental reassurances, she increased her speed until she was almost running. Just before she passed the final line of trees, she stopped again.

"What is it?" Cal called across the yard, starting to make his way toward her.

"Nothing," she said, walking toward him and holding out the branches.

He took them from her, but his serious expression didn't change. "Why'd you stop back there?"

"It was just my imagination." Hooking her hand in the crook of his elbow, she urged him back toward the snowman. "I thought I caught a whiff of Smelly Jim."

"Huh." Turning his head, he raked the trees with his gaze.

The sound of a vehicle engine approaching caught both of their attentions.

"Expecting someone?" Lou asked.

Shaking his head, he dropped the arm sticks next to the snowman and walked around the side of the house. After gathering a handful of snow, she hurried to catch up with him. When they rounded the corner to the front of his house, Lou saw a sheriff's squad car parked on the street. Chris left it running and climbed out of the driver's side. As he rounded the hood, lifting his hand in greeting, Lou threw the snowball, hitting him square in the chest.

Stopping abruptly, Chris eyed the remains of the snowball plastered to his coat before looking at Lou. "Assaulting an officer is a crime," he said.

She raised her hands. "It was completely unpremeditated, with no malicious intent."

He rolled his eyes. "Tell that to the jury."

"Chris." Callum stepped closer to Lou, draping a possessive arm over her shoulders. Although she lifted her eyebrows, she let it stay.

"Hey, Cal." The deputy looked amused as he eyed them. "Do you two have a minute? This won't take long."

"Sure," Lou answered. "C'mon in."

They went in through the front, all of them staying close to the door. Although she felt more comfortable in Callum's house now than she had the first time she'd been there, the expanse of immaculate floors was still intimidating, especially when she was wearing snow-covered boots.

"Thank you for the tip—about the murder victim's first name," Chris said as soon as Callum closed the door behind them. "That proved to be really helpful. I was able to ID him."

"Really?" Lou bounced on the toes of her boots. "That's great! Who is he? Do you know what happened to him? Do you have some new leads now about who the killer is?"

Chris blinked at her, speechless for a moment.

With an amused snort, Callum muttered, "Welcome to my world."

"Ah…" Chris shot Callum a glance that Lou translated as a look of masculine solidarity. "This hasn't been confirmed. DNA testing's been done, but that takes some time to get back from the state lab."

"Who is it? Can you tell us?"

After a second, he nodded. "You need to keep this under your hats until the tests come back and it's released to the media."

Lou made a zipping-her-lips motion.

"His name is—probably—Willard Alan Gray."

"Will Gray," Cal said thoughtfully. "I know that name."

"He lived on the outskirts of Simpson, off of Esko Hill Road."

"Right." With a nod, Cal added, "Kind of an odd guy. Kept to himself, except when that new development was about to be built right by his place a few years back. He came to a couple of city planning meetings to protest it."

"That's him," Chris agreed. "The sheriff actually lives in one of the new Esko Hill houses. Said that after the development was built, Gray hardly ever left his cabin."

"Was he reported missing?" A flood of questions poured through Lou's brain, triggered by the new information.

"Not officially," the deputy said. "His old army buddy showed up a couple of weeks ago, though. Baxter Price."

"Uncle Baxter!"

Chris gave Lou an odd look and then continued. "Anyway, Price said he and Gray communicated through email and occasional phone calls. After months of silence, Price became concerned and came here to check on him. He's staying at Gray's place for the time being."

With a frown, Lou asked, "Why didn't Baxter make the connection between his missing friend and the body found in the reservoir?"

"Apparently," Chris answered with a grimace, "Price is not a fan of law enforcement officers. It was like pulling teeth to get him to talk to me. He never officially reported Gray as missing, but just started poking around on his own, like some people do." His pointed gaze fell on Lou, but she just blinked at him innocently. "As far as knowing about the body, I got the impression he doesn't interact with the other people in town much, so he missed out on all the gossip."

"His friend was all Willard had?" That struck Lou as sad. "No family, then?"

"Not that we could find. Price doesn't know of any, but I don't know how reliable he is."

Callum gave the deputy a sharp look. "You think he's lying to you?"

"Not intentionally," Chris said. "But he clearly has some mental issues."

"Did no one local know that Willard was missing?" Lou frowned at the thought. "I know he rarely left the house, but I would think the neighbors would notice when he went from reclusive to completely gone, especially when an anonymous body is discovered."

"Apparently not," the deputy said. "No one reported it to us, at least."

Her brain was racing with new theories and questions. "If he was pretty much a hermit, why would anyone care enough to kill him? Is there any connection between Willard and the Liverton MC?"

Chris's expression shut down. "I can't discuss this case with you any further, Lou. In fact, I shouldn't have told you what I did, but I thought you deserved it for giving me the information that led to a probable ID."

"Okay," Lou said, deflating. Callum reached over and squeezed her shoulder. "Thanks for telling me. It's good to know who he is, at least."

With a short nod of acknowledgment, Chris reached for the doorknob. "Please keep this to yourselves."

"Of course," Callum said, and Lou nodded.

"Enjoy the rest of your weekend." Stepping outside, the deputy closed the door behind him.

Lou and Callum eyed each other for several long, silent moments. The sound of Chris's squad car faded into the distance.

"Whiteboard?" Callum asked.

A grin spread over Lou's face. "Yes, please."

Chapter 18

THERE WASN'T MUCH TIME TO SCRIBBLE MORE THAN the basics before Lou had to head to work. The warm, sunny day brought in locals and tourists alike, and her shift flew by quickly. Tyler Coughlin stopped in for a hot chocolate, but she didn't have the time or the privacy to ask the sheriff's son for the latest gossip on the HDG case before he flipped his boy-band bangs out of his eyes and left.

She frowned. It really wasn't the HDG case anymore. He had a name now. Willard Alan Gray. But as much as she would have liked to ponder how knowing who the victim was changed the direction of the murder case, a family with four small kids trooped into the shop, asking about the menu and distracting her from a whole new flock of theories.

There was a short lull around five when the shop emptied, and Lou frantically cleaned, not sure if the rush would start again. She'd had only a few minutes to tidy the day's mess when an SUV pulled into the lot. With a heavy sigh, she returned to her spot behind the counter, watching as a couple got out of the vehicle. The man opened the rear door and clipped a leash to the collar of what looked like a golden retriever mix.

Callum pulled up, distracting her from her potential customers. She watched him back into his usual spot at the far end of the lot. As he walked toward the front door, she had to repress a stupidly lovesick sigh. Even in multiple winter layers, the man was just mouthwatering.

With a snort, she forced her gaze away from him. She was being ridiculous, worse than a junior high girl with her first crush. If she'd been a cartoon, her pupils would be heart-shaped. The bells on the door jangled, jerking her out of her self-mockery.

"Sparks," Callum said. "Get out here." He stepped back outside, the bells ringing again as the door closed.

"Okay," she said slowly. That was odd. Although she didn't like to jump when Callum ordered her to jump— unless it was something dive-team related—curiosity had her heading for the door.

He was talking to the couple when she stepped outside, and she made her way toward them. As she approached, the dog began to wag his tail so hard that his whole body wiggled. All three people looked at her, and she slowed, not able to read their expressions.

Handing the end of the leash to the woman, the man crossed the short distance to Lou and grabbed her in an enveloping hug, lifting her off her feet. She stared over his shoulder at Callum, giving him frantic eye signals to come save her from this inappropriately affectionate stranger, but he wasn't moving. Not only didn't he rescue her, but he was smiling.

The man put her back on her feet but kept his hands on her shoulders. There were tears in his eyes, she noted with awkward horror. What was happening here? "Thank you."

She just blinked at him.

"You don't recognize me?" He gave a watery

laugh as he released her. "I guess I am drier now. And conscious."

"Oh!" She bounced on her toes as realization struck her. "You're the one we pulled out of the water the other night. And your dog."

"Yes. Howard Spalding. And that's Moses. We'd be dead if it hadn't been for you guys, so thank you." He laughed again. "It's such a small thing to say after something like that, but I still wanted to say it. Thank you."

"You're welcome." She wasn't sure what else to do in this situation. "I'm glad you're okay. That you're both okay."

The woman came over with Moses bounding ahead of her. Once the dog reached Lou, he didn't slow his forward momentum, but jumped up and planted his paws on her middle.

"Moses!" the woman scolded. Tears flowed freely down her face, and Lou felt a sympathetic burn behind her own eyes.

"It's fine," Lou said, focusing on scratching the dog behind his ears so she wouldn't have to look directly at the crying people. "He's beautiful."

"Thank you so much," the woman sobbed. "I would've lost them both if it wasn't for you and the other rescuers."

Howard put an arm around her and pulled her in to his side. "This is my wife, Trudy."

"Nice to meet you," Lou said, wincing inwardly at the trite words. "And you're welcome. I'm just glad they're okay."

Overtaken by sobs, Trudy grabbed her in a hard hug. Lou patted her back awkwardly. She met Callum's eyes over the other woman's shoulder and mouthed, "Help me."

He shook his head and grinned. "Enjoy it," he mouthed back.

Once Trudy's tears had eased to the occasional sniffle, she took a step back.

"Um…do you want to go inside and have some coffee?" Lou asked.

"No," Howard answered, draping his arm around his wife again. "Thank you, but we have to be going. We're headed back to Colorado Springs tonight. I wanted to stop by to thank you before we left, though."

"How'd you know to come here?" Lou asked.

"The EMTs said you two would probably be here," he explained. "Could you thank the other guys on your dive team for me, too?"

"Of course," she said.

After additional hugs and thanks and yet more tears, the Spalding family drove away, waving and honking as they left. Once they were out of sight, Lou and Callum entered the shop as small, sharp flakes of snow began to prick their exposed skin.

"*Brr*," Lou said as she stepped into the warmth of the small building. "I didn't realize how cold it had gotten."

Callum ran his hands briskly over her upper arms. As she began to thaw, she smacked him on the belly.

"What?" he asked, looking offended.

"You just left me to those people's crying and hugging and gratitude!"

He laughed. "You deserved it."

"I didn't know what to say," she admitted. "I mean, what *can* you say when someone is thanking you for saving their life? I really didn't do anything. You and Wilt went into the water. I just pulled on a rope. They were acting like I'm a hero or something."

"You are a hero." Leaning in close, he kissed her temple. "Get used to it."

—␣—

"Holy cow," Lou breathed later that evening, standing close enough to Callum's living room window that her exhalation fogged the glass. After peeking over her shoulder to see if he'd noticed, she used her sleeve to surreptitiously rub away the smudge.

"What?" he asked.

"The wind is just crazy," she explained, taking a half step away from the glass. "It's not snowing anymore, but it might as well be, the way it's blowing around. I can't even see that spindly looking pine tree in your yard. What's the visibility—two feet?"

"Ground blizzard," he said, crossing the living room to stand behind her. His arms crossed over her upper chest as he pulled her back against him and rested his chin on the crown of her head. Casual physical affection from Callum still surprised her, but Lou had to admit it was really, really nice. "Glad I don't have to drive in this."

When the radio sounded, Lou sighed, giving his forearm a light smack. "You just *had* to say that, didn't you?"

His only response was a groan of his own as he grabbed the radio off the breakfast bar and headed for the mudroom. Lou followed, automatically pulling on her outerwear as fast as she could as she listened to the dispatcher.

"Dive Rescue One, there's been a report of an unidentified victim falling through the ice on the west side of Mission Reservoir. Caller is on scene and witnessed the victim enter the water less than one minute ago. Victim is conscious and attempting self-rescue. Dive Rescue One, do you copy?"

Callum depressed the button as he grabbed his gear bag and charged into the garage. "1210 copies. En route with 1244 to Station One. ETA three minutes."

"Copy."

After waiting for the paramedics to call in their status, Callum spoke into the radio again. "Dispatch, can you see if Fire and Sheriff are available to assist?"

"Affirmative."

As they hopped into the truck, Lou waited for other dive-team members to speak, but the radio stayed ominously silent. Callum backed out of the garage as soon as the pickup had an inch of clearance below the rising door.

"Are we it?" Lou asked, wishing her voice didn't sound so small.

"Wilt's still gone," he said grimly, peering through the white sheet of blowing snow. "Derek and Chad ran to Denver this morning to pick up that part for the van, and the pass was closed before they could get back. Phil lives over in Burne, which means it'll take him two hours to get to Mission in this weather. So, yeah. We're it. Hopefully, Fire and some deputies will make it out to help."

"Okay." Her knee jerked nervously up and down. "Poor Derek."

"What?"

"He has to share a hotel room with Chad."

"If he's lucky. Otherwise, they'll have to bed down in the truck cab."

Her laugh was too loud for the joke, revealing her nerves. "They'll need to cuddle, in order to share body heat."

He snorted as they pulled up to Station One. Grabbing their gear, they ran for the building. The cutting wind stole Lou's breath, and she burst through the door into the warmth of the station. As Callum donned a dry suit, she started the van and opened the overhead door before fastening his suit for him. Even by the time they left the station, no firefighters had made it in yet.

Thanks to the clumsy nature of the suit, with its attached gloves and boots, Lou drove the van. It was hard to find a balance between urgent speed and care, and the wind gusted hard enough to rock the van, adding to her tension. Clutching the wheel with both hands, she leaned forward and tried to peer through the white curtain of snow in front of her.

"Let me know if I'm going to run into anything, okay?" she tried to joke, although her voice shook.

"Steady," he said in a calm voice. She could almost feel her blood pressure dropping just listening to him. "Slow down if you need to. If we wreck, we can't help anyone."

"Okay." Taking a deep breath and then letting it out, she forced her fingers to ease up on the steering wheel. The reservoir was only five miles away from Station One. She could do this.

"What I don't get," Callum said, still in that composed, easy tone, "is how anyone managed to go through the ice on Mission. Verde, I'd get. There are always weak spots on Verde once the temps start warming up. But Mission? What'd this guy do? Chop a hole before jumping in?"

Her laugh came out in a nervous rush. "Thanks." When he cocked an eyebrow in question, she explained, "For settling me down, I mean."

"You're doing fine, Lou." His dry-gloved hand reached over and squeezed her leg above her knee.

"Thanks," she said again, her gaze fixed at the tiny portion of road she could see in front of her. "Now keep your hands to yourself and quit distracting the driver."

It was his turn to laugh. "I thought you liked how I distracted you."

"I said 'settling me.' Your touch is more unsettling than settling."

He laughed again but removed his hand from her leg. The horrible visibility didn't allow her to dwell on how she missed the weight of it.

They were quiet for the remainder of the drive, the silence broken by short, stressed transmissions from the other emergency vehicles trying to make their way to the reservoir. Callum managed to convey their progress over the radio, even wearing his clumsy gloves, for which Lou was thankful. She didn't need one more responsibility, not when her entire focus was keeping the dive van on the road.

When the van's headlights reflected off the sign for the reservoir turnoff, she almost burst into tears of relief. Instead, she bit the inside of her lip hard enough to send a shock of pain through her. Lou reminded herself that this was just the beginning of the call, and the hardest part was yet to come.

Although she knew, thanks to the radio transmissions, that none of the other first responders were even close to the reservoir, it was still a disappointment not to see any flashing lights through the blowing snow.

"Where do I go?" she asked, leaning even closer to the windshield. "I know I was just here, but it looks different in the dark and with the snow flying."

"Take a left."

She did, bumping across the frozen ruts in the gravel road. The wind had blown most of the snow clear, leaving only a few hard-as-rock drifts to maneuver. Lou was concentrating so hard on navigating the narrow road that Callum's voice made her jump.

"Dispatch, are you still on the line with the caller?"

"Negative," she replied. "I lost the connection four minutes ago. I've been trying to call him back, but he's not answering."

Lou's stomach clenched. If the complainant wasn't answering his phone, there was a good chance he was doing something stupid, like going onto the ice to help the victim. She braced herself for the likelihood that she and Callum were going to have to pull two hypothermic people out of the water.

"Fuck," Callum muttered off the air before he depressed the mic button again. "Copy. Let me know if you reach him. 1210 and 1244 are on scene. I don't see the caller on shore, but visibility is sh—uh, not good."

"Copy."

"Park up there," he said, pointing to a section of shore mostly blown free of snow.

"Copy," Lou said, making him send a wry look in her direction. She shrugged as she eased the van into the spot he'd indicated. It was hard not to fall into the radio pattern of speaking when on a call.

"There!" he said abruptly, and Lou jumped, hitting the brakes. "There he is."

She squinted through the blowing snow, realizing that the cover had lightened slightly between gusts of wind. A dark circle of water surrounded an even darker spot before it disappeared under the surface.

"Oh shit!" she yelped. "I think he just went under."

They both climbed into the back of the van. Callum sat to slide his arms into the buoyancy control device that was strapped to the oxygen tank. Ripping off her gloves, Lou secured the BCD, arranging the regulator and gauges to hang over his shoulders for easy access. Lifting the weight belt, she paused, frowning.

"Is this going to be enough with the buoyancy of your dry suit?" she asked.

He shook his head. "I already have weights in the BCD pockets," he said, motioning for her to attach the belt. She did, as he checked the tank pressure and tapped the regulator button, getting a burst of air in response. His mask was next, and she tucked the edges beneath his hood, trying to ignore how hard her hands were shaking. He stood, lifting the oxygen tank from its stand as he did so.

"Harness," he said, and she scrambled to fasten it around him. When she crouched to slide on his fins, he shook his head and held out his hands for them. "I'll put them on closer to the entry point."

She nodded, following behind him as he exited the back of the van. Before he opened the door, he stopped.

"Gloves and radio," he said.

Shaking her head at her scattered brain, she hurried to yank on her gloves and grab her portable.

The wind was a shock as they left the van. "Stay on shore," Callum shouted over the howling gusts. "Call it in once I'm in the water."

She nodded silently, her eyes fixed on his masked face. He leaned in and kissed her, quickly and firmly.

"You've trained for this," he yelled as he walked onto the ice. "You've got this." And then he was gone, swallowed by a wall of snow.

Lou stood, frozen, until a tug at the rope coiled in her hands jerked her out of her paralysis. She hurried to release the next loop, giving slack until Callum's forward movement stopped. After she counted to twenty-eight, there was forward pressure on the rope again. She guessed he'd been putting on his fins during the pause.

Although she squinted toward where she'd momentarily glimpsed the hole in the ice, all she could see now was snow. She fumbled for her portable radio and pushed the mic button.

"Dispatch, 1244."

"Unit calling, you're unreadable," the dispatcher's voice responded.

Turning so her back was to the wind, she curled around her radio and tried again.

"1244, go ahead."

"Diver One is in the water," she said in a near shout as the wind gave an extra-hard blast.

"Copy. Diver One in the water."

"Do you have an ETA for other responding units?" Lou asked, desperation creeping into her voice.

There was a pause, and then a different voice said, "Fire Rescue Four. We're approximately twenty minutes out."

"Ambulance Two. We're right behind Fire Rescue Four."

"County 401." She recognized Rob's voice. "Two squads en route. ETA twenty-five minutes."

"Fire Rescue One," another person said. "Just leaving Station One. Eighteen minutes out if we manage to stay out of the ditch."

Lou closed her eyes. Eighteen minutes felt like a lifetime. "Copy."

Dropping her radio into her coat pocket, she released another loop of rope. "You've got this, Cal," she muttered, squinting through the snow. "You've got…"

She trailed off as the rope went slack in her hands.

Staring at the suddenly limp line, she started recoiling the rope, her movements getting jerky with panic as she pulled it in with no resistance. She gasped when the end appeared, sliding across the ice and then bumping along the shore. Dropping the coils, she grabbed the end, yanking it off the ground.

It had been cut. The nylon fibers were sliced evenly across the end. There was no way it could've snapped so cleanly. She stared for several precious seconds, trying to comprehend why his safety rope had been cut. Had the line gotten hung up on something and he had to use his diving knife to slice himself free?

She stared through the snow until her eyes stung, but she couldn't see anything beyond the sheet of white. *He's okay*, she told herself. *With all his gear, he'll stay warm, even in the freezing water*. Without the rope, though, getting the victim—or victims, if the caller had decided to try to play rescuer—out of the water was going to be difficult, if not impossible. She had no idea what to do.

But she had to do something.

With sudden determination, she ran back to the dive van. She scrambled into a dry suit, twisting awkwardly to fasten the back. The hood pulled at her hair as she used gloved fingers to poke it back out of the way. Getting into her BCD and weight belt took much too long, thanks to her nerves and the dry gloves. As she tested her regulator, she looked at the unfamiliar-looking breathing apparatus and remembered reading that cold-water regulators were required so they didn't freeze and allow oxygen to free-flow, releasing her precious air supply. Her previous tropical diving experience had definitely not prepared her for this.

Eighteen minutes, though. Eighteen minutes until help arrived, and that help wouldn't include any trained rescue divers. Eighteen minutes was too long for the victims. If something was wrong, it would be too long for Callum, too. Lou beat back that line of thinking and the panic it induced.

Stupidly enough, her mask was the hardest thing to manage. Her gloved fingers were useless at tucking the edges under her hood, and she finally gave up in frustration, leaving the mask as it was while hoping it would still form an airtight seal. After fastening a harness around her, she dug her portable out of her coat pocket. Carrying it and her fins, she headed back out into the howling wind.

She tied the end of the safety line to a metal bracket

on the dive van and stepped onto the ice. It was solid beneath her feet. Cal's ice-rescue training lecture skipped through her mind then, about how no ice was safe—ever.

Although she tried to keep a straight line, she was walking blind. The dive light hooked to her BCD reflected off the sheets of sideways-driven snow. Her stomach twisted with the fear that she'd walked right past the hole when the wind settled for just a few seconds—just long enough for her to glimpse the dark smudge of water against the whitish-gray surface of the surrounding ice.

Her steps grew cautious as she approached the hole. She dropped to her hands and knees and then her belly, despite the growing urgency demanding that she hurry. The ice was firm beneath her, with no cracking or signs of weakness, and she frowned as she slid to the edge, suddenly remembering Callum's throwaway comment during the tense drive over.

There are always weak spots on Verde once the temps start warming up. But Mission? What'd this guy do? Chop a hole before jumping in?

The edges were uneven, but smooth...and had *definitely* been cut by some kind of tool. What the hell was going on?

Staring at the dark water as if it would tell her the answers, she reached for the radio and pulled it close to her face.

"1244, Dispatch."

"1244, go ahead."

"Diver One's safety rope was cut," she said. "Diver Two entering the water."

There was a startled pause, and then the dispatcher responded, "What is the status of Diver One? 1244, do you copy? Do you have another dive tender on scene? Is there someone else on shore?" Her questions increased in urgency as Lou fumbled to pull on her fins. Lou picked up the radio again.

"Status of Diver One is unknown. No one else is on shore. It's just me." Her voice wobbled on the last words, and she placed the radio back on the ice.

Closing her lips around the regulator mouthpiece, she slid feetfirst into the black water.

Chapter 19

ALTHOUGH THE MAJORITY OF HER WAS COVERED with the dry suit, the frigid water on the exposed skin of her face made her gasp. She sank quickly—too quickly—and fumbled to inflate her BCD. Although her thick gloves made her clumsy, she finally managed to add air, and her descent slowed. The light attached to her BCD cast an eerie glow, illuminating a short distance directly in front of her. When she turned her head without also rotating her body, the darkness was absolute.

Her breathing was too quick, too shallow. If she kept panting like that, she knew she would use up her air much too quickly. She counted to four on her inhale and then exhaled for four counts, tipping her light up so she could watch her bubbles ascend. The sight calmed her a little, that evidence of her ability to still breathe, despite her nightmarish surroundings.

Her ears ached, and she pinched the rubber over her nose and blew, equalizing the pressure. That familiar action settled her nerves even more, reminding her of all those sunlit sea dives she'd gone on before Brent became a fourth on their family vacations to the Caribbean.

Lou checked her depth gauge, which showed her at eighteen feet. She turned in a circle, careful not to get tangled in her safety line. Her light penetrated less than eight feet through the murky water and revealed absolutely nothing. Forcing her breathing to slow once again, she tugged her dive knife from the sheath attached to her dry suit.

Reaching back, she tapped it against her tank, creating a pinging noise. Sound traveled through water four times faster than through air, and the sharp ding of metal against metal cut through the reservoir better than her light. Lou paused, waiting for a response. Once again, she had to force herself not to hold her breath. There was nothing, though, and she quickly cut off panicked thoughts about what was keeping Callum from answering her signal.

Lou attempted to ease the knife back in the sheath, but the tool refused to cooperate. After several unsuccessful tries, she gave a frustrated grunt and kept the knife in her hand, telling herself sternly not to cut anything vital, like a safety line, regulator hose, or an artery.

As she'd messed with her knife, she'd descended another ten feet until her light glanced off the weedy bottom just beneath her. The reservoir averaged eighty feet in depth, so she was relieved this was a relatively shallow area. After equalizing the pressure in her ears again, she turned onto her front and began searching in larger and larger circles.

The bottom was littered with junk—from beer cans to umbrellas to fishing reels—everything that fell or was thrown into the reservoir during the summer months when the water warmed to a balmy forty-two degrees Fahrenheit. Her light created odd shadows around the waterlogged objects, turning everyday items into ominous shapes.

The image of HDG's body kept flashing in her mind, no matter how many times she forced the visual from her brain. The possibility that she'd stumble upon another body in this eerie darkness made her breathing quicken, forcing her to consciously slow it down, again counting her inhales and exhales. There were two victims in the water, she reminded herself, plus Callum—although she refused to think of him as a victim. It would be a *good* thing to find them. Despite that, she shivered beneath the thermal layer under her dry suit.

Systematically scanning for a glimpse of Callum or the victims, she turned her light and gaze from left to right and then forward again. Every so often, she would rotate to look upward, shining the light into the murky, endless water, which brought a stifling rush of claustrophobia each time. It was hard to believe the surface existed less than thirty feet above her.

She checked the pressure gauge and saw that her tank was half-full. Giving a near-hysterical huff of laughter into her regulator, she commended herself on her optimism. It wouldn't be good to start thinking about her tank being half-*empty*.

Lou refocused on her search, sweeping her light to the left. She moved it past the figure before it registered. With a jerk of delayed reaction, she aimed the light back at the dim form as she turned, kicking her fins as hard as she could to propel her toward the human-shaped shadow.

As she grew closer, the shape became more defined, and her muscles tightened with excitement as she recognized the back of a figure in a dry suit—Callum! Her light reflected off his oxygen tank, and she renewed her forward plunge. Kicking closer, however, Lou had a moment of confusion when she saw a second dry-suited figure in front of Cal.

It appeared that they were grappling, which didn't make any sense. Lou stared, confused, as the second diver shoved Cal, making him stumble back. His fins kicked up clouds of sediment that fogged the water, adding to the surreal image.

It had been just a couple of seconds, but time felt stretched to Lou, like she'd been watching the horrifying tableau for hours. The second diver's dry suit was green and black—definitely not one of the dive team's.

And he was attacking Callum.

At that realization, she kicked forward toward the pair, plowing into his shoulder and knocking him away from Cal.

As she glanced back to check on Callum, she saw he was swimming toward them, shouting something into his regulator. Distracted, she didn't see the stranger's swing until her head was jarred to the side, knocking her face mask askew.

The shockingly cold water hit her eyes as her mask filled, paralyzing her for a frozen second. Lou couldn't see, blinded by the twisted mask and the rush of water. Squinting, she barely caught a blurry black-and-green arm swinging toward her, and she threw her left arm up to block the anticipated blow. His bellow of pain reverberated through the water, amplifying the sound, and she realized she still held her dive knife in her hand.

Callum's blurry form darted between her and the other diver. Fumbling, her heart pounding in her ears, Lou managed to straighten her mask and partially clear it by pressing on the top with her non-knife-holding hand and exhaling through her nose. Air filled the top two-thirds of her mask, allowing her to see the other two divers were locked together, struggling. The water and sediment churned around the fighting pair, turning them into hazy shapes. Frantically, Lou swam around them, knife clutched in her fist. Her heartbeat thundered in her water-blocked ears as she tried to figure out how to help Cal. She jerked back as a fin almost connected with her face.

Diluted blood turned the water light red, and Lou felt a sob creep into her throat. As the two divers flipped and turned, a green-and-black target would open to her before disappearing again. She darted toward them but pulled away as the fighters rolled. Her fingers gripped the knife so tightly they cramped, but she didn't strike, not wanting to hit Callum by mistake.

The other diver's fist slammed into the side of Cal's face, snapping his head back. As the aggressor pulled his arm away, it caught his regulator hose, ripping Cal's mouthpiece from him. The regulator bobbed, bubbles floating uselessly toward the surface. As Cal swept his arm through the water, trying to retrieve his air supply, the second diver wrapped gloved hands around his neck and forced his back against the reservoir bottom. Callum's struggles were losing power.

No! Lou lunged toward the person trying to kill Cal— *her* Callum. Releasing his hold, the diver turned and kicked, his fin hitting her in the stomach. She folded, breath knocked from her lungs, caught by the physical memory of another kick to the stomach, into fire rather than ice water that time. Fear turned her body to useless rubber for a second, but she forced herself to push back the terror. Callum didn't have any air. She needed to save him. Scrambling upright, she saw the other diver barreling directly toward her.

Screaming into her regulator, her hands extended defensively, Lou fell backward in slow motion. The other diver followed her down, and she pulled her knees to her chest before kicking her fins toward his belly.

Let's see how you like it, she thought viciously. The ends curled under, muffling some of the impact of the kick, but it got him off her. She scrambled upright and pushed off the bottom with both feet, tackling him. The water robbed her of much of her power, but the knife sank into his side. As she pulled it free, her light illuminated a cloud of red as his blood mixed with the already-murky water. Lou felt a bloodthirsty thrill of satisfaction.

He reached for her again, but pulled back when she slashed at him, this time aiming for his regulator hose. His eyes widened as he saw her intent, those crazily familiar brown eyes she'd looked into so many times in the past. A sense of unreality washed through her. This was Brent, ex-boyfriend Brent, who was trying to kill her and Cal in the freezing depths of Mission Reservoir. At the thought of Callum's weakening form, she shook off her distraction and fought with renewed ferocity, aiming her knife at the hose supplying Brent's life-preserving air.

The blade sliced through the hose, and he immediately dropped his regulator and reached for his alternate air supply. Her brain flashed to Callum, inhaling water behind them, each second increasing his chances of brain damage and death. The fight felt like it had gone on forever, and desperation tightened her throat.

As his arm lifted to fumble for the second air supply, it exposed the right side of his chest. She plunged in the dive knife, feeling it scrape against something hard and then slide in deep. Brent stared at her, eyes wide behind the mask, his hand frozen, before he folded like a lifeless rag doll.

Yanking the knife free, she turned toward Callum, panicking in the few seconds it took to locate his limp form. Relief flushed through her as she finally spotted him, and she half ran, half swam the short distance to his side. Cursing her gloves, she fumbled for his regulator, which was still burbling oxygen. She pressed it to his mouth, clearing it of water and inserting it between his slack lips, but it fell free the instant she released it.

She cut the fabric of his weight belt and then dropped her knife, not wanting to accidentally stab Callum as she worked over him. Unhooking the carabiner attached to the safety line from her own harness, she hooked it to his. After she inflated his BCD, he began to float upward, and she scrambled to stay with him.

She noticed they were passing her exhaled bubbles, and every dive-safety lecture she'd ever heard about ascending slowly—no more than thirty feet per minute—ran through her head. What if she thought she was saving his life, when actually she killed him from the nitrogen building up in his system? But Lou didn't slow their ascent. Oxygen was the priority. They didn't have time for a three- to five-minute safety stop on their way to the surface.

When the slab of ice appeared above them, she almost sobbed with relief. A rush of panic quickly followed, since the hole where they'd entered was nowhere in sight. Although nightmare visions of being trapped under the ice as Callum died and she slowly ran out of air flashed through her mind, she shoved the images into a dark closet in her brain and slammed the door. She could have bad dreams about it later. Right now, she needed to *think*.

Grabbing her safety line just past where it connected to her harness, she started pulling in the slack. It was a hundred-foot line, and she had no idea how far from the hole she'd drifted in her search for Callum. She pulled in the rope, hand over hand. When she hit tension, it took several tugs for her to realize she'd removed all the slack. Once she did, it took another moment for her to feel someone on the other end of the rope was tugging back.

This time, she did give a sob of relief into her regulator. She gave two answering pulls and wrapped her arms around Callum. Whatever guardian angels were on the other end of the rope hauled them both through the water until the dark shape of the opening came into view. Lou actually laughed in relief. She never thought she'd be so glad to see a hole in the ice. With a squeeze around Cal's middle, she allowed herself to hope he'd make it.

It was just in time, since Lou could feel the increased tightness of each breath that indicated her tank was getting low on oxygen. She kicked her fins, helping to move them through the water toward the opening. *Hold on, Cal,* she thought. *Almost there.*

Something closed around her left calf and yanked. Her heartbeat stopped as she plunged back into the deep. Startled, Lou opened her mouth, releasing the regulator and sucking in a mouthful of reservoir water. Her arms flailed, releasing Callum to churn at the water. Looking down, she saw Brent, his fingers wrapped around her lower leg as he towed her deeper.

She kicked and fought, terror ripping through her as she struggled, but she was pulled deeper and deeper. With a desperate upward glance, she saw Callum's body floating away from her, his limbs outstretched like a starfish, until he disappeared into the murky darkness above her.

Another jerk on her leg made her renew her fight, kicking out at Brent uselessly. His hold on her dragged her farther down even as the fin on her free leg just bumped against him harmlessly. Her lungs started to burn with the need to expel the water she'd inhaled, and she swung an arm out to the side, hooking the regulator hose and sweeping it back in front of her.

Jamming the regulator into her mouth, she pushed the button to clear it as she coughed into the mouthpiece.

The image of Cal's limp form getting farther and farther from her burned in her mind, igniting a rage like she'd never felt before. Twisting her body, she reached for Brent. She grabbed for him, but her gloved fingers slid uselessly against the slick material of his hood. Knocking away her grasping hands, Brent yanked her down so they were mask to mask.

Desperately wishing that she hadn't dropped her knife, Lou thrust her hands toward his chest, attempting to shove him back. His fingers gripped her arms, pulling her closer to him, and she swung her fists, trying to strike him where she'd buried the blade beneath the skin. The resistance of the water robbed her blows of any power, however, and his hold on her didn't lighten.

Their sides bumped something, and Lou realized they'd hit bottom. She wanted to wail and cry at the unfairness of it. She'd been so close to the surface, and now Brent had ruined her chance at survival. She inhaled, feeling the squeezing pinch of an almost-empty tank. She had nothing—no weapon, no air, no way of freeing herself from Brent's hold.

Their faces were so close that she could see his expression. He looked smug. Brent thought he'd won, that she'd accepted the inevitability of her death, just as she'd come so close to resigning herself to marrying him. He was going to have her, even if that meant they both drowned.

Oh, *hell* no. He wasn't going to win. Lou had a new life now, a good life, and she was going to keep it. Remembering the shock of cold after he'd hit her the first time, she grabbed his mask and pulled. He reared back as the water made contact with his face, stretching the band that had held the mask in place. Lou twisted in his grip, fighting to get free with everything inside her. The image of Callum filled her mind until there was no room for panic. She hammered at Brent's chest, trying to break his hold, but he was already recovering from the cold-water shock—and he was furious.

He shoved her against the bottom, his hands wrapping around her throat in the same way he'd choked Cal. Still she fought, trying to hold on to her fury. Each of her breaths was getting tighter, harder to suck into her lungs. Her arms flailed to the side, hitting against the rocks scattered over the bottom with bruising force. That new pain brought her out of her frantic haze for a second, just long enough to close her fingers around a fist-sized stone. With the last of her strength, she brought her arm up in an arc. When the rock connected with his temple, she saw his moment of startled shock. His hands didn't loosen, so she struck again, and then a third time. Finally, *finally*, his grip eased as his eyes rolled back, and she managed to shove free. Choking and coughing into her regulator, she scrambled away from him, knowing at any second he could lunge for her again. His body was completely still, though. As she stared, his regulator floated free of his mouth. No bubbles emerged from his mouth or nose, but she still watched him carefully as she pushed off the bottom and swam upward. She couldn't resist turning her light toward Brent one last time, but the clouded water showed only the bare outline of his lifeless form.

She turned away. Kicking her fins, she moved toward the surface—and Callum.

Her gloved fingers worked at the weight belt, but her coordination was off. Odd sparkles appeared at the edges of her vision, and she increased her upward pace. There was nothing left in her tank, forcing her to spit out her regulator and break the cardinal rule of diving—she held her breath.

Finally the buckle gave on the weight belt, and it fell, leaving her more buoyant. Her upward velocity increased as she kicked harder, her lungs burning with the need to breathe. She almost hit the ice before she realized she was at the surface, and she flattened her hands against the hard crust to keep her skull from bouncing off it.

Her feet floated toward the surface, reminding her of her first dry-suit experience. It had been only a few weeks ago, but it felt so much longer. The light on her BCD reflected off the layer of ice above her, and she pushed herself back to get a wider view.

It didn't matter. The ice stretched, unbroken, in all directions.

Her heart pounded in her aching lungs, reminding her that she had to get out. Without an opening, though, she was trapped, imprisoned by the thick slab above her. Her hands thumped against it in a futile attempt at what, she didn't know—breaking it? Attracting someone's attention?

Lou tried to think of a plan, but her brain could process only how much it needed air. She moved to the left, knowing it was futile. The hole was nowhere in sight. Despite all her attempts, she was going to die with Brent. He'd won after all.

The first glimmer she dismissed as a trick of her oxygen-starved mind, but then the glow brightened and steadied. She turned toward the muted light, that one break in the vast darkness that surrounded her. Forcing her legs to move the fins—up and down, up and down—she focused on the illumination that got brighter with each stroke of her feet. Her vision narrowed until she felt like she was swimming through a tunnel, focusing only on the beam of hope in front of her.

She was almost underneath it before she saw the hole. At first, she didn't believe it was really there. It was a mirage, a taunting tease for a desperate, drowning woman. It didn't fade, though. It didn't move or shift or disappear, and a kernel of hope grew in her tight chest.

A diving light attached to a safety line dangled a few feet in the water, and she kicked her way toward it, giving a final surge of effort. Her head popped up into the frigid air, and she dragged in painful yet amazingly wonderful breaths—breaths that smelled like Smelly Jim.

Someone behind her grabbed her under the shoulder straps of her BCD and hauled her out of the water. She landed on her back on the ice and was dragged away from the hole. After the initial shocked moment, she started to struggle, twisting like a banked fish in the unknown person's grip.

"Settle down, missy." Smelly Jim leaned over her so she could see his face. "Just getting you out of that water."

Lou was so happy to see his familiar—albeit dirty—face that she almost kissed him. It took only a fraction of a second for her relief to change to frantic worry.

"Callum," she croaked, yanking off her mask and attempting to turn. Her oxygen tank kept her on her back like a turtle shell, and she fought to undo the fastenings on her BCD. When she finally managed to work herself free from the vest, Lou rolled over and pushed herself to her hands and knees. Her head spun, forcing her to pause before standing. Her fins got in the way, and she impatiently pulled them off. Once she was on her feet, she swayed. "We need to get him out!"

"Already did." Jim nodded at a blanket-draped form several feet from them. "Barely. He's a heavy bastard."

A cry caught in the back of her throat as she ran to Cal on wobbly legs. He was on his side, his eyes closed. When Lou started to turn him to his back, Jim spoke again.

"Wouldn't do that. He puked up a couple gallons of that reservoir water already. Not sure if he's done with that."

"Is he breathing? What if we need to do CPR?"

"Already did that, too."

Cursing the gloves attached to her dry suit that made it impossible to take his pulse, Lou shoved the malodorous blanket aside and leaned down to put her ear against Callum's chest. When it moved beneath her cheek, she started to cry.

"No time for that." Smelly Jim pulled off the blanket and stretched it on the ice next to Cal. "He's breathing, but he's not walking yet."

His words reminded her that they weren't in the clear. Distant emergency lights pierced the gloom in the direction Lou assumed was the shore. With shaking hands—an entire shaking body, actually—Lou helped Jim roll Callum onto the blanket. Grabbing one corner, she waited for Jim to take the other, but it remained limp on the ice. When she looked at him in surprise, he'd already started backing away.

"I tried to stop him. Been following him, watching so he didn't hurt you. He got away from me in the woods, though." He gave her an apologetic grimace. "Sorry."

"You've been watching him?" She didn't think anything could surprise her anymore, but she was completely shocked by Jim's admission.

He twitched his shoulder in an affirmative half shrug.

Lou wasn't sure what to say. "Thank you."

Without responding to that, he took another backward step. "Wish I could help you more, Lou," he said, giving the faint red-and-blue flashes a hunted look. "They're waiting for me over there."

"Just the good guys, Jim," she pleaded. "He's too heavy for me to drag on my own. Please?"

"Sorry." Ducking his head, he backed away a couple

of steps until she could barely make him out in the gloom. "And they're not all good. They've infiltrated, so they can watch me."

"Jim!" she called, but he was gone. Looking at Callum's unconscious form, she firmed her shaky legs and her bottom lip. "Guess it's just you and me, Cal."

Gathering one side of the blanket, she gave a heave. Cal's body didn't move, and despair struck hard. Bracing her feet, she hauled on the fabric again. This time, she felt a shift that she desperately hoped was Cal moving and not just the blanket pulling out from underneath him, like a magician's tablecloth.

The next pull slid the blanket across the ice with an immobile Cal still on board. The earlier wind had scoured the snow from the ice, so the surface was slick and mostly smooth. Once she started moving, it got easier, and Lou sped up to a shuffling backward jog. Every so often, she'd turn her head to find the flashing lights and readjust her direction. Each time she looked, they were a little bit closer to shore.

"We're coming!" she yelled when the lights had gotten close enough that she figured she could be heard. Answering shouts made her want to dissolve into tears again, but she bit her cheek hard to stop them. She wasn't there yet. The ice roughened as she approached the edge, making it harder to pull Cal. They were so close. Lou tightened her fists around the handfuls of blanket and yanked. The blanket caught on an uneven patch of ice, rumpling under Cal.

Swearing under her breath, she looped her arms under Callum's and pulled. He moved with surprising ease, throwing her off balance with the unexpected lurch.

Although she stumbled backward, she didn't fall. She shuffled back, pulling his limp form with her.

Before she could make it to the shore, it felt like a hundred people surrounded them. Relief took all the remaining strength from her body, and she toppled backward, pulling Callum on top of her. Shouting voices and flashing lights overwhelmed Lou's senses, and she clung to Callum as hands tried to separate them.

"Let go, Lou." Ian's face came into focus in front of her.

"Not until he's about to be lifted into the ambulance," she said between chattering teeth. "Or Callum will yell at me like he did when I let go of Phil in training."

"That's now. Let go."

She allowed herself to be pulled away from Cal, and then he was gone.

"Anyone else down there?" Ian asked, helping her to a sitting position.

An image of Brent's lifeless form flashed through her mind, and her shaking increased. "A body will need to be recovered."

"Phil's on his way," Ian said, shooting a grim look at the reservoir. "It'll take at least an hour before he gets here, though. We put a call in to the Mercer County Dive Team, but they'll be even longer. Right now, they're stuck in the snow in their fire station parking lot."

"He's dead."

Ian gave a single shake of his head, still staring out over the ice as if he could pull the guy out of the water with pure strength of will. "There's a possibility he could still be revived if we could get him out. There just aren't any other trained divers here."

"No, Ian." She grabbed the sleeve of his coat, waiting until he looked at her. "He's dead. I stabbed him. Then I watched him stop breathing."

Although his eyes sharpened, he just stared at her for a long moment before giving her a short nod. "I'll let Phil and Mercer County know to stand down."

Her muscles relaxed at his easy acceptance. She didn't think she could handle horrified accusations or demands for explanations, at least not until she'd had a chance to mentally process what had happened. "Thanks, Ian."

He just nodded and helped her to her feet. "Med needs to check you out."

"I'm okay," she protested, but Ian shook his head. He urged her into the back of an ambulance, ignoring her protests. The young, dark-haired EMT, whom Lou was pretty sure had introduced herself as Amy, ignored Lou's insistence that she was fine, as well.

"Really," Lou said for the tenth time. "I'm okay. Go help with Callum."

"He's already on his way to Denver. He got the luxury ride," Amy said with a smile, helping her free her arms from the dry suit. She'd first moved toward Lou with scissors, as if to cut the suit off of her, but Lou had put her foot down. She was conscious and fully able to remove the dry suit—there was no reason to ruin an expensive piece of equipment. "Flight picked him up."

"Flight for Life? Of course." Her brain seemed a little sluggish. She remembered the limpness of his body and swallowed. "Was he conscious when he left? Still breathing okay?"

Amy ducked her head, focusing too hard on the dry-suit sleeve she still held. "They grabbed him and went. I don't know what his vitals were, but they'll work on him in the helicopter."

"Oh." Desolation washed all the warmth from her body, and shivers overtook her, despite the thermal underlayer she still wore. "He was without air for so long. I should've been faster."

"Don't give up on him yet," Ian said, sticking his head into the back of the ambulance. "Remember, there's no such thing as a cold, dead person. There's only a warm, dead person."

"She doesn't need to hear that!" Amy snapped.

He just rolled his eyes. "Save all that PC shit for the tourists. Lou gets it—she's one of us. Cold water is the best water to drown in. They've revived people up to an hour later—much longer than Callum was in the water. Besides, he'd come back from the dead rather than let someone else manage his dive team."

With a watery laugh, Lou said, "True."

"Need a ride home?"

"I need to check her out first," Amy protested.

"Well, go for it. I'll be back in five."

As he pulled his head back and started to close the door, Lou called, "Ian?"

"Yeah?"

"Can you grab my clothes from the dive van?"

"Of course." He shut the door quietly behind him.

As Amy wrapped the blood pressure cuff around Lou's upper arm, she rattled off the standard questions. Lou hoped she was giving the right answers, the ones that wouldn't get her stuck overnight in a hospital—a different hospital than where Callum was headed. Amy seemed satisfied, though, so Lou must've passed. She was rushing to dress when a knock sounded on the ambulance's rear door.

"Busy place," Lou muttered, zipping her coat as Rob opened the door, apparently not waiting for an invitation.

"Hi," he said with that rare smile that always made her smile back. "How're you doing?"

"Depends. Have you heard anything about Callum?"

"Yep." His grin widened a few notches. "By the time they landed at Presbyterian St. Luke's, he was conscious and alert. Nice save, Lou."

"Seriously?" She blinked as the information settled, and then launched herself at him, wrapping him in a hard hug. "That's awesome! Thanks, Rob." She shifted to slide past him.

"Wait." He grabbed her arm. "Where are you headed?"

"Denver," she answered, although a "duh" was implied in her tone. "To Callum."

"Now? Is that a good idea, for you to be driving?" He looked around, as if searching for someone to support his attempt to keep her from leaving.

"Very. Amy cleared me medically."

"I need to get your statement."

Now that she knew Callum's status, everything else that happened crashed through her brain. "You're right, but I need to go. Can I call you and give you my statement over the phone while I drive?"

Shaking his head, he said, "I don't want you driving at all, much less while talking on your cell."

She resisted the urge to stamp her foot in frustration. "I can—"

Ian opened the other rear door of the ambulance, interrupting her. "I'll drive her."

"To Denver?" When he nodded, she grinned. "Thank you!"

"Okay." Rob released her arm. "Call me with your statement, then, as soon as you're in an area with enough cell reception not to be dropping the call every few seconds. This isn't the usual way we do things, but you've earned an exception tonight."

"I will," she promised. "Thank you." When she grabbed Ian by the sleeve of his coat, the stiff material reminded her that he was still in his bunker gear. "Did you want to change first?"

"Sure. I'll just take a minute. Meet you at the dive van? Thought we could run by Station One to drop it off and pick up Callum's truck."

She nodded, circling around the ambulance on her way to the dive van. Firemen and deputies still milled around the scene. As she wound her way through the rescue workers, each one gave her a shoulder squeeze or a quiet "good job." She accepted each accolade with a smile of thanks, even though she wasn't sure her inept fumbling under the ice merited the praise.

"Callum is alive," she muttered under her breath. "And that's worth something. That's worth a lot."

Firefighter Steve caught her by the arm as she passed. "You did a good thing. I would've missed the surly bastard."

She grinned at him, knowing her relief and thankfulness were shining from her. "Me too."

Ian didn't say much on the almost three-hour drive to
Denver, but Lou was grateful for his strong and steady
presence—as well as his excellent driving skills. If
they'd had better road conditions, the trip would've
taken closer to two hours, but the ground blizzard had
glazed the highways with ice where the wind had blown
snow across the road.

As soon as they reached a flat stretch of high plains
where she knew she'd get cell reception for a good
twenty minutes or so, she called Rob to give him her
statement. He put her on speaker so Chris could listen
to her as well.

Lou didn't know if it was sheer exhaustion or if she
was still in shock, but she told her story in a dull, unemo-
tional voice. Neither Rob nor Chris interrupted her. After
she finished, there were several seconds of silence.

"Brent Lloyd was the one who called it in, then?"
the sheriff finally said. It sounded as if he was working
it out in his head, rather than actually asking Lou the
question. "He was the only one at the reservoir?"

Lou rubbed her forehead. Her brain was lethargic,
and her thoughts were slow to form. "I guess. So he
lured us there to, what? Kill me? Or Callum? That
makes no sense, though. He didn't even know Callum."

"He was watching you, though," Chris said. "He saw
that you were spending a lot of time together—living
together, even. Since he was fixated on you, your relationship with Callum probably enraged him."

Rob interrupted Chris's theorizing. "Could you identify
Lloyd's voice if you heard a recording of the 9-1-1 call?"

"I don't know. Maybe." Lou squeezed her eyes together and then opened them. They felt gritty, as if sand had worked its way under her lids. "My stepdad would be a better one to ask, though. He worked with him every day for years. You still have his number, right?"

"Yes, I'll contact him."

"Okay." She noticed they were on the curve approaching the south side of the pass. To her relief, there were no flashing lights indicating that the pass was still closed. "If you have any more questions, you'll need to ask them quickly. I'm going to lose cell reception in about one minute."

"We'll call you back in a couple of hours. You can give us an update on Callum at that time, too."

"Okay. Talk to you then."

The two men said their good-byes and disconnected the call. Lou let the phone drop into her lap, her fingers suddenly too weak to hold it.

"Holy shit," Ian said, his first words since she'd called the sheriff. "Fucking bastard set up an ambush."

"Yeah." Her head fell back against the seat. "Mind if I sleep now?"

"Go for it." Although he sounded truly pissed, she knew it wasn't directed at her. It was all meant for a dead man. Shutting down any thoughts of Brent, she allowed her eyes to close. There would be plenty of time later to process the events of the night. Right now, she just needed to sleep.

Chapter 20

WHILE THE FIREFIGHTERS ON THE SCENE HAD commended Lou for her unauthorized dive, Callum had a different take on it. "What's Rule Number One?"

Taking another step into his hospital room, she grinned at him. It was one thing to be told he was conscious and alert, and quite another to actually see him scowling at her. Unable to stop herself, she rushed over to his bed and hugged him as best she could without disturbing any tubes, IVs, or equipment. When she pulled back, he was smiling.

"Rule Number One?" he asked again, despite his tender look.

"Um...don't hold your breath when you're diving?" she guessed, sitting on the edge of his bed so her hip rested against his. She couldn't stop staring at him. Seeing him awake and talking and a normal, healthy tan color seemed like a miracle.

"No," he said with a snap that didn't do anything to dim her smile. It was even wonderful having him bark at her. "It's *go home*."

"What?" Her eyebrows drew together. Did he not want her there at the hospital? If so, that was just too bad. They'd have to call security to boot her out of his room. She settled her rear more firmly on his bed.

"Go home. That is the first rule that every rescue worker needs to follow—to go home at the end of the call."

"And we did!" She beamed. "Well, at least we *will* go home. Eventually. Once they spring you from this joint. Eventually qualifies, doesn't it?"

He scowled even as he took her hand and ran his thumb across the back. Lou wasn't even sure he was aware he was holding it. "You're missing the point."

"What's the point, then?" she asked absently, her eyes tracing his features. She loved his stubborn chin and the way he set his jaw when he was irritated or frustrated. His mouth was even better, its soft curve not disguised by the firm way he pressed his lips together. Even his nose—

"The point," he gritted, interrupting her catalog of his features, "is that you were not qualified for what you did. You didn't have a dive tender on shore. You disregarded so many SOPs..." He trailed off, shaking his head as if overwhelmed by the sheer number of rules she'd broken.

No matter how long he lectured her, Lou knew she wouldn't be able to dredge up an ounce of contrition for going under the ice after him. With a shrug, she said, "But if I hadn't, you would've died. This way, I get to keep you. Rules, schmules."

His face unreadable, he stared at her.

Cupping the side of his face with her free hand, she leaned over to kiss him lightly on that stern and beautiful mouth. As she pulled back, she stroked her thumb over his bottom lip. "I don't think there's any rule I wouldn't break for you," she admitted. "In the same situation, I'd do it again."

With a frown, he mirrored her movement, laying his large, rough hand against her cheek. She leaned into it, loving the warmth it radiated. "I don't want you to sacrifice yourself for me," he said.

"How about we both live, then? That'd be a win-win." This time, he answered her grin with a tiny one of his own.

"Don't think you're off the hook, though." His smile disappeared into the familiar hard lines of his face. "I'm going to think of an appropriate punishment."

"Yeah?" she breathed, kissing him again.

He returned the kiss but then scowled when she pulled back. "Don't make it sound so sexy. It will be a real punishment. Something bad."

Having Callum alive and talking to her made it impossible to dread whatever penance he could impose. "Will you send me on a week-long, out-of-state training with Chad where the only sleeping quarters available is a pup tent we have to share?"

"No." Lines formed between his eyebrows. "You won't be sharing a pup tent with anyone but me."

"Well, that's good." She couldn't stop kissing him, marveling at the warmth of his lips. His eyelids were drooping, though, so she reluctantly pressed her mouth to his a final time and then pulled away. "The guys want to see you. Think you can stay awake for a few more minutes?"

"Yeah," he said. "Send them in."

An anxious crowd filled the waiting room—the fire chief, Derek, Chad, and Phil among them—and Callum was visibly flagging when Lou slipped into his room after the last visitor had left. Dragging a chair next to his bed, she picked up his hand again and gave it a squeeze.

"How'd you get here? You didn't drive, did you?" he

asked, his words loose with exhaustion. Lou supposed that almost dying would tire out a person.

"As if I'd do something that stupid," she scoffed, ignoring the fact that, before Ian offered to bring her, she'd been insisting on doing that exact stupid thing. "Ian drove me in your truck. I called the sheriff and gave him my statement, and then kept almost dozing off before everything that happened hit me again and jerked me awake."

"What did happen?" He was definitely slurring now, his eyes barely open. "I remember feeling a tug on my line after I started to descend. When I looked up, the end was floating. By the time I'd figured out it'd been cut and looked around for the person who did it, he was far enough away just to be a shadow. It was dumb, I know, but he was too far away for me to see the dive gear at that point, and I was still thinking he was a victim. I swam in that direction but lost sight of him."

He paused, and Lou thought he'd given up the battle with sleep, but he picked up the story again after a few seconds. "That kept happening—I'd spot him and then lose him again, like this weird game of hide-and-seek. I followed him for a while, but then he must've circled around behind me, because something hit me hard on the back of the head. After that, everything got mixed up in my mind. I know I turned and struggled with him. He had a knife in his hand, and I managed to get him to drop it, but then he hooked my regulator hose. Fighting him like I was, I couldn't get it back. The last thing I saw before I lost consciousness was you. I was so pissed at you for coming after me. So pissed, and so scared you'd be hurt."

"I'm fine." Her voice wavered, and she swallowed hard, trying to steady herself. "It was Brent. He must've been the one to report someone falling through the ice. I don't know why he attacked you, though. I mean, everything so far had been aimed at me. Why did he want to hurt you?" Her hard-won control broke, and her voice cracked on the last word. Lou was glad he was almost asleep, so he didn't see the tears begin to track down her cheeks. She scrubbed at the wetness with the back of her free hand.

"Because," he mumbled, even as his eyes closed completely, "I got...the girl."

Standing so she could lean over him and kiss his forehead, she whispered, "Yeah, you do."

A ringing sound jerked Lou out of her restless doze. Her neck straightened from its kinked position with a painful crack, and her hand pressed against the side. Her phone rang again, and she fumbled to pull it out of her jacket pocket. She answered it without looking to see who was calling, whispering, "Just a second," with her gaze on Callum. Although he stirred, he didn't wake completely, and Lou slipped out of his room before speaking again.

"Hello?"

"Louise. What on earth is going on?"

Rubbing her eyes, she walked through the quiet hallway, heading for the far side of an empty waiting area that she hoped was far enough away from everyone that her voice didn't disturb any patients at—she checked her watch—two in the morning. "Mom?"

"Why is some Podunk sheriff calling Richard in the

middle of the night?" she demanded. "Is it true that poor Brenton is really dead?" Her voice caught on the last word.

"Yeah." Lou sighed. "He attacked Callum. I had to stop him."

"What? You killed Brenton?" Her mother's voice rose to an uncharacteristic shriek.

"I had to, Mom." Despite her words, Lou's stomach felt heavy, and her throat was so thick it was hard to speak. "Or Callum would've died. And I would've, too."

"Who is this Callum?"

This was not the time or the circumstances which Lou would've chosen to reveal her new relationship status to her parents. "My boyfriend."

"Your *what*?" The piercing shriek was back, and Lou winced, pulling the phone away from her ear. "You were cheating on Brenton?"

"What? No!" It was Lou's turn to get a little shrill. "How could I be cheating on someone I wasn't dating anymore? He was *stalking* me, Mom. He tried to kill me—twice! He burned my house down, and my truck, and everything I owned." To her disgust, Lou was crying again and couldn't seem to stop. Between her sobs and the still-present throat lump, she could barely understand her own words. "He tried to murder Callum!"

Several seconds of silence ticked by as Lou tried to control her tears, which only made her shuddering breathing more uneven.

"He wouldn't," her mother finally said, although her tone was uncertain. "He just wanted you back. He said you were finally talking with him, going out with him, that he'd almost convinced you to come home."

"When did he say this?" Lou demanded, the slap of betrayal stopping her tears. "Were you talking to him while he was here? Did you know about all the things he'd done to me? Why didn't you warn me?" She'd gotten loud, loud enough for a nurse to stick her head into the waiting area and frown. Lou gave an apologetic wave and lowered her voice. "I can't believe you knew he was doing this."

"What 'this'?" Her mother's voice had gotten some of its snap back. "All he wanted was you. He followed you all the way to those godforsaken mountains because he cared about you."

"If you care about someone," Lou said flatly, exhaustion weighting her so heavily she sank into a nearby chair, "you don't burn down her house. You definitely don't try to kill her and her loved ones."

"I can't believe Brenton would do any of those things." Her mom's tone was now back to her usual level of confidence.

"Well, he did." Leaning back in the chair, she fought to keep her eyes from closing. "I can't believe you were talking with him the whole time."

"I wasn't." Her mother sniffed. "We emailed a few times, but that was all. He wanted to share his progress in getting you to come home."

"There was no progress." Lou forced herself to her feet. If she spent five more seconds in that chair, she'd be sleeping there for the rest of the night. "Not after he slashed my tires or cut my propane line or peeked in my windows while I was sleeping or kicked me back into my burning house or after he tried to kill me and Cal. I wasn't going to leave, I'm still not going to leave, and I'm probably never going to leave. This is my home now. I have a new family here. Goodbye, Mom."

With a shaking finger, she disconnected the call. After hesitating a moment as she looked at the clock on the wall and the uncivilized hour it displayed, she tapped on the sheriff's phone number. He answered after only a couple of rings, sounding alert and awake.

"Rob, it's Lou. Sorry to call you so early."

"I wasn't sleeping," he confirmed her impression. "What's up?"

"I just talked to my mom. Brent had been emailing her." Saying the words out loud made betrayal twist again in her belly. "You might want to look at those emails. They could explain why Brent did what he did— or what he tried to do."

"Thank you, Lou. I'm already working with local law enforcement in Connecticut. I'll see if we can get a warrant to search your parents' house and seize your mother's computer."

Even after the conversation she'd just had with her mom, she cringed at the thought of the police searching their home. Then, she pictured Callum's lifeless body floating in the water and hardened her heart to her parents' upcoming distress. "Thank you."

"How's Callum?"

She smiled, despite her misery and exhaustion. "Better. He was lecturing me earlier."

"Good. And you deserve worse than a lecture, after that foolhardy stunt."

With a shrug he couldn't see, she said, "Like I told him, I'd do that again and worse if it kept Callum alive."

The sheriff's response was just a disapproving grumble, and she grinned again. "Good night, Rob."

"Good night, Lou. I'll probably need to talk to you again tomorrow once Brenton Lloyd's body is recovered."

"I'm not sure when Callum is getting released, but until then, I'll have my phone on me."

"Let him know everybody's thinking about him."

"Will do."

Pocketing her phone, she walked back to Callum's room. He watched her as she entered.

"Sorry," she whispered, moving back to her chair next to the bed and taking his hand. "I didn't want to wake you."

"I just didn't know where you were," he grumped, although he squeezed her hand. She thought how hard it must be for a control freak to be incapacitated, even for just a short time.

"My mom called," she explained with another grimace. "Turns out that she was email buddies with Brent. I yelled at her and got in trouble with a nurse for being too loud. And then I called Rob to let him know about the emails. Maybe they'll shed some light into the mind of a crazy guy."

Callum nodded, already looking like he was about to fall asleep again. His fingers tightened around hers. "Don't leave, okay?"

"And miss out on this supercomfortable chair?" she gasped with mock horror. "As if I would." When he just watched her out of half-closed eyes, not smiling, her own teasing expression fell away. "Go to sleep, Cal. I promise I'm not going anywhere."

Chapter 21

BY THE END OF HIS HOSPITAL STAY, HE PROBABLY regretted making her promise not to leave. She stuck to him like Velcro, only prying herself from his side when a staff member kicked her out of the room. As he improved, his mood took a drastic dive, and Lou was pretty sure everyone at the hospital gave a deep sigh of relief when Callum was finally discharged two days later.

While she was driving them back to Simpson, they passed through one of the few sections with cell reception, and her phone rang. Callum plucked it out of the cup holder and glanced at the screen.

"Rob," he said.

"Would you?"

He accepted the call and put it on speaker. "Hello."

There was a short pause. "Callum?"

"Yes, but Lou's here, too. You're on speaker."

"Good. I just wanted to update you on those emails we found on your mother's computer."

Lou winced, thinking of the seventeen calls from her mom's phone she'd ignored when the search warrant was executed. "What'd you find?" she asked, dreading the answer. Callum took her hand in his, and she shot him a smile.

"He'd created quite a fantasy world for himself. He wrote about conversations the two of you had, going on dates with you, even how you were discussing living together when you returned to Connecticut."

When she realized her mouth had fallen open, she closed it with a snap. "The fantasy me is kind of a fast mover."

"He also mentioned another guy, who I'm assuming is you, Callum, but Lloyd didn't see him as a lasting threat to your 'relationship.'"

"Relationship?" She choked on the word.

"In his final email, he makes a reference to needing to 'deal with an impediment to Louise's happiness.'" Rob sounded as if he were reading directly from the email. "Your stepfather identified the voice of the caller who made the 9-1-1 call that night as Lloyd's. Between that, these emails, your and Callum's testimony, and his dive gear, this is a pretty clear ambush. There will be a hearing where you will both need to testify, but I can't imagine anyone seeing this as anything but a solid case of self-defense."

Because she'd been so focused on Callum's recovery—as well as avoiding thinking about her mother's betrayal and the way the life faded from Brent's eyes—it hadn't even occurred to Lou that she might be accused of murder. The idea slammed into her chest, and she couldn't talk for several long moments. She tried to concentrate on just breathing.

Shooting her a concerned glance, Callum broke the silence. "Thanks, Rob."

"Not a problem. I'll keep you both informed about the details on the upcoming hearing. Oh, and Lou?"

Still rattled by the image of Brent's face as he died—as she killed him—she only managed a grunt in reply.

"I hate to give you more bad news," he started, making her cringe, "but I figured you'd want a heads-up. During the investigation into Lloyd, the Connecticut investigators found some suggestion of illegal activity involving your father's business."

"Stepfather," she corrected automatically, still sounding as if she'd been punched in the belly. "What kind of illegal activity?"

"Misuse of funds and possible money laundering," Rob answered, sounding tired. "It's been turned over to the FBI."

She couldn't answer, couldn't manage to speak, so she was relieved when Callum thanked Rob again.

By that time, Lou was able to wheeze out a good-bye that was semicoherent before Callum disconnected the call.

"You okay?" he asked mildly, tucking her phone back into the cup holder. His other hand slipped from hers so he could gently massage the back of her neck.

"Yeah. It just feels like everything is crashing down on me. I can't believe that Richard…" Even as she said the words, she knew they weren't true. Although he'd married her mother when Lou was twelve, she didn't feel like she really knew him. He'd always been a remote figure, a workaholic.

"It's been a hard month for you." He was quiet while his hand worked the muscles connecting her shoulders to her neck. "You'll need to talk to someone."

As blissed-out by his mini-massage as she was, it took a moment for his meaning to register. "Talk to someone—like a professional someone?" She snorted. "I don't think so."

"Not optional."

"Yes. As the one whose brain is supposed to get shrunk, I definitely get a say in this."

"I'm not telling you as your boyfriend. I'm telling you as your team leader what the official policy is. Technically, you should have had to go after you discovered HDG."

Although she grumbled under her breath, she didn't push the argument further. It was a lot harder to debate official policy with her team leader than it was to blow off a well-meant suggestion from her boyfriend. Besides, she couldn't keep shoving any thoughts of that night in the reservoir into a dark corner of her brain forever. Eventually, as terrifying as the thought was, she'd have to deal with it.

Since she'd conceded the point, he tipped his head back against the seat. In short order, he began to snore quietly. Even though she knew it was probably a short-term symptom of her current ecstatic condition that he was alive, she reveled in the sound. It was a clear sign that he was breathing. If he'd dozed quietly, she probably would've had to poke him every so often so he'd swear at her, proving his non-deadness.

Grinning, she pointed the truck up the north side of Lever Pass. Callum was alive, and they were going home. Rule Number One...accomplished.

—⁓—

Once they arrived at Callum's house, he blearily stumbled to the loft. Shortly after he collapsed on the bed, the rhythmic snoring began again. Left to her own devices for the afternoon, Lou decided to spend some quality time with the whiteboard. It had been neglected since the incident under the ice. It also took her mind off memories of that night, and the question that kept repeating in her mind—why? Why had Brent tried to kill her? What had pushed him from being a slightly unstable ex-boyfriend to a completely off-the-rails stalker and murderer? The questions looped through her brain, making her nervous and potentially weepy, so she seized on the distraction of their murder board.

She couldn't stop staring at HDG's name. Willard Alan Gray. It still seemed foreign to her, as if her brain couldn't wrap around the idea that the bloated, headless corpse had been a person, someone's son and friend. Giving her head a shake to force herself to focus, she picked up an orange marker and found an empty space on the board.

After writing his name again, she listed everything she could remember Chris telling them about Willard. She jotted down *lived alone* and *how long?* to remind herself to ask Callum once he woke. Although he never gossiped, Cal seemed to know everything about everyone in Simpson.

Baxter Price, Army buddy was the next item she listed. Under that, she added *emailed/called*. It could be important that Willard had communicated with the outside world, even if it was through the Internet and phone. She was having a hard time imagining how a hermit could enrage someone badly enough to lose his life and his head over it.

"Willy," she muttered, tapping the cap of the marker against her bottom lip. "Who'd you piss off?"

She wrote *protested nearby home development* and

then took a step back to eye the words. Leaning back toward the board, she added *unsuccessfully* to the front of the phrase. His protests could've been annoying to someone or some company, but the development was built. His city planning complaints had been brushed off like a pesky but ineffectual fly.

Glancing at the area of the whiteboard dedicated to the motorcycle club, she frowned. As tenuous as the connection between Willard's protests of the new development and his murder seemed, there didn't appear to be *any* link between the reclusive loner and the MC.

She tapped her marker tip next to Baxter's name, leaving several orange dots. Talking to Willard's friend was next on the agenda. First though, she thought, capping her marker and tucking it away with the rest, was making dinner. And then maybe a nap with the not-dead guy sawing logs upstairs. The last thought made her smile. Since Lou wasn't sure how long Callum was going to sleep, she decided to take a modified page out of his book and fire up the Crock-Pot. Finding ground beef in his freezer was easy, not only because it was so extremely neat, but also because each section of shelving was labeled with the food item it contained.

"That's just not normal," she muttered, resisting the urge to switch the bag of frozen broccoli with a package of chicken breasts, just to see what would happen. Due to Callum's very recent hospital stay, she restrained herself.

Opening his fridge, she was surprised everything still looked fresh. She had to remind herself that, even though it felt like they'd been gone for weeks, it had only been a few days since that horrible night. The image of Brent's wide-eyed look of disbelief as she'd killed him flashed through her mind, and she squeezed her eyes closed until the mental picture faded. Her eyes eased open again, and she blindly stared at the inside of his fridge. His extreme organization wasn't enough to make her smile this time as she grabbed a green pepper and an onion from the vegetable drawer.

By the time she'd browned the meat and chopped veggies, she'd managed to shove the mental movies of that night back into that dark closet in her brain, slam the door, and lock it. Although she figured it probably wasn't the most mentally healthy way to handle it, she was able to add the rest of the chili ingredients to the Crock-Pot with a modicum of calm.

Once she'd cleaned up the kitchen and left the chili to simmer, she climbed the stairs to the loft. When she saw Callum, fully dressed and sprawled on his belly crossways across the bed, she smiled, her heart giving a little lurch. Grabbing a fleece blanket that had been folded over the footboard, she shook it out and spread it over his snoring form. After shedding her jeans and hoodie, leaving her in a long-sleeved thermal shirt and underwear, she crawled beneath the blanket and pressed against him.

With a grunt, he turned onto his side and gathered her close. "Sparks," he grumbled, still sounding more than half-asleep. "Where've you been?"

"Cooking." Shifting her head so one of his shirt buttons wasn't indenting itself onto her cheekbone, she snuggled closer.

"D'you clean the kitchen?"

Lou laughed softly. "Of course. It is spotless perfection. You'll ask me for cleaning lessons once you see it."

His grunt, even as sleepy as it was, sounded skeptical. She just laughed again and closed her eyes.

"Love you, Sparks," he mumbled.

Her fingers clenched around handfuls of his shirt. "Love you, too."

His only answer was a snore.

After tipping her head so she could kiss the top of his sternum, she turned her cheek to its original position on his chest. "Glad you're alive, Cal."

Her eyes started to slide closed when a knock from downstairs popped them open again. Mentally swearing, she checked to make sure the sound hadn't disturbed Callum. Since he was still happily snoring, she slid out of bed, pulled on her jeans, and hurried down the stairs, hoping to get to the door before the person knocked again.

Heavy knuckles pounded just as she was reaching for the doorknob, and she quickly jerked open the door.

"Richard?" She gaped at the sight of her stepfather standing in the doorway. Her cell phone rang in the kitchen, but she ignored the sound, too startled by the unexpected visitor. He was the last—well, second to last—person she'd thought would ever be visiting Simpson.

"Louise." When he moved forward, she automatically retreated, allowing him to step inside. As she studied him, he raked the interior of the cabin with his gaze. At his disdainful expression, Lou felt a flare of defensiveness for her cozy, tidy new home. Although he was wearing his usual suit, which made him seem even more out of place in the land of flannel and log cabins, he looked mussed and pale.

"What are you doing here?" she asked warily. The

news Rob had shared about her stepfather's legal troubles ran through her mind, making her wonder crazy things. *What if he wants me to hide him here?* Mentally, she started thinking of a firm yet gentle way of turning him down. Her unfortunate history showed she wasn't very good at going against Richard's wishes. She was stronger now, though. She'd faced down a killer. Telling her stepfather "no" would be a piece of cake. Despite her stiffened spine, though, her stomach churned with nerves.

"Do you have a will?" he asked abruptly.

She blinked at him and swallowed the *sorry, but I won't hide you from the FBI* hovering on her lips. "Uh… that's a bizarre question."

Stepping forward, he loomed over her. "Answer me. Do. You. Have. A. Will."

Her mouth opened, but nothing emerged. All she could do was stare at the stranger wearing her stepfather's face. His hair was rumpled, his comb-over flopping to the wrong side. There was a few days of patchy scruff on his cheeks and jaw. The most alien part of the man in front of her, however, was his intense, furious expression. The Richard she knew was remote and emotionless, not this rage-filled person standing in front of her.

His hands landed on her shoulders, squeezing hard enough to make her yelp. "Tell me!"

"No!" She yanked out of his hold and retreated until she collided with the back of the whiteboard. "Why would I have a will? The little I owned was burned by your psycho protégé."

That seemed to calm him a little, although his eyes still looked wild. "Good. Okay, good. Let's go."

"Go?" Was everyone in her life losing their minds? "I'm not going anywhere. It's been...uh, great seeing you, but you need to go now. Without me. Because I'm staying here."

His hand slid into his coat pocket, and he pulled out a black handgun. She stared at it blankly for a long second, her brain refusing to make sense of her boring stepfather holding a deadly weapon. Her vision narrowed on the gun until it was all she could see. Her breaths were coming in rapid puffs, but she couldn't get enough oxygen.

"No," he said evenly, sounding more like his usual self. Weirdly, the normalcy of his voice calmed her a little, and she was able to suck in enough air to stay conscious. "You're not. Now let's go."

Despite her pounding heart and the sweat prickling her skin, she tried to think. If she went with Richard, he'd kill her. It didn't take a genius to figure that out now. If she stayed, she could be putting Callum at risk. It took a great effort of will not to glance up at the railing of the loft bedroom and give away his presence.

"Why are you doing this?" she asked, hoping to stall while her thoughts stopped racing and she could think of an operable plan.

"My assets have been frozen," he gritted. "I don't want to hurt you, but I don't have a choice. There are ruthless men—really ruthless—who need their money. This is the only solution."

"It's not a solution!" Despite her efforts at staying calm, the words came out too loudly. "I told you—I don't have any money. I work as a barista, for Pete's sake! Killing me won't accomplish anything." Her voice shook, but she was too terrified to be embarrassed by her tremors.

"There are accounts under your name." Richard dragged a hand over his head, disheveling his hair even more. "I needed that bit of insurance, in case something like this happened, but things got complicated. You were supposed to marry Brent. That was the plan. He'd have control of the accounts, and you wouldn't have to know anything about it. But then you went crazy, broke up with him, and moved to this godforsaken place!"

Although her thoughts still spun like a hamster on a wheel, an idea managed to click into place. "You sent him after me."

"And you killed him." His tone was only mildly disappointed, very similar to the one he'd used when she'd gotten a B on a calculus test in high school.

"He tried to kill me first," she protested, hearing the ridiculousness of the complaint even as it left her mouth. "Twice!"

"Let's go." Not even acknowledging her defense, Richard gestured toward the door with his free hand, all while keeping the barrel of the gun trained on her.

"I'll sign the accounts over to you!" She rushed out the words, not moving from the back of the whiteboard. Maybe it was selfish of her to put Cal in danger, but she wasn't taking a single step out of the cabin. She thought of HDG and how easy it was for people to disappear in the mountains. There was no way she was becoming one of those undiscovered victims.

"They'll just freeze those as well, *and* they'll add charges of tax evasion and fraud." It seemed as if the more scared Lou got, the calmer Richard was.

Because he has a plan, she thought. *I need a plan. Think! Think! Think!*

"Move, or I'll shoot you here," he stated flatly, completely obliterating any chance of rational thought in a wave of utter terror. "I'd rather not have to deal with a body, but I will if I have to."

"And *I* will deal with your corpse if I have to." The clipped words made both Lou and Richard whip their heads around to look up at the loft. The barrel of a shotgun was leveled over the railing, aimed directly at Richard. A mixture of relief and complete fear for Callum's safety rushed through her, weakening her knees.

Richard set his jaw. "Action beats reaction. She'll be dead before you can pull the trig—" A blast from the shotgun cut him off midword, and he stumbled back, the gun falling from his hand and spinning across the floor. Lou lunged for it, throwing her body over the pistol as if it were a live grenade. All she could think was that her stepfather couldn't get hold of the gun again, or he'd shoot Callum.

There was another bang, and Lou wrapped her arms over her head, pressing her face against the floor.

"Sheriff! Down! Get down! Arms to your sides!" Although Rob's words were louder and gruffer than usual, speaking faster than his normal thoughtful pace, Lou recognized him and raised her head. Her stepfather was facedown on the floor, and Rob had planted a knee in Richard's spine as he handcuffed him.

"Sparks!" Callum's shout had her scrambling to her feet so she could run to him. He'd beat her to it, though, and she made it only two shaky steps before he snatched her against his chest. The minute she was safely tucked against him, Lou burst into tears.

"I'm sick and tired of people trying to kill us!" she wailed against his shirtfront.

His arms tightened around her as he pressed his lips to the top of her head. "Me too, Sparks," he muttered, his voice shaking. "Me too."

"It would help if one of you would answer your damn phone once in a while," Rob snapped as he hauled Richard to his feet. "An FBI agent called to let me know that they'd discovered Chilton had been funneling money into accounts in Lou's name. He'd gone AWOL, so the agent figured he'd come here. I tried calling both of you, but evidently, no one answers a goddamned phone in this house."

As she tried to absorb Rob's explanation, Lou looked at her stepfather. He appeared more disheveled than before, and a trickle of blood slid down his neck, but he was standing and conscious. He didn't look at all like he'd just been taken out by a shotgun blast. She frowned and poked Callum. "Didn't you just shoot him?"

"When I overheard what your fuck-face stepfather was saying," Callum said without loosening his grip on her, "I just grabbed a gun and some shot and ran."

"Squirrel shot?" Rob asked.

"Yep."

Looking down at Richard's rumpled, wilted, only slightly bloodied form, Rob said, "Guess it was your lucky day." He sounded a little disappointed.

The cabin gradually filled with more and more people—local deputies, FBI agents, and others Lou couldn't identify. Honestly, though, she was beyond caring. Even stiff-spined Cal was drooping as he sat next to her on the couch. Their shoulders braced each other, and Lou knew Cal's support was the only thing keeping her semi-upright. They'd told the story over and over, had been asked endless—and often repeated— questions, and now Lou was beyond tired.

"Rob!" she called across the room where the sheriff was talking to someone wearing an FBI jacket. He moved through the crowd until he was standing in front of them. "Please make everyone go away."

Apparently, Rob was a magician as well as a sheriff, because he had the house cleared of everyone except her and Cal within ten minutes.

"The stairs look really steep," she sighed, leaning harder against Callum.

"Yep."

"And tall."

"Uh-huh."

"Almost insurmountable."

When he didn't respond to that one, she turned her head to see that he'd fallen asleep. Smiling tiredly, she kissed his relaxed jaw.

"Thank you for shooting my stepdad, Cal."

——⟿——

Something was tickling her cheek. Lou gave a sleepy grumble and buried her face in her pillow—her very hard, moving pillow. A male chuckle made her eyes pop open as she jerked up her head. Somehow, she couldn't remember how, they'd obviously managed to get up the not-quite-insurmountable stairs and into the bedroom.

Callum was smiling at her. Despite the rude awakening, she couldn't help but grin back at him.

"I'm happy you're not dead. Again." She couldn't seem to keep back the words.

"I'm just happy," he responded, playing with a few strands of her hair. When he flicked the ends against her cheek, she realized that had been the tickling sensation that had woken her.

Smothering a yawn, she said, "You sound surprised by that."

He shrugged, concentrating on brushing her hair along her nose. "Just not used to it. It's nice. Being with you is very nice." He dropped the strands and kissed the tip of her nose.

"Yeah?" she asked. Whenever he started kissing her, her brain shut down. Lou wondered if there was some kind of scientific explanation for it—maybe he caused an overdose of serotonin or something.

"Yeah." His lips met hers and clung. As sweet and gentle as the chaste, closed-mouth kiss was, her heart rate increased until it felt like a hummingbird fluttered inside her chest. Callum could give her a heart attack just by holding her hand.

He deepened the kiss, drawing her out of her thoughts about how he made her feel and just making her *feel*. With a sigh, she relaxed into him. Her hand burrowed between them until she could press against his chest and feel his heart beat under her palm. Just like him, the rhythm was steady and calm, although it started to pick up when his tongue touched hers.

A jolt ran through her at the contact, and she shivered, tossing her leg over his hip in an effort to get closer. His warm hand settled on her knee, tracing over her thigh and back down to its original spot. He seemed content with kissing, and so was she, until her blood began to heat. The three points of contact—their mouths, her hand on his heart, and his fingers around her knee—warmed her entire body from the inside out.

Finally, after what could've been minutes or hours of kissing, she couldn't hold still anymore. Lou squirmed, trying to push him to move faster, to touch more, but he wouldn't be rushed. Every kiss, every touch on a spot that *shouldn't* be an erogenous zone but seemed to light up anyway, was deliberate. When she finally gave in and stopped trying to hurry him, she allowed herself to appreciate every contact as the gift it was. They were alive. They were together. They were home.

Once she stopped pushing, he started advancing, although still at that slow, easy pace. Callum eased their clothes away, piece by piece, touching each newly revealed area of skin as if it were precious. The curve of her shoulder, the inside of her elbow, the cup of her hipbone—all got the same careful attention.

By the time he eased inside of her, her entire body was alight. She couldn't stop staring at his face as he moved, looking uncharacteristically but deliciously rumpled with his three-day scruff. Cupping his face in her hands, she led him down to a kiss. It was one of his gentle kisses, but it quickly detonated, matching the intensity of their bodies' movements as the pleasure built.

Lou came first, although she tried to delay her climax, wanting this intense and gentle lovemaking session to last forever. He pressed into her hard, his hands pushing hers into the mattress, and found his own pleasure.

They took a long time to recover. Lou didn't want to move. Callum's weight and heat were comforting, creating a cocoon of safety. Once they left their snug nest, everything would return—death and danger and bad dreams of Brent and Richard. Her family's betrayal. The continuing search for Willard's murderer.

Callum ran his fingers down her sides and then slipped his hands under her so he could hug her close.

"You hungry?" she asked. Since her mouth was so close, she couldn't resist brushing a kiss under his ear. He shivered at the touch, and she smiled, liking that she could draw out that reaction. "Or still tired?"

"Tired," he sighed, the word sounding a little slurred.

"Then sleep," she said, stroking the back of his head as his body went limp and heavy. Lou smiled. Her cocoon was safe—for now, at least.

Chapter 22

"OH!" LOU PAUSED IN THE MIDDLE OF POURING steamed milk into a cup, twisting her head to look at Callum. Even though her stalker was no longer a threat—and *was* no longer, full stop—Callum still kept the habit of coming into The Coffee Spot for the last hour or so of her shift. Lou thought he might be addicted to the cranberry white chocolate scones. "The insurance agent called earlier this afternoon."

He flicked a look at the couple impatiently waiting at the counter. Although she wrinkled her nose at him, Lou finished their drinks and rang them up before continuing.

"They're basically giving me enough to erect that pup tent you were about to stick me and Chad into for the training week."

"I wasn't going to…" He shook his head, cutting off his defensive objection. Lou grinned. She always counted it as a win when she was able to send Callum on a verbal detour. "Not enough to rebuild your cabin then?"

The couple lingered, sipping their beverages. Apparently, Lou and Callum's conversation was interesting enough to delay their trek back to civilization.

"A closet, maybe." She tipped her head, thinking. "I could build one of those tiny homes. Actually, I don't think I could afford that. Maybe a teeny-tiny home, if they make them."

"They do. It's called a tent."

"That's what I thought." Frowning, she warmed up the scone she'd saved for Callum. "I could get a pop-up camper to pull behind my truck. When I get a truck, of course. That way, I could move my house every few days and experience different views."

"You're not living in a camper." He bit into the scone and chewed angrily.

"Excuse me." The female half of the eavesdropping couple took a step closer to the counter. "Are there any more of those scones?"

Lou pasted a regretful smile on her face. "Sorry, no. This was the last one."

"I didn't see it in the display." The woman scowled. "I specifically asked if you had any scones, and you said you were out."

"I had to hold this one back. It was defective."

"Defective?" Her eyes darted between Lou's expression of fake sympathy and the small bite of scone Callum hadn't eaten yet. "It looked fine."

"I licked it." Lou heard Callum choke on the last piece of scone, but she couldn't look at him or she would start laughing. If his airway was blocked, he was going to have to give himself the Heimlich.

The woman's suspicious expression didn't ease. "Why did you let him eat it then?"

"Oh, his tongue is in my mouth all the time," Lou said sweetly, and Callum's coughing increased. "I didn't think he'd mind my germs."

With a sound of frustration, the woman stormed out of the shop, followed closely by the male half of the couple. The bells rang merrily as the door closed behind them, as if celebrating their absence.

"Sparks," Callum rasped once his coughing died down. "You're going to kill me."

"But what a way to go."

"True." Grabbing her hand, he pulled her closer and leaned across the counter. "Now give me some of those germs."

Her burst of laughter was interrupted as his mouth met hers. The kiss was short but intense, and she was dreamy-eyed and breathing hard by the time it ended.

"Stop talking about living in a camper," he ordered, although his crooked smile softened the harshness of his command. "You're staying with me at my house, and that's final."

She studied him, trying to throw off the brain-numbing aftereffects of his kiss and think logically. "Okay."

"Okay?" He looked a little startled. "That was, well, easier than I expected."

"There are conditions."

"Ah." Sitting back, he crossed his arms over his chest. "Shoot."

"I want to contribute. Financially."

He grunted. Lou was beginning to be able to translate his nonverbal sounds. That grunt was not agreement. She narrowed her eyes. "Nonnegotiable. You know, my neighbor has this nice little pop-up camper parked by his woodpile. I bet he'd let me buy that baby for a song. It's only, what, fifty years old or so, and once I got the packrats to move out—or at least tamed them a little— it'd be a cozy little nest for me."

"Fine. *Some* financial contribution."

The emphasis on "some" concerned her, but she

accepted the concession. "I'll need complete control of the whiteboard until we solve the Willard situation."

His grin was back. "Agreed."

Tapping her chin in thought, she gave a nod. "Okay."

"That's it?"

"For now."

He still looked wary. "I'd never try to take away your independence. You know that, right?"

"Of course," she said. "In the hospital, I had a lot of time to think, and I realized that loving you doesn't make me weaker. To save you, I dove into a frozen reservoir, killed a guy, and almost died." He flinched, and she gave him an apologetic grimace. "Loving you actually made me into kind of a badass."

He extended his hand, as if to shake to cement their deal. When she put her hand in his, he pulled her toward him instead. This time, the kiss was even longer and more thorough. It didn't end until someone cleared their throat. Loudly.

Pulling back, Lou put on her customer-service smile as she turned to look at the throat-clearer with eyes that didn't want to focus. "Sorry about that. What can I get... Oh, Ian. Hey."

He gave a short nod. His expression was grim, even more so than it had been at the bar in Liverton. Out of the corner of her eye, she saw Callum stiffen, as if bracing himself for trouble.

"Lou. Callum." Ian practically growled the terse greeting. "We've got a problem."

*Keep reading for an excerpt from the
next book in the Search & Rescue series*

FAN THE
FLAMES

It had started out as such a promising day.

"What?" Ian bellowed when the roar of the fire and the rumble of the pump-truck engine drowned out the chief's words.

"The homeowner said he stores a propane tank in the northeast corner of the barn!" Fire Chief Winston Early yelled.

Closing his eyes for a moment, Ian sighed. *Of course he does*. "This barn? The one that's on fire?"

"That would be the barn."

A torrent of profanity rose in his throat, but he clamped his jaw. A few weeks ago, he'd promised Steve's youngest, Maya, he'd stop swearing. Once he gave his word, Ian stuck to it, even if he and his fire-fighting brethren were all going to be blown to bits thanks to a flame-happy serial arsonist Ian couldn't even call a *fucking asshole*.

Swallowing the curses that desperately wanted to escape, Ian yanked on the hem of his borrowed, too-small bunker coat. "I'm on it."

Soup fell in next to him and spoke over the radio

incorporated into their SCBA—Self-Contained Breathing Apparatus—gear. "Got your back, Beauty."

The hated nickname deepened his scowl. With a wordless growl, Ian stalked toward the flaming barn. The heat was incredible, and sweat beaded beneath his mask. A backward glance showed Steve and Junior at the trucks, hurrying to hook up the hoses.

"What's the plan?"

Studying the barn, Ian noted that, although the south side of the old storage building was fully engulfed, the northeast corner looked relatively untouched by the fire—it wouldn't stay that way for long, though. The house where the homeowner and his two grandkids lived was only ten feet north of the burning barn. If the propane tank blew, they'd be screwed.

"Hey? Ian?" It was like Soup was incapable of silence for more than a few seconds at a time. "Plan?"

"We go through that door"—Ian pointed to the entrance on the north side—"get the propane tank, and get out."

"Short and sweet." Soup's good-natured chuckle echoed through the speaker in Ian's mask. "I like it. Let's go save the day...again. Because we're awesome like that."

This time, Ian was unable to hold back a snort of laughter. That was Soup—cracking jokes right before walking into a burning building. Despite Soup's tendency to run away at the mouth, Ian couldn't ask for a better, braver partner.

Heat scorched his skin, even through his bunker gear. The door was locked, so Ian kicked it, cracking the ancient wood and sending the door slamming into the interior wall. He blocked it with his body before the door could rebound and slam shut again.

"Aww," Soup complained. "You get to do all the fun stuff."

"The next door is yours," Ian promised before stepping into a burning building for the second time that month. After six years with the Simpson Fire Department, it still surprised him how dark it was inside a structure fire. The smoke in this one was especially thick and black, probably due to what appeared to be a pile of smoldering tires covering most of the east wall.

Once inside, he moved as quickly as possible across the debris-strewn floor. Stacks of boxes and other junk obscured the northeast corner, and Ian clenched his jaw as he started shoving them aside.

"Fucking packrats," Soup grumbled, breathing hard as he shifted boxes, helping to clear a path.

Tossing an armful of lumber, Ian snapped, "Watch your mouth!" He moved another stack of boxes and uncovered the propane tank...the hundred-pound propane tank.

"Why? You were the one who told Steve's girl you'd stop swearing. I made no such promise." Soup groaned, obviously spotting the container. "Hell. It couldn't have been a twenty-pounder?"

Ian was already bending, preparing to hoist the cylindrical tank onto his shoulder.

"Heads up!" Soup shouted as Ian started to rise, looking up just in time to see a large chunk of burning plywood falling right on top of him. With the weight of the tank, his shift to the left was turtle-slow, and he braced himself for impact. Soup lunged forward, knocking the flaming wood aside, so it only grazed Ian's free shoulder before falling to the floor. Pieces of what had been the roof crashed down around them, smoldering chunks of wood and asphalt shingles blocking the path they'd just created.

"Thanks, Soup," he said, breathing hard. Adrenaline was ripping through him.

"No problem." Despite his words, Soup's voice was tight, and he was holding his right arm against his side. "Let's get out of here before the *rest* of the roof crashes down on us."

Knowing that he couldn't do anything about Soup's injury until they were clear of the fire, Ian adjusted the propane tank on his shoulder, feeling his muscles bulge under the strain. *This* was why he worked out religiously, even on days he would've killed for an extra hour of sleep instead. In his job, that little bit of extra strength could mean the difference between life and death—his own or someone else's.

Soup moved as fast as he could, using his good arm to clear a new path around the burning debris. Following, Ian tried not to obsess about how the tank of explosive gas he was carrying was just a spark away from turning into a bomb. Smoke thickened around them as the flames leapt closer.

The barn was burning quickly, red and orange light smothered by the rolling black smoke. His boot caught on something, making him lurch forward and almost crash into Soup's back. The tank slid, threatening to overbalance him. As he heaved it back into position with a grunt, he squinted through the darkness. The barn had looked so small from the outside that he hadn't bothered to bring a hose with him to help them find their way back out. Ian was regretting that decision now.

"What's the problem, Soup?" Even to Ian's own ears, the strain in his voice was obvious.

"Just trying to find the shortest route to the door." He paused. "Or any route to the door."

"Need me to lead?"

"Nope. It's straight ahead." There was a pause before Soup spoke again, this time with a lot less confidence. "I think?"

"I'll lead." As Ian passed Soup, peering through the gloom, his heart pounded in his ears. Being in this barn—being in any structure fire like this—always made him understand why images of hell included fire. The blackness, cut only by eerie flickers of orange, the constant roaring, and, worst of all, the intense heat…everything combined easily brought to mind eternal torture.

A crash in front of them made Ian lurch to a halt, the tank sliding forward again. He caught it and shifted it back into place as his muscles screamed a protest. The sound of splintering wood came again, loud enough to be heard over the fire's roar, and Ian craned his neck to look at the roof, expecting to see it falling on them. If something hit and damaged the tank… He quickly cut off that train of thought. There was nothing to be gained by allowing deadly scenarios to run through his brain. The only thing he could see above them was a heavy layer of smoke.

He refocused on the darkness in front of them and saw a glimmer of light fighting through the gloom.

"There!" Ian readjusted the tank on his shoulder

before charging forward. After each smashing sound, the light got bigger, until it was almost the size of a doorway. A hulking figure, silhouetted by the light, filled the hole.

"Get your dawdling asses out of here *now*!" Steve's voice echoed through the radio speaker in his mask.

Relieved, Ian couldn't hold back a gasp of a laugh as he carried the tank toward the backlit, ax-swinging rescuer. "Hey," he protested. "You're her dad. If I can't swear, then you definitely can't."

"I'm a single father of four kids." Steve helped them through the improvised opening and away from the barn, giving Soup's cradled arm a concerned look before turning back to Ian. "If anyone deserves to swear, it's me. You need a hand with that?"

"I'm good," Ian said, although "good" might have been overstating it. Now that they were out of the burning barn, the pressure of the tank made him realize that his shoulder and back were screaming protests. Ignoring the discomfort, he carried the tank a safe distance and then went another twenty feet, just for good measure. As he lowered the tank to the ground, he couldn't hold back a grunt of effort.

Another gloved hand reached out and steadied the wobbling tank. "Nice job, Walsh," the chief said, clapping his free hand onto Ian's shoulder. Unfortunately, it was the shoulder that had carried the brunt of the weight. Ian swallowed a pained sound.

"Thanks." His voice was only slightly choppy. "Where do you need me?"

After a sharp look—as if checking his physical status—the chief gestured toward the tender truck. "Can you and Steve dump the water into the portable tank and then refill the tender? We might not need it, but I want to make sure not to leave any hot spots."

"That's a go, Chief." Ian jogged toward where Steve had already started setting up the portable tank. He scanned the scene until he saw Soup, standing next to the ambulance. Even from thirty feet away, it was pretty obvious that Soup was flirting with the EMT. With a huff of amusement, Ian refocused on the tank. Soup would be fine.

Hours later, after mopping up was done and they were absolutely positive no embers were left to flare to life after they'd gone, Ian straddled his motorcycle. All the strength seemed to have oozed out of his body, and he was trying to force his arm to lift and start his bike.

"Beauty!" Soup yelled from the passenger seat of the engine. "Leave that beast and hop aboard this lovely vehicle. It has an enclosed cab, a heater, me—everything your little heart could desire."

"It's supposed to snow. I don't want to leave it out all night."

Soup frowned in exaggerated confusion. "Why not? It's an old piece of junk."

Forcing himself not to react to Soup's goading, Ian kept his face expressionless. "It's not old. It's a classic. And it's not *junk*." Despite his best efforts, Ian heard his voice dropping to a growl on the last word.

"Why'd you ride it here anyway? Spring's still months away."

"It was nice earlier." It had been one of those rare, balmy days that hinted of warmer weather to come… right before winter slammed back into place. He'd been unable to resist a ride, just a short one to tide him over until spring arrived for real. Unfortunately, he'd been far away from the station when the fire call had come in, resulting in borrowed bunker gear and the prospect of a chilly ride home in the wee hours of the morning.

Obviously hearing Ian's irritation, Soup grinned. "Fine. Freeze your ass off, Beauty. Just know I won't be bringing you any chicken soup when you get sick from riding that piece of crap in the snow."

"Don't call me that." Ian didn't know why he bothered protesting. The more he complained, the more the guys teased. "And no. I'll take my *vintage BMW work of art* home."

As soon as the engine rumbled down the drive, Ian started to regret his decision. No good wasting time mulling over it, though—he had miles of freezing highway to go before he was safe in bed. He pulled off his fire helmet and ran his hand through his hair, grimacing when he found it still damp with sweat.

"That bunker gear covering up your gang colors?" a snide voice interrupted, making Ian stiffen. Now he *really* wished he'd taken Soup up on his offer of a ride.

"Lawrence," Ian greeted the deputy, wanting, as usual, to wipe the smirk from the man's face with his fist. Suppressing the urge took a heroic level of restraint. "Run into any bison lately?"

Deputy Lawrence turned an unhealthy shade of purple that clashed with his reddish mustache. "I was responding to a call. A short response time is critical. People's *lives* depend on it. That crash wasn't my fault."

Although Ian tried to behave, he was tired, and his shoulder hurt from carrying the tank. Baiting the deputy was just too tempting. "It was a bison-in-the-road call. Didn't that give you a hint that there might be, I don't know, a large animal standing in the middle of the highway you were speeding down?"

Lawrence narrowed his eyes. "At least I'm not killing people and tossing their headless bodies into a reservoir."

Exhaustion forgotten, Ian stood abruptly, sending the deputy scurrying back a couple of steps. "Yeah," he said, straightening and crowding closer. "I heard there was some 'evidence' linking me to Willard Gray's murder. Tell me about that."

All color disappeared from Lawrence's face. "What? How did you... Who told you that? It was that bitch at the coffee shop, wasn't it? She twisted my words. I never—"

"Watch your mouth." Ian shifted forward, forcing Lawrence back another step. It had indeed been Lou who'd shared the information, but Ian wasn't about to let Lawrence know that—or allow him to insult her. "The source doesn't matter. What matters are the details. Exactly what did you find in that reservoir?"

"I'm not telling you anything." Lawrence turned to leave but Ian shot out a hand and grabbed him.

"Yeah," Ian snarled, tightening his grip until he felt Lawrence flinch beneath the pressure. "You are. Let's start again. What did you find that made you think *I* was involved?"

"You're a member of a motorcycle gang," the deputy blustered, although his darting eyes gave away his nerves. "Killing is what you people do."

"No." Ian let his voice go silky smooth and felt

Lawrence begin to shake. "There was something else. Some physical piece of so-called evidence. What was it?"

"You'll find out at your murder trial."

A small smile touched Ian's mouth, and Lawrence cringed. Sometimes, fear was stronger than a very real threat. Shifting his body, Ian let a fist swing toward the deputy's midsection, trusting fear to do his work for him.

Sure enough, before he could connect, Lawrence yelped, "Okay! Okay! I'll tell you."

Ian pulled the punch, barely touching the deputy's doughy belly. By the way Lawrence whimpered, it was as if Ian had pulled off his arm.

"It was your necklace," he wheezed.

"My necklace?" Ian repeated the unexpected words. Ever since Lou had informed him that the sheriff's office had found something linking his MC to the murder, he'd racked his brain, trying to figure out what it could be. He'd never considered that his lost pendant would come back to haunt him.

"Yes, your necklace, the one with your gang's symbol on it," Lawrence spat, regaining a little of his bravado when Ian let his fist drop to his side. "The chain was caught on the weight holding down the body. Everyone in town has seen you wearing that thing until you…*lost* it." The deputy's accusing gaze lowered to Ian's chain-free neck. "Maybe next time you kill an innocent man, don't drop any identifying jewelry at the crime scene."

Yanking free of Ian's grip, the deputy hurried away, heading toward the sheriff. Ian watched him, a small part of his brain wondering if Lawrence was getting reinforcements to return and arrest him for assault. The rest of his mind was running over this new information.

"Damn it," he growled under his breath. And damn *him*, for not trying harder to get that pendant back.

Lawrence was talking to Sheriff Rob Coughlin, and both men were looking at him. Although Ian was ninety percent sure that Rob, a stand-up guy, would take his side over Deputy Lawrence's, he figured they could chase him if they really wanted to drag him to jail. Besides, he needed to talk to Lou and Callum. Not only were they unofficially looking into Willard Gray's—the headless dead guy's—murder, but they were two people he knew for sure were on his side in this whole mess.

After donning his helmet, Ian started his bike. Despite everything—the murder investigation, his inconveniently missing pendant, his exhaustion and aching shoulder, the threatening snow—Ian felt a thrill at the familiar sound of the engine firing. He'd done that. He'd taken a broken-down bike and rebuilt it, giving it new life.

Too bad not everything was that simple to save.

With a final glance at the blackened ruin that had been a barn earlier that day, Ian roared off into the icy mountain night.

About the Author

A fan of the old adage "write what you know," Katie Ruggle lived in an off-grid, solar- and wind-powered house in the Rocky Mountains until her family lured her back to Minnesota. When she's not writing, Katie rides horses, shoots guns, cross-country skis (badly), and travels to warm places where she can scuba dive. A graduate of the police academy, Katie received her ice-rescue certification and can attest that the reservoirs in the Colorado mountains really are that cold. A fan of anything that makes her feel like a badass, she has trained in Krav Maga, boxing, and gymnastics. You can connect with Katie at katieruggle.com, facebook.com/katierugglebooks, or on Twitter @KatieRuggle.